EON CREATED, DESIGNED AND WRITTEN BY:
DANIEL ALDEN SOPP
ARTWORK BY PROFESSIONAL COMIC BOOK ARTISTS:
RON ADRIAN, ANDRE PINHEIRO AND ED SILVA

DEDICATION:
TO ALL THE GREAT COMIC BOOK CREATORS AND ARTISTS THAT KEPT ME DREAMING FOR ALL THESE YEARS, THANK YOU.

BOOK I: EVOLUTION

Chapter 1

The bright light slowly pierced through the opening eyes and the sting of the cold metal table became apparent. It took a few moments to come back to reality, as if coming out of a dream.

"OK Toria, one more time."

The voice said over the intercom as the whirring of the CT scan kicked into place.

"Well Doctor we've been testing all day, has your curiosity been piqued?"

"Mr. And Mrs. Kayden, I've never seen anything quite like this, her cells, muscles, bone structure…"

"What does all this mean Doctor, why was Toria pulled from school to a top research laboratory like this?"

"Folks, I know you're concerned with your daughter's well being. I can assure you that it's nothing bad; in fact I'd say she's quite remarkable. After this last scan I'd like to talk to all three of you together about these findings."

The room was small, but comfortable as Toria and her parents waited for Dr. Marks to enlighten them. Just when they were getting comfortable, the door opened and in walked Dr. Marks with a file in his hand.

"Toria Kayden, you were asked to come here to undergo testing because your teachers have noticed, to say the least, above average physical and mental attributes. However, I never expected anything like this."

Dr. Marks sat at the table and opened the folder.

"The cell walls in all your tissues are very thick and durable, neither do they breakdown when introduced to dangerous chemical substances. They seem to also be operating at an advanced state compared to normal cellular function, breakdown and repair. This phenomenon is all the cells in your body. You were given memory stimulation, hand-eye coordination tests, strength tests, agility tests as well as a variety of others."

"Doctor what does all this mean for our daughter?"

"Mr. Kayden, I had the computer recite pi out to 1,000 places and your daughter recited it back perfectly without missing a single number. On the resistance platform I asked her to keep lifting up on the handles until she couldn't lift them up anymore, she failed at 850lbs. The contraction and tensile strength in her muscle fibers are incredible. The elasticity of the tendons is 234% higher than normal for her age. She was able to go over backwards and with her hands walk through her legs."

Dr. Marks stopped reading and took off his glasses.

"The list goes on and simply put Toria has the strength of a power lifter, the flexibility of a gymnast, the balance of an acrobat, the eyesight of a hawk, sense of smell like a bloodhound, can dunk a basketball with ease and catch a fly out of the air just by hearing it; as well as having the intellectual capacity of a genius. There is also something else amazing about this girl. Because of the thick cellular walls especially in her skin, it's very resistant to pressure. We had to take blood from her femoral vein with a large gauge needle because when we tried to puncture her arm, the needles snapped off on several tries. Catheter sites had to be replaced on multiple occasions because the puncture wounds to her body were closing up and pinching off the catheters. Her cellular regeneration is 678% faster than ours. What would take us a week to recover from, takes her a single day."

"So what you're telling us is that she's some sort of freak."

"On the contrary Mr. Kayden, Toria is the next step in evolution---she's just seemed to skip quite a few steps. There is nothing abnormal or supernatural about her, her body simply runs better and more efficient. She's eons ahead of her time or mankind for that matter."

There was a pause and a silence in the room for a while; Dr. Marks letting the gravity of Toria's abilities sink in.

"Mr. And Mrs. Kayden and especially you Toria need to keep this all confidential. Information like this could be dangerous with certain people."

Dr. Marks, right as he was, couldn't have known about the ears that were listening on the other side of the door. As a man in a white lab coat quickly and quietly makes his way from the door and down the hall. The man makes his way to the parking garage and gets in his car. He makes the drive across town to the infamous "Tower of Power" as the locals of Harborside City call it. Armed guards let the vehicle pass as well as let the man enter the hallway that leads down to Mr. Powers's secretary, who presses the intercom.

"Mr. Powers, Mr. Sitchell is here."

Meanwhile a meeting is being held with Mr. Powers at the head of the table. A commanding presence with his large frame wrapped in a pristine black suit. He places down his cigar and presses back the intercom.

"Please send him in. If you'll excuse me gentlemen, I have a very important visitor."

The men all file out of the office all dressed in back suits as Mr. Sitchell enters in his contrasted white lab coat.

"Were you followed over here?"

"No, Mr. Powers."

"Good, I hope you have some useful information, that was a very important meeting. Any reports on the Kayden girl?"

"More than you could possibly imagine sir."

3 months ago:

Toria Kayden was a normal senior at Harborside High, decent grades and active in sports. It's a winter day outside, the school year well under way, third period history class, test day.

"What is the first sentence in the Declaration of Independence? God, I don't have a clue! Hold on, I just looked at it last night."

Toria closed her eyes to think back and from her pencil came forth a torrent of writing. She used another piece of paper as she ran out of room. Ignoring the rest of the questions on the test, she kept writing just to see how far she could go. At the end of the period, she'd written word for word the entire Declaration of Independence.

Later that day, intramural indoor field hockey in the gym:

"I've gotten a lot better at this stick handling, these defenders are useless. There's an opening, the very top right corner just over the shoulder."

Toria shot with such accuracy and precision, the goalie never saw the ball go over her shoulder. There was a loud sound as the ball hit the wall leaving a gaping hole in the goalie net. Toria stood in disbelief with just the top half of her stick in her hands. The other half was snapped off 20ft down the field.

Now:

Toria shook her head snapping out of the fog, she was back in the little room in the genetics lab with Dr. Marks. Her parents were speaking with Dr. Marks across the room. However, she could hear them as if they were whispering in her ear.

"Doctor, why all of a sudden are we now seeing these changes in Toria?"

"As you know, the human body takes time to mature. This July Toria will turn 18 and the cells in her body, like her, will be matured. I believe they were always there, you just never saw the potential till now. This is only 2 months away; by that time her physical and mental capabilities will be at their peak level. I suggest we keep this under our hats, let her finish out her schooling next month and then do some more thorough testing to make sure she's not a danger to herself."

Back at Mr. Powers's office, Mr. Sitchell has just finished describing the tests that Toria underwent.

"For now Mr. Sitchell continue to monitor her progress. We'll let her finish her schooling and let the genetics lab continue their tests. They can do the work for me, but as it approaches her birthday of July 18th; then I will act."

The days went by and the Kayden's carried on with every day normal life. Toria graduated with honors and with the coming of July, so did Dr. Marks. Testing continued and progress was being made until the morning of July 13th.

"Hi Mr. and Mrs. Kayden, my name is John and I'm with the Department of Defense. I'd like to have a few words with your daughter."

"She's with Dr. Marks right now John, but if you want to have a seat out here with us and wait that's fine. Why does the Department of Defense want to speak with my daughter?"

"I'm afraid that's a matter of national security Mr. Kayden, I'll come back another time perhaps when she's not busy. Good day."

Around the back of the building, John pulls out a radio.

"Alright, she's in with Marks right now, the parents are in the lobby; initiate the pick up."

Mr. Sitchell receiving the message on his radio goes to a rear entrance of the facility. After entering the security code, 5 armed men walk in and proceed down the hallway. Meanwhile, on the second level Dr. Marks is conducting a balance test with Toria. She's progressed to standing on a steel strip no thicker than a thread. Dr. Marks looks up to see the armed men coming this way through a security camera.

"Toria, this session is over right now; we need to get out of here."

"What do you mean; I just got into a groove?"

"No, I mean it, there's men coming for you and they're with Mr. Sitchell. I had him followed; he's working for Mr. Powers. I had a hunch, but the board is still investigating it."

"Mr. Powers the crime lord?"

"Yes, now come on out the emergency exit I showed you."

Dr. Marks and Toria make their way down a long corridor to a door with a control panel. He starts to type in a code when a shot rings out and he falls to the ground with a loud cry.

"Toria, the last 2 digits are 7 and 4."

Toria in a panic pushes the last buttons and the door opens, running as fast as she can to the door that leads outside the lab. Meanwhile in the lobby, Toria's parents hear gunfire ring out.

"What the hell was that, I bet it has something to do with that guy that came in here."

They burst through the doors that lead to the labs with laboratory workers behind them. They are met with security officers around a corner.

"Sir, madam, you need to come with us there were shots fired on the second floor."

"That's where our daughter is, now let us through!"

"I'm afraid I can't do that sir."

By this time laboratory personnel are running in a panic to the nearest exits. Alarms are sounding throughout the entire lab. The armed men chasing Toria reach the door where Dr. Marks lay dead.

"Come on, she's a fast one; we can't let her get away."

He gets on a radio and calls to a team waiting outside to keep their eyes open for her. Toria reaches the stairwell door, but more men are coming up the stairs. She turns and runs further down the corridor now in unfamiliar territory. She kicks out a window, climbs out and drops to the next window ledge below, bruising her shin and cutting her arm in the process. She makes the easy 10ft jump down to ground level, and then takes off around to the front of the building to where the lobby is. As she rounds the corner, shots ring out from the team that was radioed. Security guards go down and there is mass panic as laboratory workers run to their cars. Toria's mother and father see her rounding the corner.

"Toria, get back they're after you!"

Her father picks up one of the guns on a fallen guard and starts firing back at them. Toria runs into the streets and down an alleyway, but it's a dead end. Just then a steel door slides open on the side of one of the buildings.

"Hey Kid, get in here quick before they catch up."

Without much of a choice, Toria takes the stranger up on his offer as he slams shut the steel door and locks it with a chain and padlock.

"The name's Jax and if you want to live, come with me now!"

Almost immediately there was a pounding on the steel door. Without warning an explosion erupted from the door, and then all went black…

Toria woke up on an old musty cot in a damp, dark place. There were dozens of candles lit to give just enough light. It looked like a basement to an abandoned building. By her side was the mysterious man named Jax.

"That was a hell of a hit you took, thought it killed you."

"What happened?"

"Those men were after you and blew the door off the track with explosives. You were caught in the blast radius, should have killed you. Damn, now I've gotta fix the front door. I've made a few hidden trap doors around here. I grabbed you and hid in one of them before the dust and smoke settled. Don't worry, they won't find you here."

"You don't understand we have to go back and see how my parents are."

As Toria sat up, she felt woozy and the room started to spin. Holding her head, she fell back on the cot.

"You're in no shape to go anywhere, just thank your lucky stars you made it out alive. Not too many people escape Mr. Powers."

"Well, since I'm bedridden right now, how about telling me who you are, what this place is and why you live here."

"That's fair enough; I told you my name was Jax. Long ago, probably before you were born, I was an architectural strategist for a hired mercenary group that worked for the Soviets before the collapse in '91. The satellite countries were getting unruly, it was our job to suppress any uprisings and take out their leaders. It was my job to infiltrate structures and know where best to put the explosives. I became pretty good at maneuvering around old buildings and staying hidden. I guess that's why I feel comfortable here. After '91, I came to the States. Things were pretty ugly back home. I'm not a legal citizen and would probably be wanted by the U.S. Government if they knew I was here. Nobody knows I'm here, nobody asks questions and I get left alone."

"I know where you live now, aren't you worried I'll tell someone?"

"You're wanted more than I am, why would you say anything? We're in the same boat, eh? Here, you want some fruit?"

"Thanks, I haven't eaten today or really slept well for that matter. I'm still curious how you knew I was in the alley, have you been following me, like them?"

"I heard commotion outside my building, I saw you through a periscope I have set up that scans the whole alley. I was simply lending a helping hand."

"You don't have much of an accent."

"I've lived here for many years, it fades in time. Now what about you, what's your story and why does Mr. Powers want you?"

"Well Jax, lets just say I'm a little. …advanced."

Toria fills Jax in on what Dr. Marks tested her on and her school stories. She even demonstrates some of her abilities.

"That's amazing, if only we had you during the Soviet era. Now I understand why Mr. Powers wants you and he won't stop till he finds you."

"Jax, I can't live in hiding my whole life, you have to help me fight back."

"Oh I do and why do I have to do that? You have all the tools, but you lack any fighting knowledge."

"That's why I need you, you know all about that. I'm not looking for a fight; I just want to defend myself."

"Sigh, I should have left you out there, easier on my part. Fine I'll help you, but we have to limit you going topside. I'm sorry, but you can't even go back home; these guys mean business. Unfortunately, there's no going back now."

"Thanks Jax, you really saved me; those guys would have killed me."

"No Toria, it would have been much worse than that."

In the Tower of Power, Mr. Sitchell finds himself in a binding situation. Both hands and feet bound with mouth gagged in a chair sitting in front of the pacing Mr. Powers surrounded by his men.

"Mr. Sitchell, you had a simple task to deliver the girl to me. I'm a man not accustomed to failure."

While Mr. Powers speaks to the terrified Mr. Sitchell he is slowly taking off his suit jacket and dress shirt to reveal an enormously muscled physique in a tank top. With a chest as thick as a barrel and arms the same circumference as his head, he's the most imposing sight Mr. Sitchell has ever seen.

"You see Mr. Sitchell with failure there also comes consequence and that consequence can be very severe. I hope this teaches you a valuable lesson."

With the speed of lightning and the power of thunder, Mr. Powers throws a right cross punch at Mr. Sitchell's face. Mr. Sitchell and the chair he's tied to fly back and skid across the floor 15ft. Mr. Sitchell's head twisted in an unnatural way, revealing an obvious broken neck. His face a horrible caved in disfigurement with missing teeth, a broken jaw, obliterated nose and crushed cheekbones.

"Find a way to cover up the true intent of this botch up in the media. Clean up this mess as well and find me that girl, or I'll hit somebody else."

As for the media, the death count was being tallied from the day's horrific events. Among them were the bodies of Mr. and Mrs. Kayden.

"Wow Jax, I can't believe I slept that well, I must have been exhausted."

"I figured you would be, I've made some breakfast for us."

"How did you do that in a place like this?"

"The same way I do everything that resembles domestic life, I have a small generator. I even have a place to shower with hot water if you'd like. There's a small alcove over there, we can hang a curtain over those pipes and that can be your room with a little privacy."

"Ok Jax, I'll take it. You know in 4 days is my 18th birthday, I never thought I'd be spending it like this; living in a dungeon, learning to fight from an old Soviet mercenary. I really wish I could go back to the house; my folks are probably worried sick. Hey, how did you get a newspaper down here?"

"Now and then, I'll get one off the stands early in the morning to see what's going on in the city. I haven't had a chance to look at it yet, is there anything in there about the genetics lab break in?"

Toria picked up the paper and started to flip through it; she let out a shriek and dropped it to the floor. She sat back and began to cry. Jax ran over to see what the matter was, and then he picked up the paper to see for himself. Those that died were listed in the article. The press was labeling it the laboratory massacre.

"Oh Toria, I'm so sorry. I can't imagine what you must be feeling, but know that they stood and fought so that you could live. Their deaths were not in vain, you're here and you're safe."

Jax was only met with a blank expression, silent tears and glazed eyes.

"I'm gonna leave you alone now Toria, but if you need me just to talk or a shoulder to cry on, I'll be right over there."

Jax began to walk away, but was stopped as Toria spoke up.

"Dr. Marks said that it could get dangerous if word got out about me, but nothing can justify what happened that day in the lab. I don't know who this Powers is and I don't care what he controls or what influence he has. He can't go around taking whatever he wants. Jax, remember when I said I wanted you to train me to fight for self-defense? Well, I changed my mind, you're gonna train me for revenge. Somebody needs to take this Powers down and it's gonna be me!"

Chapter 2

"Now hold on Toria, you don't know what you're getting into. Powers is the head crime lord of all the gangs in Harborside. The city has gone to hell in the last 5 years; you can't even cross the street now without looking over your shoulder. All this is because of him and he controls everything. You'll never even get close to him and even if you did, he's not your average Joe. There are rumors about him, but we don't need to get into that."

"I'm not exactly your average Jane either."

"You're not bullet proof Toria and these guys mean business. You can't just go kick in the door with guns blazing; they'll cut you to ribbons faster than you can blink."

"Please Jax I need your help, I have nowhere to go."

After a long pause Jax finally nodded his head.

"Alright, we'll train for combat, but this is no game; remember that. You said your genetic potential reaches its peak in 4 days, at least the timing is right."

Thus it began, Toria trained with an intensity that could only be fueled with the power of determination. When July 18th arrived, there were no presents, no friends and no celebration, just more training. They stayed hidden day after day in training, but they were safe. Toria was allowed to go outside during the daylight in the alleyway 1 hour every day to keep her sanity, as long as Jax stayed on look out. Jax was going to the corner store every other day. Toria was eating huge amounts of food. Not only was she exercising 10 hours a day, but her metabolism was so incredibly fast that she could eat an entire chicken and be hungry again in 3 hours. She was looking leaner and more toned by the day.

As far as the training went, she remembered every word to every description Jax told her and it didn't take her long to execute the moves with perfect accuracy. In 2 months she had mastered what would take most dedicated people years.

"You know Jax if I'm gonna be acting the super-hero part, I need an outfit and weapons. Stealth is going to be my best asset, so no guns."

"I have some things down here from the old days in boxes, let's go take a look and see."

Jax and Toria go through old Soviet weapons that Jax still has. Like a kid in a candy shop, Toria pulls out her favorite weapons. She piles up a batch of throwing knives and throwing daggers, then reaches in to pull out 2 long Bowie knives.

"Oh my God, look at these, they're the size of small swords; I gotta have 'em!"

She continues to pull out bits and pieces of material including a pair of old leather pants.

"Are these your Jax?"

"Those were not for fighting, they were for the discos we went to. You know I have a lot of memories of those pants, I was about your age then."

"Can I have them, I want to make them part of the outfit?"

"Well I'll never fit into them again, so I suppose. Call it a hand-me-down to the next generation of fighters."

"Thanks Jax, do you mind if I cut it up and alter it some?"

"Go ahead, they're yours now."

Continuing to dig through the last of the boxes, she pulls out pieces she can't make sense of.

"What are these things?"

"Those are some welding tools and some detonators. Remember, my main job was to infiltrate and set up bombs."

"You're a pretty cool guy Jax. I have an idea; can you teach me how to weld?"

"Sure, we can hook it up through the generator, but it has to be used sparingly. Speaking of power I need to pick up more candles."

Excited, Toria grabs some more bits and pieces of weapons and runs off to the little alcove that acts as her room. Jax showed her how to weld and while he stocked up on more supplies, Toria worked in her room for 3 days straight on her new outfit.

"Hey Jax, how do you get money to buy food and supplies?"

"I grabbed what I could when the Soviet Government collapsed and I fled. Mercenary jobs paid well, I've got it hidden and have been using it sparingly. That is until you came along; you eat so damn much that it's going to run out prematurely. I suppose it's a small price to pay to have someone around during these dark times down here."

"Jax, I'm ready with the outfit, I'm gonna come out and show you."

"It must be amazing; you've been in there for days."

Toria walked out of her room dressed to kill. She had cut up the leather pants to make a thick band across her chest which held throwing knives. Bands around her arms that held a throwing dagger each on her forearms and bands around her thighs that held throwing knives in little grooves she made in them. She strapped the Bowie knife holsters to the outside of her boots. She even carved out a leather mask around her eyes. Her hair was up in a high braided ponytail with a metal spike on the end of it. In her hand she held a concoction that she welded together. The handle was from an old steel rod, attached to that was a crescent shaped blade and at the end of that was a double-sided axe blade welded to the other side.

"So, what do you think?"

"You look very impressive! Now is distraction part of your strategy, I feel like I need to put a sweatshirt over you."

"Well, I didn't have much material to work with, just the leather pants."

"You know it's fall out there right now; don't you think you'll get cold?"

"Remember that whole advanced cell thing I have? I'm pretty tolerant to temperatures either way, unless it's pretty extreme."

"Ok I believe you, you certainly look the part; but is it functional? How about a demonstration of you in action on the targets and dummies we set up."

Toria smiled, turned and faced the 3 dummies and 1 target that were set up for her training the past months. She ran at the first dummy, swinging the axe over her head and cutting it in half across the chest. Dropping the axe, she somersaulted in front of the target releasing a throwing knife in each hand, both hitting the bull's-eye 30ft away. Flipping to her feet, she starts to run at the other 2 dummies; taking out the 2 Bowie knives and simultaneously cuts off the heads of both of the dummies with 1 swipe of each knife. Holstering the Bowie knives, she does a forward flip; turns in the air to land facing the way she came looking back at Jax.

"That's very impressive Toria, you've learned incredibly fast. You really are special, a true one of a kind."

Jax sat back in his chair, crossed his arms and smiled.

"You have the look and you obviously have the talent, all you need now is a name. What will you call yourself?"

"Dr. Marks already gave me a name. He said I was well ahead of my time. To all those that would know me both friend and foe, they can call me --- Eon!"

"Eon, I like it. However, hold on little miss superhero. There are things you need to know about Mr. Powers and his gangs before you play the wild cowgirl. You need a plan of attack Toria; you're not invincible by any means. One thing that I have that you don't is wisdom and that can only be gained through time and experience. I like your choice of weapons. I'm a believer in the old ways when you had to stand in front of your enemy and strike him down. With the technological advances in warfare any Joe can pull a trigger or push a button, it's taken the honor out of combat. That's why there aren't any heroes anymore. The warrior of old can still be victorious as long as the warrior uses his wits and his skill. Do you understand me Toria?"

"I think so, that's why you took my cell phone away right; you said it clouds the mind."

"That's right Toria, not to mention that without it they can't track you. Using the old ways means you threw a wrench in their system. You'll still face a great uphill battle. I'll do what I can to help you, but in the end it's you that has to stand in front of your enemy."

"I will Jax, thanks; I'll listen to everything you say. What do I need to know about these guys?"

"First of all Mr. Powers's scientists work in the tower engineering an enhanced drug that can't be grown. Powers has all the police force of Harborside in his pocket, so they'll be no help to you. In fact, they may even try to stop you. The effect of this drug is that you see things in more vivid detail, you feel like a God, very vibrant. It also makes you more reckless and violent as well as immune to pain. Most people that take it don't live too long, but it's a great drug to give to an army. The effects last for 2 hours and the street name of the drug is called Surge. Powers has business deals with multiple drug lords and cartels from Central and South America. It's a multi million-dollar business and his gangs around the city control the local law enforcement behind the scenes to make sure his business stays operational. It's rumored that Powers's scientists have developed a refined version of Surge made for him and his particular DNA that allows him to control his actions while under the effects of Surge, but still enhances all of his physical and mental attributes. Where your abilities are natural and evolutionary based, his are chemically enhanced to the same result."

"How do you know all this Jax?"

"Surge is common knowledge out on the street and when you walk these streets in the wee hours you hear things. I'm not sure about the rumor on Powers, but I wouldn't put it past him."

"So, I need to shut down this operation from within the Tower right?"

"It's not that easy, you'd have to deal with all his gangs coming after you as well as the law enforcement. On top of it all, the Tower is like a fortress unto itself to get into. What you need to do is use guerrilla tactics and take out the system piece by piece before you strike the Tower. If you can take out these so called guard dogs, maybe you can get the law enforcement on your side, but no promises."

"Who are these guard dogs then?"

"There are 4 gangs that each runs a district of the city. Now these names are common knowledge on the street, but I've never seen them. They have underlings that do their work for them and these guys I have seen. I've also seen what they do to people that get in their way.

First is Sal the Snake, he has multiple venomous snakes that he uses to kill subtly. He had his teeth filed to points and small vials of poison in his mouth that gets delivered when he bites you. His right hand is Slither, an expert whip master and they rule south Harborside.

Second is Johnny the Smasher, supped up on super steroids derived from Mr. Powers's scientists. He wears steel plated gauntlets and I hear that he can punch through brick walls. His right hand is Hammer and this guy is just outright mean. He carries a 50lbs sledgehammer with studded spikes on it, they rule west Harborside.

Third is Carmine the Cannon, a gun and artillery designing genius. I hear he's collaborated with Mr. Powers's scientists to create some sort of super guns. His right hand is Berserk and if you'll excuse the term loose cannon, this guy is crazy. He usually carries as many guns as he can, including a huge side hip cannon. I've seen his work first hand, there's a lot of clean up with this guy. In fact those piles of rubble you passed to get to this alleyway, used to be a gas station. These guys rule the east and we're right in the heart of their territory.

I have no love for Mr. Powers because like you he took something from me as well."

Jax turned around and sat in the chair, turned away from Toria and stared off at the wall.

"Jax? Who is the forth gang leader?"

"Her name is Natasha Slicer, an ex-Soviet officer and was once a teammate of mine as a mercenary. There used to be something there, but not after Powers got to her. She's as deadly with 2 swords as she is beautiful. Her right hand is Blade

Master, like you, he's an expert with anything sharp. Her gang rules the north side of the city."

"I'm sorry to hear that Jax."

Jax got up and turned around from his chair.

"That's all water under the bridge now. Just remember that each one of these people I mentioned is incredibly dangerous and ruthless as well. Each gang is from my estimate 125-200 thugs strong and that doesn't include what's in the Tower. Toria, you're asking to go to war with a small army."

"I know Jax and even if I don't win, I'll promise you this much; I'll take as many as I possibly can. So, where do I start looking?"

"You're the super hero, go do some research. However, right now it's dinnertime, bread and hot soup for this fall day. Eat up and get a handful of hours of sleep. It's a good thing you have great eyesight because most of your work is going to be at night."

Chapter 3

That night Toria got up at midnight, her first night as Eon. As she tiptoed out to one of the manhole exit tunnels, Jax's voice rang out.

"Toria, just remember not to lead any of them back here or you and I really will have no place to hide. One more thing, once you step out there be extremely careful and focused, it's the real deal."

Toria smiled, nodded and continued on. As she lifted the manhole cover she made sure nobody was looking and she climbed out. With the streetlights and her evolved vision, it would seem nearly daylight to a normal person. She stuck tight to one of the streets, staying close to the buildings; walking with her eyes and ears open. She spots 2 guys walking the opposite way, she ducks partially down an alleyway and listens in on their conversation from across the street.

"I think Berserk is getting even crazier, thinking he can take out Powers."

Toria lets them go by, and then she starts to trail them. They don't even hear her approach as she reaches up and grabs one from behind, holding a Bowie knife to his throat. The other guy pulls out a gun and points it at her head.

"Let him go or you're a dead girl! What are you supposed to be?"

Toria becomes nervous, her heart pounding in her chest. She freezes and her captive slips free and pulls a gun on her as well.

"Hey, I bet this is that girl that Mr. Power's was looking for. He's got all the gangs around the city doing a search, lucky for us. Yeah, this chick is supposed to be some sort of evolved human. You know Billy, if chicks in the future are gonna look like this, I say bring 'em on."

With anger and frustration building up inside Toria, she suddenly finds her Zen moment and remembers Jax's words: "…this is the real deal." With lightning fast reflexes she flings a throwing knife into Billy's throat and tumbles to the side of the other guy. As he watches his friend go down, Eon brings down the Bowie knife and cuts off the hand holding the gun. Screams of pain fill the night as he drops to his knees next to his dead friend. Eon collects the throwing knife and replaces it, then holds the Bowie knife to his throat once again.

"Where is Berserk? Tell me and you'll live!"

"West Thompson street #132, it's one of the hideouts. We just came from a meeting, but he might have left already. Don't kill me!"

"Put some pressure on your arm, you'll need a hospital."

With that Eon takes off towards West Thompson Street at about 30 MPH with adrenaline fueling the fire. The wrong types of people were out at this hour. Hearing the jeers and catcalls from the bums gave her a feeling of isolation. When she arrived at her location, she slowed and calmed her breathing. Her recovery was quick, in minutes; it was as if she hadn't been running at all. She had covered a span of at least 5 miles. It was a 2-story house looking like any other on the street. Of course this wasn't the greatest neighborhood and the conditions of the houses were poor. She didn't notice any signs of movement and the lights were out. Approaching the door, she tests the doorknob and it's open. The door cracks ajar a few inches, it's quiet inside. It's too dark in the house even for her to make out. The streetlights shed enough light through the windows to see only 10ft. As she makes her way down a hallway, she hears voices on the other side of a closed door. Leaning closer to the door she hears a voice.

"Hello dear, you really don't think we leave things unguarded here do you?"

Eon spins around and once again she's staring down the barrel of a gun. The silhouette of the figure lit up by the lights outside through the windows.

"Come on out boys, we got ourselves an intruder, a good lookin' one at that."

The door swings open and light streams into the hallway from the room. At that moment Eon grabs the first guy that comes through the threshold. The guy holding the gun has an itchy trigger finger and fires hitting the guy Eon pulled in front of her. She throws the dead body at the guy holding the gun knocking him to the ground. She's grabbed from behind and thrown into the room. A quick count reveals 5 guys all pulling out guns and the sound of more coming down the stairs.

Eon does a swirling sweep kick, knocking all 5 guys to the ground before one guy gets a shot off, and swipes her axe in a wide arc killing all 5 at once. Immediately she's struck in the back of her right shoulder, knocking her to the ground. The axe clanging to the ground and one of the guys that came down from upstairs standing over it with a smoking gun. Eon realizes she's been shot and thanks her lucky stars that she's ambidextrous. With her left hand she throws one of the knives at the guy with the gun, it embeds itself in his forehead. The sounds of the others coming into the room flood her ears. Wincing from the pain, she forces herself to get up and dives out of the window. Gunfire erupts as she crashes through the window. She puts her back against the outside wall just to the side of the window and pulls out one of the Bowie knives. When the thug that shot at her stuck his head out the window to see where she went; Eon brings down the Bowie knife on his neck.

    The sound of running is heard behind her, she quickly turns just in time to catch a steel baseball bat to the ribs. Eon screams in pain as she hears at least one wet snap as she takes a knee. Before the bat can come down again, she swings the Bowie knife at his leg cutting it clean off just above the knee. As he goes down, she drives the knife through his head under his chin. Eon gets up slowly and makes her way around to the front of the house in time to see 2 more guys run out at her. One guy is holding her axe and throws it at her. Doing her best to dive out of the way, the blade circling in the air still slices a large gash in her right hip. Laying on the ground, woozy from the blood loss she turns to see the 2 thugs approach pulling out guns. She pulls out 2 throwing knives and in a single amazing swipe of her arm; she releases the knives at different times. With each of her knives stabbing the heart of each guy as they both drop down dead.

    Getting up slowly, she limps in pain back into the house to collect her blades and look for more clues. The house is empty, but before she can do a thorough search, she drops to the ground with the room spinning. Involuntarily, Eon closes her eyes and slumps against a chair out cold.

    She opens her eyes to the familiar sight of "Jax's dungeon". Her wounds are dressed and cleaned as she wakes up on a mattress on the ground. Jax appears with some soup in his hand.

    "Here eat some of this; you lost a lot of blood. You're lucky to be alive; you should be dead. You're also lucky I followed you. I stayed back quite a ways and I'm sorry I didn't help, but I had to see what you could do. I couldn't see inside the house, but I saw what you did by the window and the front of the house. The good news is there's nobody in the house left to identify you, so we can still keep them guessing. The bad news is that you would have died had I not brought you back here. You need to learn when enough is enough and I know it's hard to call it. There are times you push it and times you don't. There was nobody important at the house last night, but you can be sure Carmine is going to hear about it and so is Berserk."

"On the way there I ran into 2 guys. One's still alive and missing a hand, but he could identify me."

"Let's just say he didn't make it to the hospital. You took out a dozen of Carmine's goons last night and you should be proud of that. You were also wounded badly; learn to listen to your senses more next time. I know if you were more in tune it would have saved you from those broken ribs, I'm not sure about the gunshot. Now I know you're a fast healer and you want to get back out there in the war, but even you need time to recover."

"Jax, I don't know where I'd be without you, you saved me again."

"You'd be a prisoner in the Tower of Power being experimented on or worse yet, they'd use you as one of the gang leaders. You'd be helping further his cause, but instead we have a chance to stop it. You just keep doing well like you did last night and don't get yourself killed. I'll keep you going as best as I can."

Jax continued to treat Toria's wounds; she was healing nicely. Meanwhile, topside other happenings are taking place.

"Thank you Carmine, this is indeed most interesting news. It's got to be her, the Kayden girl I lost in the labs months ago. I thought she was dead, but nobody in this city could have done that. It seems she's started a little war, but she's limited in resources. You say there weren't any bullet wounds, which means she had to resort to primitive sharp objects. Her little rebellion won't last long, I will have her. She must be living underground, tell the other gangs about this. I want her flushed out and brought to the surface, she can't hide forever."

Back underground; Jax is giving Toria a chemistry lesson.

"As I said before, I took what I could before I left the crumbling Soviet Union. I haven't opened this in over 20 years."

He started to pull out laboratory equipment with vials and bottles that held liquid.

"I went out last week and picked up a few items I'll need."

"What is all this Jax?"

"Remember I was a demolitions expert? This was all part of my job and I bring it out now because I'm gonna teach you how to even the odds a little bit. Now I don't have a lot of material, so you'll have to use it sparingly."

"Use what sparingly?"

"You'll see, just help me with the mixing and the measuring while I instruct you. If something happens to me, you'll be able to do this on your own. One more thing, please be careful when handling these liquids and mixtures; they need to be respected.

I also put in while you were resting, some cables with pulleys and handles. There are also some horizontal bars for you. As far as weight goes, there are some old pieces of machinery laying around down here. I can't budge them, but when you're better you can drag them over and rig them up with chains and hooks. It's good to keep up on your skills, but you also need to work on the physical training. You need to keep your agility and strength in tip top shape."

"Thanks Jax, I will. I've set up everything you wanted, I'm curious to see what you're doing."

Toria watched as Jax chemically treated glycerol with the tube labeled nitric acid.

"Now we add a little nitrocellulose to increase the viscosity, there. This small vial here is all I can make without breaking into a chemistry lab. It's colorless, oily, viscous and extremely deadly. This Toria is what's called nitroglycerin in its base form. A smokeless explosive, but very sensitive; a little bump and this little vial will leave a crater where we're standing. Because the 2 throwing daggers on your arms can be thrown further, we're going to coat those with this."

"Hey wait a minute, if I get bumped or punched or whatever, my arm will blow off!"

"I was getting to that, now please let me finish. I chose your arm daggers for more than the fact that they're a little heavier, you also only carry 2 of them at a time. I only have enough here to coat 10 blades, that's why I told you to use them sparingly. In liquid form it's very volatile, but the weather is on our side. It's fall now and winter is coming. Nitroglycerin has a high freezing point and will become a solid at less than 45 degrees Fahrenheit. This will desensitize it. To get a detonation, you'll have to throw the knife hard at something; which I know you can do. We'll coat it here in its liquid form and let it freeze topside near the metal door I fixed, hidden of course. Since there are only 10, you must use them only when you absolutely need to."

"Alright so it's safer to wear in its solid form, I feel somewhat better. So, this stuff will let me blast open a door if I need to?"

"Toria, with this you can make a door wherever you like."

They coated 10 blades and put them upstairs by the steel door hidden behind pipes.

"I put a thermometer up there; it's reading 38 degrees. Let's just hope we don't get a warm spell. When nitroglycerin thaws it becomes very unpredictable."

Topside days pass as word of the mysterious girl spreads out to all 4 gangs of Mr. Powers.

"How do we know what she looks like?"

"I don't know, I guess she's some sort of super girl. So if she throws you across the room, then you'll know."

"Guys, I heard she was over in Carmine's turf. She makes it over here to the west, Hammer's gonna put a hole in her the size of a basketball."

"I hear there's a reward Mr. Powers is puttin' out, don't know how much, but it's gotta be good."

"Wherever this little girl is, she'll pop up sooner or later and when she does we'll get her. She can't hide for long all the gangs are lookin' for her."

"Toria, how are you feeling?"

"Great, it's been 3 weeks and there's no more pain in my ribs anymore and there's not even a scar on my hip now. As far as the shoulder goes, I tried to put it through some workouts yesterday. I wrapped a chain around my waist and ran it through 7 old car batteries I found down here and did 20 one-handed pull-ups without a problem on one of the bars you put up. I feel like I'm ready to go back out there."

"Alright, unfortunately we've somewhat lost the element of surprise during your recovery time. The word on the street is that all the gangs are on the lookout for you. Are you sure you want to do this?"

"Jax, I can't stop now; there really is no turning back. I can't just stay down here; I want to be able to walk in the city again. I just don't know where to go next, do I strike again here, or do I keep them guessing in a different territory?"

"It would be great if we could keep them guessing, but if you get caught in trouble across town…"

"I know it's hard to get back here through all the others. We've got to take out Carmine's gang first and give ourselves some breathing room before we branch out. The unfortunate part is they'll probably pick up on the fact that I'm staying in the east part of the city. That makes it more dangerous for both of us, but it's better than getting caught behind enemy lines."

"Well you're more prepared now; you know what's out there to a degree. You're in better condition and you have some firepower now. Remember when enough is enough and get back here when the odds look too great, I won't always be there to get you."

"I know Jax, you're my best friend and I've listened well. Tonight I'll go up and grab 2 of the nitro blades to put in my armbands. Then I'm off to take on my second mission."

Jax watched as she walked to her room to get some sleep. He smiled because he knew she was a warrior now and was ready for this. However, he could never stop worrying till all this was over. He blew out the candles and pulled the ratty blankets over him on the old beaten mattress. Ignoring the scurrying rats and dripping pipes, he closed his eyes and went to sleep.

Chapter 4

That night around midnight, Toria changed into her Eon outfit. She went upstairs and grabbed 2 nitro blades and put them in her armbands, they were frozen. She went back down and out one of the 3 manhole covers that leave Jax's lair. She took a deep breath; here she was out on the street again remembering what happened last time. It was a cool night in the mid 30's. She felt a little of the cold, but not bad. She quickly ran to the cover of a building and away from the manhole cover as not to let anyone see her. Only 2 blocks down, it didn't take long for trouble to find her.

"Hey girlie, you look lost. I think we found the mystery girl boys, go get Berserk!"

Eon saw 3 thugs take off in different directions in the streetlights. At a quick glance there were 20 thugs running at her with guns, chains and knives. Looking down, Eon picks up a manhole cover and throws it at the group with such force that it crushes the chest cavity of 2 thugs. She then takes off down an alley where it's dark running past a streetlight. Knowing that they can't see her, but she can see them as they pass under the light. Eon lets out a barrage of throwing knives with each one finding its target as 6 more go down. The remaining thugs open fire as Eon ducks behind the corner of the building in the alleyway cursing them for making noise.

"Well boys, so much for stealth you ruined that for me."

During the gunfire, Eon takes off at nearly 30MPH all the way around the building to come out from behind them. She watches them from behind as they cautiously sneak into the alleyway with guns pointed. Eon sneaks up to where the 6 dead guys fell. She picks up their guns and unloads on the rest of the thugs till any has a chance to turn around. When the gunfire stops, all are dead but her.

Meanwhile, the 3 thugs that ran to go find Berserk have found him.

"Hey Berserk, we found her boss!"

Berserk is loaded to the hilt with guns, including his hip cannon. He has a crew of men with him.

"Where is the little bitch? We heard gunfire and came running."

"She's 3 blocks down here; the boys might have gotten her by now."

The gang comes upon their dead comrades in a matter of minutes all out of breath from running.

"Holy shit! Look at what she did, there's no sign of her now."

"Maybe she split boss, got scared and took off."

"Well, just to make sure I want everybody to fan out and search the area. If she's here, we'll find her and keep your weapons at the ready."

Before the men spread out too far, a lone figure crawls out a 2nd story window to the fire escape of a nearby building. On her stomach, Eon pulls out 2 guns she picked up from the other thugs and starts raining down bullets in the street.

"Boss, she's up there on the fire escape!"

The sounds of gunfire and screams erupt in the night. Eon takes out 10 thugs before they pinpoint her. Quickly she crawls back into the 2nd story window.

"Oh no you don't, none of this cat and mouse shit."

Berserk turns his hip cannon towards the window and fires 3 blasts. The noise is deafening as the fire escape blasts apart in twisted metal. The whole corner of the 2nd floor in a 10ft radius is blasted apart with bricks flying. Eon is caught in the crumbling bricks. Though she eluded the impact, she falls 15ft to the ground below, hitting pavement and debris.

"Just stay down girlie, this'll be an easy shot."

Eon quickly fires her 2 remaining shots at Berserk, which knocks him back, the cannon shot hitting the 3rd floor. The remaining 8 thugs bear down on her as she gets up and starts running towards the alleyway. Diving into an alley, she lets loose 4 knives that all find their targets. Pulling out her axe and a Bowie knife, she stands at the ready while being surrounded by 4 guys. They can't get a fix on her because of the darkness in the alley, but enough light is being let in for Eon to see just fine. She dives at the thugs, the axe cutting across one's neck. The Bowie knife slashes open another's chest. She whips her head and the metal spike at the end of her ponytail embeds in one guy's forehead. Landing on her feet next to the last guy, she twists his head, breaking his neck. Meanwhile, Berserk gets up from being knocked down from getting hit with 2 bullets in his bulletproof vest.

"You can't hide in the alley from me girlie. Since I can't see in there, I'll have to make some light."

Across his right shoulder he pulls over a flamethrower and lights up the alley. Eon dives back as far as she can go, but this alley is a dead end.

"There you are, now I can see you."

Berserk takes another gun from his left shoulder and blasts at the back of the alleyway. This gun spreads an array of bullets, making chunks of bricks spray like shrapnel. A stray bullet hits Eon in her left calf. She screams out as she crawls behind a dumpster, blinded by the intensity of the flamethrower. It's throwing her senses off and she can't get a good read on him. Berserk then fires the hip cannon at the dumpster; the blast sends it flying back crashing into the bricks behind it and turning it to scrap metal. The impact nearly knocks Eon out; she's spitting up blood and is pinned under a pile of bricks and metal shards that used to be the dumpster. Berserk holds the flamethrower high, shooting flames up into the night air, walking up to Eon within 20ft.

"You can't hide forever girlie. You put up a good fight, now it's time to eat some hot lead."

Berserk brings around the hip cannon and gets ready to fire.

"Eat this you asshole!"

Eon, amazed that her nitro blades are still intact, pulls one out. She throws it as hard as she can from a prone position, hitting Berserk in the stomach with it. As soon as she throws it, she pulls one of the sheets of metal from the dumpster in front of her to act as a shield. The impact is enough to set off the nitroglycerin as the blade hits it explodes. The explosion hits the gas tanks of the flamethrower to create a fireball with a concussion that could be heard throughout the city. The sides of the buildings in the alleyway are blown out and Eon is put through the wall behind her shield. After a while when all that's left are small fires and smoke, Eon slowly crawls out from the debris. She's badly cut and bruised from the blasting and limping on her left leg from the gunshot wound. Finding the remains of Berserk's body, she leans forward to spit on what's left of his burning carcass. She forces herself to move quickly to get back to Jax, falling multiple times. She starts to fade in and out of consciousness. Finally crawling back into the lair, she calls out for Jax, but there is no answer.

Earlier that night at 1:00am:

"I can't sleep knowing she's out there. Damn, this is starting to become a bad habit!"

Jax grabbed some weapons and was out one of the manhole covers to the street. Before Jax can get anywhere, a limo pulls up and rolls down the window. Jax not wanting to look suspicious continues to walk. However, guns clicking at the ready make him stop. Then the car door opens on the other side of the limo. Out steps a pair of long legs wrapped in tight leather, followed by 2 long swords across her back.

"Jax, I can't believe it, what a coincidence running into you! Isn't it a little late to be out on a walk?"

"Natasha, what are you doing here?"

"Haven't you heard? Mr. Powers has all of his gangs out looking for a trollop of a girl. It seems she's done some damage here on the east side. I was going to send out some of my lackeys to look for her, but then I heard she was an expert with blades. You know, I just had to see for myself. Especially since I hear she moves in ways that are so familiar to me. Then I thought how could a girl so young have this kind of fighting knowledge? Then your name popped into my head, but I didn't think an old bat like you'd still be around. Did you train her the same way you trained me?"

"How's the traitor business going?"

"You had a choice too, but you hung onto your precious old ways. Don't be angry with me for being opportunistic. Now why don't you tell me where she is and I might forget that I saw you out here. You won't like the other way Jax."

Three other men get out of the limo with machine guns trained on Jax. Natasha pulled out one of her swords and pointed it at him.

"Please get in the limo and we'll talk, it's cold out here."

Without much of a choice, Jax reluctantly gets into the limo.

"Natasha, what makes you think I know who this girl is or what you're talking about?"

"Don't play stupid Jax, I know when you're lying, we were on the same team once. You can tell me now or we can draw this out at my place."

"I don't know what you're talking about, but I do know I'm getting to old for this shit."

"Fine Jax, be like that, you'll talk either way. You were too old for this even in the old days."

The limo speeds down the streets towards the north side of town. Entering inside a steel gate with armed guards, the limo stops in front of a mansion.

"This is where I live now because of the choice I made, where are you living now? I can't wait to show you the basement; I've got a special place down there just for you."

Meanwhile back under the city:

"Maybe Jax went on one of his nightly shopping trips. I need to eat something and rest; I can barely walk. Well, I'm sure I'll see him in the morning."

Toria fell asleep instantly on the old couch in the "living room" and there she stayed sound asleep till the next morning.

When Toria finally woke up, her muscles were stiff and ached. She had caked on dried blood matted all over her. Rising slowly to the makeshift shower, she turned on the radio to the local news. This was a custom Jax did on most mornings.

"Jax isn't back yet, I hope nothing's wrong."

As Toria climbed into the shower, the radio announcer came on:

"We have a special bulletin; it seems the mysterious vigilante struck again last night. Thirty-six were found dead last night near Eastern Boulevard as well as damage to multiple properties. There are no confirmed sightings of the person or people responsible. Police are calling it gang violence and are assuring citizens that they will take care of this situation at once. Locals have mixed emotions about these killings. Some are calling it a tragedy, while others are calling it justice. Whether the nature is good or bad, police are putting extra patrol cars out at night."

Meanwhile in south Harborside someone else is listening to the same radio broadcast. In the kitchen of the famous Harborside Diner, Jason Card is focused intently on the radio.

"Come on Jason, these people out here are hungry. What's taking so long?"

Jason scoops up the hash browns and eggs, sends them out and rings the bell.

"Geez, I'm 25 years old and still working in a dead-end job. I really gotta do something with myself."

Later that afternoon when Jason gets out of work, he goes to his favorite hang out, the Southside Boxing Gym.

"Hey Jason, how's it going, you promised me a few rounds today."

"Yeah Eddie I know, but look I gotta talk to you about something. It's not too safe to talk out here, but get some of the boys and meet me in the locker room."

In 10 minutes Eddie assembles 6 other guys and the 8 of them are sitting on the benches in the locker room.

"Guys listen, I had an idea today. I was listening to the radio today in the kitchen and the killer struck again. I don't know this guy is, but he's certainly against Powers and his gangs. This city has been going downhill ever since Powers took over. None of the streets are safe and he's got the police in his back pocket. Now I know most folks are scared to death of just saying the name Powers, but I think now is the time to do something. All of us here are great fighters and we should help make a stand."

"Hold on Jason, the Snake rules down here; we can't even get out from his grasp and you want to take Powers out! Yeah, 8 guys unarmed against about 200 alone here in the south."

"Look Eddie I know it sounds crazy, but if we keep our eyes and ears open; we might have a chance to get armed. You know they traffic Surge through here all the time. Now if any of us hears anything, we need a codeword to keep this secret. It's a phrase that says that we need to have a meeting and that phrase is Wild Card."

Later that evening underground, Toria is taking out here aggressions about Jax not coming back on her workouts.

"I can't believe you're not back yet Jax. I didn't want to go back out tonight because I'm still a little sore, but I'll have to. I just hope wherever you are, you're all right."

Toria gets some dinner and rests before tonight's outing.

On the north end of town in Natasha Slicer's mansion, Jax is tied to a chair in the basement bloody and beaten.

"Jax, you're making this difficult for yourself, just tell me where she is and I'll let you go.

One of Natasha's thugs raised the Billy club to bring it down on Jax again.

"Wait! He's had enough for tonight; we don't want to kill him. We'll continue this in the morning. Sleep well in the chair Jax and remember, we're coming back down here in the morning. There will be more pain old friend if you don't give her up."

"Is this how you treat all your friends, you heartless sellout bitch!"

Natasha simply smiled and walked away. Jax was left with a single light on, tied to the chair. He was hungry, thirsty, tired and in pain. Natasha had left 1 guard to watch over him. Everything that they had taken off him was laid in the corner of the room. Jax sat in silence with the guard for 20 minutes before speaking.

"Excuse me, could I be allowed to use the bathroom?"

"No, you can just go right there and sit in it."

"I'm an old man for Christ's sake, what could I do. It's not number one and I don't think you want to smell that all night."

"Fine old man, but one false move and you're getting the back end of the gun to your head. I'm leaving your hands and feet tied; I'm just untying you from the chair. Your hands are tied in the back, so you shouldn't have a problem cleaning up, he, he."

The guard untied Jax who stood up slowly wincing in pain.

"Oh, thank you sir."

"You won't be thanking me tomorrow."

"Oh, one more thing that I really have to do..."

Without warning Jax lunged at the man's throat, teeth bared with lightning speed. His teeth sank into the man's throat, crushing his trachea and killing him in a matter of moments without any screams.

"I really have to kill you and get out of here. I may be old, but I don't have false teeth yet. Your soldiers are weak Natasha; I never would have been able to get away with that in the old days."

Jax bent down to get the man's knife from his belt to cut his bonds, and then he ran to his gear in the corner.

Chapter 5

That night Jason and his Wild Cards overheard a tip about some of Sal's goons going out to look for some girl.

"So Jason, I thought these guys were in the drug trade, not girls."

"I don't know, maybe it's just for kicks. I do know when this guy leaves the gym we have to follow him. It can't be much longer; the gym closes at 11:00pm."

Jason and his Wild Cards were parked outside the gym. Each guy was wearing a ski mask, was armed with a bat and was a damn good brawler. Jason looked around at his brothers in arms and thought they looked more like the bad guys. Then the lights went out in the gym and the last remaining people all filed out to the parking lot. They were looking for a guy driving a tan Cadillac.

"There he is boys, remember don't follow too close. I don't now about you guys, but I'm a little nervous. I feel a little like one of those super heroes you see in the comics."

"You don't look like one; more like you should have your picture hanging up in the post office."

"Very funny, hey this other guy might show up tonight too. You know, the one that's been taking out goons on the east side. I'll say one thing, that guy's gotta have some pretty big guns to take out that many guys including Berserk."

As the tan Cadillac pulls away, so do the Wild Cards.

Back underground Toria is just getting up for tonight's escapades. She's still sore from her encounter with Berserk and not looking forward to another harsh night.

"Jax isn't back yet, now I know something's wrong. I don't even know where to look. On top of that this puppet police force is out looking for me. Christ, I'm the good guy and everybody wants to kill me!"

Once ready, Toria enters the streets to look for answers to Jax's whereabouts. The nightly trash and bums are out on the streets, but it's pretty quiet for the first hour. Then out of an alley, one of Harborside's finest blue and whites flicks on the sirens.

"Excuse me miss, where are you going dressed like that?"

"Look, I'm on your side; I'm just trying to find my friend. Why don't you try to break up these gangs in Harborside, or are all the cops corrupt?"

"Hey it's you! You're the one we've been looking for. Just put the blades down and come with me quietly."

"Hold on I hear something. There's a group of guys coming down the next street. I really have to find my friend and they might know something.

I'm sorry I can't comply with you, but you gotta believe that I'm one of the good guys."

With that, Eon takes off in a sprint down the street while the cop gets in the car and goes after her. Toria arrives first to see 5 guys making their way into what looks like a hidden door in the side of a building down an alley.

"Stop right there I need to talk to you."

Eon is answered back with a spray of bullets. She leaps to the side of the alleyway and presses her back against the building around the corner. As the cop car rounds the corner, he sees the shots fired and makes a U-turn back down the street. Eon watches as the cop high tails it out of there and shakes her head.

"I can't believe it, Powers really does own all these guys; that's all gonna change. I count 5 of them, no problem."

Eon pulls out 5 throwing knives from her leg bands and tumbles into the alley. Each revolution of the tumble, she lets one knife fly. Because of the darkness in the alley, she's nearly impossible for them to see and the shots go wild. Each blade finds its target on the other hand. Eon walks up to the hidden door that was behind a dumpster on wheels and examines it.

"This enhanced vision really comes in handy at night; now let's see what's so secret about this."

She quietly slides the door back and peers into a stairwell leading down. As she creeps slowly with weapons at the ready, she hears voices from the steel door below.

"Look, I heard some shots fired, just go take a look and see what's going on."

Eon is able to walk up the sides of the stairwell with her hands and feet and go all the way up till her back is touching the ceiling. She lets the man pass by her and look around outside. Then she climbs down and goes through the steel door. She walks in unnoticed and hides behind a large wooden crate. Taking in her surroundings, she's impressed with the size of this place. It's as big as a warehouse, only underground.

"Holy shit, this must be Carmine's super gun operation. It's like a factory down here and I bet that's what's in the crates. I gotta shut this place down, but it looks like the whole gang is here and I'm not feeling my best."

Over on the north end of town, Jax has been planting C-4 explosives around the mansion, careful to avoid the guarded areas. As Jax works his way outside towards the gates, all the floodlights come on. There are 10 guards in a semi-circle all pointing machine guns at Jax and in the middle of them is Natasha with both swords drawn.

"Well, well Jax; somehow I knew you'd escape. You're a resourceful old man. A little piece of me wanted you to escape; I haven't had a good fight in a while. It's too bad you're not in tip top shape, but it'll be fun anyway."

"I may be old Natasha, but I don't sit around and get lazy here in America like you have."

In an instant Jax dives behind a small rock wall in the gardens. While doing so he releases a grenade from his vest. Natasha reacting equally as fast spins behind one of her men just as the blast goes off. All the guards are blown down like bowling pins. Natasha pushes the dead guard off her body just in time to see Jax running toward a machine gun that a guard dropped. Natasha lets loose one of her swords and knocks the gun away and at the same time dives at Jax with the other sword raised above her head. Jax rolls away as the sword clangs on the flagstone. He reaches out and grabs a steel flagpole and rips off the flag to use it as a bar. Natasha casually picks up her other sword.

"I'm not going to shoot you Jax, I'm going to savor this."

Natasha comes at him in a barrage of flashing steel. Jax does all he can to block. He counters with a swing to the head, but Natasha is too fast and she does a back flip out of the way.

"You're too slow Jax, that pole has to be really heavy."

Natasha throws one of her swords at Jax's leg; he goes down to block it only to be clubbed in the temple with the side of Natasha's other blade. Jax falls to the ground on his back, dropping the flagpole. Natasha stands over him with the other sword raised over her head.

"I've waited a long time for this Jax, I always knew I was the better agent. I want you to see this coming and have that be your final thought as I send you to the next life."

Jax was holding the side of his head obviously in pain.

Over on the east side of town, Eon is sneaking around to get a better vantage point when the silence is broken.

"Hey Jimmy, go get Carmine! When I went to go check out the shots, I found 5 of our boys dead. It looks like they were stabbed, but I didn't find any blades or anything for that matter."

"Alright, alright, I'll go get Carmine. You stay here and watch that door, he's not gonna be happy about this. We got one of Sal's boys comin' over to make a pick up of guns; Carmine wants everything to go smooth. The guy is drivin' a tan caddy."

"That's right go get Carmine Jimmy; I'll just hang out right here and see what else I can learn."

Jimmy comes back with Carmine behind him, a short man with a nervous twitch.

"Look you half wits, get up there and clean up that mess and be on the lookout for Sal the Snake's boy. I don't know what happened, but I just got some important news. I got a call from Natasha Slicer, it seems she's picked up one of her old comrades. She thinks he might know something about that girl Mr. Powers is after. I told her I couldn't leave the operation, but it seems she's got the situation under control. That's great news boys; maybe we'll get rid of this meddling brat."

A look of horror comes across Eon's face.

"Jax, what are you doing over there in the north side of town? Damn, now how am I gonna get out of here without these guys seeing me? I didn't see any sign of a struggle in the lair; Jax must have gone out tonight. I hope he wasn't coming out to help me, hold on old friend."

Jason and the Wild Cards follow the tan Cadillac to the east side of town. It pulls up to an alleyway. The Wild Card's vehicles keep a safe distance with the lights off.

"Come on boys, he's cornered in that alleyway. Maybe he's getting rid of a body. We'll get on either side of the alley, when he comes out we'll let him have it."

Each one of the Wild Cards, a formidable opponent in and out of the ring takes up the sides of the alley near the car. Each man a well-muscled brawler armed with a steel bat. When their target never comes out, Jason peeks around the corner and decides to investigate.

Down in the warehouse factory, Carmine greets the man.

"Remember if Sal wants more of these, he knows what to do. These are prototypes. Our 2 gangs will own this city and we'll take out Powers in the process."

"I can't let these bastards get those guns out on the street, I've got to act and get to Jax as well. I can't believe I'm actually gonna do this, here goes."

Eon steps out from behind the crate and throws a blade that hits Sal's guy in the chest and he goes down.

"I can't let you take that gun outta here. While I'm at it, I'm gonna shut down this operation and take out you bastards as well."

"It's that little bitch that took out Berserk, kill her!"

Carmine runs in the other direction as his goons close in around Eon.

"No shooting you morons, you might hit the gunpowder tanks!"

Eon draws one Bowie knife and starts twirling the axe over her head.

"No guns guys; now how is that fair for you?"

The goons are armed with machetes and lead pipes, but they're no match for Eon. She hacks her way through a dozen before they even know what's going on. Carmine climbs into the cockpit of a large crane and moves the long arm above Eon and throws a switch. All the machetes fly out of the goon's hands, but with all the metal on Eon's legs; she flies right up too. She's stuck to the giant magnet off the end of the crane 30ft from the ground. She struggles to free herself, but the blades have pinned the leather bands around her legs right to the super magnet. Carmine lowers the magnet to ground level.

"Have at her boys; she did a lot of damage."

The thugs close in on her and bring down the lead pipes with no mercy. Just then, the doors burst open and Jason and his Wild Cards come running in.

"Let her go you sick bastards! Come on boys, she must be the one the goon we followed was going after."

As the Wild Cards get closer, their bats are ripped right out of their hands. Not that it helped the goons much, each bone shattering punch from a Wild Card sent the thugs sailing to the ground. Just as it looked in the Wild Cards favor, at least another 50 men came running out from behind the machinery all armed with clubs. The Wild Cards were being overwhelmed.

"Try to hold them off a little longer, I'm going to get the girl; then we're outta here!"

Jason ran to the cockpit, which was now empty as Carmine was running to the other side of the warehouse. Jason released the magnetic lever and Eon dropped to the ground. Running over to Eon, Jason picks her up in his arms.

"Are you all right? We've gotta scram, they're killing us."

"I've been better, but I've got some more juice in the tank. Go get your men out of here; I think I know how to take out this operation."

With a puzzled look, Jason calls his men back to the steel door and up the staircase. Eon slashes into the thugs with her axe and Bowie knife to help the Wild Cards get away. She then tumbles out of combat and runs towards the large grouping of barrels and sets down one of her nitro blades on the edge of a barrel in the center. Eon breaks into a dead sprint towards the door, hacking goons along the way. She picks up the wooden crate holding the prototype gun and smashes it on the ground. The gun looks still in tact as Eon picks it up.

"Let's see how well your handiwork is boys."

Eon points the super gun at the gunpowder barrels, aiming at the barrel with the nitro blade on it from 200 yards away.

"My blade was too light to cover the distance, but I bet I can hit it with this."

The thugs hit the deck as Eon fires a deafening blast from the gun that directly hits the center of the barrels. The nitro blade goes off and sets off a chain reaction explosion. Eon was able to get a glimpse of Carmine running towards the door, just as the flames engulfed him. The explosion blew out the entire bottom of the building as it came toppling in on itself with Eon diving from the collapsing rubble to join the Wild Cards in the street outside. All the Wild Cards staring in disbelief as Eon gets up to dust herself off and look at the crumbling building behind her.

"Well, I think it's safe to say the east side gang is no more."

"Excuse me, but who exactly are you?"

"I'm the wrench in the works, the name's Eon. Thanks for getting me off that magnet, I owe you one."

"No problem, are you the one that took out the 36 guys last night including Berserk?"

"Yeah and I'm still feeling the aftershock from that one."

Eddie elbowed Jason in the ribs and leaned in to whisper in his ear.

"Well Jason looks like you were wrong about the tough guy with the big guns. However, you had part of it right; this broad's got some pretty big guns of her own, he, he."

"I can hear everything you say, but we don't have time to stand out here and ogle. A good friend of mine is being held prisoner in the north side of town by Natasha Slicer, come on."

"Hold on Eon, Natasha's mansion is like a fortress, there are armed guards all over the place."

"Oh come on Jason, I just blew up a building, shut down a major operation and took out 75 guys in the process. I'd say I'm feeling a little lucky tonight."

Eon and the hurt Wild Cards got into their vehicles and screeched off down the road towards Natasha Slicer's mansion in the north side of town.

Just outside Natasha's mansion, Jax is in a tight spot.

"Any last words old comrade?"

"Yeah I do. You know Natasha, you never did have any foresight or you'd have seen this coming."

Without another warning Jax pushed the detonators in his pocket as the C-4 incinerates Natasha's mansion. Natasha is knocked off her feet and prone on the ground. Jax takes the opportunity to pick up the steel flagpole and drives it right through her abdomen with tremendous force, pinning her to the ground! As the blood comes bubbling up from Natasha's mouth, Jax leans over and whispers in her ear.

"You chose the wrong side Natasha, Powers is next."

"I don't think so old man; you're the next one on the list."

Jax looked up to see Blade Master come out of the burning wreck, coughing. Dressed to the hilt with swords and knives, Natasha's right hand man was ready for action. Before the Blade Master could make a move, the front gates are smashed off the hinges by 2 large vehicles speeding towards the burning mansion.

"What the hell happened here?"

"Jax is a pretty resourceful guy Jason, but I don't like the looks of the guy standing on the stone steps with all the gleaming sharp objects."

Eon leaps out of the vehicle and runs towards Jax, the Wild Cards right behind her.

"Are you all right Jax?"

"I'm fine Eon, but be careful; they call him the Blade Master. He's as deadly as he looks."

"You're the Blade Master; I've been looking forward to meeting you. We'll just see who the real Blade Master is. Nobody interfere with us, I want this fight all my own."

"Toria, you're in no shape to take him on, you're hurt."

"It's fine Jax; I've had a really good night so far."

Eon and the Blade Master faced off in a slow turning circle. Eon was holding her trusty axe and Bowie knife. The Blade Master holding a scimitar in one hand and a curved dagger in the other hand with the blade pointed down. Both combatants sized each other up, waiting for the other to make the first move. The Blade Master launches at Eon bringing the scimitar low at her legs and the curved dagger in an overhead strike to her chest. Eon hooks the axe around the scimitar and snaps the blade off at the hilt. She catches the dagger with her Bowie knife. Both of the combatants locked with blades overhead, the Blade Master just flicks his wrist changing the pressure on the dagger as it rolls off the Bowie knife and cuts deep into Eon's forearm. With a kick to the midsection, the Blade Master sends Eon tumbling to the ground. He immediately draws a katana sword from his back and leaps at the prone Eon. She throws the axe like a bolo and the hooked blade wraps itself around the katana, ripping the sword from his hands. Eon rolls to her feet in time to see the Blade Master pull out 2 shuriken throwing stars from his belt and fling them her way. Pulling 2 knives from her leg bands, she knocks the stars out of the air. She then counters with 2 more throwing knives. The Blade Master is able to knock 1 out of the air with the curved dagger, but the other embeds itself in his right thigh. Using the slight momentum, Eon pulls the other Bowie knife from her boot and lunges at the Blade Master. He pulls out another curved dagger and they meet with both of their weapons clanging against each other. Both combatants enter into a dance of flashing blades with blinding speed, until the Blade Master sees an opening. The curved dagger hooks like a talon and rips open Eon's side from her ribs to her hip. She was able to shift mostly out of the way as not to get disemboweled, but the blade still bit deep. Eon staggers back and they both disengage, eying each other and breathing heavy. The effects of last night's antics and today's are catching up with Eon as she starts to sway on her feet. She makes a sacrifice move and fakes a lunge with both Bowie knives towards his stomach. The Blade Master brings down a curved dagger to the top of Eon's head. She moves to the side and lets it embed in her shoulder. Wincing in pain and running on adrenaline, she brings both Bowie knives under the Blade Master's arm in a scissors formation. With great force she rips her blades apart, severing the Blade Master's hand right off. A wail of pain sends the Blade Master back as Eon pulls the curved dagger from her shoulder. At this point she is staggering badly and tries to focus on one last attempt. During the moment the Blade Master is doubled over holding his wrist, Eon lets fly both of the Bowie knives. They tumble end over end looking like 2 deadly pinwheels both embedding to the hilt in the side of the Blade Master's head. The Blade Master immediately drops down dead and Jason runs over to catch Eon from falling to the ground.

"You look as pale as a ghost; you're losing a lot of blood."

"We have to get her to the lair and patch her up now, follow me and hold pressure on the wounds."

Running to their vehicles, they race back to the east part of town. Jax leads the Wild Cards down to the lair.

Working through the night Jax and Jason stabilize the wounds of their comrades. Four of Jason's men have broken bones and the others are badly beaten. Jason himself sustained minor injuries and Eon was still out cold. Jax looked about the lair with wounded bloody men in the sewers and shook his weary head.

"It looks like a damn third world infirmary down here. I'm gonna turn on the radio for the morning news, and then I'm sleeping for the next 3 weeks. I'm just too damn old for this shit."

"Police now have a visual of the self proclaimed vigilante. Last night a police officer took this video footage from the camera mounted on the dash of his car. Be on the lookout for this girl, she is extremely dangerous and report any sightings. The explosions last night in the east and north part of the city took the lives of 137 people reported thus far. Police believe the vigilante girl probably has accomplices throughout the city. If you have any information pertaining to this investigation, please contact authorities at once."

"Ha, ha, ha, you hear that Jason, we cleaned house last night. I know one guy that's gonna be real pissed off. Well, let's get some shuteye. Since you look the least beat up out of all of us, can you make a run topside tomorrow? I used most of my medical supplies last night and I'm low on food. Just be sure to go to multiple places, it'll take longer, but you won't attract attention."

"No problem Jax, I'll take care of it first thing after some sleep."

With that Jason blew out the candles and lay down on the mattress next to Toria.

That morning in the Tower of Power, Mr. Powers is greeted with last night's troubling events.

"I was going to use those guns in future plans of mine. Now the whole factory is destroyed, 2 of my 4 gangs are wiped out and I've lost drug influence over half the city. This girl will pay dearly for this; she also has help. I smell a sewer rat and his name is Jax, Natasha's old mentor. I can't efficiently run the Surge operation with trouble like this around. I'm temporarily suspending operation in the city for defense here, so I can continue with business abroad. I have a feeling they'll be looking to come here next. Sal, I want you and your men in the sewers night and day, I want them flushed out. Johnny, I want you and your men around the compound, added to my personal guards. We'll make the Tower impenetrable and be rid of this little runt, she's more trouble than she's worth."

Chapter 6

It was about midday until everyone started to wake up. Jax was first and started to make what he had left of food. He walked over to Jason to wake him up to get some supplies and saw that he had his arm around Toria and she was sleeping on his chest. They were both still sleeping and he knew they needed it, so he let them be. Some of the other guys started to wake up; many were in pain. Jax had splinted some broken bones and had given them what he had to take the edge off, but they needed a hospital. A couple of guys called friends to meet them topside. Jax helped them up the manhole exits. At this point he knew that the location of the lair would be compromised, but these guys needed help and they earned it. Eddie was one of the last ones to go topside.

"Jason wake up man, we're gettin' outta here."

"Hey Eddie, what's going on?"

"The boys and I are going to the hospital, but don't worry, we won't say a thing about any of this if it comes up."

"Alright Pal, I'll catch up with you guys later. You did a hell of a job last night, we really made a difference."

"I hope so, because I'm in some pain. Miss Eon I never saw anybody fight like you. Take care of this guy here, he's my best buddy."

"I will Eddie, thanks for your help last night."

Eddie limped off as Jax came back to the lair. Jason and Toria got up to help Jax back in.

"I'm not feeling too bad this morning besides being a little stiff and bruised. I'll go make the supply run for us Jax."

After Jason left, there was a silence between Jax and Toria. Jax started laughing and eased back in his chair.

"He's a good boy Toria."

That was all she needed to hear, she ran up and gave Jax a big hug.

"Look Jax, I don't know what's going to happen next or what Powers plans to do. I do know that I need to have a little sense of what my life used to be or I'll go insane. All I've done for months has been a killing machine. I want to continue, but I..."

"Say no more Toria, I understand. It's hard to say what Powers will do next, maybe we should lay low and recuperate a while and see what he does. You and Jason go have a good time away from all this as best you can. Just promise you'll get back here the first sign of trouble. I think I was young once, I just can't remember that far back."

"You're the best Jax!"

For the rest of the day the three of them went through inventory on what they had with the new supplies that Jason brought. They slept another 12 hours that night and felt a little more refreshed on the next day. At least they were a little more functional instead of being dead to the world. That evening they all sat around a steel drum fire eating canned food.

"I've been down here 3 days and I don't know how you do it day in and day out. You can't tell if it's light or dark, warm or cold."

"You get used to it my boy."

"I've been meaning to ask you Jax, you're Russian and the name Jax doesn't sound too Eastern European."

"That's because it's not it's a codename my boy. My real name is Igoranovich Peroshencovich, but you Americans butcher it."

"You're right, I'll stick with Jax."

They all had a good laugh, and then Toria spoke up.

"Jason, I want you to take me out dancing tonight. I've been down in this place so long; I just want to get out a bit."

"Do you think that's safe?"

"Out here crossing the street's not safe, but I've got to chance it. I've already spoken to Jax about it."

"Go see my friend Ivan who runs the clothing store near 46th and Jones Street. You'll be safe there and he'll find you a nice dress."

Later that night Toria and Jason were on their way to a night out on the town. Toria was dressed in a form fitting sparkled red dress, high heels and her hair down. They walked by one place with heavy metal blasting out from it.

"Come on Jason, this is my scene; they even have karaoke here!"

"Toria, I don't know how to dance."

"It's Metal Jason, you don't dance; you rock!"

Toria burst through the doors, fists pumping and head banging. Jason joined right in.

"Hey Toria, check this move out; I call it the Boxer."

As Jason and Toria have some fun, 3 guys in the corner are watching them and walk outside. They make their way to the south end of town, not too far away.

"I'm sure it's them Sal, we even saw them come out of the sewers. We've been following them for a while now."

"Good work boys, here is the plan. I want 20 of you to go down that end of the sewers and see what you can find. I want 20 of you to come with me, we're going dancing."

Back at the dance hall, Toria is stealing the show as the crowd watches her sing karaoke to "All for Nothing" by Lullacry.

"When you came crawling into my dreams,
That's all I've left or so it seems.
I can't erase you from my memory,
I think I'm ready for eternity."

At the same time Sal's thugs burst in on Jax in the underground lair! Caught off guard, Jax can't get to any weapons in time and is overwhelmed in a struggle against the thugs.

"Cause of you I've cut my wings,
Peace for me it hopefully brings.
I'm in this pain,
I've craved for love in vain."

Jax throws punch after punch, but there are just too many and he is knocked unconscious by the end of a club.

"I've never wanted to,
Burn my bridges down.
Gasping for air,
I'm left to drown."

Back in the lair all is silent as the last thug leaves out the manhole.

Just as Toria finishes up the song, the crowd erupts in applause. Toria throws the microphone and calls out to Jason to catch her. She leaps off the stage into his arms.
"So, you can sing and dance too, is there anything you can't do?"
"I can't read minds and I wish I could read yours. So, how about getting me another drink handsome?"
"Alright, you're lucky they're not checking ID's here; I'll be right back."

Jason gets a drink for him and Toria. In a matter of moments Jason unexpectedly collapses and starts coughing. Figures in the dance hall move towards him, while Toria is by his side.

"I don't understand it boss; we gave each of them a double dose. The guy went down like a ton of bricks and she's as right as rain."

"I don't know, Mr. Powers said this girl was special. You boys take the girl, I'll handle Mr. Hero."

Toria is tackled to the ground by a group of thugs as Sal the Snake moves in on Jason.

"Just go to sleep Mr. Hero."

Sal bites Jason on his right shoulder, sinking his sharpened teeth in his flesh and injecting him with poison. Just then Sal is sent across the floor from a kick to the back. Toria is standing over him with a group of thugs on the ground around her. She grabs Jason and jumps up on the stage, and then crashes though the windows out onto the street. She takes off running towards the lair.

"After her you fools, she's heading back to the sewers."

Toria reaches the lair before any thugs can catch up to her. To her horror she finds that Jax isn't there with signs of struggle everywhere. Immediately she goes topside near the steel door and hides with Jason, who is now unconscious, in one of the small tunnels that Jax created. It takes an hour for the thugs to search and leave. Leaving Jason in the tunnel, Toria ventures out in the lair to make sure they're gone. Once she's sure she runs back to the hiding tunnel and brings Jason to the mattress in the center room. As soon as Toria lays him down, he begins to wake up.

"What the hell happened, I'm pretty dizzy."

"We were jumped by one of the gangs at the dance hall. You went unconscious and there was a creepy guy standing over you. It looks like you were shot in the shoulder as well."

Jason felt his right shoulder with a look of fear on his face.

"That's not a bullet wound, that's a bite wound. That creepy guy was Sal the Snake. Nobody ever lives to tell the tale after he bites them. You saved my hide back there; Sal would have done me in."

"Lay back and I'll clean out the wound for you. That's not the worst part Jason; they took Jax. When I came down to the lair, he wasn't here and it looks like he tried to fight them off. I don't know where they took him, but I'm going to pay a visit to the Tower. I'm just glad they didn't find my stash of extra blades."

"Alright Toria, it's crazy, but I'll go with you. First thing in the morning, I'll talk to Eddie and see if he wants to go. I know it's not safe down here anymore, but maybe they won't be back tonight."

The next morning over at the gym, Jason runs into Eddie.

"I know it's dangerous as hell Eddie, but I know you and a couple other Wild Cards still are able to fight."

"Jason, I was talking it over with the boys and we all feel that it's just too dangerous. None of us wants to die Jason; we were almost beaten to death in that underground gun factory. Half of the guys are in the hospital, you have to understand."

"I hear you Eddie and I can't make you go. Tonight I'm going to the Tower with Toria. If something happens to me I want you to tell the guys that I'm proud of what they did."

"I will Jason, but you take care of yourself and you won't need me to tell them that."

Just as Jason is about to leave, he spots 2 guys walking the street outside the gym.

"Hey, I recognize those guys from the dance hall. Do me a favor Eddie and go get Toria; she's in the lair. Tell her to get down here as fast as she can as Eon. I'm gonna follow these guys and see if they take me to Sal."

Eddie takes off towards the east end of town in his truck, while Jason follows the 2 thugs. Jason is led down a series of alleyways deep in the southern heart of the city armed with only a metal bat. They enter into a large rundown mill site by a large river. Jason notices sidewalk chalk on the ground, probably left there by neighborhood kids. He picks up a piece of chalk and writes on the alley walls where he's going. After back tracking some he returns to the mill site that looks abandoned, but he knows better. There's a loud raging river in the back of the mill, which makes it impossible to listen for anything. It's a crisp day in the low 30's and Jason is glad he brought his jacket; he only wished he had his gloves too. Grabbing the cold drainage pipes, he climbs up to the roof to scout out the back of the area. The steam was thick in the air from his heavy breathing. The roof was made of corrugated steel, which was making noise as Jason walked on it. His large 240lbs frame was buckling the roof as he decided to re-think this maneuver. Jason started to climb back down the steel drainage pipe to the ground and go on foot. Unfortunately, with the noise from the river, he didn't hear the footsteps coming behind him. Just before he touched down on the ground, he felt something press into the small of his back. He knew all too well that it was a gun as he turned around with his hands up. Six guys surrounded him with guns pointed at him.

"You got a pair of brass ones snooping around here alone, why don't you come on inside and hang out for a while."

Jason was led into the mill at gunpoint by the thugs. Inside Jason saw Sal sitting in a big chair with Slither, his right hand man, standing next to him. Slither carried a coiled whip on each hip, both ending in cruel looking barbed hooks. Jason could see out the windows in the back and saw armed men patrolling around the river; some were also in other rooms that he could see through open doors. In the main room where he stood there were at least 30 guys. Most of the south side gang was right here; this had to be headquarters. Sal stood up with a toothy smile and walked over to Jason.

"I'm surprised you're still walking around, I thought the venom would have killed you. Then again, you do have a large frame. I'm glad to see you took the bait, I hope it wasn't too hard following my men here. I was hoping you'd bring your little friend with you, it seems we lost her in the dance hall."

Sal is interrupted by gunfire outside, he runs to the windows to see Eon hacking up his men left and right. With a sneer he slams his fist down on the table and starts to bark orders.

"Tie Mr. Hero here up tight, the rest of you prepare the steel net for our young lass. Slither why don't you go out and reel her in, she's quite a catch."

Jason watches chaos break out as the men prepare for Eon and watches Slither uncoil his whips and go out a back entrance. Jason is then tugged to the ground and has his hands and feet tied. Outside Eon has dropped a dozen and a half men when she sees something out of the corner of her eye. The rest of the men back away as Slither approaches. The grotesque man in front of her who stands easily 7ft tall with long gangly limbs wielding 2 long barbed whips surprises Eon. Slither hisses at Eon to show a tongue that has been cut up the middle to resemble a forked tongue. Eon throws a knife at him, but with surprising speed, it's knocked off course by the whips. Slither lurches forward towards Eon with whips snapping. Eon tumbles backwards and starts spinning the axe over her head. As one of the whips comes down on her, she meets it with the axe; which gets tangled in the whip. With her other hand she cuts the whip with her Bowie knife. Slither fires off the other whip that latches around her leg and he pulls. The barbed ends bite into her leg and rip at her flesh as she's yanked off her feet to the ground. Eon lets out a scream as Slither jumps on her, driving his foot into her stomach. Slither brings down the butt end of the whip handle on Eon's head, which has a metal spike on the end of it. She catches his hand and kicks him off of her, but he lands on his feet. Eon goes to back flip to her feet as well, but at the same time Slither throws out the whip and it wraps around her torso pinning her arms to her body. Slither raises the butt end of the other whip handle above his head and yanks her closer to stab her with it. As he pulls her in, he hisses at her before bringing down the handle. With her arms bound and being pulled through the air, she makes a last effort and whips her head forward. Her pony tail launching forward and just before Slither can bring down the spiked handle, Eon's hair spike goes into his mouth and right out the back of his skull. Slither drops down dead as Eon lands on the ground still wrapped in the whip. As she starts to untangle herself, the thugs fire off 2 guns. Each one firing a harpoon and attached in the middle is steel netting that wraps around Eon and holds her tight. The thugs close in on her; unable to move they carry her inside the mill. Sal walking over to Slither's body caresses his hideous face with a gentle touch, and then comes back inside.

"You certainly live up to your reputation young Eon, consider this a gift I'm about to give you and your friend."

As he talks, his goons are pulling back a rug to show a metal grate in the floor.

"You see, I haven't fed my pets today and they're hungry. Please consider it an honor that you get to be their meal. Men, throw them both in the pit and take their bonds off. My pets like prey that tries to fight back."

Eon and Jason are forced at gunpoint to get into the pit by 20 thugs. Dropping 15ft, they land on a ramp made of pavement. It's slippery and leads down to a pool of water. The room is dark and wet with slivers of light being let in by steel barred grates in the top of the room 15ft up at outside ground level. The room itself is about 30ftx30ft and the entire room is flooded with water. The walls are stone block and smooth to the touch.

"It looks like you've got some flooding in your basement Sal."

"Very funny Miss Eon, but it's preferred that way for what lives down there. If you have any incline to try to jump up here and try to work this locked gate free, my men will shoot you. You've been a worthy and amazing opponent, but now I must say goodbye."

Sal's men cover the grate with the rug and leave Eon and Jason in very little light. Jason makes out little ripples on the surface of the water by the little light coming in through the 3 barred grates on the ceiling.

"Toria, do you see those ripples on the water?"

"Yeah Jason, just be happy you don't see as well as I do, there's tons of water snakes in here!"

Chapter 7

"I don't have any weapons, they took the bat from me and we can't climb these walls."

"I used half of my throwing knives on the thugs outside the mill and my axe is laying near Slither's body. I've got the 2 Bowie knives, you take one and aim to cut the head off; these things are probably venomous. I'll go see if I can get to one of those grates."

"Toria, you can't wade in there, the snakes!"

"Don't worry Jason, they can't penetrate my skin; it's too tough. Even if they could the venom wouldn't hurt me. One of the tests Dr. Marks did was to expose my cells to blood born diseases and venom. He told me if we were in the Middle Ages that I would have survived the Plague. I guess you could say I have a super immune system, don't worry about it."

Jason watches as Toria wades into the water. The snakes swarm her as she hacks at them with the Bowie knife; the water starts to turn a reddish brown. True to her word, the snakes can't penetrate her skin. After a good 5 minutes of thrashing around, the snakes stop coming and Eon wades out into the room. The slope drops off and Eon is swimming through the water towards the grate near the river.

"The water's a little cold and deep, don't come in it'll be a shock to your system…"

Eon is cut off as she disappears under the surface in a thrash of water.

"Toria! What the hell's happening under there?"

Jason's question is answered as Eon pops up again gasping for air and he sees the dark glinted scaly skin of a huge green anaconda bite Eon in the back of the neck and take her down again. The snake's head is nearly the size of Eon's and the body as thick as hers. The snake was a monster that Jason estimated around 450lbs and was helpless as he watched. He didn't dare go in the water as he saw that the smaller 5ft snakes had returned to the surface. Eon had been under for a good minute when out of the water came the huge tail of the anaconda slapping on the cement ramp next to Jason. He quickly dove onto it, hacking at it with the Bowie knife; cutting clean through it in a matter of seconds. The snake erupted from the water and came after Jason, who cut its head off with a single swipe out of mid air. Eon bobbed up to the surface coughing and choking. She swam back to the ramp shivering and bloody, holding her side. Jason could see that the snake had bitten her multiple times as she had hundreds of teeth marks all over her, she was bleeding quite a bit.

"Jason thanks, I think the bastard bruised my ribs pretty bad; maybe even broke a couple. Don't worry, I'll get us out of here; I'm just glad it's still cold."

Eon grabs a nitro blade from her arm and throws it at one of the sidewalls just under the grate. The explosion shatters the stonewall as water comes rushing in from the river outside.

"Jason we've got to swim for it before this place fills to the top with water! Just wrap your arms around me, I'll swim us out."

Eon does just that, the icy sting of the water nearly taking Jason's breath away. They make it outside and across the river, once into the woods Eon collapses. She looks pale from her wounds inflicted by the barbed whip and snake.

"I feel out of gas Jason, I don't know if I can push on."

Jason shivering from the water and now in 34-degree weather outside picks up Eon in his arms.

"There's no bridge over the river, that should hold them off for a while. I'll take us down stream through the woods and look for a way to cross back into the city and get you to the lair."

Gunshots fired through the trees as Jason carried Eon deeper into the woods before going down stream. Keeping himself moving is the only way he stays warm. Jason drapes Eon over his shoulder, so she's easier to carry and finally decides to cross the river near the outskirts of town. Getting winded, Jason needs a moment before proceeding. He sets Eon on the ground and notices that her wounds have stopped bleeding from both the snakebites and the barbed hooks.

"You are one amazing girl Toria, just let me catch my breath and I'll get you back to the lair."

Once Jason comes to the river, he doesn't see any of Sal's thugs. However, the river is even bigger at this point, as it gets closer to the harbor. Jason takes a deep breath and braces himself for the cold and difficult crossing. The sting of the river is nearly unbearable as he makes it to the halfway point. The river at this point is 50ft across and raging. Jason sinks in up to his waist as he holds Eon over his head. The current is so strong that it threatens to topple him at any second. Jason's feet dig into the rocky bottom to keep his footing with every step. His breathing becomes more rapid and shallow as the sting of the water saps the life out of him. Only will alone and the feelings he has for the girl he holds push him on to the other side, where he sets Eon down and collapses in a curled position shivering uncontrollably. As Jason tries to get up, he's forced back to the ground from his muscles locking up. Then to his horror, he spots a group of Sal's goons coming down the street that parallels the river. Realizing that this is it, tears of frustration well up in his eyes, as he still can't control his movements. As if by some miracle, from a side street comes a familiar pick up truck. It pulls to a screeching stop by Jason and Eon. Eddie jumps out of the truck and runs over to his friend's side.

"Jesus Christ Jason, I heard gun shots and started driving around looking for you. I thought you were a dead man!"

"E-E-Eddie, t-they're c-c-coming, h-help!"

Eddie quickly picks up Jason and puts him in the back of the truck and places Eon in the front seat. As he runs around to get into the driver's side, gunshots start to ricochet around the truck off the street. Eddie slams the accelerator while losing a tail light to a bullet. The truck pulls away and out of sight around a corner. Free from danger, Eddie drives back to his place in the south side of town and parks behind the garage, so his truck isn't visible. He takes Jason and Eon inside his apartment and wraps them both in blankets and puts on some tea. Eddie checks Eon's pulse as she's still unconscious and it's very slow. He looks over to see Jason start to lose consciousness himself.

"Look man, you need to stay awake and drink this. I'm gonna put you in the hot shower, you're going into hypothermia."

Eddie piles blankets on top of Eon with a hot water bottle on her neck, he takes her temperature and it reads a low 95.2 degrees. Eddie takes notice of the bloodstains on her and her pale complexion.

"Come on girl, I've seen you come back from this state before when you fought the Blade Master, but I bet you weren't this cold either."

He runs back to check on Jason who is starting to respond to the heat and has stopped shivering and can talk now.

"Thanks Eddie I owe you a big one for this, we were done for."

"You probably owe me more than one, but this was for me. Who am I gonna hang out with if I lose my best buddy?"

"Eddie how's Toria?"

"She's not looking good, we need to get some warm fluids in her."

Both of them knowing that a hospital is out of the question; they wait for her body temperature to come up. Within half an hour she starts to wake up shivering.

"Jason where are you? Where am I?"

"I'm right here Toria, we're in Eddie's apartment, just stay still. You need to drink this hot tea to warm up."

Toria took small sips at first coughing if she went too fast. Gradually she was able to drink normally as she woke up a little more. She set the mug down with a sad look on her face.

"Well Jason, that was a hands down winning battle for the bad guys."

"Oh, I don't think so Toria. You killed a third of Sal's gang, killed his right hand man Slither, killed his pet snakes and flooded his headquarters by blasting a big hole in the foundation. I'd say they lost quite a bit as well."

That brought a smile to Toria's face as she finished the rest of her tea.

"I guess you're right, but I lost my axe and need to restock my other blades in the lair."

"Both of you need to rest up and get your strength back before you do anything. You should be safe here, those guys don't know where I live."

"Alright, but only till nightfall; then I'm going back."

"Toria, that's crazy look at you!"

"Jason, I heal 7 times faster than you do. That means just sitting here talking with you two for a few hours is like a full day and night of bed rest. I lost a good deal of blood, but my wounds have already scabbed over and within a week there won't be any evidence that I was even wounded. I just need to keep drinking Eddie's tea and rest a little bit more. There is one other thing Eddie. Since my cells regenerate so fast, it causes my metabolism to skyrocket. So, I was wondering if you had anything to eat?"

"It's true Eddie, I've seen this girl put away food like you wouldn't believe."

"I'll see what I have in the kitchen, hold on."

Eddie goes into the kitchen and pulls out a supreme pizza and a dozen chicken wings. He heats them up and brings them out to Toria who devours them like a snack.

"Wow, where does it all go?"

"I'm full now, but it'll be gone in a few hours. Jax used to complain that I was making him go broke. Speaking of which I hope he's all right."

"Hey, try not to think about it Toria, he's a tough old bird."

"Guys I gotta go out to the truck, I left my phone out there."

"Oh I got it Eddie, my legs are stiffening up sitting here anyway."

Toria gets up, walks downstairs and out to the truck. Just before she opens the door she stops to listen more closely. There are footsteps and whispers among a large group of people. Toria ducks around the other side of the truck. It's starting to get dark at this point, the "magic hour" and Toria waits.

"One of the boys got a fix on this guy's license plate, we tracked him here. I tell you boys it's a lot easier having the law on your side. You get to use all their fancy equipment. We're gonna plug all 3 of them for what they did back at the mill, good thing we got the back-up hideout. Well, here we are boys, let's lock and load."

Toria waits till they pass the truck; she has 6 knives left and 1 nitro blade. She grabs all 6 throwing knives and lets them fly, all embedding in the back of 6 necks. As the others start to turn around to see what happened, Eon is already upon them with the Bowie knives. She hacks 3 of them down and pins the last one to the ground holding a Bowie knife under his eye.

"I've killed your whole hunting party in less than 7 seconds and unless you tell me where the other hideout is, your joining them."

"I'm no rat, you little bitch!"

Toria starts to dig the point of the blade under his eyelid.

"Alright, alright!"

She stops pressure with the blade.

"Look, it's in the basement of the old clothing factory on the south end. You gotta believe me, now let me go!"

"Yeah, I'll let you go."

Eon drives the Bowie knife through his eye and out the back of his head. She collects her blades, gets the phone and grabs all their guns before running back upstairs to the apartment.

"I ran into some trouble out there, had to take down 10 of them. They know where you live now Eddie; it's not safe here anymore. The good news is I found out where they are now. Do you know where the old clothing factory on the south side is?"

"Yeah, it's actually not too far from here."

"Good. Eddie, do you mind if I use your shower to clean up and get the blood off? Oh, by the way here's your phone."

Eon tosses the phone towards Eddie and walks into the bathroom. Both Jason and Eddie look at each other in astonishment.

"Jason old friend, you've got your hands full, she's the real deal. It looks like we've got some fire power as well, I have a feeling we'll need it."

Once Toria finishes cleaning up, the 3 of them get into the truck and head out to the old clothing factory.

"I'll park here just down the other street while you 2 go in. I'll stay here unless they come after me, but I'll try to circle back around to grab you if there's any trouble."

"Eddie, there's 3 pistols loaded on the seat and keep this one on you, I hope you don't need to use them. Hopefully we'll be back soon."

"Who are you fooling Jason, it never goes according to plan."

The men both exchange smiles and Jason and Eon take off towards the old clothing factory.

Inside the basement of the clothing factory, Sal is barking orders.

"The hunting party isn't back yet, that means they won't be coming back. We need to assume that one of them talked and get ready. I want the front door bolted and you guys ready with the steel net. That really was a useful tool Carmine came up with. I want 20 of you up in those chain rafters they used to hang clothes and act as snipers. The rest of you hide on ground level behind the machinery. Get ready to finish the job boys, we're putting them down here and now."

Eon and Jason make it to the factory and start heading down the stairs to the basement, where they run into a locked steel door. Jason shoots out the lock and kicks open the door. There are lights on inside, but nobody visible.

"Hold on Jason, let me take a quick look around in there before you go in."

Eon checks around the door frame and notices the men in the rafters and the 3 support chains holding them in place.

"Jason there's about 20 guys in the rafters with guns. There's no way we'll get in there with them waiting to pick us off. I'm gonna open things up with a bang, when I do roll behind that crate and stay down till you have something to shoot at."

Eon takes aim and let's loose her other nitro blade into the central column in the rafters. The explosion blasts out the supporting chain, killing a few guys in the process. The weakened structure with the added weight of the men starts a chain reaction of bolts snapping and giving way until the whole chain structure collapses. All 20 gunmen fall to their deaths as the chains fall on top of them. Jason tumbles behind a crate just to the left of the door. Eon starts doing super fast flips hand over feet down the middle of the factory. She draws fire from behind the crates. Once the men pop out to start firing at her, Jason targets them and starts to pick them off. Eon is untouched by the bullets, the flips making her a near impossible target to hit. The nearest 4 guys that she sees all get throwing knives stuck in their foreheads. From behind her 2 guys pop out with the steel net guns. This time Eon is ready for it and as they fire, she flips over the net towards them. When she comes down, she brings down the Bowie knives and cuts both their heads off. The gunfire from guys behind pieces of machinery and crates sends her diving behind a crate for cover.

Meanwhile, Jason sees Sal running towards the door out from behind some machinery. He lets him go and follows him out to the street. Once Sal starts to run Jason holds up the gun.

"Stop right there Sal, you're not going anywhere."

"You going to shoot me, what sport is there in that?"

Jason puts down the gun and rolls up his sleeves.

"No, I'm not gonna shoot you; I just wanted to get your attention. What I am gonna do is beat you to death. You ruled my part of Harborside for too long, I lost friends to your thugs. Not to mention you gave me a real nasty scar on my shoulder. You've got this coming Sal and I'm gonna enjoy every bit of it."

Sal hissed at Jason, showing a mouthful of razor pointed teeth. Jason knew just one bite would render him unconscious and Sal would kill him. It was just the 2 of them out in the road under the streetlights in the dark, cold night. Jason ran at Sal, who surprised Jason with his speed in ducking out of the way. Sal grabbed his arm and flipped him over his shoulder to land on his back, nearly knocking the wind out of him. Then Sal grabbed Jason's leg with intent to break it at the knee. Jason kicked down hard and yanked his leg free from Sal's grip. With a powerful kick, he knocked Sal off his feet. It was a race as both men tried to get up first, a race that Jason won. He grabbed Sal and threw him into a light post, as Sal lay motionless. As Jason approached him Sal sprang to life and bit down hard on Jason's calf. Jason screamed in pain as Sal started to laugh with blood running down his face.

"It won't be long now, too bad you didn't get a chance to say goodbye to your little girlfriend. Don't worry though, she'll be joining you soon enough."

Jason let out a scream of anger and grabbed Sal by the ankles. With tremendous strength, he picked Sal up and started spinning with him through the air till Sal's body was completely horizontal. With all the might Jason could muster, he connected Sal's head with the metal light post. There was a loud crack as Sal's skull split open killing him instantly. Jason was starting to sway and the world was starting to spin, but he picked up Sal's body and made his way back down to the basement. With his last bit of energy he threw Sal down the stairs, then collapsed unconscious. Sal's body flew through the air, landing hard on the pavement of the basement floor. The impact threw Sal's brain matter out the back of his cracked skull with a large bloodstain on the floor. Sal's body was all the diversion that Eon needed. As the men looked at the gruesome site before them, Eon was upon them with blades flashing. There weren't many left and the entire gang was wiped out this night in the basement of the old clothing factory. Eon ran upstairs to see Jason's body. In a panic she checked his pulse, he was still alive, just unconscious. Eon picked him up and ran back to Eddie who started up the truck.

"He'll be fine Eddie, lets just get back to your place. I have a feeling we'll be safe there tonight."

As Eddie speeds away back to his apartment, word of another gang's demise spreads to Mr. Powers.

"Your girl is most impressive Jax, she's taken out 3 of my gangs. I have no doubt she'll be coming here next. Johnny, I'm putting Jax in your care as a little insurance. When she shows up here, we'll ask her to surrender. If she refuses, make sure she sees you kill him."

"With pleasure Mr. Powers, I'm looking forward to this little meeting."

Chapter 8

Two days pass as Toria, Jason and Eddie lay low in Eddie's apartment; a much needed rest for all of them.

"My ribs are finally starting to feel better from that snake bite."

"It was more like a sea monster than a snake, Sal must have had that thing down there for years. Speaking of Sal, he left me with a pair of killer scars."

"Hey you're a hero Jason for taking Sal out like that. Once word spreads, things are gonna start changing around the south end of the city. Hell, things are already changing around the whole city. You can see it in the papers, the news or just walk outside the front door. Community centers are opening back up again; kids can play outside and Surge on the street in now non-existent. I hear it in the gyms from the people, they're rooting for you guys they want Powers to fall too."

"Thanks Eddie, but I'd be dead next to the river if it weren't for you, we all played a part."

The conversation is interrupted by a knock on the door. They all look at each other in confusion. Toria and Jason hide as Eddie cautiously approaches the door.

"Who is it?"

"This is Special Agent Taylor, I need to talk to an Eddie Scora."

Eddie held a gun in one hand and cracked open the door with the deadbolt in place.

"What's this concerning?"

"Mr. Scora, we at the agency know that you have ties with the fugitive known as Eon. We just need you to pass on a message to her. The agency has been tracking your movements and there is a reason that we haven't stepped in. Mr. Powers controls the law enforcement behind the scenes, but we have to make it appear to the public that we're against his gangs and operations to keep the peace. The thing is, we want Eon to take Powers out. That's why we haven't tried to step in and stop her. Powers has seen to it that we purposely don't have the firepower to defeat him. With Eon wiping out his gangs, it's the edge the law enforcement needs to overthrow Powers."

"Are you saying that we now have the backing of the police force to help us?"

"No we can't do that, it's not that easy. Powers could take over this city by force if he wanted to, then it would become a Federal problem. The whole thing would escalate to a bloodbath that we don't want to happen. We all have homes and families…what I'm saying is that we won't stand in the way. Look, it's dangerous for me to be standing here like this as it is, will you pass on this information?"

"Yeah, no problem."

Eddie shuts the door and Jason and Toria come out.

"I heard everything he said from across the room Eddie and that's great news."

"I think it sounds too good to be true, how do we know we can trust this so called agent?"

"Jason, do you really think that the police want to be puppets to a madman?"

"Didn't you here him Toria, the police won't even help you."

"Guys, they're just looking out for their families as best as they can. He said they don't have the firepower to take out Powers. Together we've defeated 3 gangs in this city and already things are changing. Now we have a chance to liberate the entire city from this tyrant. There's only one more guard dog as Jax called them over in the west part of town, then there's nothing stopping us from going straight to the central Tower."

"No need Toria, all operation in the west has been suspended. I've got some friends over there, they said Johnny pulled all his men out and shacked up with Powers. I really think it's a smart move on his part, divided you were beating him. Now, he's united what he has left and the Tower is more powerful than ever."

"If that's the case then there's nothing standing in our way now. I don't care how powerful he is, Jax is in there and I owe him everything and more. I have to go out and at least try. I say we let things calm down some, right now the Tower's on high alert. If we let them relax some, maybe they'll be more likely to slip up when we attack. Somehow I know they won't hurt Jax as long as they know they can use him as a bargaining chip. What we need to do now is a little reconnaissance work and see what we're up against."

Over the course of the next month, the 3 of them all stayed at Eddie's apartment. Eddie and Jason continued to work their jobs, pooling the money to help Eddie. Jason gave up his little, expensive one room apartment. Toria on the other hand continued to train and hone her skills down in the lair. Sometimes she even spent the night down there. Her supply of throwing knives was running critically low and she had 6 nitro blades left. On a good note, during the clean up of the mill site battle; Agent Taylor had found and returned Eon's axe to Eddie. Each night Eon would scout around the Tower looking for the best way inside. Unfortunately, she didn't find any, Johnny's gang served as armed guards all around the perimeter of the Tower. On a late November night, Toria decides to get a closer look. She brings it up around dinner at Eddie's place.

"Jason, I've decided to try to get into the main grounds around the Tower. The guards aren't letting up it's as if Powers knows I'm just waiting to strike. I've seen Hammer out patrolling with his men; he's a mean looking son-of-a-bitch. I've got a plan to breach the surrounding wall, but it will take all 3 of us to pull it off. I'll call out Hammer, I wish I could just pick him off; but he wears a body armor suit. While I'm keeping him busy, Jason you're going to cover Eddie by picking off the thugs. Eddie, I'm giving up one of my nitro blades that I keep in the lair. While Jason covers you, you need to run straight at the wall and throw it as hard as you can. Stand a little ways back, it makes a big boom. Once that happens, I should have taken care of Hammer by then and I can come to your side so all of us can go through together."

Jason and Eddie nodded, each of them had a bullet proof vest that Agent Taylor had given them; as well as automatic assault rifles. That night they geared up for the attack on the perimeter.

On foot the 3 traveled to the center of the city that night. It was cold and Jason and Eddie felt weighted down with all the layers they were wearing, but most of all they were nervous. They took up positions behind parked cars outside the outer gates. The Tower looked like a prison, with 2 guard towers and thugs on foot patrolling around the gate. Hammer was walking with a small patrol around the wall's perimeter. Eon made the first move.

"Hey tack hammer, you boys looking for me?"

Like an angry bull Hammer turned around and charged at Eon.

"It's her, go alert Mr. Powers now!"

Eon dodged out of the way of the 50lbs sledgehammer as it cracked the pavement. She swung the axe overhead to bring it down on

Hammer, but he got the steel sledge up in time to block it from taking his head off.

    Just then gunfire erupted from behind parked vehicles as Jason and Eddie unloaded on the guards in the towers and on the ground in the front. Eddie dropped the assault rifle and started running for the gates as more thugs started to close in from the surrounding areas. Jason was doing the best that he could to pick them off, but there were so many, he was just slowing them down. He hoped it was enough time for Eddie to get close to the gates and use the nitro blade.

    Hammer noticed this out of the corner of his eye and started to move towards him. Eon jumped at him with the Bowie knife and tore into his left arm with it. With a loud scream Hammer grabbed Eon by the ponytail and threw her off. He swung the hammer and knocked down a telephone pole that came crashing down on Eon, pinning her to the road and crushing her. Hammer took off towards Jason just as there was a loud explosion. Eddie had blasted open the gates with the nitro blade. Jason was so focused on Eddie's progress that he didn't see the giant steel hammer out of his peripheral vision. The hammer came down shattering the assault rifle and knocking Jason on his back. Jason stayed down holding his arm and wincing in pain as Hammer stood over him and raised his weapon.

Meanwhile, Eon had lifted the telephone pole off of her and saw Hammer standing over Jason. She was upon them in a flash, all she saw was red. Eon lowered her shoulder and tackled Hammer to the ground. Eddie started to run back to behind the vehicles to regain his assault rifle and return fire, but was shot from behind by all the men pouring out of the gates and went down in the street.

Eon in a blind rage was stabbing Hammer in the face repeatedly with the Bowie knife till it was just a bloody paste. Jason had to grab her off of him and bring her back to the present.

"Toria, Eddie's been hit we've got to get out of here. There's at least 100 men coming out of those gates after us, we'll never make it in there alive. I think my arm is broken, but I can run. You need to get Eddie and get him to a hospital now!"

Eon climbed off of Hammer's corpse and ran to get Eddie who was gasping for air, but still holding on. The men were closing in and shooting at them. Eon and Jason took off through the streets of the city. Jason was trying to hold them off by shooting behind him with one arm using Eddie's assault rifle. Soon, they were far enough away that the men weren't chasing them anymore. They went on another 10 minutes before they reached the Central City Hospital. Bursting through the doors, they ran to the front, Jason was going into shock at this point and wasn't too responsive.

"Somebody help us immediately! This man was shot multiple times and this man may have internal damage as well as a broken arm!"

Nurses responded immediately, taking Jason and Eddie back into the hospital. Eddie was still wheezing and looking paler, sweating profusely. In a flash all that Eon could see were the double doors swinging shut and all of a sudden she was alone.

Meanwhile, inside the Tower men are reporting the damage.

"The gates are blown apart and we lost 38 men including Hammer."

"I want a team repairing the gate right now, I want the tower guards and men replaced as well. You say you hit 2 of them, but not the girl. It may not be a total loss, she could be all alone now and that means she'll become desperate."

Toria waited in the hospital until the Doctor came out.

"Your friend Jason is stable with a broken left arm with some internal contusions, but he'll be fine."

"What about Eddie, the other guy that was with him?"

The Doctor looked down and thought before he spoke. He placed a hand on Toria's shoulder.

"His ribs and lungs were crushed from the impact of so many bullets. We had him on a ventilator, but he lost so much blood from other gun shot wounds. I'm so very sorry, but he didn't make it."

The Doctor walked back behind the double doors as Toria sank down into a chair with a blank expression on her face. After a few moments she got up and slowly walked to the reception desk.

"I need to see Jason."

"I'm sorry Miss, but he's still in critical care."

Toria's voice rose in anger and she slammed the counter so hard that it split down the middle.

"Where is he, I need to see him now!"

"Please stay calm Miss, I'll page the Doctor."

Toria walked into Jason's room and the look on his face told her that he knew. She ran to him and embraced in a long hug, through painful tears she chocked out the words.

"He's gone Jason, he's gone!"

Jason started to cry and just hung onto Toria with his good arm. After a long moment Jason was able to compose himself for a brief time.

"Listen to me Toria, you need to get out of here. You need to stay away in case Powers sends men after you. You're the only one that can stop him; you need to get Jax back. All the pain, all the suffering, all the death needs to come to an end.

Everyone believes in you Toria, Eddie did and so do I. The entire city needs you."

Jason painfully leaned in closer and sternly looked into Toria's eyes.

"Bring Powers down."

He lay back into the bed, his eyes started to close as the pain medication kicked in and he was asleep.

That night Eon stayed in the lair, she took a shower and sat back on the mattress on the floor. With only a few candles lit, she was left alone with her thoughts. She thought of Eddie and the hole that would be left from his absence in every aspect of his life. She wondered about her home that she was forced to leave. Was there another girl living in her room by a family that bought it from the bank? She thought about Jax and how he was faring in the Tower. She thought of how she missed her family and Jason. She thought of the uphill battle that she'd be fighting with Powers and how the Tower seemed an impenetrable place. She started to cry and lost hope, how could Powers be taken down? She lay down on the mattress and closed her eyes tomorrow was another day.

In the morning Toria scrounged what she could find in Jax's pantry. It wasn't much, but enough for now. Her thoughts drifted to what Eddie had said about the city changing. "Just step out the front door", he had said, Toria did just that. Putting on one of Jax's old coats, she went topside just to look around at the city that she never really realized was there. Caught up in her own ambitions for revenge, this was the first time she really took a step back. The streets seemed livelier than before, people now walked places and stopped to speak to each other on the street. There weren't as many sirens going off and people had smiles on their faces. Then she realized that all the hardship that she had endured had actually made a difference. She knew that she had to find a way to finish the job that she had started. Returning to the lair, she took inventory of what she had left. There were enough throwing knives to fill the 12 slots on her suit, but that was about it. She had 5 nitro blades left and her trusty 2 Bowie knives and axe. She had to laugh; this was all she had to take on the most powerful man in all of Harborside in his fortress full of guards. All this would happen tonight, she would use the darkness and her evolved vision to her advantage. For the rest of the day, she practiced and prepared physically and mentally for the task ahead. She had to come to terms with the realization that she may not ever be coming back to the lair.

Chapter 9

As nightfall came, Toria forced herself to eat something just in case it was her last meal. It was December 1st and a cold night with light snow coming down. Even with her tough skin and evolved thermoregulatory system, she would still feel chilly tonight. It was good she thought; it would keep her on her toes. She took her time eying and feeling the blade of each knife as she put on the gear once again and was ready to go. Before going topside, she paused to take a last look at the lair. It was calm and tranquil like a calm before a storm. How she wished Jax was there right now and she didn't have to do this alone. Mustering her courage, looking at the underside of the manhole cover she emerged onto the street.

She started to jog to keep warm at about 17MPH. There was traffic out, but not too many people walking the streets. In about 20 minutes Eon could see the Tower in the distance and she started to pick up speed. She was focused now; nothing could stand in her way. As she got closer she could see the men patrolling about and the 2 guard towers on either side of the now repaired gate. Eon increased her speed to an all out sprint reaching just shy of 40 MPH. She came out of the darkness of the night and threw one of her nitro blades at the gate. The gentle falling snow in the dark clear night had its majestic tranquility broken by an explosion that sent men and steel flying. Eon ran by the men so fast, they didn't have time to react to shoot at her. As she ran by them through the hole she had created, she threw 2 throwing knives, one knife for the guard in each tower. Once through to the other side, she jumped 15ft straight up to catch the bottom platform of one of the towers and flipped into it. She picked up the fallen M-16 next to the dead guard and unloaded on the thugs on the ground. A mass of bullets sprayed in all directions from above and below. The stone and steel sanctuary that the tower provided protected Eon.

She had killed all the guards in the immediate vicinity and ran out of ammunition. Other thugs were running to the gate for back up. Before they were able to get there, Eon did a running leap from one tower to the other crossing a span of nearly 20ft. She picked up the other M-16 by the other fallen guard and waited for them to come closer. She breathed a small sigh of relief.

"So far, so good, but this is just the beginning."

Up in the furthest reaches of the Tower, Mr. Powers is observing the action from video cameras in place all around the grounds.

"She's slaughtering my men Mr. Powers!"

"They're my men Johnny! There's nothing I can do about that right now. Take up a defensive position at the Tower entrance and take Jax with you. Offer her the choice to surrender, if she refuses, then you can kill him. Stop her from entering the Tower."

"Yes Mr. Powers, I look forward to crushing her skull. I'll have revenge for what she did to Hammer."

Johnny the Smasher grabs Jax, who is tied by the hands and feet as well as gagged. He looks tired and lifeless as he's thrown over Johnny's shoulder.

At the perimeter gate, the shooting has stopped. Eon climbs down from the tower to ground level where nearly 100 men are dead and not a single police siren. She picks up another machine gun, from a fallen thug and proceeds cautiously across the Tower's courtyard grounds making her way to the entrance.

Mr. Powers observes her progress from multiple video screens and starts to push buttons and flip switches on a large control panel on his desk.

"Well, little Eon you've made it this far. You've defeated all my gangs and taken out my best men. Now you dare to take me on in my own domain. We shall see how good you really are."

As Eon made her way across the snow covered lawn, she heard a humming noise that grew louder. In the lights of the Tower she noticed little black things coming out of the ground all around the entire length of the section she was on. Not knowing what it was, at the height of the noise that sounded like something charging up; she jumped into the air. Just as she jumped a latticework of electrical current appeared beneath her in a grid like pattern of small squares made of electricity. She landed with each foot in a square; the latticework of electricity was the size of a football field with each square only 1ftx1ft and Eon was caught in the middle of it. Holding her breath to assess the situation, she didn't dare move. The humming and sparking was nearly deafening. She slung the machine gun over her shoulder and began flipping through the grid pattern. She made it all the way to the end of the electrical grid pattern when her foot caught a patch of ice and she fell on her back, catching the very edge of the current. She was blasted into a group of nearby bushes with enough force to kill a person! Eon lay there breathing sporadically in gasps, her eyes wide and her body shaking uncontrollably. Her heartbeat was irregular and panic started to set in. She forced herself to stay calm and try to re-gain her breathing. She closed her eyes hugging herself and trying to stop the shaking. Eon lay there battling internally for a good 10 minutes before her shaking began to cease and her breathing and heart rate were normal again. She walked out from the bushes, looked at the electrical field and shook her head.

"If I had slipped in the middle of that mess, I'd have been fried to death. What else have you got for me Powers?"

She continued on to a clearing that led up to the front entrance. She began to walk through it cautiously, when it sounded like a sprinkler system was coming out. From the corner of her eye, she saw a stream of liquid shoot at her. She instinctively pulled out the Bowie knife and blocked it with the flat of the blade like a shield.

"Oh, it's just the sprinkler system. Come on Powers it's the middle of winter, you can turn it off now."

Then a drip fell from the knife and landed on her knee, making her jump as it sizzled.

"Jesus Christ, it's acid!"

Looking around, she found that once again she was in the middle of a field of trouble. Her only chance was to run for it, using both her Bowie knives as shields as it was shooting from both sides. It was a sprint of about 150ft before she was out of the acid sprinklers. She had small burn marks here and there from the splashing of the acid to match the large red electrical burn on her back.

"I wonder how long it will take for these burns to heal and I'm not even in the Tower yet. Something tells me I'll look like I went through the grinder if I make it out of this alive."

Eon goes to replace both Bowie knives and catches a glimpse at the blades and the holes in them.

"Holy shit! That acid ate right through my knives. With these holes in them they're about as strong as a tin can."

Eon was able to bend the blades over with the tip of her finger. Angry and disgusted, she throws the Bowie knives to the ground. She still had her axe that was strapped across her back and the machine gun. She grabbed the machine gun and walked forward to the front entrance of the Tower. There was a lone figure standing on the steps. The entrance way was all white marble with bushes surrounding the 30ft wide semi circle stone steps to the grand entrance way. The entire place looked like a palace, complete with a stone fountain in the center of the platform on the top of the 12 steps. Two large pillars stood on either side of the fountain and by one of them stood the figure. As Eon cautiously got closer, she could see that it was an enormous man with steel gauntlets over his hands. She knew this was Johnny the Smasher, representing what was left of the 4 gangs in Harborside. She had remembered what Jax had told her about him and how he could punch through a brick wall with those gauntlets. Kneeling in front of Johnny was Jax bound and gagged. Johnny held his hand around Jax's neck as Eon approached.

"I've been waiting for you little girl. Send over the gun or I'll kill him with a flick of the wrist."

Eon knew it would take multiple bullets to bring down this giant. By the time she fired even a killing shot, she didn't want to tackle the chance of losing Jax.

"Alright I'm putting down the gun."

"No, no, no, toss the gun up here and give it to me."

Eon hesitated, and then tossed the gun up the stairs to Johnny who caught it and looked it over.

"This is one of Carmine's designs, he always hid behind his guns. I could kill you in an instant with this, but I don't hide behind guns."

With a wicked smile, Johnny set the gun down in front of his feet.

"I like to be more direct, up close and personal."

Johnny made a fist and with tremendous force punched the gun in front of him, smashing it to bits. Eon swallowed hard and stood wide eyed at this display of strength.

"Now little girl, you got 2 choices. You either surrender now to Mr. Powers or you refuse and I kill Jax here and pound the shit out of you. Personally, I hope you refuse the surrender."

"No, that's fine, let him go and take me to Powers."

"Toria, you will not surrender, don't worry about me. You're the only one that can bring down this tyrant."

"Jax we can fight another day, lets just get out of this one."

"Ha, ha, ha, tough decision to make isn't it little girlie? It's too bad life didn't turn out to be your perfect little world."

"No Johnny, it's not a perfect world. In a perfect world I'd be doing what I like to do instead of killing people. In a perfect world I could walk into a clothing store and actually find a bra that fits. In a perfect world I wouldn't be standing here at night talking to a loser like you. Now let him go and you'll get your answer."

"You want me to let him go? Alright, you got it, I'll let him go."

Johnny picks up Jax by the neck and throws him like rag doll into the stone fountain. Jax crumpled to a heap and lay there bleeding in silence.

"Jax! Oh my God!"

Eon runs up the stairs to Jax's side, not knowing what to do with a look of horror on her face. He looked bad, really bad. It was obvious he had multiple broken bones as well as other injuries.

"Listen to me Toria, you will finish this. Powers will not get away from you, free this city. Because of you the breath of life filled me once again. I felt like I did in the old days, you gave me a reason to fight back and live at all. Thank you Toria, I always knew you'd be something great. You take care of Jason and have a good life together. You say that you owe me, but you've given me more than I could ever want. You brought me happiness again Toria in my dark days, I'm forever grateful. Finish this job and don't worry about me, I'll be watching you always."

"Jax, I'll get you out of here, just hang on!"

Jax held up a hand to touch Eon's face.

"I love you…remember me."

Then his hand fell, the life of this great man had come to an end. Eon burst into tears, hugging Jax's body. She picked him up and carried him down to the bushes and covered him with branches.

"I'll come back for you old friend and give you a proper burial and recognition."

"Hey where do you think you're going, I'm not gonna let you walk outta here."

Toria stood up and faced the giant man as she strode confidently up the stone stairs. Then she started to take out her throwing knives and lay them down on the fountain where the snow was stained red. She removed her axe and even took off her other nitro blade.

"You don't like hiding behind guns do you Johnny? Well, I'm not hiding behind my blades."

"You're going to fight me? Ha, ha, ha, that's absurd!"

"Oh, I'm going to do a lot more than fight you Johnny, a lot more."

Eon slowly walked towards him with a look that could burn through iron.

"I'm going to beat you until you're broken and I'm not stopping till you're dead."

"I'm no push over like Carmine or Sal little girl. So come on, lets see what you've got."

Eon charged at Johnny and he went to swing at her with the massive steel gauntlets. Eon ducked out of the way and slammed her fist into his stomach with enough force to dent the front end of a car. Johnny staggered back and lunged at Eon, she dove through his legs and kicked him in the back of the knees. Johnny buckled down to his knees and Eon unleashed a torrent of strikes to his back. Johnny stood up and swung his arm in a backhanded fashion and again Eon flipped out of the way. She grabbed his arm and tucking with all her strength, she flipped him over her shoulder into the fountain. Johnny's massive body smashed into the stone fountain, cracking it. He started to get up and Eon did a roundhouse kick to his face, knocking him back to the ground. Then she stepped back and let him get up; he was a little wobbly in the legs.

    She stood there and watched him with calm breathing and relaxed posture. As Johnny stood up, he wiped the blood from his face and looked back at Eon. He didn't know what to make of this as he looked around nervously. Johnny gritted his teeth and came at her again, Eon dropped down on her hands and kicked with both feet into Johnny's solar plexus. Then she stood up with an upper cut to his nose, breaking it. Johnny stumbled back holding his face with the wind knocked out of him. Again Eon stood there and did not attack. Johnny picked up a piece of the broken fountain over his head to bring it down on her. Eon flipped to his side as the stone piece came crashing down and she kicked at his ankle. With a loud crack, Johnny went down to his knees, with his tibia broken. From his knees, he took a swing at her; she caught his arm and with a severe wrench dislocated his shoulder. Johnny leaned up against the fountain unable to stand, fight or see with the blood in his eyes. Eon walked around him in a slow circle as he suffered in agony.

    "I told you I would break you. Now that you're broken it's time to pay for your crimes against humanity, me and especially Jax!"

    Eon stood in front of the massive brute and he eyed her back.

"Go to Hell, you'll never win!"

Eon let out a half smile, then unloaded kick after kick and punch after punch until finally Johnny was knocked right off the stairs and landed in a broken heap dead as a doornail. Eon walked over and put her blades back on and took out the axe. She walked over to Johnny's body and with a single powerful swipe, took his head clean off. She picked up the head and walked over to one of the cameras that were mounted on the Tower and held up the head high to be seen.

"Is this all you've got Powers? Is this the best you've got to send against me to defend yourself?"

Eon threw the head out into the acid field in which she had come. She turned back to the camera and got as close as she could.

"I've defeated every one of your gangs Powers, nothing will stop me from coming after you. There is no place to run, no place to hide from me now. I am Eon, I am the wrath of God sent upon you, I am the scourge sent to destroy you and there's nothing you can do about it."

Eon began to walk away from the camera towards the door, and then she stopped and turned around quickly pointing her finger at the camera.

"I'll kill you all!"

She stood there staring at the camera a good 30 seconds before turning back around and walking towards the front doors.

On the other end of the camera, high in the Tower, Mr. Powers watches the display on his video screens. He leans back in his chair drumming his fingers on the desk and for once the great and powerful man was speechless.

Back outside, Eon walks up to the very entrance of the Tower and pauses for a moment.
"I'm here, all the guard dogs are dead Jax. Whatever is on the other side of this door, I'll give it my all and more. This is my final test."
Eon reached out her hand and opened the door, nothing happened. She walked inside and the heat from the furnaces greeted her. As she stood in the doorway she was staring down a long hallway and all was silent.

Chapter 10

She pulled out her axe and slowly walked down the hallway, she stopped as she heard a small beeping sound go off. Immediately, from behind her as well as every 50ft in front of her, steel bars came down to block the hallway. From tiles in the roof, small machine guns with motion detectors dropped down and targeted in on Eon. Reacting quickly, she threw a throwing knife at the gun able to knock it off course long enough to smash it with the axe. There was a door at the end of the hallway, but there were 3 portcullises in the way of getting there and 3 more machine guns. Looking up, Eon smashed out one of the tiles and jumped up into the ceiling, which had about a foot and a half crawl space. She just hoped that the machine guns couldn't detect her above them.

    Eon held her breath as she passed over the mounted guns. Luck was with her as the tiles blocked the motion sensors of the guns. When she got to the end of the corridor, she made a hole in the wall with her axe. Cautiously peering into the next room, she saw a series of elevators. Eon dropped down on the other side of the door and decided not to take the elevators, but instead the stairs. She was faced with 2 choices of up or down on the stairs. A gut instinct told her that Powers would be on an upper level. Making her way up the stairwell, she stops suddenly as she hears the hammer click back on a gun. Diving back down the flight of stairs, gunfire erupts from a sniper a level above. After the bullets stop, she waits for a few moments and hears nothing. Sneaking up the stairwell inches at a time, she makes out the barrel of the gun poking out from the next level up directly above her. The barrel of the gun is poking out through vertical steel bars that line the railing. Eon jumps the 10ft up and pins the barrel of the gun between her axe and the steel bars so it can't move. The gunman pulls the trigger, but can't pull the gun free. Eon using her other hand to hang onto the landing ledge vaults herself over the railing to land on top of the sniper. The sniper rolls over on his back to fire at Eon who is standing above him, but Eon's reflexes are faster. Just as the sniper turns around, the axe comes down and cuts off both of his arms just above the elbows. To silence his screaming, Eon jams the spike on the head of the axe into his forehead and picks up the sniper rifle. Eon holsters the axe onto her back and continues to make her way up the stairs with the gun at the ready.

    Passing up the next 2 flights of stairs, without warning an explosion erupts blowing apart the next section of the stairwell. Eon dives back down the last flight of stairs as debris hits her in the shoulders and back. The gun is knocked from her hands and falls all the way down the center of the stairwell to the ground floor smashing as it hits. Wincing from the concrete chunks that fell on her, Eon manages to get up. The whole next section is blown out; Eon takes a running leap at the ledge to the next level. She barely makes it, hanging on by her fingertips. Just then, bursting from the door to that level come rushing out 10 thugs with machine guns. If Eon lets go, she'll fall too far and break something or worse. If she flips up to that level, the gunmen will take her down.

"Freeze! Climb up slowly and you won't die, make any sudden moves and we'll blow you right off that ledge."

Without a choice, Eon slowly crawls onto the ledge as 2 gunmen run to hold a gun to her head and drag her through a door to a level filled with office cubicles. Looking through the windows of the Tower, she can tell she's up a ways. The room is filled with desks and what looks like a huge table used for meetings. Down at the end of the room is the elevator shaft.

"Well, well, the notorious Eon in the flesh. Boys, tell Mr. Powers that the infiltrator has been caught. I don't think you'll be needing these little lady."

The thug walks over to Eon and starts to take out her throwing knives and tosses them on the large table 10ft behind them. Then the realization hits Eon, it's warm in here. She immediately remembers the remaining nitro blade on her arm and that when nitroglycerin thaws out it becomes very unstable and unpredictable. She can feel the coating on the blade starting to thaw out and holds her breath.

"What do you have to say now little lady, Powers is gonna tear you to pieces."

Eon ignores the thug and starts to look at her surroundings. As the thug pulls out the arm blade, Eon gets ready. He tosses it, just as he'd done with the other throwing knives. As it flies through the air, heading for the table with the pile of knives, Eon dives behind some desks in a cubicle just as the nitro blade hits the table. The explosion blows out the windows, blasts apart the table and knocks Eon back through several more cubicles. The eruption also sends the throwing knives rocketing through the air in all directions, half of them embedding themselves into several gunmen and killing them. In the commotion, the 3 remaining gunmen not killed by the blast start to look for Eon. All that she's armed with is her axe. She also has a large cut on the top of her right thigh from a piece of metal flying through the air during the explosion. Her head was also the first point to make contact through the cubicles. Eon lay there disoriented and in pain. She hears one of the gunmen approaching closer to her position, which is hidden under a pile of rubble. Eon musters the strength to burst from the pile and grabs the man's gun, ripping it from him and opening fire. She takes out the remaining guards and once again finds herself in possession of a gun. She stands there in silence as the winter wind comes in through the window, fluttering papers from desks onto the bloody bodies on the floor. Eon limps with the gun towards the elevator with blood running down her right leg and the side of her head. Once in the elevator, Eon goes for the top level. However, 3 stories before the last floor the elevator stops and all power shuts down. Eon is left there in the dark inside a steel box. She takes out her axe and smashes at the roof of the elevator, until it makes somewhat of a hole that she can crawl through. Climbing up through the hole she sees nothing but blackness. Although she can feel the cables of the elevator, she'll have to guess her way up the shaft to the top floor.

Deep in the basement levels of the Tower, Mr. Powers has his scientists working on multiple projects. The main project is of course Surge to sell to his foreign business partners, but there are other more secretive workings. Watching what Eon has done just several floors beneath him; Mr. Powers calls over the intercom into the sub levels of the Tower.

"Anthony, are you available?"

"Yes Mr. Powers, what can I do for you?"

"Anthony, what's the status of Project: Claw?"

"Well, it's still in the testing phase, it's not ready yet."

"Desperate times Anthony, call for desperate measures. I want you to release the project."

"Sir, that is not advisable at this point in time. The test subjects are not yet under our control, the consequences could be severe."

"I'm counting on that Anthony, now do as I say. I need to buy some time and get this little vigilante off my back. Oh, a little tip for you Anthony, you might want to skip out of town in the near future."

"Yes Mr. Powers, consider Project: Claw operational."

Mr. Powers leans back in his chair with a smile on his face.

"This will be just a temporary set back."

Mr. Powers pushes another intercom and leans forward.

"Stewart, get the helicopter ready, we're heading south."

Anthony briskly walks down a corridor in the underground lab into a room marked "caution Project: Claw". He pulls out some vials of liquid and prepares some syringes. He places the syringes in a holder attached to a long stick. After letting out a long sigh, Anthony reluctantly approaches another part of the room full of deep, guttural growls.

Back in the elevator shaft, Eon is climbing up the cables in the darkness. She tries not to think how high she is or what's around her. Her goal is to make it to the top and pry open the doors at the top level. Once her head bangs into the ceiling, she stops and tries to orient herself.

"Lets see, when I left the elevator the doors were on my right and I don't think I've turned at all on this cable."

Eon reaches out to try and touch where she thinks the elevator doors should be, but all she gets is open space.

"Damn, I can't reach the door."

Using the length of her axe she is able to touch the wall, hoping that it's the door. She drags the axe along the wall until the tip of it hits a seam. The axe head finds a groove and sinks in half an inch. Eon slides the axe up the groove to make sure it could be something resembling a door. Unfortunately, her arm is getting tired of supporting her weight. She holsters her axe and wraps her braid around her waist and ties a knot. The remaining length of the braid, she ties around the cables to use as a rope.

"I'm so glad I never cut my hair, who knew it could be a life saver."

Eon tests out her make shift "rope" and is able to hang there with the pressure on her waist and not her head. Using the length of the axe in both hands, she tilts her body horizontal so her feet touch the opposite side of the elevator shaft and the tip of the axe head is in the groove that she hopes is the door. With all her might she jams the axe head into the groove and it sinks deeper. Eon works the axe deeper into the groove until a crack of light shines through. Holding in a sigh of relief, Eon works the steel axe as a pry bar to manually open the elevator doors just enough for her to squeeze through. Untying her hair from her waist and the cable, she leaps to the small opening she has created and pulls herself through.

She's standing face to face with an enormous set of steel double doors.

"Well, there's only one way to go and it's through these doors."

Before turning the door handle, Eon examines the doors and the surrounding area for a trap of some kind. When she doesn't find anything, she feels confident enough to try the doors.

"Great, it's locked! I wish I had brought another one of those nitro blades with me. Of course with the heat in here, I probably would have blown myself up. Now how the hell am I supposed to get in there?"

Eon looked around the door casing; the whole thing was solid steel. She swung the axe at it, but it just clanged off harmlessly. Eon sat back against the wall to take a moment to think about this. She checked her leg and felt the side of her head and the bleeding had stopped, but her leg still hurt and she had a headache. There weren't even any windows to climb out onto and frustration was setting in. However, she didn't stay frustrated for very long. The large steel doors started to open by themselves and Eon stood up slowly with great anticipation of what would be on the other side.

When the doors finally opened, Eon was looking at an enormous desk in a massive office overlooking the entire city through giant windows. The room was dark and uninviting. There was a chair with the back facing her behind the massive desk. Eon walked into the room and the large leather chair swiveled around to reveal a very large man in a business suit.

"Hello Eon, I am Mr. Powers and this is my Tower. I've been trying to get a hold of you for a very long time now."

"Cut the bullshit Powers, you know why I'm here. It's time that justice is served out."

"You know Toria, you've caused me a lot of trouble and set me quite a ways back. You've killed my men and because of you, I've lost control of this city."

"All for the greater good you bastard and now your time has come."

Eon grabbed the machine gun from her shoulder and fired at Powers. The bullets seemed to have hit some sort of unseen shield and start to ricochet all around as she hits the deck. Looking up Eon sees the shield; it's a 2-inch thick incredibly clear wall that runs the length of the room.

"Please Toria, be careful that wall is bullet proof. I wouldn't want you to shoot yourself and deprive me of that pleasure. How ironic that would be, I controlled nearly 1,000 men and none of them could kill you, but you shoot yourself ha, ha, ha."

Eon got up and set the gun down, she had rage in her eyes. She reached back grabbing her axe and ran at the clear bulletproof wall, bringing the axe down on it. Instantly she is blasted back with the axe flying right out of her hands. Eon stayed on the ground trying to catch her breath as her pulse raced.

"Poor Toria, so head strong and so eager to get to me. You silly girl the wall is also electrified, it holds the same current as my field outside you so perfectly navigated through. Now please act civilized before you really hurt yourself."

Eon painfully sat up and crawled over to her axe and stood up wincing.

"Everything Powers. All I've ever had or loved you took it all away from me and I didn't even know you, all because you wanted me to join your little cause. Well now I've taken from you, I've stolen all you've cared for. Your empire has fallen and I'm going to take you with it. That's the difference Powers, I'm going to win."

"Yes, it would have been nice, you could have brought so much to the team. Now look at you, making empty threats and you can barely stand up. No Toria, I don't think you win. In fact I think you're very close to losing."

Mr. Powers stood up and started to walk towards a door in the center of his office, carrying a briefcase.

"I have to go now Toria, it was good to finally meet you face to face. You really are quite stunning, but duty calls. I am a gentleman though; I wouldn't leave you alone like this. My personal guards are here to show you out permanently. If by chance Toria you do survive them, I believe you'll be a very busy girl. Take care in your next life Miss Kayden, you were a worthy adversary ha, ha, ha, ha."

Mr. Powers started to walk towards the door and Eon turned to look behind her. There were 4 guards all dressed in red suits with their faces covered like ninjas. They had already taken the gun, one cutting it in half with a katana blade he pulled from the sheath on his back. Each guard was armed with 2 katana swords and moved in closer to Eon. Eon was leaning up against the axe for support, now held it firmly in both hands. She was still a little wobbly on her feet, but held fast through gritted teeth.

"Come on boys lets play, I'm not dead yet."

Eon was twirling the double-headed axe over her head to try to keep them at bay. Two charged at her, there was a shower of sparks as steel clashed on steel. Looking up to see that the ceiling was high enough, Eon jumps high over the heads of the 2 that charge her and swings the axe in a downward motion between her legs to stab one through the middle of the back. She lands in front of the other 2 and one attacks high and the other low. She turns the axe vertical to catch both attacks, but was slashed across the back by one of the 2 she jumped over. Screaming, Eon dives to the side away from the 3 of them and throws the axe hard at one of them. The bottom part of the axe shaped like a crescent cuts clean through one's neck, leaving his head to roll onto the floor. Eon flips over to the first fallen warrior that took the axe to the back and she picks up both of his swords. She brings them up quickly, just in time to meet the advances of the other 2 guards. Eon wields the blades twice as fast as they do just to keep up with them both. At the same time she throws out a foot jab to one of the guard's midsection that knocks him back into the clear wall. Electricity bursts forth as the man screams, with his body falling to the ground dead and smoking.

    Eon stands with both swords circling the last guard, who makes an attempt to swing one blade in an upper cut like motion, which is blocked by Eon. She slashes a sword across his eyes and he immediately staggers back holding his face. She approaches the wounded guard and drives her sword into his stomach just under the rib cage and out through the side of his neck. The last guard drops down dead and Eon retrieves her axe. She quickly looks up to hear a helicopter in the distance and Mr. Powers voice hailing it down to the roof.

"You're not getting away from me Powers, if I could only find a way around this wall!"

Eon stepped back to think, while she felt how bad the wound was across her back.

Chapter 11

Eon had an idea; she grabbed her axe and ran down to the elevator. There was enough light coming in through the hole to see the cables, so she jumped to them. Climbing down the cables, she returns to the dark elevator and uses her axe to pry open the door just as she had done on the top floor. She was down 3 stories, but at least this floor had windows. Running to the nearest window, she smashed it out with her axe. She was greeted by the cold gust of winter. The wind was really blowing at this elevation with nothing around to block it. Cautiously Eon stepped out onto the 6-inch ledge and pressed her back to the outside of the building. The chill of the wind was even cutting through her skin. She could see the next ledge above her, but didn't want to risk jumping to grab it for fear the wind would knock her off balance. Instead she used the length of her axe to find the ledge with her axe head. The head of the axe hung onto the ledge above like a grappling hook. Eon used it like a pole and started to climb up the axe. As soon as her feet left the ledge, the wind made her body sway on the axe. She went as fast as she could, but deliberately hand over hand to not make a mistake. When she made it to the next ledge, she breathed a sigh of relief. The cold was starting to get to her now and she starting to shiver and chatter her teeth, but she had to keep going.

She swung the axe up as she had done on the ledge below and began to climb up the axe. When she was half way up the axe, a large gust of wind came across the side of the building and broke the axe loose! Eon fell; fighting the instinct to let go of the axe she held it firmly in one hand, while the other reached out for the ledge. Her fingertips connected with the ledge and she hung there by the tips of 3 fingers as her body moved in the wind. The sting of the cold was biting into her and her fingers were numb. She hauled up the axe and put it on the ledge. At this point she needed 2 hands to pull herself back up onto the ledge.

She smashed the window near her to let out the heat, and then she put the axe up again to climb it. This time the hot air blew out at her, helping somewhat. She wanted to get back inside; she was in pain and freezing. Doubling over, she closed her eyes in hopes to find renewed strength to get her up this ledge. She was shaking nearly uncontrollably as she smashed out this ledge's window and put the axe up again. It seemed she was moving in slow motion, but she couldn't help it. Eon knew that if she stopped then she would freeze and worse yet in her mind would be that Powers would get away. She could still hear the chopper on the roof, which gave her renewed hope. She painfully and slowly climbed up to the next ledge. This was the top level and she could see inside Mr. Powers's office.

    Eon saw all the video screens behind the desk and the control panels. She smashed out that window and knew that just above her was the roof. Practically falling into the office, she lay there for a long moment as the heat tried desperately to warm her up. Still shaking and in pain, Eon gets up and pushes on making it to the doorway that Mr. Powers had walked through. Making it out to the roof, Eon gets there just in time to see the helicopter start to lift off. She holsters her axe and tries to run after it, but the joints are so stiff and her legs feel like lead in the cold. Anticipating where the chopper will go, she makes her way to the edge of the building and pulls out her axe. The chopper starts to lift off the roof and starts to fly horizontally away. As it passes by where Eon is standing on the ledge of the roof, she jumps into thin air with all her might.

Meanwhile inside the chopper, Mr. Powers breathes a sigh of relief.

"Stewart, set a course for our port in Columbia. This might be a little set back in Harborside, but think of it as a little vacation in a warmer climate. We'll meet up with some business partners and commence operations there until I can return here again."

"Yes Mr. Powers, I could use a little warm weather for a while. These Harborside winters can be harsh near the coastline. Other than a few refueling stops; I'm looking forward to a nice relaxing trip down to South America. Just sit back and relax Mr. Powers, it's all smooth sailing from here."

As soon as Stewart finishes his sentence, there is a loud clanging sound as the helicopter starts to rock slightly.

"What was that Mr. Powers? It felt like we were hit by something."

"I'm not sure, I'll take a look."

As Mr. Powers leans over to look out the window, he's shocked to see Eon's axe attached to the landing rails with her hanging onto the end of the axe. The wind was whipping her all around, at times bringing her dangerously close to the tail rotor. She looked like a paper doll in a windstorm.

"I don't believe this! How is this even possible? Stewart, we have some baggage that needs to be shaken off."

"What is it?"

"My tenacious little problem."

Stewart starts to move the chopper side to side, up and down. However, Eon holds fast and Mr. Powers notices that she's starting to climb up the axe.

"Never mind Stewart, I'll take care of this myself."

Outside, the wind was hammering Eon. She wasn't sure how she was holding on she couldn't feel her hands. All she focused on was putting one hand in front of the other up the axe. When she was a little better than half way, the door to the chopper slid open. Eon looked up through frost-covered eyelids to see Mr. Powers leaning half out of the chopper.

"You know Toria, I thought you were a bright girl, a genius even. Since we've met I've seen you nearly kill yourself with ricocheting bullets, electrocute yourself and now here you are out in the cold dressed like that."

"Keep joking Powers, it won't be so funny when I bury this axe up your ass!"

"Really Miss Kayden, I already have what I need from you. You don't have to keep following me like this. Oh, don't look so confused Toria, your DNA is all over my building."

Eon realized that Powers was talking about his scientists. They would collect blood samples of hers that she left as she fought her way through the Tower.

"They'll never get to use it Powers, I'm staying one of a kind."

Looking down, Eon noticed that the chopper was starting to leave the city and starting to fly over the coast. After this was nothing but ocean for miles. Then she noticed Mr. Powers climbing out onto the rails with his foot raised over her axe blade.

"Happy landings Toria and goodbye."

His boot came down before Eon could climb up the rest of the way. Striking with tremendous force, he knocks the axe free and sends Eon sprawling into the air.

"I'll get you Powers!"

Mr. Powers watches as Eon falls into the water, he can't help but admire her spirit.

"Defiant to the end, I like that. I believe you will try to kill me again. Somehow I doubt that we've seen the last of each other."

As Eon falls through the air, she clasps the axe with both hands and holds it vertically and tight to her body with the blade extending past her feet. She makes herself as straight as she can as her body hits the water. The impact would shatter the bones of anyone lesser; Eon plunges down into the water 30ft before slowing to a stop. The sting of the water's icy touch nearly paralyzes her as she realizes that she needs to swim back to shore as fast as she can before she can't even move. Bobbing up to the surface, she holsters her axe and starts to swim towards shore. Luckily the nearest shoreline is only 200ft away, but seems like an eternity in this environment.

Making it back to shore, she fights to stay moving because stopping means death. Eon starts to run faster and faster, the only things that can produce heat and keep her alive. She doesn't stop until she reaches the Tower again and enters back inside it. Thanking her lucky stars that the electrical and acid fields had been turned off. She crawled back through the ceiling to bypass the machine guns and this time took the stairs that led down into the sub levels.

She kicked in the door with renewed strength that it flew right off the hinges; it felt good to be warm again. However, the feeling was fleeting as she was met with gunfire from the revolvers the scientists had.

"Hold your fire, you'll destroy the equipment!"

Eon dove at 2 scientists, hacking at them with the axe and picking up their revolvers.

"Well that's exactly what I plan to do and I'm destroying it all."

Eon opened fire on the scientists while at the same time leaping and flipping from one aisle to the next. With the inexperience that the scientists had at shooting, she was an impossible target to hit. It took only a matter of minutes to complete the slaughter in the giant underground laboratory. Eon slowly walked around the lab stopping at a few choice tables with equipment on them.

"You know, I could use these, but the rest of you have got to go."

With a smile of satisfaction and nobody to stand in her way, Eon smashed the entire laboratory with her axe. When she was satisfied she returned outside, the early morning light was now cresting over the horizon. Walking over to where she had placed Jax's body, she knelt down and cleared away the bushes.

"You look so peaceful now Jax, just like you're resting. I can't believe I'm still alive, what a night. You would have been proud of me old friend, I did it. All the gangs, all the scientists, all the equipment, his personal guard, it's all destroyed. The evil grip that Powers had on this city is over now, we won. Powers got away, but if he comes back then I'll be here to deal with him. I just have this feeling that we're going to meet again someday. I'm so exhausted Jax, I could sleep for a week straight and I feel like I've been hit by a truck."

Eon picked up Jax in her arms and walked away with him.

Back in the hospital Jason was just waking up for the morning when the Doctor walked into the room.

"Hello Mr. Card, we'll be discharging you today. Besides some lumps and bruises, your broken arm is the worst of it. There's no reason to keep you here any longer. Though I'd lay low for a while if I were you. We'll need you to come back for radiographs in a few weeks to see how things are healing. The nurse will be in to go over the discharge instructions with you in a little while. Take care of yourself Mr. Card and I'll see you in 3 weeks."

Jason sat up with a smile; he couldn't wait to see Toria again. It was driving him crazy not knowing if she was all right and what had happened in the Tower. The first place he was going to go was the lair. Just as Jason started to get lost in his thoughts, the nurse walked in the room.

"Hello Mr. Card, I have your discharge instructions here if you're ready?"

"Lady, get me outta here!"

Toria had brought Jax to the morgue and returned to the lair where she fell straight down on the mattress in the center of the large room. She desperately wanted to sleep, but the gnawing hunger pains wouldn't let her rest. She got back up with one last task before she could sleep. Finding the last bit of food that Jax had packed away, she ate all of it in a matter of minutes.

"Maybe I'll go out tonight and do some grocery shopping, but right now it's time to sleep."

That morning the local news crews and police gathered around the Tower.

We're here live at the infamous Tower of Power, where police received a tip from the self-proclaimed vigilante known as Eon. It seems that this prowler of the night has single handedly taken down Mr. Powers and his underground operation of the drug known as Surge. Police are still bringing out bodies and are calling it a massacre of justice. The body of Mr. Powers has not been recovered and there has been no sign of him anywhere in all of this. Police speculate that he may be hiding possibly somewhere in the city. One thing is for sure; the silent reign of terror that the city of Harborside was in has been eliminated for good. Wherever you are we thank you Eon.

Later that morning Jason came down the manhole cover to the lair. He made sure to take extra care on the ladder with just one good arm. There were a few candles still lit, a custom that Jax had put in place. He always wanted at least 2 candles burning at all times or else it would be pitch black down there. Jason crept over to the mattress where Toria was sleeping.

"Toria, wake up it's me!"

Toria opened her eyes and blinked a few times not believing what she was seeing.

"Jason! I'm so glad you're here, when did they let you go?"

"I left the hospital just a couple hours ago. You don't know how glad I am to see you. Even though I knew how dangerous it was going to be, somehow I knew you'd be all right."

"Oh, you don't know the half of it. I'll have to fill you in on it later. Just know that we did it, this city is no longer under that madman. Jason, do me a favor and just lay here with me."

"You got it, there's no place else I'd rather be."

Jason climbed in next to Toria on the filthy mattress, under the ratty, hole-covered blanket and was the most content he'd been in a long time. The 2 of them slept peacefully as if a great weight had been lifted from their shoulders. While outside, the city was waking up to great news as the headlines had already been printed.

Chapter 12

A month had past since the Tower had fallen. News of Eon had spread like wild fire throughout the city. It was also a time to remember their fallen comrades. First they had Eddie's funeral with people coming from all over the city. Many people spoke highly of him and of the deeds he had done. Then came time for Jax's funeral, which was held in the center of the city as Toria had requested. She had also requested that a monument be built in his honor over his gravesite. There was an engraved plaque on the bottom of the monument, which read:

"Here rests Igoronovich "Jax" Peroshencovich, hero, mentor and friend. May the sun shine upon you. May your spirit live forever. May the world never forget you."

Toria would often visit the gravesite at all times of the day and night. She would talk to him, other times she would just sit there in silence. Today was one of those days that she came to visit her old friend.

"Hi Jax it's me again, hope you're not getting sick of me. Things are really going well, you should see what the lair looks like now. We just started the New Year and the mayor of the city wants to kick off the New Year with a celebration in my honor. Can you believe that? So, today they're having a ceremony, actually right here in the city center, which means you won't miss a thing. I was told that the Mayor and the city are going to officially recognize me as Eon. Unofficially it's been that way for a month now, but it's pretty cool. Jason went out and found me a really nice dress and even had it altered for me. Well, I just wanted to come by and tell you what was happening today so you weren't surprised. I have to go and get ready now. Oh, I've been using your old ratty jacket every day; it's officially cold as hell now. Anyway, I miss you every single day Jax; you'll never be forgotten. I'll see you later today, bye."

    Toria returned back to the lair and Jason was busy getting ready. The lair had been sectioned off and really cleaned up. All pipes were covered, sewage was rerouted and actual doors had been put in. Toria had added many household items to make it feel like a home. They had even constructed a bed since a mattress or box spring didn't fit down the manhole (they were always unsure how the old mattress had gotten down there in the first place). The bed sat up high and new blankets covered the new sheets. They had also brought in small appliances and 2 new generators. Eon's area took up half of the lair. She left up all the training equipment that Jax had put up for her and she added in an alcove a small forge and metal working tools. In her old room she had put chemistry lab equipment together from the Tower's basement. Except for the door being a manhole cover, you'd never know this place was inside a sewer.

"Toria, I understand why you put in the forge and the metal working tools to replace your blades, but what's with all the lab equipment in the corner from the Tower?"

"Well Jason, I'm working on new types of arm daggers."

"What do you mean types?"

"You know how I have my nitro blades. Now I'm working with other chemical compounds to create different kinds of blades for different occasions."

"That's way over my head Toria, but speaking of occasions; you need to get that dress on and we need to get our butts over to the city center. It's 11:15am and the ceremony starts at noon. Don't think you'll wait till the last minute and run over there, you'll destroy that dress. Besides, I can't run as fast as you, so we're leaving in 15 minutes."

"Alright, alright give me the dress I'll put it on."

Fifteen minutes later, the 2 of them headed to the city center. There were people everywhere; Eon had become a household name in Harborside. People recognized Toria immediately and wherever they went people waved. Some people even stopped them on the street to take pictures others wanted autographs.

"Jason, I feel like I'm going to the premier of my new opening film in Hollywood."

"You're the biggest hit in town now. You liberated the entire city and the people love you for it. Next we'll have to start merchandising. I can see it now, Eon the action figure, Eon the comic book, not to mention there will be a poster of you hanging in every boy's bedroom."

"Very funny wise guy, I guess you get the last laugh because you've got the real thing. Hey look we're almost there, they've got quite a set up here."

As they approached the city center, large tents were set up with space heaters and refreshments. There were hundreds of people out on the streets and the tents were shoulder room only. It seemed that everyone in the whole city came out on this cold day to see the events. Once Toria and Jason made it to the main tents, the people started to let them through.

"Look Hun, I'll stay back here and watch, I'll catch up with you after the ceremony."

"Alright, you know I've gone through some pretty rough things these past months and it's now that I feel the most nervous, go figure."

Toria made her way up to the front of the tent where the Mayor and other city officials were standing on a raised platform. When the officials saw her making her way up, they all greeted her with smiles and open arms. The Mayor stood up to the podium and took the microphone.

"Ladies and gentlemen, I'd like to call your attention to the front of the tent. We'd like to begin the proceedings now of welcoming Eon into our city."

The people in the tent grew silent and all eyes were on the platform at the front of the tent.

"People of Harborside, today we recognize a great accomplishment of an even greater individual. Growing up right here in our city, Toria Kayden was gifted with certain evolutionary qualities. With these gifts, she has single handedly defeated the crime lord known as Mr. Powers as well as eradicating all of his gangs that controlled the streets here in the city. Over the past month the crime rate has decreased significantly and for the first time in years people aren't afraid to leave their homes. Toria you have made this city safer and a much happier place to live. The bank of Harborside has set up an account in your name with $500,000 dollars in it. Anything you need in this city is available to you. It gives me great pleasure to announce you to the entire city as our champion and defender. On behalf of the whole city, and myself we'd like to say thank you Miss Kayden for your courage and monumental effort. Ladies and gentlemen, let me introduce to you for the first time officially as the Harborside Heroine Eon!"

Applause from the crowd erupted, even outside the tents where people were listening to the speech over loudspeakers. The whole city gave Toria an ovation that lasted a good 5 minutes before people started to settle down and the podium was passed over to Toria to speak.

"Thank you Mayor and all of you out there, I really can't describe how amazing this feels. You know when I first started this; it was a personal vendetta against Mr. Powers. To me it didn't matter who or what was in the way only that I had to get him back for what he did. His men killed my parents during a raid last summer at the genetics lab, including Dr. Marks who became a friend to me. My world was turned upside down and I had no place to turn. All of a sudden I couldn't go back home, I couldn't see my friends and all communication had to be cut off from the world as it was my only chance for survival.

During that dark time, the man that took me in is buried right over there. Jax took me in, kept me alive and taught me how to fight back. As far as

I'm concerned Jax is the real hero. It wasn't just me that did this; credit needs to be given to others like Jax. Especially to Jason, Eddie and the Wild Cards, without you I wouldn't be standing here at this podium.

Somewhere during the course of my blind revenge, I noticed the people of the city. It wasn't just me alone in a great world of buildings against the tyrant in the Tower. I realized that I had support and that hope, not just revenge was riding on my shoulders. Thank you for being there for me and taking me in. I gladly accept the role of defender of the city until I can do it no longer."

Again there was an eruption of applause. Toria basked in her glory, this was her moment and she would remember it forever.

It was several hours before the crowds started to disperse and people went back to their homes. Toria had spoken to many people on the street and received copious amounts of praise. Once in the lair her and Jason changed into regular clothes.

"Today has got to be the greatest day of my life Jason. I'm going over to the cemetery and visit mom and dad's grave site, they should share in this as well."

"Sounds good, I'm gonna stay here and work on a few things. So, what are you going to do now Miss Heroine, you've beaten the bad guy?"

"He's out there somewhere Jason and besides, you never know. It's a city there's always some sort of crime going on. I'll be keeping up on my training, creating new blades and working on my new designs for blade types. Trust me, I'll be plenty busy, but I'll try and save a little time for you."

"Oh thanks, I wouldn't want to bother you too much. Hey, what's that thing the Mayor gave you?"

"It's like an alarm/radio that has a direct line to the Mayor and police chief. If it goes off, I have to respond and see what's up. It's about the size of a quarter, so I can wear it anywhere."

Later that night Scott Oris was doing his nightly routine jog on the outskirts of town. He liked the peace it offered being next to the woods away from all the people in the city. Lost in thought and enjoying the crisp, clear night, he didn't notice that he was being followed. Large luminous eyes watched him until it was time to strike. Scott was listening to music while he ran and it's probably a good thing. This is something he didn't want to hear coming, something so terrifying that it would cause shock. No, it was better this way for poor Scott.

One moment Scott was running and the next moment he wasn't. Something rushed him from the trees with such speed and force that his spine snapped in several places killing him instantly. At least poor Scott's last thoughts were peaceful.

That same night in the lair, Toria's alarm went off. She was asleep, rolled over and answered the radio.

"Hello, this is Eon, you guys just checking to see if this thing is working all right?"

"Hi Eon, this is police Chief Dixon and I wish this were just a test."

"What's the matter Chief? You guys are working late tonight, it's 1:00am."

"I know and I'm sorry about that, normally I'd wait till morning; however this seems urgent. We picked up a tip from a driver on the edge of town. He thought maybe a deer was hit in the road, but then he saw a man's head and blood that splattered all the way to the tree tops."

"Oh my God Chief, I'll be right there!"

"I hate to say it with all the festivities we had today, but we've got a problem. Judging by the looks of what's left of this guy, it's a damn big problem."

End of Book I

Book II: Primal

Chapter 1

Toria rushes over to police headquarters and meets up with Chief Dixon.

"Thanks for coming on short notice, well this is what we have left of the guy."

"Holy shit! What's out there in the woods that could do something like that, a bear attack?"

"I don't think so, we had the boys examine it and the bite marks are too big. We were able to line up the torso and as you can see the bite diameter from the tip of mandible to maxilla is 12 inches. It also looks dog like in nature, here could be the canine punctures. It's not just the teeth that did the damage; this guy's bones are crushed to bits. The power of this thing's bite is incredible. These slash marks here indicate very large claws and a wide paw. I've never seen anything like this except in monster movies. In fact this scares me to death that there's something like this out there so close to the city."

Eon looked over the mutilated body, trying to hold down her dinner.

"Did you find anything else at the seen, any other clues to what we're dealing with?"

"We did get this photo of a few paw prints that we found, the ruler's next to it for scale."

"That paw is over 8 inches in diameter Chief."

"I know Eon, this thing, whatever it is, is bigger than a tiger and mean as hell."

"Well, it happened at night, maybe this guy is nocturnal. I'll check it out tomorrow night, we have a ¾ moon so I should have enough light to see."

Eon returns back to the lair and tries to go back to sleep, but just keeps thinking about those size dimensions. In the morning, she fills Jason in on what she saw last night.

"Toria, you can't be serious. You're going to go check out some Bigfoot creature in the woods at night, alone? Why didn't you tell the Chief that dinosaurs are a little out of your league?"

"Jason, it's my duty to the citizens here in the city and besides I'm pretty sure I'll fare better than some jogger. Also, what's with the little faith, I could take out a dinosaur if it was a little one."

"I'm serious Toria, this thing doesn't really sound natural. All I'm saying is that don't you think you should learn a little more first before you go jumping right in?"

"How am I supposed to do that, go ask the dead guy for details? Don't worry Jason, I'm just going to check it out, at the first sign of trouble I'll bolt."

"What if it can catch you?"

"I can run nearly 40MPH, I doubt it can catch me. I have to do this, it's my job."

That night Toria geared up as Eon and got ready to go, Jason stopped her just before she left.

"Be careful out there Toria, remember what that thing did; stay on your toes."

"Geez, are you trying to scare me! I know, I'll be careful and with a little luck this won't take too long."

Toria climbed out of the lair and started to run towards the outskirts of town where the attack happened. It didn't take her too long to get there, around 15 minutes. She entered the woods holding the axe tightly. The night was clear and cold, she wore extra socks in her boots and had an old vest on zipped halfway up. She was too focused on the task at hand to let the cold get to her. The moon shed enough light for her to see fairly well, but the trees hid things and cast shadows. She could hear nothing but the wind in the trees overhead as well as her own footsteps.

She walked on into the woods for about 20 minutes, and then she stopped. She thought she had heard something. Scanning the woods, it was hard to make out anything because of all the trees. After a few moments she continued on across a small stream.

Back in the lair, Jason was working on a project he had started a couple weeks ago. It was slow going because he still had his arm in a cast, but the Doctor had told him that it was healing very nicely. He was reinforcing a shirt made of thick spandex material with sections of Kevlar and steel plates. The elbows and shoulders were also reinforced with extra material and a cover for the neck was added. Jason also had pants of a similar design and boots to match. Next to it on the table were 2 semi-long steel bars 1 inch thick with grips put on them.

"Once my arm heals up and I can put it through a range of motion again with some muscle, this suit should be ready. Then once again the Wild Card will be back on the streets."

In the woods, Eon stalks deeper and deeper, but still hears nothing. She stops again and scans the woods, but the shadows are thicker here. Then the slightest noise, like the wind rustling a little bit catches Eon's ear.

"That's not normal wind, too fast."

Eon dives forward on the ground, just missing her is a large mass that lands 20ft beyond her. Getting to her feet quickly she can only make out the eyes and shape of her attacker. The eyes are a good 10 inches apart and taller than her. Once again it bears down on her and pounces. Eon meets the attack with her axe, but the creature bats it out of the way and sends her flying through the air. Quickly getting to her knees, she fires 2 throwing knives at the large mass, but to her surprise it moves incredibly fast and they embed in the tree behind it. Not hearing anything again, Eon slowly gets up and walks over to the tree to retrieve her blades. She looks around nervously and is a little uneasy at the fact that she actually missed her target and that she still can't make it out fully. There is no sign of it anywhere now and she begins to head in the direction that she last saw it move.

In the lair Jason is working steadily on different pieces of his suit to stitch it up. He's converted an old lacrosse helmet for his purpose as Wild Card, using the machining tools to reinforce it with steel plates.

"Boy, this thing has got to weigh 10 pounds. I don't want to carry an more weight than that on my head, but the armor turned out great."

He sets the helmet down, taking a break from it and picks up one of the steel bars. Each one was 2 ft long including the handle. Jason started to practice swinging it with his good arm at the dummy set up in Eon's training course.

"Just because I have one bad arm, doesn't mean I have to sit around and wait for it to heal."

The hits are hard as he puts his weight behind the strikes. Each hit is strong enough to break a 2x4 piece of wood. After 10 minutes of that, Jason continues to work on his suit.

Eon has gotten at least another mile deeper into the woods chasing the beast. This time the sound of snapping branches gave away its location only 15ft away from her. In a single leap, the beast was upon Eon with lightning speed, pinning her to the ground. Claws digging into her shoulder, she lets out a wail as she thrust the axe upward into its chest. The beast cries out and leaps off of her.

Eon rose to her feet only to be hit from the side. The creature bit down on the side of her abdomen and ribs, picked her up and threw her into a tree. She knew she was bleeding and at least one rib was cracked, she held her side as it hurt to breathe. The axe had been knocked right out of her hands and lay under the beast's feet. Again it leaps at Eon, she quickly threw 3 throwing knives straight at it and dove out of the way. The knives distracted the creature long enough for Eon to regain her footing and pull out the Bowie knives. Although they did little to stop it, it was like throwing a pin at a rhino. All the beast did was change direction and it was upon her again in a single second.

Eon slashed it twice across the face and it slashed at her arm, opening a large gash and taking her off her feet. It was momentarily dazed, Eon took advantage to get up and start to run back towards the city.

"This thing is too dangerous out here, I need to get away and come up with a strategy."

Eon was running full speed after grabbing her axe as she heard thunderous foot falls behind her and trees cracking out of the way. She looked back behind her and saw to her horror that not only was the beast chasing her, but it was also gaining on her. Knowing that she could never outrun the beast in time, she turned and ran straight at it. In a daring and hopeful attempt, she unloaded the rest of her throwing knives at the beast and dove behind a rock.

The creature snorted and shook its head, sniffing the air to try and find her. Eon tried to get a bearing on the creature, but as soon as she stood to attack it was upon her in an instant. She let loose a nitro blade, but was off balance because of the fast counterattack. The blade missed its target, hitting a tree and blasting chunks of wood everywhere! The blast knocked her on her back and she could hear the creature rushing through the woods as branches snapped around it. Eon sat up slowly and didn't see it anywhere, guessing the blast scared it off.

"I'll call that one a draw, but I don't want to stay here for another round."

Eon was wounded, but nothing too serious. She started to jog back in the direction she had come back to the city.

When Eon finally crawled into the lair, she saw that Jason was already asleep. However, he woke up when she climbed into the shower and doubled over holding her side. Jason climbed out of bed and looked at her with the "I-told-you-so" facial expression and she picked right up on it.

"How bad is it?"

"It's not too bad, but I'll need to lay low for at least 3-4 days. I still don't know what it is; I could never get a clear view of it. I know that it's big, powerful and fast. It was even able to dodge out of the way of my blades and when I did hit it, it was like a distraction to it. It flung me around like a rag doll and on top of it all, it can run faster than me. I really don't feel like getting a lecture right now either."

"I'm not going to give you a lecture Toria, I'm just glad you made it back."

Jason walked back to the bed and climbed in it to go to sleep. Toria sat in the shower lost in thought at the night's events. She had never missed before, let alone thrown around like that. This creature wasn't natural by any means, but then what the hell was it? Well, she'd have time to think about it while she was recuperating. In the meantime, first thing in the morning she had to get a hold of Chief Dixon and fill him in on the details.

Chapter 2

Later the next morning, Toria spoke with Dixon. Right after hearing the severity of the beast, Dixon ordered that a curfew be placed on the city until the beast could be brought down. Toria had taken it upon herself to do just that. During the next few days Toria stayed in the lair, metal working in the forge and in the chemistry lab. Her wounds were healing while she kept busy; Jason entered the lair on one of the evenings bringing back groceries.

"Toria, you've been working non stop for 3 days, are you building a bomb or what?"

"I'm trying to perfect 2 new types of blades, but the construction is harder than the nitro blades I made with Jax."

"What do you mean by blade types?"

"That thing out there is dangerous, so much so that I'm not sure that I could stop it without coming up with something else. My normal blades are enough to slow it down or distract it, but it moves so fast, I can't get a good shot in on it. There's a lot of collateral damage with the nitro blades if I miss, so I wanted to create something where all I had to do was come close. As in, if I hit it anywhere on the body; it should really hurt it."

"Sounds like a near impossible task and how do you know what you come up with will work?"

"I don't know till I actually try it out, but I'm pretty confident on what I've come up with.

The first blade type I'm calling my fire blade. I take calcium phosphide and when it reacts with water, it releases phosphine that ignites spontaneously. The idea is that all I have to do is hit the creature anywhere and the blade will ignite buried into it. This will cause the flames to spread no matter where it goes because it's attached. It follows the same principle as Greek or alchemist's fire. The trick was creating a breakable chamber filled with water to reside inside the dagger handle. So, when the blade strikes and the chamber breaks, the water will rush out and ignite the fire. Creating these types of daggers are very time consuming and have to be perfect. The good news is that I can use this same dagger with the breakable chamber design for both of my new blade types.

The second blade type, I'm calling my poison blade. When I was developing this concept, I thought about using a poison that works in the bloodstream, but if I hit this guy in the muscle or fat the effect will take 15-20 minutes. By that time I could be dead already. I needed to find something that was much faster and still worked regardless of where I hit it. There's a fantastic chemical mix of a linear molecule with a triple bond between carbon and nitrogen and I'm setting the concentration at 600mg/m3. It's an inhalation poison and can kill a person at half that dose, we'll see about this thing. Even if it doesn't kill it, it will disorient it enough so that I can finish the job with my axe. No matter where I hit the beast, the poisonous cloud will erupt around him and all he has to do is breathe in. With the size of this guy, let me tell you, he takes some big breaths. However, as there's a temperature problem with the nitro blades, the same can be said for this blade type as well. At temperatures over 80 degrees Fahrenheit, the mixture will start to boil. This will cause it to expand slightly and possibly rupture the breakable chamber in the dagger handle. I really don't want that to happen while it's attached to my arm. However, like the nitro blades we should be alright because it's winter out right now."

"That's all over my head Toria, but it sounds like you've got it all under control."

"I made a few prototypes for the chambers on the dagger, but I don't like how they came out. I'm close though; I think the next batch should be right on the money. Plus, I'm making a lot of my regular throwing knives since I'm going through them faster than usual. These are the reasons I've been working down here non-stop for days and because it hurt to breathe, but that's fine now. I really want to get this down, but I've got to take a break, my head is throbbing with all the work I've done."

Toria started to get into her Eon outfit, while Jason unpacked the groceries.

"What are you doing now?"

"I'm getting some fresh air and if I see people out on the streets, I can tell them to get inside."

"What if it's not people you run into and something else?"

"That's a chance I have to take, I'll go crazy if I stay down here any longer."

Eon grabbed her axe and was out through the manhole cover 30 seconds later. She started to patrol around the east side of the city, not venturing too far from the lair.

An hour later Jason had finished dinner and now had a chance to work on his suit for Wild Card. He was finished with the pants and tried them on. The spandex like material allowed him to move easily while everything stayed in place. He had built pockets all around the thighs in 6 long tubes for better contouring. He did the same thing around the shins and calves. The knees took the longest as he meticulously placed small pads all around the knee joint that offered protection, but wouldn't impede movement. He also did this around the groin and glutes.

"These pants feel great, I can't wait for this arm to heal and get the top on. I've still got a little bit more work to do before I'm ready to try it on anyway."

He changed out of the pants and began to work on the top. After a while he took a break, picked up one of the steel bars and started to twist it in his hand. He sat back and relaxed while he became lost in thought.

Eon had made it to the outskirts of the city on the east side. She found a small group of people crowded around something, so she went to check it out.

"Good evening folks, you should really be inside right now. We have a creature on the prowl near the city."

"Hi Eon, we were just heading home from the coast and found this."

Eon walked into the circle and saw to her surprise another mutilated body.

"Did any of you know this person?"

"No, but it must have happened while we were down by the water. I'm just surprised we didn't hear anything."

"Alright, everyone head home now, I'll take care of this. You should probably stay away from the coast until we get this thing, it's very dangerous."

The people dispersed quickly and Eon was left alone with the body. She scanned the area, but didn't see or hear anything.

"So, you killed another victim, you bastard. What are you doing all the way over here near the harbor? This spot is a lot further away than the last death."

Eon picked up the body and carried it all the way back to police headquarters after wrapping it in a tarp by the harbor. When she arrived, she expected to see a skeleton crew since it was 9:00pm at night, but the station was bustling with officers including the Chief.

"What are you doing here so late Chief?"

"We just got a report of another death. A body was just found on the north edge of the city. The boys are just hauling it in now, what's in the tarp?"

"It's funny you should say that Chief because I just found this body while patrolling near the harbor on the east end. That means this guy covered a lot of ground in a short amount of time."

"You know, I can issue the curfew warning, but it will take a little while for everybody to get the message. If we don't get this beast under control, meaning killed, we're gonna have a city wide panic on our hands. Have you been able to come up with any ideas or clues as to how to stop this thing?"

"I'm working on developing some things that will help. I'm on my way back to the lair right now. I need at least another 24 hours before it'll be ready. Tomorrow night I'll go back out to hunt it. I'm going to go back to where the first victim was near the woods. Something tells me that it's living out that way."

"I certainly hope you can find and kill this thing for all of our sakes."

Eon returned back to the lair, where she found Jason lost in thought staring at one of his steel bars.

"It's not good Jason, we found 2 more dead bodies tonight."

"What are you going to do?"

"I have to get back to work on the new blades. I'm going back out there tomorrow night to see what I can find. I'm feeling better from our last encounter and ready for round 2."

The next day while Jason was at the gym taking over for Eddie as best he could with a broken arm, Toria stayed in the lair perfecting her new arm daggers with the breakable compartment. Late that afternoon, she finally finished a design that she liked. Now that she had the design and mold down, she could start to produce them. Unfortunately, because they're so time consuming she only had time to create one more before it was time to go back out tonight.

Jason had brought back a couple pizzas when he finished up at the gym. Toria came out to greet him, took one of the pizzas and went right back into the chemistry lab to finish up her work. A few minutes later, she popped her head back out of the lab.

"Hey Jason, sorry I can't eat with you tonight, I'm almost there and then I have to get going. I promise when I get this thing, we'll do some normal things again like board games, dinner and a movie."

"I understand Toria, do what you have to do. I've got some things of my own to work on down here. So, good luck tonight and I hope you get that thing. As always remember to be careful, you might have gotten lucky last time when that thing ran off and left you alone."

"Thanks Jason, I'm pretty confident this time around."

Toria popped her head back in the lab and continued to work. She was going to fill both her arm blades tonight with the poison. It had to be inserted into the dagger components very carefully with a syringe since it was an inhalant poison. Toria wasn't sure how it would affect her, but she sure as hell didn't want it in the air down here with Jason around. This was a highly concentrated dose of the poison and she had made just enough to fill the daggers so there wouldn't be any left in the lab.

Once the poison was inserted, the compartment was closed in the blade by a small metal piece at the top of the handle. On impact this small metal piece would give way because of the sudden stop of the dagger. The inertia of the contents would force out the top of the handle, down the blade and onto whatever it made contact with. She had also replaced all of her throwing knives and at 8:00pm started to get into her Eon outfit, plus the vest and extra socks. After she was finished with strapping on all the blades, she grabbed her axe and went out into the main room where Jason was eating his pizza and working at the table. Toria sat next to him while she braided her hair in her signature long ponytail.

"So Jason, what are you working on anyway?"

Jason had laid out the top to his suit and was working on designing more padding compartments.

"I'm designing a suit for when I go out as Wild Card. I thought that running around with a metal bat and a ski mask might give people the wrong impression. I'm getting pretty excited about this new outfit and I go back to the hospital tomorrow to hopefully get this cast off my arm. Once that happens I can start to focus on building back up the strength I lost this past month and a half."

"I like it Jason, it's pretty cool looking. So what are we, the crime fighting couple?"

Jason picked up another slice of pizza and laughed.

"Yeah, I guess you could say that, I just do what I can you're the real hero."

Toria finished braiding her hair, stood up and put her arms around Jason's neck.

"Well Mr. Wild Card, you're my hero. Alright I'm off, time to go bag this beast."

Toria and Jason smiled at each other, and then Toria was off out on the streets as Eon once again. She made her way back to the place where the first victim was found on the west side of the city near the woods. She walked into the woods a little ways, keeping alert. After 30 minutes of retracing her steps, she came across very large paw prints in the snow.

"I knew you were staying out this way big boy, now we'll see if you come back out for another nightly prowl."

Eon climbed a nearby tree up about 15ft and waited for the beast to return. She figured she would either catch him going out or coming back.

Chapter 3

Eon sat in anticipation of the beast. The moon was a little fuller tonight and she wasn't as deep in the woods as last time, so her visibility is a little better this time around. She ends up waiting for an hour and fifteen minutes in the cold on an uncomfortable tree branch, but fighting to stay alert the whole time. After that time had past she heard a faint rhythmic sound behind her. She turned to look and there standing some 200ft-250ft away was the beast just standing and staring right at her.

In the better light and the sparse foliage, Eon saw for the first time the full physical stature of this creature. It looked like a giant Timber wolf, mostly gray fur with some white. It easily stood as tall as the biggest of horses. Its canines came out from under its lips and Eon estimated they were 3.5-4 inches in length. The size of its head was bigger than a grizzly bear's and there it stood not moving, only waiting. Eon sat there in awe at the sight before her, she spoke quietly to herself.

"Well you found me, but you won't come any closer will you? That's too far of a shot to risk missing; I want to be sure I hit you. I know you remember me; I can see the slashes on your face are healing well. Well, I'm here to make new ones."

The beast stood there for a good 5 minutes and then it turned and ran back into the woods. Eon leaped from the tree and started to run after it. The terrain dropped down after rising up over a knoll. When Eon had reached the crest of the knoll and looked down, she had lost it. She looked down and tried to follow the tracks, she realized they started to turn back around. However, she realized too late as the incredible speed of the great beast had caught her unaware from behind and hit her with a clawed paw so hard in the back that she flew through the air as the ground fell away from her. Eon covered a distance of more than 30ft before she hit the ground tumbling to ease the blow. She had no time to recover as the huge wolf was upon her. The giant maw was coming down on her head; she couldn't roll away as the creature had her pinned on her back. All she could do was put up her hands in a desperate attempt to stop the enormous teeth from biting down. She put the palm of one hand on the upper incisors and pushed, while she pulled down on the lower incisors with the other hand to keep the mouth open. It was a struggle as the wolf continued to bite down and the teeth sunk into her hands. She winced quietly and took the pain in silence, but she was able to hold open the wolf's mouth.

With tremendous speed and strength, the beast lifted its head along with Eon's body and slammed her into a small tree so hard the tree split. The hit jarred Eon to the core and she couldn't hold the jaws anymore. The wolf took a swipe at her leaning up against the tree. She rolled out of the way a split second before the claws took out 3-inch grooves from the tree. Eon countered with 6 throwing knives to the face, which made it look away and rear it's head. This was the opportunity she was waiting for, she unleashed the poison blade and it embedded in the top of its shoulder.

During the beast's momentary distraction, Eon took off back up to the knoll to recover her axe that was knocked from her hands when the wolf hit her from behind. However, before she could make it up to her axe, the wolf caught her from behind. It's teeth sinking into her rear shoulder and the top of her chest. The beast reared back its head and flung Eon 25ft through the air, her trajectory stopped mid flight by slamming into a large tree.

The wind had been knocked out of her and she lay there in a heap unable to move her right arm very well. She had visions of the wolf finishing her off and there was nothing she could do about it. She could hear the wolf coming, but she just couldn't look up; her body was still in shock. Then she heard a change in the wolf's gait, it was a stumble. The air was now returning to her lungs and she was able to look up and see the horrible wolf shaking its head as if getting out of a daze.

Eon started to get up, but the pain in her back was too much and she fell back down again. The wolf seemed to be clearing its head and slowly it came after Eon again. It made a weak lunge at her, but she couldn't move and it slashed open a large gash down the side of her thigh to the side of her calf. She screamed in pain and took out the other poison blade and stabbed it right in the side of the face. Eon rolled to her stomach, covering her nose and mouth with her bad arm and trying to crawl along with her good arm. She made it 5ft before rolling over an 8ft drop off down onto an ice-covered stream below. She lay there on her back and pulled out both of her Bowie knives and made ready for a final stand. She had nothing left, the wolf had nearly broken her and she wasn't sure if she could walk. Her only hope was that the beast was just as bad off as she was.

She looked up to see the wolf crawling and wobbling uncontrollably, the poison obviously affecting it. Its eyes rolled back and its mouth started to foam and in one last effort it leaped down onto Eon. Both of Eon's Bowie knives stabbed it straight into the chest. The sheer mass of the beast landing on top of her drove her body crashing through the ice onto the rocks below and dislocating her left shoulder momentarily and then it popped back into place. The icy sting of the frozen water hit her body like a pile driver. She was in so much pain; she just closed her eyes and crawled out of the water out from under the dead beast. Both of her arms weren't functioning and there were sharp shooting pains up her back. She lay into a snow bank and grabbed the tiny little radio from her top leather band.

"Help me! Please respond, I'm in the woods on the west side of the city around 1-1.5 miles deep. I'm near a small stream, send help immediately, I can't move! Send a crew as well, the beast is dead, I repeat the beast is dead!"

An immediate response came over the radio.

"This is Chief Dixon Eon, we're sending help right now, just hang on a little longer. We'll be there within an hour, we know your whereabouts, just hang on!"

With the blood loss, extreme pain and the fact that Eon's core temperature was dropping rapidly, she started to fade in and out of consciousness. She tried her best to crawl back on top of the huge wolf and buried herself in the long, thick fur for warmth. That was the last thing she remembered as her eyes closed and she fell unconscious. Once again the woods were tranquil and all that could be heard was the sound of the small stream and the gentle blow of the wind in the tops of the trees.

"Alright men, the tracks lead down that knoll into the stream. My God, there's blood in the snow everywhere! Everyone fan out and search that stream."

Flashlight beams penetrated the darkness of the woods as Harborside's finest scan the stream.

"I found her Chief and the beast too!"

"Come on help me get her back to the ambulance, she's ice cold and it looks like this thing hacked her up pretty bad. I can't believe the size of this thing! You 2 get Eon to the hospital pronto, the rest of you get those ropes over here and let's get it around this guy's legs."

Fighting the temperature, the cold, the dark, the water and the weight of the wolf, the rope work from the men went slow. The men finally got the rope around the 2 front legs and the head. There were 10 men on the end of the rope trying to pull the wolf up 8ft out of the stream.

"Jesus Christ, this thing must weigh a ton, literally! Come on boys we've almost got him up, and then we can drag him."

After the wolf's body came over the crest and landed firmly on ground, the men sat in the snow breathing heavy.

"I can't believe we have to drag this brute over a mile back to the trucks. Everybody dig in, this is going to be a long night."

Eon was taken to the hospital, were she regained consciousness in the radiology room due to the warmth.

"Just hold on there Eon, you've been hurt pretty bad, so stay down please. You're in the hospital right now in radiology."

She looked down to see that her leg and shoulder had been bandaged up and the big imaging magnet was over her torso.

"Your wounds will heal, but it's your back that worries me. You have a fractured back Eon and it needs to be stabilized. It's not completely through or it would have severed your spinal cord. In that respect you're lucky, but it is cracked and placing pressure on the cord. We've all been educated on your fast evolutionary healing, but if you are not immobilized for at least a week then the cord could be damaged. If that were to happen, I'm not sure that even you could bounce back from that. I'm sorry, but from now till next week, you're going to stay in the hospital on complete bed rest."

"Ok Doc, the beast is dead and the danger is over."

The next morning at police headquarters down in the lab, a necropsy is being done on the wolf.

" Look at the frontal lobe of this wolf, this is a very intelligent animal. It's far more intellectually advanced than a normal wolf or dog. Its physical stature is also far greater than anything we've seen in nature for this species. The diameter of the skull is 19 inches, paws are 10 inches, height at the shoulders is 6'6", and length from the tip of the nose to the base of the tail is 8'4". The entire wolf weighs in at a total of 2,246lbs. There is dense, thick muscle tissue in the shoulders and hindquarters larger than a horse's. Looking at the growth rate of the claws, it would seem that this wolf was chemically enhanced by something to accelerate and magnify its growth rate. Take a blood sample down the hall, I want to know what's in its blood."

Back at the hospital, Jason is sitting in Toria's room.

"Well, you're half way to looking like a mummy. On a serious note, you saved the day and we're all grateful."

"Thanks, but I feel awful being in here. Though, I can already tell that I'm healing up. Jason do me a favor and go down to police headquarters and see if they picked up my poison blades from the giant wolf. I'll be making more, but they take so long I really don't want to lose those. Oh and one more thing, tell Chief Dixon that I need to talk to him. I remember something that Mr. Powers said to me just before he got on the helicopter."

"Mr. Powers? Ok Toria, I'll let him know and I'll see about your blades. Is there anything else you need while I'm out for the day?"

"No, I'll just stay here and read the books you brought from the lair."

"Ok, just hang tight and I'll be back later tonight to visit."

Jason leaned over kissing Toria and caressing the back of her hair. They smiled at each other and Jason left the hospital to go see Chief Dixon.

Later that night Jason had returned back to the hospital to see Toria, but she had been sleeping and he didn't want to wake her. He sat down at his worktable and pulled out his Wild Card outfit. He continued his work on the top part of the suit.

"If Toria is going to be staying in the hospital for a while, I might as well keep busy with finishing this suit up."

Jason glanced over at the newspaper he'd picked up and looked at the front page again. There was an article on how Eon defeated the great wolf with a picture of its corpse next to the article. It talked about how the people of the city felt safe once again. Jason smiled to himself and continued his work until it was time to go to bed.

Chapter 4

Two days pass before Chief Dixon could make it to the hospital to talk to Toria.

"Hello Eon, I'm sorry I couldn't get here sooner. Jason told me that you wanted to see me."

"Yes Chief, I'd check it out myself; but I'll be stuck in here a little longer. When I ran into Powers some weeks back before he got away in his helicopter, he told me something that's got me thinking. He said I was going to be a busy girl while he was gone. It makes me wonder if there's a correlation between him and this giant wolf I brought down. Did you guys do a sweep of the whole Tower?"

"We went through the whole place and didn't find anything that would link him to the wolf."

"What about checking the file systems that he kept in his office or down in the lab?"

"I'll have the boys check it out and let you know what we find."

Two weeks pass as the police go through the tedious work of uncovering every file that Mr. Powers had hidden away within the Tower. Toria was released from the hospital with a full recovery and Jason got the cast off of his arm. He's been starting to rehab his arm, getting the muscle back that he lost as well as the range of motion. Down in the lair is where he chooses to do most of his training work instead of the gym.

"You know Toria, I can already start to feel it coming back. My range of motion has increased as well as the strength. I even finished up the Wild Card suit, you wanna see it on me?"

"Sure Babe, I'm just mixing up some chemicals right now in the lab. When spring comes we're going to need an extra freezer down here to hold the nitro and poison blades. We don't want any gas leaks or explosions. You go ahead and put it on, when I finish this up I'll be right out."

Jason was already half way into the Wild Card outfit at that point and was excited as a kid to finally get a feel for the suit. When Toria finished up mixing a poison blade, she came out from the lab.

"Hey, you look good!"

"It took me quite a while to put together, but it was worth it. The suit's a little heavier that I'd like due to the Kevlar and steel plating, but it articulates perfectly and doesn't slide around at all. The spandex material is breathable too, so I can sweat in it and I won't overheat."

"Nice job, but you might look too good in it. That means you can't save any good looking girls wearing that."

"Geez Toria, you figured me out; that was my plan all along."

Just then the radio transmitter goes off and alerts Toria. Digging around on the coffee table, she finally locates it.

"Hi Chief, what can I do for you?"

"Well, we've had a breakthrough on the file work that we've been doing on Powers's personal projects. I think you had better come down here to the station so we can talk."

"Alright Dixon, I'll be down in a little bit."

"Well Jason, looks like duty calls and I'm curious to see what they've found out."

"No problem let me know what they find. I'm heading out to the gym to do a little work with some of the new talent. I should be back around dinner time tonight."

Toria threw on a coat and made her way down to police headquarters while Jason made his way to the gym.

Once Toria arrives at the headquarters, the Chief has a grim look on his face.

"Hi Chief, did you find anything to link Powers to the wolf?"

"Oh we found it alright and I almost wished we hadn't. Please have a seat Eon, I'll go get the file."

Toria sits down at the desk as Dixon prints out the file and slaps it down on the desk in front of her. He opens it up and they start to go through it together.

"It looks like this little experiment that Powers had going on was never fully completed. That's probably thanks to you for storming the Tower. He seemed to be working on altering the genetics of animals to enhance their natural capabilities just as it was rumored that he did with himself.

This experiment was called Project: Claw and was probably the next phase of terror that he had planned for the city. In the file it talks about how these animals are supposed to be controlled by a device that would be implanted into their brains. However, it goes on to say that part of it never came to pass."

"Chief you said these animals, was there more than one tested on?"

"I was getting to that part of it. Since this was a trial run for Project: Claw, Powers brought in 5 timber wolves to be the first in the project. When we searched the Tower, we didn't find any wolves at all."

"Then that means there are 4 more giant wolves out there. Those killings that were on opposite ends of the city weren't because the wolf can cover a lot of ground in a hurry; other wolves did it. Now that you've lifted the curfew people are starting to walk the streets again. We've got to put the curfew back in place or we're going to start having deaths again."

"I've already sent my men to the papers to put it back in the public's eye. What troubles me even more than the fact that there are 4 more wolves is another part about the experiment. It says after 90 days that the serum has been in the blood stream; the 2nd part of the serum takes effect. It seems that they become much more than they already are. They grow to be a foot taller and longer to a maximum weight of about 3,000lbs. They become faster, stronger and overall more dangerous. It says that there is a side effect to this growth. Since there is accelerated growth in the bone it will cause bony protrusions to break through the skin at the joints. If that's not bad enough, when this whole phase 2 kicks in they become maddeningly violent and ferocious. Now I'm not exactly sure when these wolves were injected with this serum, but I know that it's been about 2 and a half months since you stormed the Tower."

"Which means that pretty soon this change is going to happen. They may even openly attack the city if they become crazy in a rabid-like state. You need to have your men set up stations along the city with guns."

"I just don't have the manpower to set up checkpoints throughout the entire city as well as police it 24 hours a day. It just isn't possible, especially if we don't know where they are going to attack from."

"I was right about where I found that one wolf, maybe they have a common lair in those woods. Hopefully they haven't changed yet and I can get to them before that happens. I'll go back out tonight and see what I can find."

About half an hour after Toria left to go see the Chief, Jason left the lair with his gym bag heading in to do some work. He didn't get very far when he heard commotion and screams coming from a few streets up ahead. Jason picks up his pace towards the sound of the screaming and stops dead in his tracks. There is a mass of people running and an enormous wolf cornering a woman and her daughter in an alleyway.

"I don't believe it, I thought she killed it! Where the hell are the police, those people are gonna get hacked to pieces."

Jason looks down at his gym bag; along with other things it also contains his Wild Card suit and metal sticks.

"Talk about one hell of a maiden voyage. My arm isn't where I'd like it to be yet, but those people will die. I could die, but I have to trust the suit; it's what I made it for. I just never thought I'd be going up against something like this."

Jason quickly starts to put on his Wild Card suit, stashes his bag and starts running towards the beast.

"I really didn't think about insulation when I made this thing, but I'm sure things will heat up."

Jason thinks about how Toria looked after her battle with the wolf and he tries to block it out of his mind. He watches as the wolf slowly advances towards the mother and daughter with their backs against the wall. Jason picks up speed and there is a rush of adrenaline where he feels so intense that he could never be hurt. The wolf turns to see Wild Card running at it as the sound of heavy footfalls gives him away. The wolf turns and takes a swipe at him at the last second. Wild Card meets the oncoming arm with both steel bars. The impact sends Wild Card off his feet tumbling 20ft away. The wolf howls in pain and turns to face its attacker with a limp on its right forelimb. Wild Card gets up from the glancing blow and the two face each other in a stand off.

The wolf leaps at him with teeth bared and claws out. Wild Card manages to roll to the side to avoid the full weight of the beast. Swinging one of the bars at the wolf, he connects with its head. Wild Card is knocked off balance after putting his full weight behind the blow. The wolf's head recoils to the side, then quickly turns back to face him with a sneer and a growl. Wild Card's eyes widen at the recovery of the wolf and for a moment his body freezes with fear. Unfortunately, that's long enough for the wolf to swipe at him with one clawed paw and send him up in the air. Then the beast swings the other paw and knocks Wild Card out of the air and slams him back down onto the ground, jarring his entire body. The force at which Wild Card is hit with is enough to knock the wind out of him and he lays there motionless.

    At this point the wolf starts to hack and claw at him repeatedly until he's thrown into a snow bank near a building. The wolf turns back to its prey that is still in the alley clutching each other and frozen with fear. It takes a few moments, but Wild Card gets to his hands and knees coughing and dazed. His suit is halfway torn off him, but he's relatively all right as the Kevlar and steel plates took the brunt of the swipes. He sees a heavy chain left by a worker near a telephone pole and crawls over to it. His hands are cold, but he works as best as he can and wraps one end around the telephone pole. Taking a moment to find his steel bars that were knocked out of his hands, he takes one and slides it through the links in the chain. Taking the other end of the chain, he runs after the wolf and throws it around one of the wolf's back legs. The momentum of the chain coils around the wolf's leg like a whip. Wild Card dives onto the chain and ties it on itself as fast as his numb hands can go. The wolf turns and bats Wild Card away with another swipe of its massive claws.

    Getting up with his suit half hanging off him and running on adrenaline, Wild Card takes his last steel bar with both hands and after a running start, leaps through the air at the beast. Raising the bar over his head with the sharpened end pointing down, he falls towards the wolf. The wolf turns to see this, but can't react in time. Wild Card lands on the side of the wolf and drives the sharpened steel bar all the way into the side of its chest, hoping to hit its heart. The wolf screams in agony and grabs Wild Card in its massive jaws and crushes down on him before arching its head and throwing him 30ft across the snow covered landscape. Wild Card hits the side of a building so hard that his helmet flies off his head and his body lands in a heap with the entire world black and silent.

    As Wild Card comes around, he has a bad headache and some bruising on his sides with some cuts here and there, but nothing critical. He's wrapped in blankets on a gurney. Looking around he sees police sirens, an ambulance and then the wolf. It lays there dead with its leg still wrapped in chain and the metal bar sticking out of its chest. One of the paramedics approaches him carrying his mangled Wild Card suit.

"It looks like this thing saved your life young fella."

Holding it up Jason could see the dented pieces of steel and Kevlar in the tattered suit. Letting out a sigh looking at all his hard work torn to shreds, he's hit from behind in a large embracing bear hug.

"Thank you whoever you are, you saved both of our lives!"

Jason put a hand on her shoulder and in that moment he knew that it all had been worth it. With a smile on his face and a lump in his throat, all he could manage to say was:

"I'm just glad I was there to help."

Jason was taken to the hospital to be looked over, and then released that afternoon. He had deep bruising and multiple minor lacerations and cuts. He'd feel like he'd been hit by a truck for the next week or so, but he'd heal just fine they told him. On his way back to the lair he looked in his duffel bag at the torn up suit.

"Well Wild Card, you just can't catch a break can you? Your first official outing and you got the crap beat out of you, but at least I won."

Going down the manhole to the lair, Toria comes out of the lab to greet him.

"What happened to you?"

"It was a tough day at the gym, I'll be resting here for the week's duration."

Jason made his way over to his chair and collapsed in it. He opened his bag and pulled out an early copy of the evening edition paper and tossed it to Toria.

"By the way Toria, we're even at 1 apiece."

Toria giving him a confused look opened up the paper and read the headline.

"Local vigilante known as Wild Card saves mother and daughter from giant wolf attack."

"I don't believe it Jason, you could have been killed, are you crazy?"

"It's nice to see you too Babe."

Toria embraced Jason in a hug with a smile on her face.

"I'm proud of you, I just know what those things can do. Promise me you won't do that again, but I do thank you; that's a huge help to me."

"Don't worry Toria, my suit was trashed in the fight, I'll be out of commission for a while. I thought you already killed that thing, are there more?"

Toria sits down and fills Jason in on the conversation she had with Chief Dixon. The facial expressions on Jason's face went from surprise, to anger, to frustration and finally acceptance.

"You remember what happened last time, what makes you think you can take 3 of them on when their super steroids kick in?"

"I don't know Jason, but every time I go out there I put my life on the line. I can't back down when things get tough; at least I'm better equipped this time. I'm curious to see how my fire blades will work on them. Hopefully I won't have to fight all 3 at once, which is just crazy. If it comes to that I know I can't outrun them, so I'll have to rely on my wits and maneuverability."

"Don't even tell me Toria, I just don't want to know. During my down time this week and maybe the next I'm going to put together another Wild Card suit. The top and bottoms were shredded, I lost my steel bars and even my helmet was caved in. My first outing as Wild Card and everything gets destroyed, but it was worth it."

"Hey, those are the breaks I guess."

"Yeah that's easy for you to say, I need the protection of the suit. I can't walk around naked like you."

Toria flashed him a look as Jason sat back with a grin on his face.

"Look Kiddo, as always take special care out there tonight and I'll be waiting for you when you get back."

Toria went over to Jason, gave him a kiss and was up through the manhole and back out on the street to head across town back to the woods. Her 2 chosen arm blades were both flame blades. The poison blades had proved effective, she hoped that the flame blades would be just as good if not better. As she made her way across town the streets were empty and there was a light snowfall. She hears what sounds like yelling coming from a warehouse down one of the side streets and decides to take a small detour to check it out. She looks through one of the windows to see a group of 30-40 people giving their attention to a figure on a pedestal. Two others flank the man and he's shouting at the group of people and they're answering back to him.

"The time has come brothers and sisters, the signs of the awakening are all around us. The great wolves are coming for us and will kill all who stand in their way. Nature is rising up against mankind, we must join its cause or our lives will be taken as well. We must fight along side the wolves to prove our loyalty to the uprising. Even the great protector of this city cannot stop them; she was nearly killed by just one of the great majestic beasts. We must spread the destruction of the city, are you with me brothers and sisters?"

The group of people erupts in shouts of victory to the man on the pedestal. Eon steps away from the window and shakes her head.

"You really have to love uneducated people. I took the time to rid the city of all the major gangs. Now a cult of people worshiping those stupid wolves replaces it. Well that's not happening, it's time to nip this thing in the bud before it spreads. I should be able to wrap this up and still get out there tonight."

Eon strides towards the door with axe in hand. She takes a deep breath and swings open the steel door.

Chapter 5

All eyes swing towards the door as Eon strolls in.

"Alright people this little convention is over, you'll have to listen to bullshit somewhere else."

The man doing the speaking jumps down from the podium. He was covered in chains as they were wrapped around his chest, forearms, thighs and shins and he wielded 2 chains in each hand. The 2 men that flanked him on the podium stood up and took out handguns. The people part towards the walls as the chained man approaches an irritated Eon.

"You've interrupted our meeting of the Nature's Brotherhood."

"I'm sorry about that, I thought you were just a raving lunatic with a chain fetish."

"You may address me as the Steel Link. You see people; the defender of the city has come here to break us up. She fights for those that were meant to fall. Mankind's era is over and the new natural order is upon us. You would stand in the way of the great avatars of nature who have been sent to cleanse our race."

"I plan on doing more than just stand in their way. Those creatures are an experiment gone wrong, they're a perversion of nature."

"You blaspheme of nature in our domain, kill her!"

Eon lets loose 2 throwing knives that embed in both gunmen's chests before they can even aim their guns. They fall off the podium and lay motionless on the floor. Steel Link rushes at Eon with both chains flailing. Eon does a simple forward flip towards him, jumping over the chains. She comes down with both feet planted squarely on his chest. The blow knocks him to the ground and knocks both chains out of his hands. Eon stands over him with her axe under his chin.

"Alright people the shows over, I want everybody to go back to your homes. As for you Chain Boy, it's bad enough with the crisis that we have going on right now; we don't need you preying on people's minds. If I catch you doing this again, I'm taking you in. Clean up your act then take your ball and go home."

Eon walks out the door with the rest of the people that are leaving while the Steel Link remains on the floor watching.

"She won't get away with this, the Steel Link will rise again!"

Eon continues on her way out to the woods to see if she can pick up any tracks or clues. Entering the woods memories flash back to her near death battle with one of these beasts and she prepares herself for anything. She can't find any tracks or any sign of them anywhere. Eon decides to play the waiting game and climbs a nearby tree in the hope of catching one of them by surprise.

Meanwhile, 1 month ago in the country of Suriname on the northern coast of South America, a local scientist makes his way into the office of Mr. Powers.

"Excuse me Mr. Powers, we've found the genetic typing to match your blood with that of the blood in the vial that you gave us. Would you like to come down to the lab to test it?"

"Excellent work Juarez, let us proceed at once."

Juarez, the leading scientist for the South American branch of Mr. Powers Surge production, leads him down to the central lab room filled with other scientists and millions of dollars of equipment. Juarez prepares and delivers an injection into Mr. Powers. Almost immediately he feels different, every one of his senses is delivering heightened results to his brain. His muscles tighten even further until they feel like cords of steel.

"I can feel the change and it's wonderful, I never knew the potential she had. With the success of my operations down here in Suriname, I have no need to return to Harborside. However, I shall return for a different goal, that of revenge. I haven't forgotten what she did to my empire there. First I'll crush her spirit as I bring down the city around her, proving she can do nothing to stop me. Then and only then will I allow her to die. From this point on you will no longer address me as Mr. Powers, you will simply call me---Power!"

Laughter erupts and fills the entire laboratory.

To the present time in Suriname, Power has set his sights on becoming a monopoly in the drug trade in the entire region. He looks to expand through the country and into Columbia. He has armed men to enforce his hold on the region with the already corrupt government bought and paid for on his side. He has become a ruthless tyrant that the very mention of his name makes his own men shutter. Even those he has appointed as his lieutenants fear to look him directly in the eye when they address him. Regal and feared he lives a life of luxury in his penthouse. Nothing can touch him except his own personal vendetta against the girl called Eon. He contemplates while looking out over his growing empire on top of his balcony.

"Soon Miss Kayden we will meet again. Once my empire grows out to the borders, I'll have a new legion of men. Then none of the other drug lords will defy me. Once that happens I'll leave the operation to my lieutenants for my leave back to Harborside. My only hope is that the little gift I left you hasn't denied me the pleasure of killing you myself."

Back in Harborside Eon has spent 3 hours up in her tree. With the wind and the cold getting through even her thick skin, she decides to climb down and call it a night. She makes her way back to the lair in the wee hours of the morning only to find that the candles are still lit and Jason is up slowly and tediously working on one of the sleeves of his new Wild Card suit.

"Jason what are you doing up at this hour?"

"I couldn't sleep tonight besides it still hurts to lay on my side. I've had to sleep in the chair the past couple nights. So, I thought I'd tinker around a little with the new suit while I waited for you. Speaking of which, you look great. Either you're getting a lot better or the hunt wasn't so good."

"You're right on the second guess; I'll try again tomorrow night. However I did have a little bit of action tonight. Get this, some crazy guy with chains wrapped around his body was preaching to a group of people who worship these wolves. He called himself the Chain Link or the Steel Link, something like that, can you believe it?"

"Are you really surprised, it's the next inevitable thing."

"What are you talking about Jason, the guy's a wacko."

"Of course, we have a costumed hero in the city. It just stands to reason that we have a costumed villain too."

Toria stood and looked at Jason who had a large grin on his face. She picked up a pillow and threw it at him.

"Hey watch it, I'm still so sore even a pillow hurts."

"Well Mr. Hero, I'm going to bed. Just blow out the candles when you're done, goodnight."

As the next week went by night after night, Eon came up empty handed in the hunt. It was mid March now and people were getting spring fever. Dixon still kept his men out on patrol to cover as much ground as they could and the curfew remained in place. During the lunch hour rush at midday, the unthinkable happened. Eon was at police headquarters when it happened. A call came in across the radio by a patrol that one of the wolves had been spotted on the west side of town and is attacking pedestrians in a mad rage. Everyone scrambled to get the equipment and get out there. However, not 10 seconds later another call came in at the south end of the city with a report of another wolf attack. Dixon began to bark orders when he heard screaming coming from outside. Rushing towards the window they saw that here on the east side was the 3rd wolf attacking people on the street. Dixon slammed his fist against the wall and got on the intercom.

"Listen up people this is a full scale emergency! I need a patrol outside headquarters fully armed now. I'm splitting the rest of you in half; I want units 2-3 to head west and units 4-5 to the south. We need every available man and empty out the arsenal!"

"Dixon you have most of your men here now, I'm heading to the south end."

"Be careful Eon, if you hadn't noticed they've already changed into phase 2."

Eon tore out of the building and ran at full speed heading south. She could hear the gunfire behind her as she ran down the street. When she arrived it was a ghastly scene, people were torn to shreds and their bodies littered the streets. The rampaging wolf was even tearing them out of locked vehicles. Some stayed hidden in their cars, while others made a run for it. Eon was the first to arrive before the police units. She could see the bony protrusions and the fact that this wolf was bigger, stronger and more aggressive. Without a moment's hesitation, she ran at it and attacked.

The wolf was in the process of tearing off a car door with its bony claws and the man inside was petrified with fear. The man could see the giant maw filled with huge teeth coming at him, and then it suddenly turned away. That would have been due to Eon's axe being buried in its thigh. The creature was ravenously insane and screaming. It turned on Eon with surprising speed, teeth snapping and claws slashing. Only Eon's amazing reflexes kept her away from being hacked to bits. The 2 combatants were a flurry of attacks, Eon having to keep jumping back as the onrushing beast charged her with every weapon at its disposal. It lunged at her with its jaws, but she jumped to the side and saw her opportunity. She brought down the axe over its neck and then in the blink of an eye the creature had turned and caught the top of the axe handle in its teeth and tore the axe right out of Eon's hands. While at the same time it knocked her into a car with its paw, cutting a large gash into her side. In less than a second the wolf had pounced right on her.

Over in the east outside police headquarters, Jason Card appears in his recently finished Wild Card suit.

"I just finished this suit last night and finally was able to move around without it hurting and now here it is again."

"Wild Card I'm glad to see you, we've got our hands full. We could really use your help taking this thing down."

"No problem Chief, I heard the commotion from the lair."

Wild Card leaps into action with his sharpened metal bars. The rampaging wolf has wiped out half the patrol. They've hit it several times with the rifles, but it won't go down. The police have spread out to better their odds, but they can't just open fire because of the pedestrians; stray bullets have already hit 2 of which. Wild Card gets a shot in on one of its legs trying to slow it down. The wolf reaches down fitting Wild Card's head and shoulders in its mouth and chomps down. The steel plates spread the force across his entire torso, but the pressure is still tremendous. He winces in pain as 2 of the wolf's canines actually puncture through a steel plate. With all his force, Wild Card drives a bar into the side of the wolf's neck. Still the wolf hangs on, but now the beast has stopped to fight. That's what the police force had been waiting for to finally have a stationary target for a few moments.

The police open fire on the wolf's flank, which finally makes it let go of Wild Card, who crumples to the ground holding his chest. The beast again is moving wildly between cars, people and alleyways hacking and slashing as it goes. Wild Card picks up an assault rifle from one of the fallen officers with his bar in the other hand and takes off after the wounded wolf.

Over on the west side of town, the police units have arrived and have cornered the wolf in a warehouse. The wolf voluntarily went in there, tearing a new doorway when it heard the gunfire. The police are unsure if it has been hit and are staging a plan of attack. There are at least 15 people dead with minor vehicle and property damage.

"This is unit commander Davis, all people in the area leave immediately. Return to your homes as fast as you can while we have the wolf cornered!"

The men cautiously enter through the smashed in door that the wolf used, rifles at the ready. The lighting is poor in the building and in their hurry in broad daylight nobody stopped to get flashlights.

"It's all clear men as soon as our eyes adjust, we'll go in waves to search it out."

As soon as Davis finishes his sentence, the men are broad sided by the enormous wolf. It tears into them with razor sharp sword like claws and dinosaur like jaws. The attack is amazingly fast and ferocious. As soon as the men know what hit them, the wolf starts to run off deeper into the warehouse. Guns go off firing wildly in its direction, and then all is silent again. Nearly half the unit lay dead hacked to pieces. The men can't even look, while others scream out.

"Jesus Christ! This is worse than fighting in a war zone, we gotta get out now! This thing is just waiting for us and I'm not sticking around to get carved up!"

"Now come on men, you all knew this could be a dangerous job. We're the only line of defense this city has right now between them and this killer. We've got to stand and take this wolf down!"

The men all form ranks in a box formation with guns pointed outward and slowly walk into the darkness of the old building.

Back over on the south end, Eon is pinned under the huge wolf and struggling to get free. Loud gunfire erupts and the wolf stumbles off Eon. The police units have arrived and have their rifles trained on the wolf, but it uses the cars as a shield.

The police won't risk firing with people trapped in their cars in the way. As the wolf starts to run off, Eon jumps up and lets loose one of her flame blades from her armband. She holds her breath in anticipation; it's the flame blade's maiden voyage. The blade embeds in the back of the wolf's left thigh and the contents immediately ignite upon being exposed to the air. The wolf stops running and turns to its leg as the flames spread in its fur. It begins biting at its leg and thrashing around in the snow. The flames are put out from the wolf rolling around, but while it was doing that Eon was running to its flank. She unleashes 6 throwing knives at its head, 2 of which punctured both eyes. The wolf howls and paws at its face frantically and starts to lash out at its surroundings. Eon runs to get her axe, but she sees the wolf's thrashing has crushed a car with a man trapped inside. She calls out for the police to help the man.

"Get that guy out of there, I'll handle the wolf!"

As the police rush to the aid of the man in the car, Eon chops at the wolf with fury. The swipes of its claws are easy to avoid due to the blind flailing. Within moments the beast lay dead at Eon's feet and her axe blade covered in blood.

"You men stay here and see what you can do to help these people. I'm going to run back to the east end back to headquarters to see if they need help."

"Eon it looks like you've got a bad wound, are you sure you can travel?"

"It's not as bad as it looks and people are being killed."

In a flash Eon takes off back towards headquarters to help them.

Over on the east end, the police are helping the wounded to safety. There are firemen, police and paramedics all over and the entire scene is chaos. When Eon arrives she finds Chief Dixon up to his ears in relief work and no sign of the wolf.

"Chief, is the wolf dead?"

"I don't know Eon, it ran off wounded with Wild Card after it. We lost them in all the commotion."

"What! Why is Jason here? He said he was just starting to feel better this morning and now he's gone off after one of those monsters. You have to tell me where he went!"

"I don't know Eon, I don't know."

Chief Dixon walked away barking orders to police units. Eon stood there stunned at not knowing what to do or where to go. The world around her went silent and all she could think about was that Jason was out there and she couldn't help him.

At the west end of town, the police unit has penetrated deep into the warehouse. A loud noise startled them as equipment was knocked over and loud growling was heard behind them in the direction of the door. The men being scared out of their wits start firing wildly at the entrance until Davis can regain their composure.

"Stop firing, there's people out there!"

They watched as the wolf left the building the same way that it had entered. They watched it pick up a body in its powerful jaws and run off towards the direction of the woods. The men could do nothing but watch it disappear in the distance. Some felt anger at not killing it, while others felt relieved that it was gone.

"This is Davis to Chief Dixon, the wolf has evaded us and gone back to the woods. We've had casualties in officers and civilians. We're making our way back to headquarters with the wounded."

As the snow started to fall heavier in the afternoon, the evidence of midday was being covered. Rescue workers in all branches of the city worked into the night recovering the wounded and dead bodies. Eon stayed into the night to help, but this tragedy was going to take days to clean up, a tragedy that the press had already called the "Winter Massacre". Eon's wound was starting to get to her now and all she wanted to do was go back to the lair to heal and see Jason.

"Chief, I'm heading back to the lair to take care of this wound. Jason's probably there and may need my help."

"That's fine Eon, go take care of yourself. It's a big thanks to you that we killed one of those beasts today. Though it was a high price to pay, we lost 83 today and more are wounded sitting in a full hospital that must be a madhouse right now. I wanted to tell you that I was sent a call from Washington. They're going to send out a special team to take care of the wolves."

"When they get in trouble who's going to save them?"

"I just thought you should know, good night Eon and thanks."

Eon ran back to the lair as best as she could. She had been on the verge of tears since she heard about Jason's disappearance. He had to be in the lair because he didn't come back to headquarters and it had been hours since the attacks. When she arrived she found that Jason wasn't there. The candles burned in silence as she undid her long braid. Toria looked around with wide eyes and leaned on the table, her hair falling all around her. Her wound was the least of her worries. There had been a massacre today, Jason was gone and there were still 2 more out there. The full weight of events piled up on her shoulders and she just couldn't help but start to cry.

Chapter 6

It was late, but Toria couldn't sleep. She cleaned her wound up and took a shower. She put on her favorite Lullacry album and was lost in her thoughts and worries. She huddled over the table sitting on the couch listening to the song Feardance. As the lyrics crept into her head, she stared off into space as tears welled up.

"I wanted to believe,
But now it's crushing me."

Clearing her eyes with an exhale, she falls back into the couch.

"In your eyes I can see the blazing flame,
Once it's gone, there is no one left to blame."

Then slowly and quietly the hatch to the lair opens up and down the ladder a figure stands and looks on. Toria doesn't even notice because she's so deep in thought.

"I've danced with fear,
With fear of losing you.

It won't disappear,
So I will dance with fear."

Then Toria hears movement and looks over towards the entrance of the lair.

"There's nothing left to say,
I just let it fade away."

With a forceful sigh, Toria widens her eyes and sits up as if by reflex.

"Through your eyes,
I couldn't see hypnotized.
Once you're gone,
I've been left paralyzed."

In an instant Toria springs from the couch ignoring the pain in her side. She embraces the figure in a bear hug as 2 steel bars clatter to the floor.

"I've danced with fear,
With fear of losing you.
It won't disappear,
So I will dance with fear."

Jason caressed the back of Toria's head.

"Don't worry Kiddo, it takes more than some overgrown dog to do me in."

Toria didn't say a word; she just clung onto him with a death grip. Jason smiled and hugged her back. He said nothing more and they stood there for long moments into the night.

In the morning Jason was up before Toria looking at the puncture wounds in his chest and back as well as taking an assessment of other minor injuries. Toria woke up and rolled over to look at him. He heard her roll over and smiled as he dressed the wounds with new bandages.

"You know Toria, ever since I met you I've been in various stages of healing constantly."

"What happened?"

"I followed the trail of the wounded one that attacked near headquarters. The thing reached down and fit my whole body in its mouth and crushed down, like I was a snack. I stabbed it in the neck so it would let go, and then I guess I just saw red. I was so pissed at it, not just for what it had done to me; but for all the chaos and pain it caused. I could hear the screams of pain and terror all around me and for a moment I was out of my mind. I grabbed a rifle and ran after it, plus it still had my bar stuck in its neck. I tracked the thing all the way to the western part of the woods, as it was bleeding pretty badly. At this point I was coming back to my senses and realized it was getting late and I was all alone out there.

    I hesitated, but then I decided to push on. I'm glad I did because I found the beast, only not how I imagined. It was dead and its body was torn to shreds. My only guess is that the other wolf did it. Either that or it died from its wounds and the other wolf ate it. Anyway, I picked up my other bar and decided to get the hell out of there before the other one showed up."

    "I'll have to tell Dixon that there's only 1 left, that's at least some good news."

    Later that day Toria went to see Chief Dixon and tell him about the other dead wolf.

    "That's great news Eon, however something doesn't sit quite right with me about the last wolf. The 2 units I sent out on the west side of town lost half of their men. They said it was never wounded either. As far as damage goes there were more casualties in the west end than anywhere else and hardly any property damage. When the men entered that warehouse, they said that they couldn't hear it as if it was hiding from them. The other 2 wolves weren't like that; they were crazy and ravenously insane. These sound like the actions of something in control of itself and has thinking capabilities. If that's the case, then this wolf will be far more dangerous than the others. You say you've stalked them to the western woods, Wild Card as well. It seems this beast didn't stray to far from its lair. Well, it's the Federal Government's problem now. That team I told you about should be arriving later today and I'd like you to be here when they arrive."

"No problem Chief, just alert me when they get here."

Later that afternoon, the team arrived at 2 pm. Dixon alerted Eon and she was there in a flash to meet them.

"Eon, I'd like you to meet Captain Jarvis and his crew of elite government trained soldiers."

"Eon could see that they had the latest and greatest that the government had to offer. Not just in weapons, but in all aspects of gear from their clothing right down to their light sources.

"Hi Captain Jarvis, I'm glad to meet you. I'm Eon, I..."

"Yes, we've heard of you. You're that self-proclaimed vigilante that's been stirring up quite a commotion. Rest assured that Uncle Sam has his eyes on you. Now as far as taking the wolf down, it's best to just stay out of our way and let the professionals handle this."

"No offense Captain Jarvis, but you and your men don't know the first thing about this beast. I've had first hand..."

"I'm not concerned with that young lady. We have our own ways to deal with this wolf and we'll have him bagged up inside 2 days. Alright men, lets move out we've got a job to do."

"Listen to this Jason, you won't believe who they sent to take out this wolf. This guy Jarvis, a class-A jerk is going in with his elite team when they don't know the first thing about this wolf. However, he assured us that he'd have it killed within 2 days."

"Yeah Toria I can believe that, after all it is the government."

"Well, Captain Dickhead and his merry band of assholes are going to find they bit off more than they can chew."

Across town, sitting in his apartment is the man known as the Steel Link. Eating his dinner hovered over the kitchen table; he works feverishly on writings on multiple pieces of paper. He's working on a suit of body armor made primarily of chains.

"They'll see, all of them will see that I was right. Mankind will fall; nature's wrath is already upon us. I must get in touch with the great beast and show him that he has followers that need to be spared. Soon, very soon all will be made clear and we can all watch as Nature's Brotherhood takes its rightful place. I especially look forward to seeing that righteous wench Eon fall, that will be a glorious day indeed."

The first day out in the western woods, Captain Jarvis and his men take shifts between guard duty and setting up a perimeter security system. They have tripod-mounted machine guns with motion sensors out to 100ft from the camp. Behind the machine guns they buried mines and baited the area with 2 freshly killed deer.

"Well boys, now we sit back and wait. This thing will come along I'm sure tonight or the next. I'm confident that the perimeter security will take it out, but I want 2 on guard at all times with high powered assault rifles."

The waiting game proceeded with the men building a fire and breaking out dinner. After dinner stories were being told and laughter commenced. Then to the surprise of the men, one of the machine guns went off and they all became very serious.

"Alright men, put on your night-vision glasses and take up positions!"

All the men quickly grabbed their guns and suited up in an instant for battle running to their directed positions. Then they heard a loud crack behind them as a medium sized tree came down into their camp. Two machine guns started to go off and the top of the tree hit one of the mines that exploded. The night was lit up with so much firepower that the men had to take off their night vision as it was blinding them. The men fired wildly in the direction that the tree came down until Jarvis ordered a cease-fire. Once again all was quiet and the men could see nothing. Five minutes past, which seemed like an eternity. From a side direction one of the deer carcasses flew into the fire zone of the machine guns. Once again gunfire erupted from the tripods and the men.

"Hold it men, hold it! I don't believe it, but I think this thing is toying with us. Now save your rounds until we're sure we know what we're firing at even if something else breaks that perimeter."

Back in the lair, Toria kicks back on the couch with Jason watching a movie.

"You know Jason, maybe I should go out there anyway. I know they said not to interfere, but I'm sure they'll appreciate the help."

"Don't do it Toria, these guys will probably pull some Federal jurisdiction bullshit on you and call it a Federal offense. It's best just to let them do their own thing."

"Alright, but I have a bad feeling about it. I know they have all that fancy equipment, but you and I both know how dangerous those wolves are.

Now Dixon thinks this one is the alpha wolf and can control its rage and actually think."

"Hun, just for once can't we take the weight off and relax; just think of these guys as a gift. I'm sure they've seen worse in war zones and can probably handle this one wolf."

Back in the western woods, things aren't looking as good as Jason would have thought.

"Sir, the 2 northern machine guns have been knocked down by that 2nd fallen tree. Should we put them back in place or leave them down?"

"No, go replace them and take a man with you as guard; remember to turn off the sensor as you approach it."

Two of the soldiers turn off the perimeter sensors and cautiously venture to the 2 fallen machine guns. Both have on their night vision while one stands guard over his comrade. The other men take up points around camp since the perimeter is down. All is silent and calm except for the noise made by the soldiers replacing the machine gun. From the depths of the snow hidden and watching, covered by the foliage is the wolf. Faster than the men can react, the wolf is upon them in a burst of white powder. With 2 powerful swipes of its paws, the impact is like getting hit by a truck covered in claws. Neither man feels a thing as one's spine is snapped and the other man's head nearly comes off his shoulders. The remaining soldiers open fire, but the wolf is gone in an instant disappearing over a knoll.

"Jesus Christ! Thompson, Alvarey can you hear me?"

"They're gone, don't go over there the wolf could be waiting. I didn't get a good look at it, all I saw was a burst of snow."

"Captain we've got to get out of here that thing breached the perimeter defenses."

"No it hasn't! It's only taken out one side; we still have 6 other guns in place including the mines. We stay by the fire and keep our eyes trained on that breached section, now turn back on the perimeter!"

"If that thing decides to jump in here through the breach and misses the mines, do you think our guns can take it down before it reaches us?"

Captain Jarvis just walked back over to the fire; the look on his face said it all. He finally realized this was no walk in the park.

Morning came and the men had stayed up all night, but the wolf never came back. There they sat, tired, scared and cold with a ghastly sight in front of them. The fire had died down and one soldier got some food together while the others kept weapons at the ready.

"Alright men after breakfast we'll start to move positions. I get the feeling this wolf is just waiting. The bait didn't work and it knows we have weapons that can hurt it, so I don't think it'll try to break camp again. We can't keep sitting here night and day, lets take advantage of the daylight while we can."

"Sir, do you think we should call for some air support?"

"I've been thinking about it, but these pines are too thick and we can't go around dropping napalm around here. No, this beast has to be taken out from the ground. You know after all that ammunition last night, I don't think it's even wounded."

Back in the city the people are still dealing with the aftermath of the attacks. Hospitals are still at max capacity as well as the morgues, while city workers continue to clean up the devastation in the streets. Eon walks to police headquarters and tracks down Chief Dixon.

"Any word from the Federal team Chief?"

"No, but I was going to let them be till tomorrow. After all he did say it might take a couple days. In the morning I'll radio in and get an update on their progress, if any."

"Well I'll give them till tomorrow morning. If there's no progress or worse then I've made up my mind to go out there and help them. I know they won't want it, but I can't just sit by when I know how dangerous it is out there."

Back in the lair Jason is still recuperating from his last fight with a wolf.

"I can't believe how hard these guys crunch down. That wolf would have ripped me in half if I hadn't been wearing my suit."

Jason looks up from the work he's doing on the suit when he hears footsteps coming towards the lair. With no time to get his suit on, he grabs his steel bars and waits by the door. To his surprise he sees an older lady approaching and she calls out from the entrance.

"Hello, I'm looking for a girl named Toria Kayden, I'm a friend."

Jason decides to answer back, but he still remains cautious.

"How do you know her and how did you find this place?"

"I was told of the location, though you hide it well from the maze of sewers; I have a natural ability to find places. I don't know her, but a mutual friend sent me here. She would know him by his code name of Jax."

"Jax! Alright come in slowly and did anybody see you come down here?"

"Oh my dear boy, please give me more credit than that. I'm an old Soviet, we know more about being secretive than you Americans ever could."

"You look to be about the same age as Jax and you have the same Eastern European accent as him. How do you know him and why are you here?"

"Jax and I were old friends as well as teammates. We served on the same covert team in the Soviet Union. My code name was Rip and trust me it will be easier for you to call me by that name than my real one. Jax sent for me months ago to come here, but at the time I was engaged in working with another pupil. He told me this girl Toria was different, she's special and required my talents. You see each of us had our own special talents on the team. Though we all knew how to fight, Jax was a demolitions expert, but my primary role was combat. Believe it or not young man, this old lady in front of you once held the title of the most feared fighter in the Soviet Underground."

Rip looked off, smiled, and then looked at the ground.

"That however, was a long time ago. Jax saved my life once and now I come here at his request to repay my debt to him. He told me to continue Toria's training, to pick up where he left off. Since I found out he was killed, I would honor one of his last requests."

"Toria should be back pretty soon, she just went to check in at police headquarters. I'm sure she'll be plenty excited to meet you, Jax was like a fatherly mentor to her and she's where she is now because of him. You picked quite a time to show up though, right now the city is in the middle of a crisis. Let me get some drinks and I'll tell you all about it while we wait for her."

Out in the western woods of Harborside, what's left of the Federal team is packing up gear to move out.

"That should just about do it, we'll have to leave the rest. We can return for it when we get back in here with more men and some ground combat vehicles. I'd give anything to have a tank right now."

"Sir, I believe up and over the crest of that hill will get us back on one of the main roads back into the city."

As the 3 men cross over the crest of the hill, they get ready to take another GPS reading.

"Sir, we're right on track; the vehicles should be right over...awww!"

The other 2 spin around to see their comrade taken down by the wolf that was hiding just over the other side of the hill crest. They quickly draw out their rifles, but after the quick attack, the wolf disappears into the underbrush. That doesn't stop either man from firing anyway in hopes of at least wounding it. After some shots are fired, they run over to their fallen soldier.

"Oh God, I can't feel my legs!"

The soldiers back has been torn open and his spinal cord severed.

"He's not gonna make it, we have to keep pushing on."

"What! Sir, we can't just leave him here, we've got to try to get him to a hospital!"

"Who knows when that thing will be back? It's not natural, it planned an ambush and it's just a canine! We risk all our lives if we try to take him with us."

The wounded soldier speaks up over gasps of pain to interrupt the other two.

"No, the captain is right. I can't move; you need to get out of here and get reinforcements. All I ask Captain is that you help my situation."

All 3 looked at each other and Jarvis nodded, he walked over to the fallen soldier and pulled out his pistol.

"Wait sir. Though it hurts, I just want to look at the trees a moment longer and feel the cool air on my face."

Through tears, the soldier looks away not wanting to see it coming. The Captain knelt down beside him and held his hand allowing the soldier a moment to find his peace and let him know that he's not alone. Without warning Jarvis fires the pistol, a clean shot to the head and it was over. He placed his hands over the soldier's eyes and shed a tear of his own.

"I'm so sorry."

The door to the lair opens and in walks Eon to find Jason sitting with an older woman.

"Toria, I'm glad you're here, I'd like to introduce to you Rip. She's a teammate and long time friend of Jax's."

"Hello Toria, it's nice to finally meet you."

All Toria could do was stand there with a shocked look on her face.

In a section of the western woods away from our troubled soldiers treks the man called Steel Link. He's breathing heavy as he drags behind him a freshly killed deer. He decides to stop here and make camp for the night. His gear isn't nearly as impressive as the soldiers, but it would do and that was all that mattered to him. After all it was the cause that was the important thing, he was doing this for the Nature's Brotherhood. He hears screams in the distance followed by shots ringing out.

"Those fools, they'll all die trying to go after the Great Avatar of nature."

Several miles away in the western woods all that remains are 2 soldiers who are running towards their freedom.

"Captain, those are our vehicles up ahead!"

The 2 men make it down the hill and race into one of the military jeeps. As they get in, both men pause with frightening looks on their faces. The faint sound in the distance of heavy footfalls is rapidly growing louder.

"Come on get in, we'll outrun it. If he gives chase then fire at him out the passenger side."

The jeep starts up and begins to accelerate down the road.

"Jesus Captain, there he is bearing down on us!"

All that was needed was 60 seconds and the 50-caliber gun would be ready, aimed and firing. Unfortunately for the 2 soldiers, all the wolf needed was 30 seconds. Before the jeep can get any speed up, the wolf leaps and hits the side of it. The impact knocks the jeep off the road into a field, but it's still on 4 wheels. The passenger door is ripped off the hinges by the wolf's jaws. Captain Jarvis steps on the accelerator hard and peels out back onto the road where the wolf is waiting. The beast reaches in and grabs the last soldier under Jarvis and tears him out of the vehicle.

Jarvis doesn't even look back as he hears the screams suddenly grow silent. He starts to pick up speed on the secondary road and begins to breathe a sigh of relief. Looking in his rear view mirror, he sees the beast is starting to run after him.

"Are you kidding me? Give it your best shot you bastard, you're not catching me!"

Jarvis keeps looking in the mirror and to his horror, the wolf is gaining on him faster than he can believe. He slams the accelerator to the floor with the wolf right behind him. The speedometer reaches 68 MPH before the wolf stops gaining on him. Not wanting its prey to get away, the wolf makes a last ditch effort leap into the air at the jeep. The incredibility powerful hind legs propel it forward just a little more and it reaches out with a clawed paw and catches one of the rear tires of the jeep. The tire is punctured instantly and Jarvis loses control at the high speed and swerves into a tree. The impact sends Jarvis through the windshield and out rolling over the hood. Stunned and wounded, Jarvis takes a moment to get up. He's bleeding and is in no condition to walk. Looking around and shaking from shock, he doesn't see the wolf anywhere. He crawls over to the passenger side and grabs the 50-caliber gun and painfully climbs back into the jeep. He and his men had walked most of the day to get down to the road and it was now 5:30pm and was starting to get dark. His only hope was that someone would drive by, but that wasn't likely with the curfew in effect. He lay back in the passenger seat that was twisted and warped looking out over the landscape through the smashed out windshield where the glass was red in some spots. He was cold, hadn't slept in 48 hours, had to kill one of his own men and was wounded to an unknown degree.

"Come on out here you son of a bitch! I'll kill you! You hear me, I'll kill you just show your face!"

Back in Eon's lair Rip has just finished telling Toria her past with Jax and why she's here.

"So you see Toria, I'm here to honor one of Jax's last requests."

"I'm honored to have you come here and train me Rip, you're welcome to stay down here in the lair with us for the time being."

"I'd like to start tomorrow and see what you can do, Jax raved quite a bit about you."

"Sure thing Rip, I just have to check in with police headquarters in the morning to see how the soldiers are doing."

"Yes this wolf I've been hearing about from you and Jason."

Jason was in the kitchen cooking dinner while Rip and Toria spoke and he was bringing it out now.

"This looks very appealing Jason, I think after dinner I will sleep. I've had a very long journey and am tired if you don't mind."

"Not at all Rip, while you're here our home is your home."

Out in the western woods it's been 2 hours now and not a single car has gone by. Captain Jarvis is going in and out of consciousness from lack of sleep and loss of blood. Only his adrenaline wakes him back up in between nods. He scans the woods one more time with the 50-caliber gun on his lap, and then once again fades into unconsciousness for a few moments. When he comes to, he's face to face with a pair of eyes the size of baseballs with 18 inches between them. Jarvis freezes with fear as he feels the hot breath of the wolf on him. All he has to do is pull the gun up and squeeze the trigger. He watches as the wolf's eyes narrow and he realizes that it's now or never. Jarvis goes to raise the gun with all the speed he can muster, but the wolf is faster. The last thought to go through Jarvis's head was how the hell did an animal get the best of him and his elite team of soldiers? He decided that it wasn't an animal at all, but similar to some demon from the depths of Hell itself. That was the last thought to go through the head of Captain Jarvis and then the head of Captain Jarvis left his shoulders.

Chapter 7

Once morning arrived Eon made her way down to police headquarters. Chief Dixon was in his office when Eon walked through his door.

"Hello Eon, I was just about to contact the team."

"Good morning, this is Chief Dixon come in Captain Jarvis, over."

As Dixon and Eon wait for a response, all that comes over the radio is static. Both of them exchange looks and Dixon tries again.

"Again this is Chief Dixon, come in Captain Jarvis or any soldier, over."

Only more static followed the radio transmission. Dixon set the receiver down with a worried look on his face. He glanced up at Eon who was already nodding her head as if she could read his mind.

"Don't worry Chief, I'll go check it out. Maybe they just have the radio turned off. I'll see what I can track down and I'll report back in later today."

Without another word Eon was off towards the western woods in a 22MPH jog. Thankfully she had geared up with all her weapons just in case she had to go out there this morning. It was a crisp morning out and she had borrowed a pair of Jason's polypropylene bottoms along with her vest.

Already in the western woods the man known as Steel Link has been up for hours. Having cooked his breakfast and already set up the freshly killed deer, he starts to howl like a wolf with remarkable accuracy. He goes in 2-minute bursts and after several attempts; he gets ready to start in again. Clearing his throat and cupping his hands, he glances over to his right and nearly falls backward in shock. There not 20ft to his right stands the great predator. The only sound it makes is the heavy breathing that creates long tendrils of steam that escapes its nostrils.

"You've arrived oh Great One! Look I've brought you an offering on behalf of the Nature's Brotherhood, please accept this humble tribute."

The wolf looks past the man to the deer and walks over to it. Ignoring the man's ranting, the wolf sits down in the snow and begins to eat its meal. The Steel Link continues to speak to the beast.

"My brothers and sisters are your followers, we know why you are here. Spare us and we will fight for your cause."

The Steel Link grows bold and walks towards the great wolf. The wolf looks up with caution as the Steel Link lays a hand along the beast's fur.

Once again the wolf ignores him and continues to eat its meal.

"Yes, you see we can be partners in this grand scheme. Eat Great Avatar and now that you have accepted the offering, phase 2 of my plans can begin. I'll start work on the Steel Link suit and when the time is right, we will wreak havoc on mankind starting with the city of Harborside."

Just making it past the outskirts of the city, Eon can see the smashed Jeep off the side of the road. Quickly making her way over to the wreck, she recoils at the grisly scene. Recognizing the uniform of Captain Jarvis is the only thing she can make out of what's left of the body. Continuing on up the road she finds the remains of a soldier along the roadside and can see their tracks going out of the woods. Taking a deep breath, she decides to enter the woods and go investigate. Eon is able to backtrack all the way to the campsite, seeing the horrendous scenes of gore along the way. It's obvious that everyone in the party has been killed. She bends down to grab some of the fallen equipment still intact from the fallen trees.

"You're a killing machine and you'll keep on killing with no remorse. These poor men never had a chance, even with all of their fancy gear the battle was over before it began."

Moving towards the back of the camp, her enhanced hearing picks up the whirring sound of the machine gun tripod. Realizing what it is, she dives out of the way just as bullets blast away the snow where she had been. Once diving out of range, everything was safe as far as the guns go. Breathing heavy and taking a moment to calm her heart, Eon gets up and scans the woods looking for any movement. Seeing and hearing nothing, her trek back to town begins.

Once arriving at police headquarters, Eon dumps what she could carry on Dixon's desk.

"That's it Chief, all that's left of the mighty soldiers. I tracked right back to their camp and not one survivor. It looks like Jarvis made a break for it, but in the end he met the same fate."

"God Damn it! I was afraid of this!"

Chief Dixon slammed the desk and leaned back in his chair while looking out the window at nothing in particular, rubbing his chin deep in thought.

"You know the government is going to send everything they've got now. Our little city of Harborside is going to turn into a war zone and there's nothing I can do to stop it."

"Tell them the wolf is dead."

"What good will a lie like that do? For one, the government will want confirmation."

Eon walked over to the window and looked out at the same nothing that Dixon was looking at.

"I'll stop it Chief, I'll kill the beast."

"Eon that's a suicide mission, how do you plan to stop this one?"

"I don't know Chief, but let me worry about that. As long as you can keep the Feds at bay, give me one week and you'll have confirmation. I'll leave tonight; this reign of terror has gone on long enough. The timing is bad, I really wanted to start something else for an old friend, but this ends now. One week at the most, wish me luck Chief."

Eon turned to walk out the door and didn't look back. More than how she was going to kill the wolf, she was thinking about how Jason would react.

Back at the lair Rip is keeping Jason riveted with old mercenary stories as Eon walks in with a somber look on her face.

"Hey Babe, what took you so long and why the long face?"

"I have some bad news, the Federal team was wiped out by the wolf. I tracked them down this morning and not one survived. So it doesn't become a national crisis, I told Dixon I'd go out there and kill it. He's going to lie and say the wolf was killed, so I can't fail on this one."

"Oh Toria, this one isn't like what we faced before. It's a lethal and cunning killing machine, I don't think you should go out there alone."

Rip stood up and walked over to Toria and put her hands on her shoulders, looking her in the eye.

"When I spoke with Jax, he said you were the best he'd ever seen. My first bit of advice to you is that you must believe in your capabilities, or you are sure to fail. Now, do you believe in your heart that you truly have what it takes to complete this task?"

Toria thought a moment, and then nodded her head that she did. Rip nodded in agreement with her.

"Then my child go and do it. Jax, myself and the rest of the team were always outnumbered and outgunned, but we always found a way. I believe you know your foe better than you think. When you succeed, I'll be waiting right here to further your martial education."

"She's right Toria and I've learned that I can't change your mind when it's set on something. So, instead I'll just ask how I can help you?"

Toria smiled, walked over to Jason and put her arms around him.

"I've got a lot of love for you Jason Card and I am going to need your help. I need you to patrol and watch the streets as Wild Card while I'm away and I also need to borrow some of your camping gear."

Jason rolled his eyes and laughed as Toria raised her eyebrows and bit her lip.

Later that night Toria had all of her camping gear lined up. All very basic: tent, sleeping bag, cooking stove, light, pot, poly pros, freeze dried food, miscellaneous gear and all of it within Jason's backpack.

"Toria that's a lot of gear and I have a lot of miles in that stuff, not to mention about $1,500.00 worth. I know you eat a lot, so I gave you all the freeze-dried meals that I have. If you kill this thing early then save me some."

Toria laughed with a quick kiss on Jason's cheek.

"You're so good to me, giving me all your freeze dried meals. It's just like giving me the whole moon."

"Hey don't joke, those things are expensive."

Toria also packed 2 of each one of her blade types, as that has been all she's had time to develop recently. She slung on the pack and turned to face each of them.

"Rip, thanks for being patient and understanding, I'll be back before you know it. Jason, I know you'll worry and that's a good thing. It lets me know that someone really important cares and will drive me that much harder to come home. Hey, we're the good guys, we have to win right?"

Eon turned and left the lair with Rip and Jason watching her go.

"You know, that's what we used to say when we went against you Capitalist Dogs."

With a laugh, Rip walked away to her guest bedroom leaving Jason with his thoughts.

"You know I've watched you go out there tons of times before and I don't think it'll ever get easier. You just make sure you stay on your toes Kiddo, this foe isn't like the others."

As Eon entered the western woods, she told herself that she was in good spirits. Then again she knew it was a nervous response because she was scared to death. She walked past the remains of the jeep with Captain Jarvis and the soldier on the side of the road. Nobody dared to venture out here as long as the wolf remained. The beast had put a blanket of terror over the whole city. People were even afraid to go to the grocery store or even work. Eon ventured into the woods to a place close to where she had been before. Always keeping on constant alert as she set up the tent and laid out her gear. It was a calm night with no wind and the nights weren't as cold as they had been. Spring was knocking at the door and winter was just clinging on. Once everything was set, she crawled into the tent while leaving the sleeping bag open like a blanket. She also forced herself to sleep with all her weapons on. It was going to be uncomfortable, but really nothing about this mission was going to be comfortable. Eon hated that she couldn't see out there, so she had to rely on her sensitive hearing to pick up anything. One thing the wolf couldn't hide was its heavy breathing. A sound that she could hear from a long way off, the sound had been burned into her mind. Letting her mind wander as she lay there, remembering the fear as the hot breath beat down on her like a harbinger of death. Sleep wasn't going to come easy this night or any night until the wolf was dead.

Elsewhere in Harborside at the same warehouse location, the Steel Link has gathered his loyal followers. He managed to get back about half of the group that he had lost the night Eon had stormed in. Fifteen men and women stood ready for his command all armed with guns that he had provided from other sources. He stood before them with a new suit on. Dressed in rust colored brush pants and a self made chain-mail shirt that had taken him weeks to make. Small linked chains had been incorporated into the fabric in the brush pants around his thighs and shins. He wore long gloves that came up to his elbows like gauntlets with the same small linked chain worked into the fabric all the way around. His boots had steel plates over the shins and a 10ft small linked chain hung coiled on his hip.

"Brothers and sisters, the beast has accepted our offering and it will only be a matter of time before he turns his attention back to the destruction of this city. Tonight let us pave the way for the Great Avatar of nature in the form of chaos. If anyone stands in our way then we will shoot to kill, our time has come. Tonight Harborside will know the power of the Nature's Brotherhood!"

Heavy laughter rang out from deep within the Steel Link's breath as his followers filed out of the warehouse for the first night of chaos.

Morning came in the lair with the fresh smell of coffee being brewed. Rip and Jason sat down for breakfast with the radio on. A customary event that Jason picked up from Toria, who learned it from Jax. The morning yawns and sleepers were wiped away from the eyes quickly as the radio announcer got to the news of the morning.

*"...With 3 accounts of vandalism to office buildings and private businesses as well as several accounts of property damage in residential neighborhoods. Six people were sent to the hospital from last night's attack from what seems to be random acts of chaos. Graffiti left on all vandalized

areas lists the name of the Nature's Brotherhood. If anyone has information for police..."*

"It sounds like the bad guys are getting spring fever already."

Jason set down his cup and began to pick up his piece of toast, when he suddenly stopped as an epiphany struck him.

"You know Rip, I think this is all that character's doing that Toria was telling me about a while back. Some crazy guy that was spouting something about the fall of mankind and the cleansing by the wolves. Yeah, I think it is, he called himself the Steel Link. It looks like he hasn't given up, in fact he's upped it a notch. With Toria gone for a while, it looks like Wild Card will be stomping these guys out. On a good note, since I became Wild Card for the first time I'm actually not injured when I go out there."

Jason raised his cup to Rip with a smile.

"Here's to small miracles Rip. I'll head out tonight and check it out, you don't mind staying here on your own do you?"

Rip flashed him a look half surprised and half insulted.

"Hey, it was just a joke. You're about as old as my mother and could probably still give me a run for my money even with the suit on."

Eon rolled awake uncomfortable and a little stiff from last night.

"Well, I'm still in one piece and that's always a good sign."

Climbing out of the tent for a bathroom break, her heart jumped in her throat at the sight before her. There directly in front of her tent were canine paw prints the size of an elephant's foot. The prints of the claws protruded 3 inches out from the paws. Eon quickly scanned the woods with narrowed eyes, but saw and heard nothing.

"How is this possible, I never heard it coming. What the hell are you and why didn't you attack me? Well, it's your mistake; you left tracks for me to follow. This is what you want isn't it? You want me to come after you like some sort of game."

Eon took her time in getting her breakfast ready as well as her gear in check. She decided to venture out with the chosen arm blades of 1 fire and 1 nitro. As she ate her breakfast in the cold morning watching her breath, she compiled her thoughts and steeled her mind. Once she was done it was time to follow the tracks and begin the hunt. The feel of her axe felt good in her hand, she was ready for this.

Eon had followed the tracks for several miles before taking a compass bearing and realized that the tracks were arcing back around in a circle.

"What's the deal, is this thing leading me on a goose chase?"

Faced with the choice to keep going or to turn back to camp, Eon chose the latter. She increased her speed from a jog to a run. The snow made it difficult and cut down her speed quite a bit. When she arrived at the campsite her fears had been confirmed. The whole site had been destroyed and the contents scattered.

"Oh my God, Jason is going to kill me!"

Eon started to scan the woods and then she spotted it, standing on an outcrop up on one of the hills that surrounded the campsite. It stood like a statue waiting in the wind, only its fur moving in the strong gusts. Eon shook her head and spoke to herself under her breath.

"Just stay right there while I come up to get you. You're the last one and I know you won't go out quietly will you?"

As Eon started to race up the hill, the wolf casually turned and walked away disappearing out of her view over the edge of the crest.

"That's my answer, you aren't going to make things easy."

Once Eon arrived just before the crest, she stopped and listened. He's waiting for me she thought just over this crest I can hear his breathing. Eon coiled her legs in a tight squat and with a powerful leap, shot straight up in the air 15ft over the edge of the crest with her axe raised over her head. The wolf took a mighty swipe as soon as she leaped. The clawed paw met the axe head coming down and hit it on the side saving the paw from being sliced and the axe blocking the paw from slicing Eon. The blow of the paw on the side of the axe sent Eon spiraling through the air and she landed 20ft away, rolling to a standing position with axe at the ready. The wolf turned to face her with a sneer and a growl. Its head larger than any grizzly with 5-inch canines dripping saliva; a guttural growl that sounded like grinding rocks on a well-muscled body the size of an elephant sent shivers down Eon as she looked on in awe.

    It was a short stand off before the first move went to the wolf. Its attacks weren't like the other wolves that were wild and chaotic, his attacks were very calculating. First he clawed high, and then immediately low. Eon ducking the high attack and doing a back flip to avoid the low. As she flipped through the air, the wolf came at her with its giant maw. Eon was able to put the axe handle in front of her in time to jam the bar in its mouth. The wolf bit down hard on the axe handle and swiped at her legs. She jumped and missed the claws, but a bony protrusion caught her on the outside of her upper right thigh opening up a large cut. The wolf immediately flung back its head with the axe still in its mouth. Eon, not wanting to lose her axe; held on tightly. She went sailing over the wolf's head and in a free fall down the hill, the ground falling away from her. As she was falling away, she grabbed a handful of 3 throwing knives from her chest band and threw them at the wolf's face. She saw them connect and the wolf recoil before she turned in the air like a cat to face the oncoming ground. Having time to take the impact with a tumble, the impact wasn't so bad for her. To anyone else they would have been lucky to come out of it with just a broken leg. When she stood up to look around, the wolf was nowhere to be seen and at least she still had her axe. Looking down and assessing the deep cut, she winced some.

"Well wolf, I'll call round one a draw."

The wolf didn't come back the rest of the day, time that Eon used wisely to gather what was salvageable of the campsite together. The tent could still be made into somewhat of a shelter and the sleeping bag could still be used like a blanket, even though some baffles had been ripped open by claws. The stove was still in tact, but she had to drink the melted snow out of a metal pot as her water bottles were shattered. A lot of her extra layers were ripped apart, but one light jacket was still in tact. She was thankful that her thick skin could endure some of the cold. At about 5:00pm the snow started to fall, winter's last death throes. Eon ate something and stayed hunkered down in the tent. She had to fold in some of the sides to cover tears and tie it off with cord. The tent space was half the size, but it was keeping out the wind and that was the important part. The sleeping bag sat loosely around her as she held her axe over her lap. The snow could be heard against the tent and it was coming down harder now. She knew the wolf was just testing her out today and that's why she didn't give away too much.

"Boy the snow's really coming down tonight, radio said this was the last storm of the season, maybe these idiots won't come out tonight."

Wild Card prowls the streets tonight looking for any sign of the Nature's Brotherhood. It doesn't take long before his question is answered with the sound of broken glass in the merchant district of the city. Using parked cars and the sides of buildings for cover, Wild Card makes his way over to the noise to find a group of 5 looting out an electronics store and smashing the merchandise on the street.

"I wish I had one of those handy mini radios they gave Toria. Well, maybe I'll try the nice guy approach and try to reason with them."

Wild Card walks out from behind a parked car and confronts the 5 Nature's Brotherhood members.

"So, you guys do know that the store is closed and besides breaking and entering you can also be charged with littering the streets."

His answer was a barrage of bullets fired in his direction from all 5 members. He dives behind a car and is hit behind the right shoulder. Luckily for him the bullet hit a steel plate. He pulls out his 2 sharpened steel bars and waits behind the vehicle.

"Alright, now I'll take the asshole approach!"

"Hey Marko and Lemme, go check it out the Steel Link doesn't want any witnesses."

Wild Card watches the 2 armed men approach from under the car.

"What the hell would Toria do? She'd probably throw a knife at each one of their trigger fingers simultaneously from 100ft away behind her back. I guess that just leaves the question of what the hell am I gonna do?"

Staying low, Wild Card crawls his way around the corner of a building as the men cautiously approach around the car. When they both look and see that he's not there, one of the gunmen falls into the car with a yell of pain as a steel bar hits him in the head that spiraled through the air. As the other gunman turns around, he's met with a smash over the face with the other bar from a running Wild Card. With both men unconscious, Wild Card picks up both guns and orders the other 3 to stop from behind the car.

"Hey, he took out Marko and Lemme; come on let's get him!"

As they approach, gunfire erupts from behind the parked car and yelps of pain as 2 go down being hit in the leg. One is a guy; the other is a girl, which makes Wild Card feel even worse about being forced to fire. The other man returns fire and riddles the parked car with holes.

"Look Pal, I'm not going away; give it up now and nobody else has to get hurt."

Getting scared, the man turns and runs. Wild Card springs from behind the car after him. The man is no match for Wild Card's speed and in under 200ft is tackled to the ground on the receiving end of a steel bar. Wild Card drags the man back and rounds up the others, collecting all the guns. The 2 unconscious guys wake up and at the end of a pointed steel bar help their friends up that were shot in the leg.

"Alright, all 6 of us are going to take a nice walk down to police headquarters and you can tell them about your little shopping spree."

Once Wild Card and his captives make it to police headquarters, guards take them away and give them the proper medical attention.

"Here are some guns I confiscated from them Chief. I was also wondering if I could borrow a small radio like the one you gave to Eon, at least while she's out of town. I really could have used it tonight with these guys."

"Sure thing Wild Card. Some of our boys picked up another group tonight, part of this so-called Nature's Brotherhood. They've caused quite a bit of damage in this city in a short amount of time. It seems their numbers are small and should be a lot smaller now thanks to you. I've heard their leader is a guy named the Steel Link. We find that guy and I think we can safely assume we shut down this little organization."

"Eon said she ran into him before, I'll keep my eyes open for him Chief. Now if you'll excuse me it's been a long night and I'm pretty tired."

The day comes to an end with Eon hunkered down for the night in the western woods and Wild Card sleeping in the lair. The Steel Link stays up brooding in his makeshift headquarters with the remaining 4 members of what's left of his Brotherhood.

"It seems that we have a new wrench in the works called Wild Card. He cost me dearly tonight and I want to switch focus before we resume our activities. All our efforts will be to find this Wild Card and to kill him!"

Chapter 8

The dawn came with mixed emotions for Eon. It represented the end of another cold uncomfortable night, but the day represented another possible dance with death. The wind had died down and the snow had stopped falling, which had left behind 3-4 inches over the night. She made a vow to herself that the next encounter with the wolf would be the last. She didn't want to make this a battle of attrition, where the wolf had the advantage. Wiping the snow off the gear and starting breakfast, her eyes constantly scanned the woods in fear. Her muscles were sore and stiff in the cold; this would be the time for the wolf to attack.

After breakfast Eon went back up to the ridge where she had last seen the wolf. The snow hid the tracks, but it wasn't enough to hide the large impressions completely. The game began once again as she followed the tracks down the backside of the hill.

"So, how did last night go?"
Rip had already been up as Jason rolled out of bed to pour a cup of coffee, rubbing his lower back.

"I'd say it went well, I put away a good chunk of the gang. Of course I probably made an enemy with the Steel Link in doing so."

"To make enemies is inevitable Jason, just don't let them get the best of you."

Jason sat down at the table to join Rip with the radio on that told of last night's events.

"Tonight I'll venture back out as Wild Card, but today I've got some work to do at the gym as mild mannered Jason Card. With all that's been happening I've neglected my responsibilities over there. If Eddie were here, he'd be jumping down my throat right now to get my ass in gear. I wish he was here to get on my case, I miss him like hell Rip."

"Death is an interesting thing Jason. It affects us all differently and brings out many different emotions in us. However, if you ever get used to it then it's time to stop doing what you're doing."

Jason nodded in agreement and both of them sat there in silence trying to shake off the sleep of the night.

Death is just what one man had in mind that was already up for the day. Eagerly awaiting the information that one of his men is bringing to him now.

"So, what have you found out for me and the cause about this vigilante that calls himself Wild Card?"

"Well, his name is Jason Card and he works at a gym not too far from here."

"Very good, we'll see just how tough this vigilante is when we surprise him at his front door."

Meanwhile in South America, the tyrant now known as Power awaits on the eastern border of Columbia with a smile on his face. He's about to become the dominant monopoly in the black market drug trade in all of the South American northern coast. His forces have pinned down the last remaining opponents to him. He's been able to buy off all the corrupt officials in 3 countries and now to top it off he's gotten a bonus. Two of his soldiers drag in a hooded figure wearing a lightweight cloak with slits up the sides of the legs, large black boots with small containers attached to them. The figure wears a belt with more of the small containers as well as a long curved knife. Power reaches over and pulls back the hood to reveal a beautiful girl in her mid 20's with long black hair and a defiant look on her face.

"Isn't this a wonderful surprise, not only am I now the supreme ruler of the drug trade in South America, but I also get the greatest rebel of all my opponents. The infamous Vapor with fighting skill as well as guerrilla combat tactics. Aided by your little drug hallucinogens have made you an excellent killing machine. It is because of this that I will not kill you; I have an idea for your talents. There is a city north of here in the US called Harborside. I'll be sending you there on a special mission, one that will make use of your talents. You've killed more of my men than any other guerrilla fighter, I think it's the least you can do for me. I know you'll be very eager to help me in this mission because now I control everything. That means if you have any intention of betraying me, I'll turn your entire village and all your loved ones in it into a giant crater in the jungle. Do I make myself clear little one?"

The girl they call Vapor thought and weighed her options; she knew he was right. Reluctantly she lowered her head with a nod and agreed.

Back in the western woods Eon follows the trail of the wolf for miles to the entrance of a cave. A large natural opening in the side of one of the hills with tracks that go in from last night, but none that show it coming out.

"Well, you don't care about hiding your tracks from me."

With some hesitation Eon listens near the side of the entrance, but doesn't hear anything. She digs in the small pack she's carrying and pulls out a small headlight that Jason gave her. Though the light it can shed will be minimal, to Eon it will nearly brighten the cave up. She cautiously enters the cave with axe at the ready just waiting for the beast to pounce on her. At about 20ft in the cave, the footprints in the snow stopped and gave way to solid rock. At this point the wolf couldn't be tracked because there was no more indication of prints, but he had to be in here. The cave started to gradually descend into the depths. She could see evidence that the wolf had been here. The smell of decayed meat and the corpses of dead animals were strewn about the area. As Eon advanced even further, the cavern opened and split off into different directions. Looking around she counted 3 possible ways on and 2 that were small alcoves.

"This is one hell of a cave system, I wonder if they know about it in Harborside? Then again I'm miles deep in these woods, it would be hard to stumble across this."

First she tries the passage that twists around to the right, which in a short amount of time leads to a dead end. The passage in the middle, which is the main passageway she decides to try next. There is a gradual incline to the cavern and after an unknown amount of time and distance Eon stops. She can smell outside air and there is a gentle breeze on her face. Turning off the headlight she notices a faint trace of light coming from up ahead. Continuing on towards the light, the passageway turns sharply upward and out into the outside world. Eon climbs up the steep section and notices in the little snow that entered the mouth of this entrance, there are fresh tracks leading away into the woods.

"So, there are at least 2 ways in and out of this cave. These tracks are fresh and it doesn't look like he's come back in, at least not this way. The tracks at the other entrance were going into the cave. Maybe that's where he enters and this is where he exits, either way he'll know I've been here. Do I stay and try to fight him in these close quarters in an ambush or do I try to catch him coming in from the outside? I'm willing to bet that the left branch of the cavern is the same as the right, just another dead end and that there are only 2 ways in and out. I hate to do this because I don't have too many, but I need to be certain that he comes my way."

Eon steps outside the entrance and doesn't see any sign of the great wolf. Stepping back, she pulls out one of her nitro arm blades and lets it fly towards the top of the rocks over the entrance. The explosion is tremendous and causes the roof to collapse in that area, blocking off use to that entranceway. Reaching into her pack, she pulls out the other and last nitro blade and puts it in her armband.

"I know you heard that beast, well come on I'll be waiting!"

Eon makes her way around to the other entrance and finds a tree to climb about 50ft away. Sitting perched on a branch, she waits for the great wolf.

Jason entered the gym saying hello to all the regulars and dropped his duffel bag off in the office. He sat down at his desk and began some paperwork when 2 men walked through the door. They walked into his office and stood over his desk.

"Can I help you gentlemen, are you looking for a membership?"

"No we're not looking for a membership, but you can help us by coming along real quiet like."

Both men pulled out pistols from under their long trench coats, just enough so Jason could see. His Wild Card suit was in the duffel bag, but how could he get to it?

"You guys mind if I use the bathroom first?"

"Sorry Pal, you're gonna have to hold it; now get up and walk out of here nice and easy into the car parked out in the back."

Jason didn't dare try to jump them, maybe if there was only one. He didn't have a choice, so into the car he went. They blindfolded him and drove to the empty warehouse. Once inside they marched him to a chair under a bright light bulb with most of the other lights off. They tied him to the chair and then took the blindfold off. With the bright light in his face, Jason couldn't make out anything else.

"So, you're the one they call Wild Card, you don't look so tough to me."

"Why don't you untie me and I'll be happy to show you."

"Humor from a man in your position, I like that. I hope you enjoyed the day Mr. Card because it's going to be the last day you ever have on this earth."

Now Jason was getting nervous and he still couldn't see who was there.

Vapor the Latin guerrilla fighter with a fantastic understanding of chemical hallucinogens sits in a chair awaiting the orders of Power.

"My dear Vapor, I had great plans to return to Harborside in the US. However, things have changed now, I run the entire drug operations of the entire north coast of South America. That is where you come in; there is someone I'd like you to meet. She has special talents like yourself you see. You have killed dozens of my men as easily as you breathe, that is why you are perfect. If you want to see your family and friends again alive, you will kill this target and bring back proof that you have done so; I'll leave that creative part up to you. Your target's name is Toria Kayden, otherwise known as Eon. If you fail, everybody dies, but if you win then it's a nice bonus for me on an old vendetta. You will be given as much money as you need for this mission and you have 2 weeks to complete it starting tomorrow. Now go little Vapor and make sure you bring your best chemicals with you, I'll see that you get across the border without any problems."

    Vapor took her new passport and papers and then left without a word. Returning to her small hut, she empties her box full of little capsules. Each one a terrible hallucinogenic mixture that she starts to slot into the small space on her belt. Grabbing 2 more daggers, she hides them under her cloak. A single small suitcase packed with clothes and travel items, she is ready to go.

    Back in the warehouse, a large man that hits like a freight train is beating Jason. His face is bloodied and his ribs bruised, but he remains conscious.

    "That's enough for now! That's for the little stunt you pulled in getting a third of my Brotherhood arrested. Don't you know what it is we are doing? It's futile for you to fight back; nature has come to cleanse the earth of its wretched parasite called man. We are the few that will be accepted and saved when the time comes."

"You're full of shit and do everyone a favor by shooting yourself in the head you asshole!"

"You will refer to me as the Steel Link! He still has some attitude left, beat some more out of him before I shoot him."

Jason had been working on the wooden slats of the chair that he was tied to and had cracked 2 of them. All he needed was a good hard force to snap them. As the man returned to beat on him some more, Jason had an idea. With the first punch, Jason exaggerated the hit and used his legs to push off the floor, which sent his chair flying backwards and splintering on the concrete. His hands were now free, but he lay still as not to let on.

"You've knocked him unconscious, go stand him up while I shoot him."

As the man approached, Jason bolted up and grabbed the side arm from the man's hip and let him have it. Gunfire erupted as Jason used the big man as a shield and no longer under the light, he could see his targets. He started to run to the back of the warehouse, firing behind him until the gun was out of bullets. He leaped, crashing through a window and onto the pavement outside. Getting up he ran as fast as he could and didn't look back. He knew where he was as he recognized his surroundings. The gym wasn't too far from here; he knew he could make it.

Back in the warehouse, the Steel Link got up off the floor. His chain links had stopped a bullet to his chest, however he was alone. The rest of his gang lay dead around him.

"You will die Jason Card, no more games!"

Jason made it back to the gym and grabbed his duffel bag and ran all the way back to the lair entering out of breath and very bloodied. Rip came running out of her room dressed in her sleep attire, as it was nighttime.

"Oh my God Jason, what happened to you?"

"The Steel Link, we should be safe here, but if he comes through that door I'm going to kill him."

Jason staggered a little, and then his eyes rolled back and he collapsed on the floor.

Out in the western woods, night had fallen and Eon still sits high up in a tree.

"I can't believe it, he's not coming!"

The night was still and the sky was clear with a bright moon. Eon could see in shades of gray for a long way off. She had to chuckle to herself, it was like an old black and white movie---a monster movie. Especially with the setting of the woods and the beast's cave in front of her, waiting in the cold night for the creature to appear. When there was a sudden jar of the tree, Eon held fast as she was nearly knocked off. Before she knew what was happening, chunks of wood were flying out of the base of the tree from terrible claws and teeth. Within a matter of a few seconds there was a loud crack as the tree was hit with a hard force. She looked down to see the wolf; there he was in an enraged state with his teeth glistening off the moonlight. He had torn through the 18-inch tree like it was paper and it was coming down in a hurry. Eon leaped out of the tree and landed on her feet in front of the cave entrance face to face with the enormous wolf. This was it she thought; it was going to be a night battle. The beast had probably wanted it that way, she was just thankful for the moonlight. Neither combatant moved for a full minute sizing up the other, knowing full well that everything was on the line in this outcome.

Another night stalker in the streets of Harborside follows his prey. The Steel Link has tracked Jason by his trail of blood to the manhole cover. Slowly he lifts the cover to enter the sewers.

"There, that should stop the bleeding, but you need to rest."
"No, I know he's coming and I've got to be ready."

Jason started to put on the Wild Card suit when he heard the sloshing through one of the sewer tunnels.

"There's no time to talk it over Rip, I can hear him coming. I'll meet him out there in an ambush as he gets closer to the lair."

Without another word Wild Card grabbed his steel bars and raced out the lair exit.

Vapor climbed into the awaiting helicopter that would take her to the States. There would be a rendezvous point in Texas at the border with guards that were paid off by Power. From here, she would be taking a commercial flight to the east coast into Harborside. Once there, she would meet up with a contact to provide lodging and food. She had some hours to kill in the noisy chopper before the Texas border. Gazing out the window at the night sky, she began to daydream about how all this started in the first place.

Several months ago:

"Welcome Miss Del Rio, please sit down. I've looked over your resume and it's very impressive. A bachelor's in chemistry and graduating at the top of your class and the winner of a pharmaceuticals scholarship in which you served several internships who all have fantastic reviews about you. I spoke to one of your professors who is a friend of mine and he said you were a prodigy. I believe you'd make an excellent addition here at Banticorp Pharmaceuticals."

    Havanna Del Rio's days were looking bright, she had a budding career by day and spent her evenings with Master Hai, studying close quarters combat and specializing in knife fighting. However, what was a hobby that made her feel good turned into a way of life. The soldiers came and destroyed everything in their path under the orders of Power. Villages to cities fell to his wake with corrupt officials looking the other way while they were paid handsomely. Many people took to the jungles, leaving their homes and building little communities. Representatives of the United Nations pleaded for help, but with the slow speed of politics it would never happen in time.

    The people took to fighting their own battles using guerrilla warfare against the soldiers of Power. On a midnight run Havanna, who gave herself a code name of Vapor; broke into the pharmaceuticals chemistry lab on a daring and near suicidal mission. She had killed at least 20 soldiers using hit and run tactics before she made it inside. Once there she stole as many chemicals as she could and as much paraphernalia as she could get along with. Making her way back to her village, one of the many hidden villages in the jungle, she set up her own makeshift lab. She began to make bullet-sized capsules that contained powerful hallucinogenic properties. Not all were the same in nature. Some caused great fear; others caused a catatonic trance, while still others caused joyful bliss just to name a few. She used these capsules to supplement her fighting skills and they worked great. Besides killing the adversary, she would also break through enemy supply lines and get much needed food and medical supplies to her's and other villages. She had been on so many raids that she had lost count. With each mission, there was always the possibility of death. As time went on, the guerrillas were losing to the soldiers and it became harder and harder to even function.

    Then came the day when her village was found. The guerrilla's fought bravely, but in the end they were just overpowered. This led to the fateful encounter with the man they called the "Great Evil", the tyrant named Power. Vapor thought she had done all she could to help her people and that this was the end for her and everyone she knew. Her village was the last of the rebel guerrilla's to fall, but Power had given her an option. She felt as though she had one last chance to save her people's lives and her own. She had to find this girl called Eon and kill her; it was the only hope she had left. Dozens had fallen against her, how dangerous could this single combatant be? Power had been detailed in his description of her, all Vapor had to do was get there and do the deed.

Vapor, snapped out of her trance and looked out the window being brought back to reality in the noisy chopper and the silent pilot. Yes, it was going to be a long ride as she let out a sigh. Deep down she didn't really want to do this at all.

Chapter 9

As Eon's personal assassin traveled many miles to kill her, she had her hands full right now. While most of Harborside was asleep, adrenaline pumped in Eon like a jackhammer. She stood in front of the beast's cave in the clear moonlight while death itself was before her in all shades of gray. In a single leap the wolf tried to pin her down. Eon knew her mobility would be her greatest asset. She jumped away while at the same time swinging the axe and catching a glancing blow across its face. Immediately Eon jumped to the side of the creature to hack at its flank, but the wolf turned 90 degrees away from her and kicked with both its back feet like an angry mule. Eon could do nothing being caught in the air; she simply balled up. The kick knocked her into the woods crashing through small saplings and finally a tree. Amazingly she sprang back up just in time to meet the wolf's next attack.

Just before leaping out of the way, Eon threw her flame blade off her armband and jumped behind a tree. The blade connected and embedded into the beast's shoulder and immediately lit up in flame. The wolf's fur was wet with snow, but still the flame persisted. The wolf turned and leaped away from her, burrowing into the snow to put out the flame that was now burning it. Taking the opportunity, Eon went after it and came down with her axe catching it in the flank. The wolf howled as Eon for the first time had given it a serious wound! She brought up the axe again for another swing, but the ravenous wolf turned on her and caught the axe with its paw on the shaft and pinned it to the ground. The creature's massive weight made it unable for her to pull it free. The flames were now out and the smell of burned flesh was in the air. Eon tried again only for a moment in a futile attempt to pull the axe free, which the wolf took advantage of and clawed at Eon's legs. She tried to jump away, but the paw had caught her ripping open wounds on her legs and the force of the paw sent her flying back into the woods once again.

    Eon rolled over to see that the wolf was gone. The footprints revealed that he had retreated back to the cave and he had taken the axe with him. Eon stopped to assess her legs, the left one was worse and she walked over to where the wolf had knocked over her tree as the small backpack was still at the base of it. There were 2 rolls of bandages in there and she wrapped one around her leg tightly to try to stop the bleeding. She realized that the wolf had gotten by her and was now inside the cave. With her mobility hindered and her axe gone, she pulled out a Bowie knife and a fist full of throwing knives. She also pulled out the headlight from the pack. It was bad enough she had to fight it in close quarters now, but at least she could see.

 Underneath Harborside in the sewers, Wild Card waits just around a bend in the tunnel for the approaching Steel Link. When he heard the sound of sloshing water he made his move. Wild Card jumped out from around the corner and caught Steel Link square in the chest with both bars. The Steel Link was sent tumbling to the ground with a loud echoing yell. The dim tunnel lights made it difficult to assess any damage. The Steel Link regained his feet and pulled out both of his chain link whips and slashed at Wild Card's legs. The steel padding in his suit protected him from serious injury, but he staggered and fell. Wild Card had lost a lot of blood and had taken quite a beating at the hands of that large thug in the warehouse and it was evident.
 The Steel Link was upon him in a flash with another swing of the chain whip. Wild Card put up one of his bars to block it. The whip wrapped around the bar and with a hard yank, it was ripped from Wild Card's hand. Still on the ground, Wild

Card attacked the Steel Link's legs with a sweeping attack, which brought him down on the ground as well. Both men rushed to regain their feet, but it was Wild Card that was there first and he tackled the Steel Link to the ground. He came down with his remaining steel bar, but the Steel Link brought up his forearm to block it as steel connected with steel. With his other forearm, he knocked Wild Card off of him and both men rolled to their feet. They stood facing each other with Wild Card holding his solo bar in front of him with the Steel Link snapping the whip in front of him and laughing.

"Come on Wild Card, you don't look so tough now do you? You've killed my Brotherhood, the least I can do it pay you back. You're going to die tonight and I'm going to make it painful."

"Come and get me you sick twisted bastard and you can join your friends in Hell!"

With an echoing war cry, the Steel Link ran at Wild Card with both whips. Hitting him in the legs, the arms, the torso and the head. All Wild Card could do was run at him head on into the fray. Taking immense punishment, Wild Card gets inside and cracks his bar over the head of the Steel Link. The Steel Link recoils and tumbles down the tunnel. Wild Card staggers into the side of the tunnel, using it to hold him up as he breathes heavy and tries to block out the pain throughout his body.

If not for his suit his bones would be shattered. As the Steel Link slowly regains his footing, Wild Card finds his other bar that was partially submerged in the tunnel.

Rip watches on as once again both men rise to their feet and face off yet another time. She sees that both of them are staggering, but Jason looks worse. This is his battle and she won't interfere, she remembers the pride and honor in a one on one battle to the death. Jason needs to dig deep and find his way.

Meanwhile in a small village in South America, the last of the rebels are being held captive by armed guards of Power. They sit huddled together rounded up and put into huts to serve as their prison. All they can do is wait and hope for their savior.

"Do you think that Havanna can do it?"

"Of course she can, it took an army to bring her in. One person doesn't stand a chance against her, she's unbeatable."

"I pray you are right, all of our lives will depend on it."

They watch as armed guards pace back and forth in the streets of the village. Their eyes wander off to the heavily fortified makeshift headquarters of Power. Behind these walls Power stands and speaks to one of his lieutenants.

"Sir, why don't we just do away with these rebels, it's just a small village? We're now the main supplier of drugs on the north coast and the demand is heavy. We should be focusing our efforts to make sure our clients are happy."

"Of course you're right lieutenant, but I've won a great victory and have earned a small break. I'm playing a game right now and I'd like to see the outcome. I've sent Miss Del Rio to track down my old nemesis Eon. I'm sure by now she's dealt with the gift that I left behind for her and is ready for something else. Consider this a vacation for you lieutenant. All you and the men have to do is keep an eye on a bunch of helpless villagers for the next 2 weeks."

Power turns and faces his desk, leaning on his hands and looking off into space.

"I wonder how you're doing dear Toria, are you having as much fun as I am?"

Far into the western woods, Eon cautiously limps to the entrance of the cave with weapons at the ready. The beam of the headlight dances around the entranceway, but there is no sign of the wolf. Eon makes her way slowly into the cave to the 3-way split and stops to listen. She spots the blood trail on the cave floor and it leads to the left tunnel, the route she hadn't checked before. With a heavy sigh she continued and realized that it went on quite a ways with a steady descent. Up ahead the end of the tunnel seemed to stop in blackness. As Eon got closer, it was evident that the tunnel led to a great open cavern larger than the entranceway. Her light beam couldn't penetrate the other side of the cavern or the ceiling; all she saw was darkness. Then she heard it, the heavy breathing above her. Quickly she looked up, but as soon as she did it was gone. All that was there was a ledge that the wolf had just been standing on. The wolf knew this cavern, it was his lair and she realized that she was the one walking around with a light on her head making her a beacon for the wolf to see coming. The smell of death and stagnant air clung to the cavern revealing this site as a terrible grave for the wolf's untold amount of human and animal victims.

 Eon took off her headlight and walked out into the blackness of the cavern and set it down on the ground with the light beam facing up towards the ceiling. This created a dome like light effect that with her eyes spread out into a 50ft radius. She crouched low to the light source with her Bowie knives at the ready looking around. At least now she had a little area of light to give her some type of warning. Her theory was tested immediately as the great wolf leaped at her from up above. She didn't have the strength in her wounded legs to move so quickly; instead she met the attack with her blades. The wolf swiped at her with both claws and into the center of each massive paw a Bowie knife went straight through. The wolf howled in pain and ran off ripping the Bowie knives out of Eon's hands and staying embedded in its paws. Eon pulled out her last 6 throwing knives and listened. She could hear that the wolf was limping; at least she could get a read on him. He was coming again and this time it was head on. Eon waited until she had a clear view as the wolf ran at her with teeth bared. She unleashed all 6 knives and they embedded in its face, neck and shoulders, but the bloodthirsty beast would not be deterred. Eon tried to jump to the side as best as she could, but her legs could only do so much. She was able to avoid the snapping teeth, but was raked across her back by the deep claws.

    She let out a scream as the wolf once again ran off into the darkness. Eon lay there on the cave floor wincing in pain and taking gasping breaths. Her eyes were closed tight, her teeth were clenched and her fingernails grinding into the dirt and rock. After the initial shock of pain, her wits came back to her. She could hear the wolf circling slowly as she lay there. It had killed enough times to know when its prey was ready to be taken. It knew that this girl was no longer a threat to it and was now time for the killing blow. She could hear the wolf climbing the rocks to a ledge. The handles of the

Bowie knives sticking out the bottom of its paws and scraping the rock gave it away.

"I'm not dead yet you son of a bitch, come and get me!"

Wild Card stood facing the Steel Link in the sewer tunnels under Harborside. Both men could barely hold themselves up; they were driven by hatred. As they eyed each other it was just a matter of who wanted it more. Wild Card just couldn't take another physical attack, so he tried to stall with words.

"I'm not letting you leave this tunnel. First it was about justice, but somewhere along the way it got real personal."

"How can you stop me, you can barely stand?"

With a laugh the Steel Link arched back over his head and snapped both of his steel whips at Wild Card. Just before they struck, Wild Card dropped his bars and caught each whip out of the air and held tightly. The sting in his hands even through the gloves was unbelievable as he closed his eyes to block out the pain. In one powerful motion he yanked and ripped the whips right out of the Steel Link's hands and threw them behind him. The Steel Link tackled Wild Card before he knew what happened and pummeled him in the face with his armored forearms. He got up off of Wild Card and went to retrieve his whips as Wild Card lay there.

"Get up Jason, you'll only be defeating yourself!"

Steel Link turned to see Rip standing in the entranceway of the lair as he picked up both of his whips with a sadistic smile on his lips.

"Well, it looks like I get 2 for the price of 1."

As the Steel Link advanced on Rip, Wild Card slowly got his bearings and recovered one of his bars. Barely able to get to his feet, he glanced over to see Rip cowering as the Steel Link raised his whips.

"No, leave her alone!"

In one fluid motion Wild Card unleashed his steel bar with all the strength that he could muster. It flew through the air like a spear from Hell! Just before the whips could come down, Rip winced as she was splattered with blood. She looked to see the sharpened steel bar that had driven through the back of his neck and had gone right through the front. With a look of shock on his face, the Steel Link dropped down dead.

Eon lay there on the cave floor next to the small headlight, she was waiting for the killing strike and she had a hunch it was coming from above. The wolf had used hit and run tactics perfectly, it was a killing machine. Eon had one more trick up her sleeve, but the timing and accuracy had to be perfect. If she failed, the wolf would rend her to pieces. She called upon her inner strength to try to focus through the pain, this meant the difference whether she lived or died as well as countless others after her. The silence was overwhelming, she felt herself wanting to slip away to unconsciousness. What was the wolf waiting for? Maybe it was waiting for her to pass out, maybe it was just watching her die. No she thought; this creature wants to kill me. Just sitting by and watching wasn't his way. So she waited with her hand clutched around her ace in the hole. Minutes went by, but still she wouldn't lower her guard.

    Without warning, without noise, the wolf was there. Through Eon's eyes it was in slow motion and surreal like in a dream. The wolf had jumped off the ledge above her and was coming down on her with claws out and teeth bared. Eon waited till the last possible second to make sure she wouldn't miss or the wolf would turn away. There was no mistaking it, this was the killing strike and just before the wolf reached her with mouth wide open and teeth dripping saliva, she acted. With precise accuracy, Eon let fly her last blade she had on her and hoped to God that it worked, or she was dead. The blade sailed through the air and directly into the wolf's open mouth. Normally this attack would just have wounded it and not stopped it, however this was a nitro blade and Eon would only use it if she were 100% sure of its accuracy.

Immediately on impact the wolf bit down and that would be the last action it would ever do. The massive head on the killer wolf exploded in a shower of blood, brains and skull! The great wolf was finally dead. The wolf's massive body landed on Eon, who did all she could to crawl and push out from underneath it. She lay there in the dark cave lit by the small headlight and looked over at the grisly scene of the headless wolf's body. Once she realized it was finally over, she slumped forward and closed her eyes in a silent prayer.

Rip ran over to Jason who was on his hands and knees looking down with blood dripping from his mouth and face.

"That was a shot to be proud of Jason, here let me help you up."

"No, I need to get to police headquarters."

"Jason you can barely stand up! At least let me dress some of these wounds and assess the damage. Then you can go, I understand all too well the need to finish something to the end."

Rip helped Wild Card to his feet and into the lair to get some dressing.

"Back there when the Steel Link had his whips raised over you, why didn't you move or act?"

Rip simply stayed silent with a smirk on her face as she cleaned out a cut over Jason's eye.

"Oh I see, you never really were in trouble, was that some sort of test for me to see how I'd react?"

"Yes and you passed with flying colors. It's what burns inside that counts Jason, it makes all the difference in the world."

"Thanks Rip, I have to go now and tell the police what's happened here. I'll be back as soon as business is taken care of and then I think I'll sleep for about 20 hours after taking 30,000mg of pain killers."

Jason got to his feet, he was shaky, but he was standing. With a slow limp, he made his way out of the lair.

Eon got up and grabbed the light to search around. First she went to her backpack and used the second roll of bandaging material to wrap around her back for whatever good that was worth. Her whole body was on fire, but she forced herself to push on. She retrieved her blades and cut off one of the wolf's paws and put it in the backpack.

"Don't worry Jason, I'll get you new gear as soon as this is all over."

The axe lay near a pile of rotting human and animal corpses. The stench was overwhelming and the sight nearly put her over the edge. She had to get out of there as fast as she could. Once outside, Eon tried to radio headquarters; but she was out of range and only picked up static. So began a slow journey back to Harborside in the eerie moonlit woods.

What would have taken a normal person most of a day still took Eon only a couple of hours, even in her injured state. As she approached police headquarters, she saw a familiar figure approaching as well and he was limping. As both of them approached each other in front of police headquarters they could finally see each other in the light.
"Jason!"
"Toria!"
There was a look of shock on both of their faces as they looked over each other's wounds. The same words left their mouths at the exact same time.
"Oh my God! What happened to you?"
"No Jason, you first. Who did that to your face and where the hell is he?"
"Now hold on Toria, it's nothing I couldn't handle. Trust me if you think this is bad, you really wouldn't want to be the other guy."
Jason let out a small laugh that hurt his ribs and he quickly got serious.
"What about you, are you all right?"

Jason held the door for Toria as they made their way to the offices.

"Boys, it's your lucky day! Call up the 3 little pigs and tell them that the big bad wolf is dead. After you're done calling the pigs, you could probably call up Chief Dixon and fill him in on it too."

Wild Card and Eon brought the police up to speed on what had transpired for both of them and started to make their way back to the lair with a police escort to retrieve Steel Link's body. One of the officers stopped them just before they left.

"Oh Eon, the Feds said they wanted to get the head of the wolf sent out for examination."

"Officer, you can tell the Feds I said good luck with that one."

They cleaned up and crawled into bed, which took each of them a few minutes due to the pain.

"Don't worry Jason, you'll be back on your feet in no time."

"That's easy for you to say, you heal perfectly in about 5 minutes."

"No, it takes at least 7 minutes."

Toria touched his shoulder and leaned in close to him for a kiss.

"I'm so glad we live down here because the sun will be up in an hour or so and it's pitch black down here. I feel like sleeping forever and we can now that this is over. I hope I go a long time before I see any sort of trouble again."

    Just as Eon was finishing that sentence, a plane was touching down just outside Harborside city limits. The raven-haired Latina that called herself Vapor, stepped onto American soil for the first time in her life. She was met with one of Power's contacts that helped her with her bags.
    "Right this way Miss Del Rio, we have a car waiting for you."
    The man opened the car door and Havanna climbed inside shrouded in her cloak. The man put her bags in the trunk and got into the driver's seat to start the car.
    "Miss Del Rio, I'll get you to the hotel immediately I know you must be very tired. Please let me know if there is anything I can get for you; Harborside can be very accommodating. Perhaps tomorrow..."
    "No, you will take me to the hotel so I can sleep and then tomorrow I would like to start in on my business of why I'm here. Since we have some time before we get to the hotel, why don't you tell me a little about this city. I've heard so much about this person named Eon."

Chapter 10

As the next day came in the lair Toria rolled her arm over onto Jason, who woke up with a start. He looked down to see that she was still asleep and realized he was starving. Looking over at the clock, it was 6:15pm. He tried to slide out of the bed without waking Toria, but it was a futile effort with someone who had heightened senses.

"Hey Babe, I'm just getting up to eat something and check these bandages."

"I'll join you, these wounds on my back and legs are killing me!"

"Rip said she was going out to get some over the counter pain killers, I could use some more myself."

"Alright it's official, I'm up. Come on I'll check your wounds and you can check mine."

Toria slowly got out of bed flashing a smile followed by a wince as she felt how sore her whole body was. Rip entered the lair with groceries and wound care products.

"Great timing Rip, we were just about to get something to eat and check the wounds. Why don't you join us for a bite? I don't know about you Toria, but I'm going right back to bed after this, I'm still exhausted."

"I'm with you there, I'll check in with Dixon in the morning."

When morning arrived Toria was up and out before Jason had even finished his breakfast. He looked over and saw Rip preparing some things in the training room.

"What are you doing in there Rip?"

I'm just setting up some things for Toria's first lesson. She should be ready to start in a few days."

"You know, I've fought by her side and I've seen what she can do. To tell you the truth, I can't imagine her being any better than she is right now. Hell, I'm scared to even get into a serious argument with her, I'll have 2 knives sticking out of my eye-sockets."

Rip started to laugh as she continued the set up for the first lesson.

"Oh Jason, I don't think you have anything to worry about. I can tell that Toria cares very deeply for you. As to her getting any better, nobody is absolutely perfect. She was severely wounded in her battle with the wolf."

"You can't be serious, that thing could tear through a tank!"

"Still she was wounded and if she was better, she could have avoided those wounds."

Jason turned back to his breakfast shaking his head with a smile on his face.

"You know Rip, you Soviets are pretty damn strict!"

Eon walked into police headquarters; she had been speaking with Chief Dixon over the radio on her way over. He had mentioned that the cave she was talking about, nobody knew existed and he wanted her to lead the way on the expedition for the body recovery.

"Hello Eon, I'm glad to see that you're up and about so soon. Like I said, I'll be sending a team of 10 men with you to recover the wolf's body and explore that cave a little more in detail. You can drive out there with them and then enter the woods on foot."

"Sounds good Chief. It'll probably take the men most of the day to get back to where the cave is. We'll camp there tonight, explore the cave and retrieve the body in the morning and then be back here by tomorrow night."

"None too soon either, I've got the Feds up my ass hounding me about the wolf's body. There's a group coming in tomorrow to get the remains of the soldiers as well as the wolf, you really cut it to the wire. I just wanted to tell you so you weren't surprised when you get back to be greeted by the Feds."

Eon walked out to where the men were loading into the vehicles with their gear. She stopped to look around and smelled the air; it was officially spring here in Harborside. The winter was over and with it the threat of these killer wolves.

Looking up and snapping out of her daze, she heard one of the men call out to her that they were ready to go.

As Eon went back to the western woods, Jason decided to venture out to see the outside world and stop at the local coffee shop.

"Hey Jason, good to see you; you want your regular?"

"Sure Bobby and can I grab one to go?"

"What happened to you, those boys at the gym kicking you around some or what?"

"Oh, I had a rough time the other night keeping these streets of ours clean."

"Jason, God bless you for what you do. I wish we had a 100 more guys just like you, here these are on the house."

"Thanks Bobby, I'll see you around."

Jason walked out the door with his 2 coffees and was approached by a girl that followed him outside. Her raven hair and striking features caught him off guard.

"Excuse me, you are Jason Card, the famous Wild Card of Harborside?"

She had a Latin accent and a beautiful smile.

"Yes, but I'm not sure who you are, do I know you?"

"Oh forgive me, my name is Havanna Del Rio and I understand you have contact with the famous Eon. I'm such a big fan, she is a fantastic role model and I'd love to talk with her. You see I'm a teacher here in town and I'd like to set up something with her if I could to come and talk to the class. I was wondering if you could set up a meeting with her for me, is that possible?"

"I'm sure she'd love to talk to your class. Let me talk to her and she can stop down to the school to get in touch with you. Which school do you teach at?"

"No, I wouldn't trouble her with that. Here is my number, just have her give me a call and we'll set it up that way."

"Alright, I'll give it to her when I see her. It was nice to meet you Miss Del Rio, take care."

Jason made his way back to the lair with his coffee and gave the other one to Rip.

"I ran into a teacher that wants Toria to speak to her class."

"What school does she teach at?"

"You know she didn't say and she had a very thick Latin accent. I wonder how long she's been teaching over here?"

Jason smiled and looked off shaking his head.

"I'll tell you one thing, she sure didn't look like any teachers I had growing up. Anyway, she gave me a number to get a hold of her for Toria."

"Can I see that number Jason?"

Jason pulled out the number for Rip and gave it to her.

"It's probably nothing, but in Eon's line of work as was mine, you could never be too careful. It's very easy to make enemies throughout your career and they can come in all forms."

"Rip, this girl is harmless, she just wants to talk to Toria. The KGB times are over, it's all right to relax."

"Just the same Jason, why don't you run the number through the police database and track it down before she calls."

"Alright Rip, but let me finish my coffee first and lay down a little. Just going to the coffee shop was a task in the shape I'm in."

The police vehicles pulled up along side of the western woods. Eon climbed out and helped grab some gear for the other men as they started to put on packs. They had brought with them a large litter to drag out the wolf's body and each man carried a component in his pack. They also had equipment for camping and exploration of the cave system. As far as weapons went, they were minimal; but why should they need them?

"Alright guys, it's a long trek into the cave location so lets get underway."

The trek was slow, painfully slow for Eon; but she had to stay with the men. With winter over at least they didn't have the snow to contend with. Small buds were well on their way to sprouting and there was a green hue in the entire forest. One of the officers walked up by Eon and she could tell something was on his mind.

"Eon, I was there when we fought those things in the streets when they all attacked and I just can't imagine going up against one alone. You took him on at his home turf as well, what was it like?"

"It was hell and torture, but the thought of what he would do to countless others if I failed kept me going. I'm just glad the threat is over and we're wrapping this up."

They carried on mostly in silence, as even though the wolf was dead, the men still felt uneasy. When they arrived it was only late afternoon, the men had kept a good pace. It was agreed that half the men set up camp, while the other half and Eon went in to explore the cave. It would save them time tomorrow morning and they could get back at a decent hour. Eon led the men back to the left branch tunnel and into the grand cavern where she fought the wolf. This time the men carried multiple large floodlights and the cavern was lit up to reveal its enormous entirety. There just off the center of the main room under a ledge, were the remains of the giant wolf. Eon couldn't help but get a chill just looking at it.

The cave was at least 200ft high at the highest point with irregular stalactite formations. The men patrolled around the wolf and talked about how was the best way to get it out of there, while others looked over the piles of carcasses shaking their heads in disbelief. Eon climbed to the top of the ledge that the wolf had been on before it jumped down on her. She could see the blood trail as she made her way up.

"So this was your point of view before you leaped to your death."

The ledge was about 50ft up and from there, other ledges could be seen up above. Scanning around even further, it looked as if one ledge were put there on purpose. The thought was absurd as there was no way to get to any of them. Still it piqued Eon's curiosity, she needed to find a way over to that ledge. She climbed down to join the others, but after 10 minutes of exploring the bottom of the cavern, she just couldn't let it go.

"Do any of you guys have some rope that I could borrow?"

"Sure, how much do you need? I've got 300ft of climbing rope, I didn't know if this cave had any vertical pitches."

"Bring the whole thing for now, come on over to this ledge."

As Eon and the officer climb up to where she had just been, she points out the ledge that she was looking at. It was about 5 ft higher and 20ft away, but a 50ft drop between the ledges to the cavern floor. Eon took the rope and made a lasso out of it and threw it to the lip of the ledge. They climbed back down and stood under the lip of the ledge with the rope attached to it.

"I'm going to climb the rope and have a look around from that vantage point, can I have your headlight?"

Eon climbed up the rope and from the perch of the ledge she could make out a narrow tunnel in the rock that she couldn't see from the other ledge. It was about 2ft in diameter and looked like it went on for a little ways. She examined the ledge and noticed 2 grooves carved into the rock as if something had been attached there. There were some officers standing on the other ledge she had thrown the rope from watching her progress.

"Hey, there's a small tunnel here, I'm going to go check it out."

The officers looked at each other trying to hold back laughter.

"Look Eon, just try not to get stuck, I don't feel like trying to climb that rope to come get you out."

"Nothing like a good boobs joke to lighten the mood. I'll try not to get stuck, but thanks for the concern guys."

Eon turned to the small tunnel with a smirk on her face and turned on the headlight. She had to crawl on her stomach with her hands outstretched. After about 20ft it looked like there was an opening up ahead. Once she got there, to her right was a carved out stone step and another cavern opened up.

"Un-be-liev-able."

Eon was able to stand up and as her headlight shone out over the stone step, there revealed an entire staircase before her right into the side of the cavern wall. Her headlight couldn't penetrate out into the cavern beyond the stairs, so she cautiously walked down the stairs until she touched down on a rock floor. From here, she could explore this cavern. Ahead of her looked like a stone table with crude chairs carved out of the stone. As she approached closer to the stone table, she noticed chains and dark stains on the table. This cavern was actually small compared to the one she had just come from. As she continued past what was now an alter of some sort that she was sure of, she noticed chains on the walls embedded in the rock. Upon closer inspection there were strange symbols carved into the rock on the walls and a large symbol carved into the floor of the cavern. It was large, so she had to scan the whole area to see the whole thing with her headlight. What she could make out looked like a giant upside-down triangle intersected by 3 lines to form 6 smaller triangles inside of it. She continued on a little ways and immediately came upon the end of the cavern as she stopped with a sudden cry. There were 3 skeletons wearing robes and a headpiece. Each one had a dagger in its chest only now hanging on by the robes. Eon approached the bodies and saw that the one in the middle was wearing a medallion around its neck with the same symbol depicted on it that was on the floor, the giant upside-down triangle.

    Eon reached out and took the medallion off of the skeleton and took a closer look. It was a circle about 1.5 inches in diameter made of what she thought was bronze. She looped the small chain that was used to carry the medallion around one of her thigh bands and went back to ascend the stairs. When she made it out of the tunnel, just before standing back on the ledge, she decided to tuck the medallion into her boot.

    "Well guys, I didn't get stuck it was close though. It goes on for a while and then starts to taper off, it got too narrow to carry on. It probably just dies off and is only a deep fissure in the rock."

    Eon climbed back down the rope and joined the rest of the men as they all walked outside. Camp was set up and the stoves were going, as it was dinnertime. Two fires were started for added heat, which would be watched all night on different shifts.

Earlier in the city while Eon was exploring the cave system, Jason got up from his nap and walked down to police headquarters to have them track down the phone number. Jason was waiting in a chair while the officers put the number through the system in the back. One of the officers came up front to get Jason after they finished running it.

"Well Jason, the number tracks back to the Sea View Hotel's private line."

"Thanks for the info guys, I'll catch up with you later."

Jason walked out and headed back to the lair. He was still feeling pretty bad from his fight with the Steel Link. He thought that possibly Rip was right, why would a teacher be staying at a hotel. Toria wouldn't be back until tomorrow night. Maybe during the day tomorrow he'd investigate if he were feeling up to it. He climbed back down into the lair and eased back in his chair.

"Well Rip, it looks like you might have been right. That phone number leads right back to a hotel's private line."

Rip listened, but just shook her head in contemplation.

"It seems too easy Jason, why would she make it easy to see her flaw. She must know that tracking the number isn't that hard to do and she's bound to think that you would do it. There may be more than meets the eye to this girl."

"Whatever it is, I'll go check it out tomorrow as Wild Card. I just want one more night of rest and then I'll grab a handful of pain killers and try not to limp over to the hotel."

Jason let out a long sigh and stared down at the coffee table in front of his chair. Rip smiled and walked over to him, placing her hand on his shoulder.

"In this line of work Jason, it seems as though there is never any rest. Only a few moments that we can catch here and there. It's better that it's you than me, I've already paid my dues."

"Yeah I know, but I just wish I could have somewhat of a normal life even for a little while. I've neglected working at the gym for what seems like forever. When I did go there, I was walked out at gunpoint and beaten nearly to death. Well, I guess all we can do is keep going because the bad guys never rest."

Rip smiled at him and nodded her head. She knew all too well exactly what Jason was talking about and how he felt.

As night fell on another day in Harborside, both Toria and Jason found it difficult to sleep. Toria was focused on her new discovery and what it could possibly be. Jason wondered who this mysterious girl who called herself Havanna Del Rio was. Either way they both had to block it out of their minds and get some sleep. It never does any good to worry at night, there's nothing you can do about it anyhow.

Chapter 11

When morning came in the western woods, Eon was one of the first ones up. She helped load up the giant wolf's body on the litter that was put together. They needed an early start because dragging the wolf was going to take a lot longer than when they had arrived. The litter was rigged with harnesses so that everybody could contribute to dragging the huge beast. Even with 10 men it was still an average of dragging 300lbs per man plus his own gear. Eon did the best she could to help, but everyone had to take frequent rest stops. They had to choose the terrain carefully because it was near impossible to drag the wolf up any hills. If fallen brush was in the way then they had to stop and clear it out of the way before continuing on.

"Well boys think of it this way, they can't get on our cases for eating donuts all day long. We're burning off the donuts we've had in the last 2 weeks dragging this bastard around."

Food supplies were just about out and the men took to drinking out of the streams. Eon had eaten enough for 4 men, but nobody complained. She was able to pull the wolf as hard as 4 men or more. Everyone had their heads in it that this was going to be a long difficult day and that's all there was to it. For Eon it would finally mean the end of the wolf threat officially.

After lunch Jason decided to pay a little visit to the Sea View Hotel as Wild Card to see whom this person really was. He was still in rough shape, but could function at least better today than he could yesterday.

"Wild Card, what brings you to the Sea View?"

"I'm here to visit a Miss Del Rio, is she still here?"

"Let me see, just hold on a moment. Yes, here she is in room number 223. Just go down the hall and take the elevator to the 2nd floor."

"Thanks for your cooperation."

Wild Card took the elevator to the 2nd floor and knocked on room 223. He waited, but there was no answer inside.

"Hello, Miss Del Rio? This is Wild Card, I have a message for you from Eon about meeting with your class."

Still there was no answer, but he had come all this way. Staring at the doorknob, contemplation had set in about just trying to open the door. He knew something was going on out of the ordinary and if Toria was in danger then he had to find out. His mind already made up, he tried the door expecting it to be locked. To his surprise the door slowly opened up.

"Miss Del Rio? Again, this is Wild Card and I'd like to talk to you about your meeting with Eon."

Wild Card knew she wasn't going to answer him, but where was she hiding? He walked into the hotel room cautiously, ready to draw out his steel bars if need be. When he got a little further inside, he could smell sweet incense. When he walked past the couch about to turn into the kitchen, he stopped in his tracks. There was a cobra coiled up at the foot of the couch and hissing at him. Stopping suddenly, Wild Card slowly backed away and turned towards the door. When he turned, to his shock, the entire hotel room was covered with cobras. Snakes hanging on the lamps, coiled in the chairs and scattered throughout the floor. Even more shocking than all of this was the fact that now the door was gone and he couldn't find it.

"Holy shit! What the hell is going on here?"

Soon after finishing his sentence Wild Card felt a bite on the back of his neck and then all went to blackness.

Wild Card lay there on the hotel floor with a small broken capsule by his body. A mere 20ft away sitting in a chair was Havanna Del Rio holding a blow gun in one hand and drinking a small vial rendering her immune to the vapors fear affects.

"Now that was just too easy Mr. Card. I banked on you looking into the number, but I never expected you to come right to me. The tranquilizer dart's effects will wear off in an hour, so I better get you tied up and gagged. Now the bait is set for this girl called Eon, all I have to do now is choose the location to kill her."

As evening fell on Harborside, the vehicles pulled up alongside police headquarters including a large flat bed carrying the wolf's body. Chief Dixon came out to greet them and was accompanied by several men in black suits. Eon was getting out of the passenger side of one of the vehicles and saw them coming. She let out a long sigh; this day was about to get a little bit longer.

"Well there it is gentlemen, feel free to take it back to Washington if you'd like. While you're at it you can thank the hero of the day for delivering it for you as well. Please let me introduce the defender of Harborside, Eon."

Chief Dixon led the Federal Agents away from the wolf carcass to meet Eon as she stood there waiting to get this over with. One of the agents stepped forward and shook her hand.

"Miss Toria Kayden AKA Eon, it's nice to finally meet you. Thank you for assisting our men in the capture of the wolf's body."

Eon and Chief Dixon exchanged looks knowing that their little secret about the Federal team bringing down the beast was still in tact.

"You're welcome, Captain Jarvis was paramount in this whole operation; we couldn't have done it without him and his men."

"That's to be expected Miss Kayden, he was trained by the best the United States Government has to offer. Although, I am curious as to why the wolf's head is missing. Our scientists wanted to conduct some lab tests on the creature's brain."

"That was due to the efficiency of your Federal team. Captain Jarvis made an excellent throw with one of his grenades as the wolf charged him. I was sorry to see him succumb to the wounds he suffered in the jeep accident just before."

"I see Miss Kayden. Even though vigilante-ism is illegal, you've done a great service to your country. However, rest assured we are keeping an eye on you and your activities. I'd like to wish you and Chief Dixon a pleasant evening, we'll take it from here."

The agents turned and walked away from both of them. The one that was talking to Eon climbed into the flat bed truck and began to drive off, while the other agents were in tow behind him.

"Well Chief, that was easier than I thought."

"Oh, they didn't want to make a big scene and have to get more press than it already has. Let's just hope that the tarp stays on until they get back to Washington."

"I'm going to head back to the lair now Chief, it's been a long day and I'm beyond thrilled that this is finally over. Spring is here and I'm looking forward to enjoying the summer."

Eon waved goodbye and walked back to the lair with a smile on her face. Her muscles were sore and another night or 2 would be needed to fully heal up her wounds from her fight with the wolf.

"Hey guys I'm home, lets eat some dinner and celebrate that the wolf problem is over!"

Rip came out of her room with a concerned look on her face.

"Oh Toria, I thought you might be Jason coming back. It's getting late and I thought he'd be back by now."

"He's not here, where could he have gone?"

Rip filled Eon in on what had happened yesterday about the girl Havanna Del Rio and how the number checked out.

"It was after lunch that he ran over to the hotel, but now it's dinner time and he's not back yet."

Eon paced the room with a terrible and horrified look on her face.

"Jesus Christ! This could be some kind of pro if Jason couldn't handle her and I'm not 100% yet. I wish I knew more about all this, I feel as though I'm going in blind. Whoever this girl is, if she's hurt Jason then she's as good as dead! Rip, I'm heading over to the Sea View right now and hopefully I'll run into him on his way back. If that's not the case, I want you to get a hold of Chief Dixon if neither of us are back within a couple of hours. Tell him just what you told me, but hopefully we won't need the cavalry."

Eon left in a hurry, right after dropping off the medallion on her dresser from her boot.

As Eon went east, Vapor and Wild Card were setting up in the south of the city.

"I heard when I arrived in your city that not too long ago it was run by gang lords pushing drugs for Power. This particular place was one of the old hideouts of Sal the Snake. I think this old billiards and gaming hall will be the perfect place to do the job, not too much trouble in the way. I'm sorry I have to do this to both of you, I really don't want to. However, if it means the difference between life and death for my village; there is no question that I have to."

Wild Card was tied up to a chair with his hands and feet bound as well as a gag in his mouth. He couldn't believe that he was in the same situation again as with the Steel Link and his goons. He wasn't sure how he could break out of this one. To top it off he was still weak and wounded from his battle not too long ago. He closed his eyes in frustration, what could he do? He watched as she put on her capsules and curved daggers. This girl was a pro and Toria was going to walk right into this trap of hers. He didn't know what she was talking about, what was this village?

Eon walked into the Sea View Hotel and there she saw a very frightened clerk behind the desk.

"Miss Eon, I have a message for you. It's from a Miss Havanna Del Rio and she says after I tell you if you go to the police, it would be a bad idea. She's threatened to kill me if I called the police after she left and held a knife to my throat. It was as if I was in some kind of fog in the jungle when I saw her and when I woke up I was back here behind the desk."

"Was she alone when she spoke to you?"

"I guess so, we were in the jungle and she came to me through the trees. I was so disoriented that I really didn't notice anyone else."

"So, she uses hallucinogens and she's not here now. Tell me what's the message she left behind for me."

"She wrote it down here for me to give to you, she said you'd stop by. Let me see, here it is."

Eon took the piece of paper, unfolded it and read the message.

"To Eon, who I've heard so much about, but have never met. This will all change very soon, meet me at the old billiards and games building on the south end of the city. I know you know where it is; I'll be waiting here playing some poker with my new friend. The game is so much easier to play when you have a Wild Card in your hands." Vapor

Eon finished reading the note and crumpled it in her hand. She could tell that the clerk was still petrified.

"Look Pal, don't call the cops on this one. I'll take care of everything and don't worry; it's not you that she's after. You already did your job, I think you can breathe easy for now."

Eon turned and walked out of the hotel and started to run back to the lair, it was on the way to the south of the city. She stopped in briefly and told Rip not to contact the police and she changed out her nitro arm blades for 2 flame blades. Then she was gone as fast as she had arrived and headed straight for the billiards hall.

Further south on the continent of South America, deep in the jungles of the northern coast, sits the tyrant known as Power.

"Sir, sorry to interrupt, but we've had communication with Vapor."

"Excellent. What does she report lieutenant?"

"She says that she's captured Eon's cohort and is using him as bait to bring Eon to her. She also says that Eon will be as good as dead tonight and she'll be coming back here as soon as she can with this girl's head in her luggage."

Power sat back with a smile on his face in amusement and began to laugh out loud.

"Little Vapor thinks it will be that easy does she? I think she'll be in for a little surprise when she finally meets up with Miss Kayden. I'm curious to see how resourceful she is when the situation doesn't go her way. Though I do have to hand it to her, she is a fast worker. She would be an incredible boon if she were working for me. I'll have to come up with a way to keep her on the payroll so to speak. That will be all lieutenant, inform me when she contacts again."

Down in one of the little huts that are being used to hold the prisoners, a man takes his ear away from one of the paper-thin walls.

"Could you hear what they were saying?"

"I could only make out some of it, but it looks like Havanna will be coming home soon. I can feel it, we'll be free within the week."

"Don't get your hopes up, how can you trust a man like Power to keep his word?"

"Hope is the only thing that we have right now and personally the only thing that keeps me going."

Back in Harborside, Eon slows her pace about a block away from her destination. She knows that this is probably a trap that this girl has set for her. What if Jason isn't even there at all? The number one question is why is this girl doing this to begin with? Eon wondered if she could enter the building another way. She made her way around the block and faced the front of the building. Besides the front door there was the big window in the front with the old business logo on it that amazingly was still in tact. It was only a single story, but the building was long. Eon noticed that it was dark inside; the power would certainly be turned off here. That was like most of the places in the south end, even ones that were still inhabited. This wasn't the part of town that you brought your girlfriend out for a Sunday stroll.

Eon made her way around the side of the building down one of the alleyways. The sound of glass clanking on the pavement from empty beer bottles and fires in barrels could be heard from the bums that lived in the area. A few of them took notice of her and stopped cooking their rat on a stick.

"Hey fellas lookie here, it's that Eon chick. Hey tootsie, you come to visit some of us bums on your night off?"

"No guys, I'm just looking for another way in this building besides the front door. I'm supposed to meet somebody in there, do you guys know another way in?"

"As long as you don't say nothin' to the cops cause we been livin' in here all winter. If you hadn't whacked old Sal the Snake, we probably woulda froze to death this winter. I'll show you the way we was gettin' in, least I can do for givin' us a place to stay pretty lady. Come on over here by the dumpster, we made our own entrance; but I don't know who you're supposed to meet'll get in there? You gotta crouch down though to get in, I'll show you the way. Hey Ray, keep that rat warm for me while I show Eon here the get in."

Eon followed the bum over to the dumpster as he removed debris and trash. Once he took away the last piece of cardboard, it revealed a small opening that looked like it was smashed in around the mortar.

"This was one of the vent systems they had here, we just opened it up a little more. You follow this short tunnel a little ways and then it goes up about 5ft. We took the grate off on the inside, so you can just climb right up. You'll pop out under one of the billiard tables in the back of the joint. Hey if this helps you and the city out in any way, maybe you'll remember us guys down here and send a little somethin' our way, you know."

"If everything goes well, I'll do just that. For right now, you and your friends might not want to stick around. This person I'm meeting here isn't exactly a close relation of mine and there might be some fireworks."

"No problem, we'll set up shop in the next alley over. There's plenty of space 'round here, good luck Eon."

The bum went back to his friends leaving Eon facing the small trash covered opening. Unfortunately, she couldn't fit her axe up through the turn in the vent, so she hid it in the dumpster.

"Great, I'm going into a trap without knowing anything about this girl, I don't have my axe and my injuries still aren't healed from the wolf. This is just fantastic, I guess we'll call this the handicapped match."

Eon began to crawl into the smashed out vent as thoughts swirled through her head. She had saved the whole city from a terrible threat, but could she save the one person that meant more to her than the entire world? When she reached the turn in the vent, she needed to stop. Her mind was clouded with the fact that this wasn't just anybody she was rescuing. She had to steel her mind and focus on her unknown opponent. She made the turn with a handful of throwing knives in her hand. When she looked up, all she could see was darkness. A darkness so deep that you couldn't tell if your eyes were closed or not.

"Well, this ought to be a blast."

Eon let out a big sigh and began to ascend into the pitch-black room.

End of Book II

Book III: Retribution

Chapter 1

It was the middle of the night at the start of spring in Harborside. Eon finds herself in an air vent coming out into a pitch-black room at the old billiards and gaming building on the south side of the city. As she comes through, she puts her hand up to feel the bottom of the pool table she was coming up underneath. Crawling out from under the pool table, Eon stands up and looks around. Everything is completely black with not even streetlights coming through the windows. This didn't seem to make sense, how could this be? Then it dawned on her, this girl was an expert in hallucinogens. It wasn't really this dark; she was just making it appear this way.

Then there was a sound to her left. This girl Havanna had taken away her sight, but she still had her other senses. Eon stood at the ready with a Bowie knife in one hand and 3 throwing knives in the other. Suddenly she recoiled her head; she had been hit in the neck by something. Putting her hand up to feel her neck, she pulled out a small dart. Knowing immediately that this was a tranquilizer dart, she began to get sleepy and her head was feeling heavy. Eon shook her head a few times and her head was clear once again. Further more, the blackness was starting to fade. Eon got her first glimpse of her opponent in a cloak with a hood and slits up the sides to reveal her legs. She had small capsules around her belt and boots and she was holding a blowgun in one hand. There were 2 curved daggers strapped to her belt. Eon looked right at her with her knives raised.

"Who are you and why are you doing this?"

The cloaked girl was shocked at Eon's response.

"How can you see me and how is it that you are still awake, the tranquilizer should have..."

"Looks like you didn't do your research about me. I can metabolize your toxins pretty quickly, now where's Wild Card?"

The girl called Vapor made a lightning fast move and snapped one of her capsules in front of Eon in the blink of an eye. Eon was surprised at how fast this girl moved and shook her head as her surroundings were starting to change again. This time she was back in the lair and Jax was there. Eon was standing in the makeshift living room and Jax was cooking some food on the old stove.

"Jax is that you? My God, now I'm in the lair."

"Yes Toria it's me, I've made you some dinner."

Jax walked over to Eon with a plate of food and a smile on his face. Eon was in so much shock at the sight of her old mentor that she put down her blades just to stare at him. As Jax got closer to her, the illusion was starting to wear off and suddenly it was Vapor who thrust one of her curved daggers between Eon's shoulder and neck. Eon was slow to react, shaken by seeing Jax's image. She staggers back holding her wound and bringing up the Bowie knife to block the killing stroke of the curved dagger.

"You're right, you do metabolize the hallucinogens quickly. Maybe it's just long enough for me to finish the job."

Eon hears another capsule hit the floor and all of a sudden she's out on the street in one of the alleyways. There is noise next to a dumpster and footsteps under a streetlight with the sounds of cars going by. Eon can't focus on where her enemy is and starts to get frustrated.

"Where are you, no more games!"

From behind her a flash of a blade cuts into her hamstring and she goes down holding the back of her leg. She quickly spins around and now the setting has changed to a forest. Besides her wounds, Eon holds her head in pain. All the hallucinogens she can metabolize fast, but they are all wearing her down and making her head spin. From one of the bushes next to her, there is movement. Eon slashes at the bush, but nothing is there. Then from her right, behind a tree she hears movement of something else. Not waiting for a visual confirmation, Eon turns and fires at the sound and hears a scream as 3 throwing knives embed in a victim. Eon knew this was a hallucination and she was horrified to think that she could hit Jason in here by accident. Eon crawled over to where she heard the scream and there was Vapor on her back with 1 throwing knife in her thigh, side of her hip and left forearm.

  Vapor tries to get up and holds a curved dagger in her other hand. Eon dives at her as best as she can with her wounded leg and her Bowie knife arched over her head. Vapor redirects the Bowie knife with her own blade, so that it embeds in a tree, which was really the leg of a pool table. After the Bowie knife sticks into the tree, Vapor's curved dagger comes at Eon's throat. Eon catches the girl's wrist just before the blade breaks her skin. Eon easily twists the knife out of Vapor's hand and pins her to the ground. The illusion starts to wear off again and she can finally see her surroundings for what they are. Looking up, Eon sees Wild Card tied to a chair off to the side of the billiards room with his head slumped down. Vapor sees the look of shock and terror on Eon's face.

"Don't worry, he's just unconscious from the tranquilizer dart."

Eon holds Vapor's wrists pinned down on the ground tightly. Vapor brings her legs up and wraps them around Eon's neck and tries to rip her off, but Eon pins Vapor's legs down with her own.

"No more breaking capsules, no more fighting, who are you and why are you doing this?"

"You must die, so that others may live."

Eon looks down at Vapor with a puzzled look on her face.

"Maybe it doesn't have to be that way, I can help you."

They both stop fighting and Vapor fills Eon in on her mission and all the details of why Power sent her.

"Before I wondered why Power was so scared of a single girl. Now I realize, you move like the wind and your strength is incredible!"

"I knew someday our paths would cross again, I just didn't think that he'd send an assassin after me. The whole ordeal with the wolves was bad enough. Look, I think I have an idea of how to help you out. Come back with me down to my lair and we can talk things out. I hate Mr. Powers just as much as you do, if not more."

"Why do you call him Mr. Powers? He is simply known by everyone as Power."

"Well that's new to me, but he's still the same bastard of a tyrant. I'll grab Jason and you can follow me back to the lair and fill me in on exactly what Power told you about both Jason and I."

Eon started to walk over to Jason and nearly fell. She reached back and grabbed her leg with her good arm. Shaking her head, she looked up at Vapor.

"So, you're from South America right? Jesus Christ, you people are dangerous!"

Vapor managed a smile through the pain of her own wounds. They both helped to untie Jason who was still unconscious and left the building through a cut out hole in the glass that Vapor had made with a glasscutter. Eon collected her axe and waved to the bum that had helped her.

"Don't worry, I won't forget you."

After a while, they hailed a cab that was more than willing to help out the hero of Harborside. He drove all 3 of them to the east side of town and didn't ask a single question. He lived in Harborside long enough with the recent happenings to know that 3 wounded people in costumes really wasn't that out there compared to giant rampaging wolves.

When they made it down to the lair, Rip was there to greet them in her sleeping gown shaking her head and letting out a long sigh.

"Well, it looks like I'll be playing Doctor for the rest of the night for all 3 of you."

The next day brought rest, recuperation and planning as well as answers. Eon fills Vapor in on her history with Power.

"I understand why he wants you dead so badly, I commend you for your actions. This still leaves the original problem of how to free my village?"

"That's simple Vapor, just make him see what he wants to see. Put a bowling ball in a bag and when he opens it, he'll see my head."

"That will work if he just looks in and is satisfied, but if he wants to keep it as a trophy then the hallucinogenic effect will wear off and he'll know the truth."

"Look Vapor, it doesn't work permanently, maybe it's enough time to at least get your people free and into the jungle again. You'll get your fighters back and you can all live to fight another day. I know that maybe it's not a solution, but it's a chance to defeat him another day."

"Yes, I'll try it. I have to be on the next flight out to Texas tomorrow, I hope this works."

Vapor looked over to see Jason sitting back on the couch listening to the conversation. She casually walked over to him with a regretful smile on her face.

"Jason, I want you to know that I'm sorry for what I did to you. I never wanted to, but now you know why I was forced to."

"I understand Havanna, in the end no damage was really done. We're all on the same side here and every one of us has lost a lot to Power. Someday he'll fall, I wish you well in your fight against him and there are no hard feelings."

Jason stood up and shook Havanna's hand then returned back to the couch. Another minute later she had left the lair and was gone. Rip turned to Toria with a smile on her face.

"Well Toria, it's time we started your training, don't you think?"

"I'm all yours Rip, teach away!"

Jason stood up from the couch looking at his watch.

"Well ladies, I've got to get over to see Chief Dixon. I promised him I'd return the mini radio that he let me borrow while you were gone Toria. Of course he might just tell me to keep it, but I have to at least make the gesture. I'll be back in a little bit, try not to get hurt while I'm gone."

Jason made the trek over to police headquarters to return the radio. He noticed all the officers, including Chief Dixon were frustrated and preoccupied.

"Hi Chief, what's wrong? You guys look like somebody else ate your birthday cake."

"Hi Jason, we're just figuring out how to handle a delicate situation. Last night we got a call in from the south side, which is no surprise in that part of town. They got a little too rowdy last night down at the Hellfire Bar. We've had countless run-ins with the owner of the bar, Damon Flame and they've all been bad. He's been in and out of jail and he's injured more than a couple officers. To tell you the truth, he's more trouble than he's worth. There are still good people that live down that way and we can't turn a blind eye to it. Nobody really wants to deal with him or the bar for that matter. I'm sure there are illegal activities that go on there, but they never make there way up here so we leave it be. I tell you, ever since the city had the gangs come in; certain sections of the city have gone to Hell."

"Why don't I go talk to him Chief and save you guys the trouble if it's that bad."

"If you're really feeling up to it Jason, this guy really isn't that friendly."

"Don't worry, I'm sure I can handle it; I came by to drop off the radio."

"Keep it, you might need it if you're going down there. Oh one more thing Jason, just trust me and go as Wild Card. He should be there tonight, the bar opens at 9:00pm."

"Alright Toria, first I want to test your offense."

Rip had set up a series of targets with agility as well as strength drills for Toria to go through. Rip sat back and watched, as the course was cleanly, quickly and perfectly completed.

"How was that Rip, you got anything harder for me?"

"It's just as I thought Toria, your offense is perfect. Now I'd like to see how your defense is."

"How are we going to do that, a sparring match?"

"No Toria, I've set up a series of daggers all in a circle behind me. What I want you to do is throw one of your blades to the outside of the dagger that I reach for. I want to hear your blade hit the board before my hand grabs the dagger. I'll be standing in the middle of this circle with the blades all around me within arms reach. You'll be standing across the lair at 50ft away."

Toria walked across the lair with a confused look on her face, it seemed a ridiculous task.

"Are you ready Toria?"

"Go ahead Rip, reach for the first blade."

As Toria eyed Rip and the circle of daggers that she stood in the middle of, Rip moved with surprising speed. Before Toria knew it, a dagger was already in Rip's hand and Toria hadn't even thrown a knife yet.

"Why didn't you throw your knife?"

"I was going to, but you had the dagger already and it seemed like a waste to throw it."

"I see Toria, we have found the root of your weakness."

"What do you mean my weakness?"

"Toria, I'm sure your reactionary defense is superbly exquisite. However, your anticipatory defense is where you are lacking. You'll never truly become a perfect fighter until you master it."

"That's impossible Rip! You grabbed the dagger in about a tenth of a second. How was I supposed to know which one you were going for?"

"That very question Toria, is where your training will begin with me. I will teach you what was taught to me so many years ago by the greatest of warriors and so forth before him. It is called the Foresight and is only taught to those that are worthy to learn it. In all my years I've never taught it to anyone. The master that taught it to me only taught it to one person. It was my privilege to learn it from him and it would be your privilege to learn it from me. It takes dedication and work, even for someone advanced like yourself."

"If you say so Rip, I'm a little skeptical about it, but Jax said you were the best. I'll try to the greatest of my ability to learn the Foresight."

Vapor climbed aboard the flight to take her to the Texan border, where she would get on the chopper back to Columbia. She had made communications with one of Power's lieutenants and told him she would come bringing the gift of Eon's head. If this ploy of Eon's didn't work, all of her village would die as well as her loved ones. The gravity of the situation weighed on her like a ton of bricks. As good of a fighter as she was and as perfect as she was at her craft, there was no way she could defeat Power and his men in open battle. This was going to be the longest ride of her life. Once she was in the chopper, there was no way back.

Jason walked back into the lair and all was silent. Rip and Toria were doing something that looked like a board game, but Toria was just staring at Rip's hands. Rip would then suddenly move one of her hands faster than Jason could believe. Toria for some reason seemed upset and sat back folding her arms. Both of them seemed frustrated with whatever they were doing.

"Toria, you need more concentration, this is something that the abilities you were born with are not going to carry you through. You will need to try harder to grasp this concept."

"I don't see how it's possible Rip, I would have to be a mind reader to do this."

Rip looked away in disgust and pushed back her chair.

"Toria, Moshet bit tee nye delat!"

"Rip, Ya kachoo eta. Eta troodny, Ya nye panemayoo, sprasteetye."

Rip looked at Toria in amazement and unfolded her arms.

"Don't look so surprised Rip, Jax taught me Russian down here during our training together. He said it might come in handy for communication if we ever needed it."

"Jax was a very wise man and I know that you want to do this. Maybe we just need to take a break, we've been at it for a while. When we start again after we eat something, I'll try a different approach with you."

Jason moved closer to them and entered the kitchen.

"Hi guys, I won't ask how the training is going. I do want to tell you Toria that I'm going out tonight after dinner though. Dixon wants me to check out a little disturbance down on the south end, so you don't have to wait up."

Toria stood up and walked into the kitchen and started to rummage through the cupboards.

"Well we're just about to eat Jason, why don't you tell me about it over lunch."

"It's really nothing I just have to talk to the owner of the Hellfire Bar. I guess they've had complaints of a disturbance down that way."

"I remember hearing things about that place, it's some kind of biker bar only it's pretty rough. You just make sure you be careful down there."

"Geez Toria, Dixon said the same thing to me; I help defend the city too. I may not be the great and talented Eon, but I can hold my own."

Toria walked over to Jason with a smile on her face. She grabbed his cheeks and pushed them together as if making a pucker face.

"I know you can do more than hold your own Baby, I just don't want anybody to hurt that precious face of yours."

Jason just rolled his eyes and didn't move. Toria kept her hand on his cheeks and started to move his head side to side making baby noises.

"Ok Toria, let me finish this sandwich. You know, you're a good-looking patronizer. We ought to go down to the gym one of these days, just you and I. You might be surprised Toria, I might give you a run for your money."

Toria started to nod her head with a serious face in a sarcastic manner. Then she smiled and gave Jason a quick jab in the ribs.

"Come on and sit down with us for a while. Rip was just teaching me how to read people's minds."

"Oh yeah, so Rip after that can you tell me the winning lotto numbers?"

"Sit down you two, the Foresight is much more than that. It's the ability to read the other person, just like you learned Russian Toria. The only difference is the medium, but the concept is the same. The ability to read a person's language of the body will dictate their minds. Just like a poker player can determine if his opponents are bluffing. There could be a nervous twitch, a raise of the eyebrow, a tensing of a muscle and so on. If we take that to a higher level, we can anticipate the opponent's next move before he even does it. The great warriors will not give away their intentions as easily as a street thug would. That is why at this level, it takes 100% of your concentration on your opponent.

The wolf you fought Toria, he was a beast with some thinking capability. Yes it was fast and aggressive, but it lacked the years of training it would take to hide its intentions from you. However, the beast was fast enough to overcome your reactionary defenses and that is why you were nearly killed. With control of the Foresight, the beast would never have touched you at all. Once more, when you are able to anticipate your opponent's next move; you can then know better where to strike them in the most vulnerable spot in the position they are in. That is what I'm training you to do Toria; I'm taking you to a higher level.

It has been said that the great masters that know of the teachings of the Foresight were considered to be spirits that could not be killed. This of course was not true, but they were so perfect in the art as well as their chosen fighting styles that they instilled fear into their opponents without even trying. That is the difference between a great fighter and a legendary warrior Toria. I teach it to you because I believe you have the potential to become such a warrior in your own time.

For the rest of today's lesson, I'll spend time telling you about the history of the Foresight. This will help you understand it better and also hold it in higher respect."

Toria sat in silence listening to Rip speak. Jason knew when Toria really wanted something; she would go into a silent state like this.

"Well guys, I'm going over to the gym for a little while and get some work done, and then I'll be back to take a little nap before I go out tonight."

Jason got up, grabbed his bag and left Toria in the capable hands of her new mentor.

Chapter 2

That night Jason went on foot down to the south end of town. He was dressed in his Wild Card suit and feeling a little nervous.

"Why the hell did both Dixon and Toria say what they did? Now I'm nervous about this whole thing, I think I'm just getting psyched out here."

Wild Card traveled for about 45 minutes alone with his thoughts before he hit the south district. There were more derelicts out this way as well as more garbage in the streets. Even the air felt different down here, but this area had been his old stomping ground with Eddie even when Sal the Snake took over the area. Since that time though, this section of the city had really gone to shit. He could hear it before he could see it and then when he rounded a corner of the street, there stood the Hellfire Bar.

The lights were on, but it still seemed dark inside. There were motorcycles outside with guys in leather and beards drinking outside the bar. There were beer bottles and crushed cans all around the outside of the building as well as some bums leaning up against the side of it waiting for the commotion to get going. It was common knowledge that this was the kind of place that you really didn't want to bring your girlfriend, but that's all Wild Card knew about it. There was neon in the windows and the noise and ruckus were equally as loud as the jukebox in the corner of the bar blasting out metal.

Wild Card stopped and looked at the bar from about 100ft away, took a deep breath and checked nervously that his trusty steel bars were by his side. He'd been through a lot worse than this and besides; all he was going to do was talk to the guy. Wild Card strode confidently towards the bar, getting looks from the bikers outside. When he walked in, the cacophony could be heard at least 10x's as loud. The doorman, whose frame and build were even with his own, immediately greeted him.

"Can I help you?"

"Yeah, I'd like to talk to the owner, Mr. Damon Flame."

The man looked over his shoulder at an even larger man, easily 6'8" and 320lbs of muscle. He was bald, tattooed and wore a white skintight shirt. His face was contorted in an angry expression that dared anyone to come his way. The doorman turned back to Wild Card with a smile.

"I don't think the Demon wants to talk to anybody right now."

"The Demon? Why do you call him that?"

It was fitting as he recognized the song that came over the jukebox. It was "Kill the Demon" by David Rock Feinstein. Wild Card watched as the enormous man approached a smaller man sitting by himself on a ratty old couch up against a wall in the corner of the bar. The man wore sunglasses in this dark place, couldn't have been more than 5'7" and 170lbs with slicked back jet-black hair. He wore a short leather jacket with ripped jeans and had small steel spikes on his belt. He sat alone with his head down drinking a bottle of beer. The large man walked right up to him and got in his face.

"Hey chump, you cheated at that pool game! You're not gettin' jack shit outta me!"

Wild Card watched as the doorman laughed at watching this scene unfold before them, he had to speak up.

"Aren't you going to do anything, it looks like there's about to be a murder."

"Hey Pal, we have our own law down here."

The doorman placed a hand across Wild Cards chest.

"Look, I'm not going to stand by and let that elephant beat the snot out of some guy just over a pool game."

The doorman folded his arms and got closer to Wild Card.

"Just trust me, you had better stay out of this if you know what's good for you, Hero."

Wild Card watched as this giant brute approached this little man, listening to the blasting jukebox.

"What does it take to survive

Life on a dream and a prayer
How can it keep you alive
The Devil will always be there."

Wild Card watched as this guy, the Demon they called him, grabbed the smaller guy's beer and threw it across the room with a shattering spray against the wall.

"It's an illusion
An evil tempter that will captivate your soul."

The big man then grabbed the sitting man and threw him like a rag doll across the bar, crashing into some tables. The smaller man gets up without making a sound and takes off his sunglasses to reveal bright red contacts.

"Kill the Demon, inside of you
Kill the Demon, or the Demon will kill you."

The big man grabs a pool stick and charges the smaller man, taking a big swing at his head. The smaller man doesn't even move, catching the pool stick in one hand and snapping the end of it off. The smaller man then retaliates with a devastating kick with his steel-toed boots to the larger man's stomach. With the larger man bent over, the smaller man delivers an uppercut to the big man's face with a loud audible crack. Wild Card knows the big man's jaw is broken and watches as his entire body soars through the air and crashes into some tables.

> "How would it feel to be free
> Free from the bondage and pain
> Strike with the force of a God
> And only the truth will remain."

The big man gets up with rage in his eyes and runs at the smaller man, who catches the big man by the neck and smashes the big man's head into the wall leaving a dent.

> "It isn't human
> It's just a Devil that will overtake your mind."

The smaller man then delivers a swift kick to the bigger man's ribs as he lay on the ground, a loud snap or two could be heard.

> "Kill the Demon, inside of you
> Kill the Demon, or the Demon will kill you."

The big man lay on the ground moaning in pain. The smaller man picked up his sunglasses and put them back on. Wild Card couldn't believe the fighting display before him.

"Who is that guy?"

The doorman turned to him with a sadistic smile.

"That's the Demon, you still want to talk to him?"

"Fight till the end, death's just a heartbeat away
Don't just pretend, the Devil won't just go away."

The Demon started to walk towards the door and stopped next to the doorman.

"Demon, this guy wants to talk to you."

The Demon looked at Wild Card through his black sunglasses on his emotionless face.

"Not tonight Junior, I'm outta here."

Demon walked past Wild Card, bumping his shoulder into his as he passed. Demon got on his motorcycle and rode off into the night.

"Kill the Demon, inside of you
Kill the Demon, or the Demon will kill you."

Wild Card left the Hellfire Bar and started to head back to the lair. When he made it out of the south district, he took off his helmet and walked a little slower.

"Well, that went well. That guy is a God Damn maniac; no wonder Dixon leaves him alone!

It's one of those nights that I just should have stayed in bed."

The chopper touched down in Columbia, carrying the nervous Vapor. There was a jeep with commandos waiting for her. She carried with her 2 bags, one was her luggage and the other was supposedly holding the head of Eon. Vapor had picked up a bowling ball from a sporting goods store before leaving as Eon had suggested. As the jeep transported her to the awaiting Power, Vapor looked down at her forearm wrapped with bandages. She instinctively touched her side and leg, the 3 places that Eon's blades had stabbed her. Of course they still hurt, so she really wasn't looking for a fight. Although the realization that she might have to occurred to her if the plan didn't work and she would push through the pain if need be. The jeep pulled up to the tent compound after 2 hours of riding. It was past midnight at this point and Vapor was tired, but she had to stay focused. She was thankful for the adrenaline that kept her going. Floodlights came on as they climbed out of the jeep. The sound of the commotion woke the prisoners in the huts, who ran to look through the cracks in the wall.

"It's Havanna! Everybody get up, we'll be free soon!"

Vapor and the 2 commandos walked into the main tent. Power was there behind his desk, flanked by a couple of his lieutenants.

"Miss Del Rio, it's a pleasure to see you; even at this hour. So let's get down to business, do you remember our bargain?"

Vapor began to approach his desk holding the bag with the bowling ball. She held her breath as she dropped a fear capsule on the floor near the commandos. As she handed the bag over to Power, she pinched and broke a capsule inside the bag as well and stepped back. Power greedily took the bag from her and looked inside with a voracious enthusiasm. Vapor still held her breath; this was the moment of truth. Power set the bag down gently on his desk and began to laugh loudly.

"You have completed your task Miss Del Rio, so I will keep up my end of the bargain. You have been given a reprieve for now, but rest assured you may find yourself in a similar situation again. As I did this time, I'll call upon your talents to aid my ambitions. You may release your village and go where you may."

Power tossed her the keys and sat back with a smile. Vapor quickly took them and headed straight for the door, only taking a moment to look over her shoulder at the guards who looked terrified at whatever sight their mind was telling them to see. A slight smile crawled over Vapor's face as she made her way to the locked huts. She didn't know how long the illusion hallucination capsule would work on Power, so she worked as fast as she could. All the while she threw out other fear capsules near the soldiers on guard around the compound just in case.

"Thank the Almighty, we knew you'd come through Havanna!"

"Quickly, there's no time for thanks right now. We are still in a dangerous situation; go south into the jungle. We need to get to civilization outside Power's grip."

"But Havanna, the jungle is dense and the terrain unknown. We'll never make it without supplies, we need to use the road system."

The road system was nothing more than clearings in the jungle with tire grooves worn in them, but it was better than forging through the jungle.

"I know. Take these capsules and through them at the drivers and guards of the transport vehicles over there near the road. The keys should be on them or in the vehicles, be sure to tell everyone to hold their breaths or they'll fall under the effects of the vapors. Have everyone climb in the cargo holds of the trucks and head south."

"What will you do here, they will kill you for sure?"

"No time for questions, just go! I will meet you all in San Guatalaharo, now go!"

Vapor turned around to assess the situation. The floodlights revealed all the tents in the immediate area. She could distinguish between the residential tents and the supply and medical tents.

Inside the main tent, Power grabs the bag again with the bowling ball.

"Lieutenant, take this head and have it mounted as a trophy for me."

When no one came, Power looked over to see his officers cowering on the floor with a terrified expression on their faces.

"Why do you not come here when I call you and what are you looking at?"

There was no response from the officers. Power's eyes narrowed at the realization of the situation. He grabbed the bag again and looked inside. With Eon's blood in his veins, the effects of the illusion had worn off a while ago. When Power saw there was a bowling ball in the bag, he threw it across the tent and right through the wall with a loud yell of anger.

Outside, Vapor cut her way through the cowering guards with her curved daggers and into the supply tents. Once inside she began to fill sacs with food and medicine as fast as she could.

Power stormed outside as he heard the sound of engines start up in the distance.

"Guards open fire, kill them all!"

Looking around, Power saw that most of them lay dead or cowered in fear. Power stormed off in the direction of his transport trucks to see why they had started up. Vapor came out of the tent just in time to see Power going towards the vehicles. She grabbed a Kalashnikov knockoff from one of the soldiers that she had killed and slung it over her shoulder. Grabbing the supply bags, she ran to the parked jeep that she had come here in. Thankful that the keys were still in the ignition, Vapor took off towards the transport vehicles. When she arrived, they had already started to take off down the road. She began to follow when she saw Power rounding the corner of the compound outskirts and taking off after the vehicles at an amazing speed.

Vapor kicked out the windshield with a shattering of glass and stepped on the accelerator. The supply bags sat in the back of the jeep bouncing around terribly on the rough Jungle Road. Vapor drove with a single handed, white knuckled grip on the steering wheel. The other hand held the machine gun resting on the dashboard sticking out where the windshield had been. There would be no accuracy on the bumpy Jungle Road, but she fired anyway in Power's general direction. Bullets ripped into the trees as Power dove out of the way into the bushes. The jeep sped past as Vapor had lost him in the headlights. She took the machine gun and rested it on the rail on the back of the jeep, looking behind her and trying to stay on the road at the same time. After a while, she decided that Power wasn't giving chase and she set the gun down. She followed the transport vehicles south to the next village, praying they had enough gas to get there. After the noise of the vehicles had passed by, Power climbed out of the bushes and brushed off his pants.

"You have sealed your fate Miss Del Rio. This was Toria's idea, I can tell. By listening to her advice, you will be given no second chance. When next we meet again, you will die."

Power walked back to the camp to collect his men. He now controlled the whole northern coast in the drug trade, there were more pressing matters right now. Vapor and her people had gotten away, but this was only a temporary reprieve from his wrath.

Chapter 3

As morning came in Harborside, Toria and Jason woke up at about the same time.

"Spring time is officially here now. Happy birthday Jason, the big 26!"

"Yeah, now I'm working on the second half of these twenties. I can remember when I was just starting them like it as yesterday."

"There's no threat to the city and we're both well enough to walk around, so what do you want to do?"

"I'd say the first part of that last sentence is a big enough gift."

"Oh come on, there must be something you want to do?"

"Let's go rent a motor boat down at the harbor and go out on the water for the day."

"I'll join you for a few hours, but then I have some more training to do."

"No problem, I'll make a day out of it and give you guys the lair."

Meanwhile in the southern Ural Mountains, the border between eastern Russia and Siberia, there sits a small group of people. They are wearing white robes belted at the waist and a black scarf wrapped around their faces. One of the men kneels down before another man sitting in a large chair with the same attire; only his scarf is red. The man kneeling holds a picture of Rip up to the man sitting.

"You're sure this is her? This is the one that killed Master Temovich?"

"Yes, our spies have tracked her to the northeastern United States. She is currently in a city there called Harborside."

"Well then, we shall have to pay her a little visit. I'll be taking a contingent of men with me, make the preparations."

In the small town of San Guatalaharo, the rebels have successfully escaped from Power. Many were malnourished and others had been diseased from being in those close quarters all together for days, living in their own filth. The guards had fed them like animals, throwing scraps into the huts. This forced them to fight over food; unfortunately some didn't make it. Vapor couldn't remember the last time she had slept, but still she couldn't rest. These people needed her and she was busy all throughout the night into the morning giving out food and medical attention to those that needed it. Those that were in charge in the small town approached her.

"We are sorry Miss, but we are low on our own supplies here. We can offer you nothing but shelter in our sheds for the night. In the morning you must move on, we want no part of Power and his business."

Vapor nearly snapped. Maybe it was because she hadn't slept, maybe it was her tone or maybe it was because when she spoke, she waved around one of her curved daggers. Whatever it was, it caught the attention of these men.

"You will help us because it's your problem if you want it or not! Power will be back for his trucks and to kill all of us for making him look bad. If we don't bond together, we will all die apart. These people have nowhere to go and they are dying. Cut down one of your livestock and ration your vegetables even more because if you don't sacrifice now, you will die tomorrow."

The men looked at each other, none of them really wanted to argue and they had pushed away the thought of Power long enough.

"Alright, bring them down here with the trucks. We will make beds in the hay and they can sleep with the animals, but at least they will have shelter. We'll butcher an animal tonight and we can all eat well. After dinner, we will help you come up with a strategy."

"Now remember Toria what I told you about body movement, anticipation and reading your opponent like a book."

Rip stood in the now familiar circle with all the daggers around her; Toria took a deep breath and was ready. There was a long pause as Rip stood there and Toria watched her. Then Toria released a throwing knife that landed over Rip's right shoulder in front of the dagger that her right arm was about to go for. Rip smiled, but still she stood there in a long pause. Then in a flash Rip reached for the far left corner, and then the right lower corner and lastly the dagger above her head. With each reach, Toria's blade landed a split second before Rip's hand did.

"Very good Toria, you're learning well now. Tell me what tipped you off in this round?"

"Your eyes, your breathing and your muscle tensions."

"That's right, I used all of those things this time. We need to become proficient at using those amazing senses of yours to your advantage. I could never have been able to see the slight movement in the eyes of my opponents at that distance, but you can. The more and more we do this drill, I'm going to start taking away elements such as the eye twitch, and muscle tensions and I'll calm my breathing. I expect the same result each time we do this; you need to become an expert. Out there you will get no second chances, if you think I'm hard on you then I think you need to reevaluate."

"I know Rip, I think I'm making some great progress on this. I just need to take a little break from it right now, but I want to run the drill again in a little while."

Out on the harbor waters, Jason cruises up and down the coastline. He and Toria had gone through a full tank of gas this morning and now he was going to burn another tank by himself. He got out a little ways and then killed the engine. Falling back into one of the seats, he takes out a beer from a small cooler he brought and looks out over the open water.

"This is just what I needed! Nobody trying to destroy the city, no being tied up to chairs, seeing snakes or having people try to kill me and absolutely no giant wolves. I think being Wild Card makes me appreciate normal things in life like this. Yeah, this is one fantastic birthday."

Jason sat there for hours before cruising around again and jumping waves. It was a sunny day with a cool wind. The water was calm and there was tranquility in the air. It was the kind of setting that makes you forget all your troubles as if the waves themselves just swallowed them up. Then you can sit back and feel like a king without a single care in the entire world.

As night fell, it was like the changing of the guard on the streets of Harborside. During the day, the streets are filled with the bustle of the daily grind. However, when night falls a different kind of people emerge out from the woodwork. Down on the south side of the city at the Hellfire Bar, a familiar figure pulls up on his motorcycle and walks in. Wearing jeans, leather, sunglasses and a goatee, the man of short stature surveys the bar and its patrons. Of course it wouldn't matter if he were 3ft tall because everyone here feared the Demon.

"Hey Demon, you come for the books?"

The doorman asked his boss with a little nervousness in his voice.

"No, I wanted to know who that was last night that stopped in here."

"That was Wild Card, he wanted to talk to you about something."

"The Kid has some guts coming down here like that, it's admirable. If he comes down here again, let me know. On second thought, you can go grab me the books. I'll be doing business tonight at my place, keep an eye on things for me."

"Sure thing Demon, see you around."

The Demon climbed back on his bike and in a loud roar he was gone.

As night fell in San Guatalaharo, those that couldn't fight were looking after the wounded and sick. While those that could fight were gathered in the main building in the town square with Vapor in the center. Everyone had a good meal, made their peace and was ready to make the necessary sacrifice. Vapor took the floor in addressing the able bodied of the town.

"What resources do you have here that we can use against Power and his men and are there any weapons?"

"We are a simple town, we have a small artillery with a handful of guns at the jail and that's it."

"That's alright, we can make use of them. We can set up 2 of your best shots in the trees along the road to shoot at tires and pick off men as they come. We'll keep the other 3 here, hidden throughout the town. These are not the only weapons that we have. You have farming tools that you can implement as weapons and we can use the horses for better mobility."

"What about Power himself, it is said that nothing can defeat him! You are a good fighter yes, but you are no match for him."

"I will do the best that I can when dealing with Power, but we can't just lay down and wait for him to kill us off. We have to hold out as long as we can and not make it easy for him. I know that we probably won't win and I know that you will all sacrifice a lot in this effort. I commend all of you; you are proud patriots of your homeland. We will use the trucks to get as many people that can't fight out of here to the next town. If we are able to weaken him little by little with hit and run tactics, we might stand a chance."

Jason entered the lair that night relaxed and whistling a tune.

"Hey guys how's it going? What a great day I had out...oh sorry.'"

Toria and Rip were both in concentration at the table; both of them were doing something with their hands. Toria watched and moved in the direction that she thought Rip would move. He honestly didn't think either of them knew he was even in the lair until after he turned around and Toria spoke up.

"Hey Jason, have a nice day out on the water?"

"Yeah, it was great! It's just what I needed as a break from all that has been happening lately. I'd really like to do that more often, the guy at the docks gave me a great price."

"Oh, I bet the fact that you're Wild Card, mister big shot superhero, super stud had nothing to do with it."

"Yes Toria, I'm sure that's exactly what he thought. How have you guys been doing in here?"

"Another day closer to getting this right, I'm really happy at how things are moving along."

Rip stood up from her chair and stretched with a smile on her face.

"Well, I'll leave you two alone tonight. Toria has earned some free time with you Jason, goodnight and we'll pick it back up in the morning."

Rip walked away to her section of the lair to get some sleep, while Toria stood up and leaned in for a kiss on Jason.

"So, do you want your birthday present?"

"Sure, where is it?"

Toria smiled, grabbed Jason by the hand and blew out the candles.

Meanwhile on the western Siberian border, the robed and hooded men have already started the next day by loading up a little bush plane with supplies.

"Very good, now let's get going we don't want to miss our next flight in London. From there we'll travel as businessmen on our flight into Harborside. The job should be quick and painless, she is much older now."

As the man with the red scarf climbed into the plane, a medallion around his neck swung out from under his robe. As he sat, he gently tucked it back inside against his chest. It was an insignia of a triangle with 3 intersecting lines.

When morning of another day came in Harborside, Jason and Toria were woken up by the police radio that Toria kept.

...Public disturbance last night at the Hellfire Bar in south Harborside, please report...

"Um, hold on Toria, I'll take this one."

"Why Jason, it's just a little disturbance. It happens all the time on the south side."

"Yeah, I know, but well, I aw...just let me handle this alright."

Toria sat up and looked at Jason with one eyebrow raised.

"Why Jason?"

"It's a dangerous part of the city, especially that place."

Toria burst out laughing not taking Jason seriously. Jason rolled his eyes and crossed his arms.

"I know you're the amazingly great Eon, but I just want to take this one. Besides it will let you spend some more uninterrupted training time with Rip and you know that's more important than this."

"Alright go take the call my 'Great Protector', but can you be back here for lunch? Rip is great and all, but I'd like to go out to eat today and get some fresh air you know?"

"Yeah, I'll be back here by lunch time, not a problem. Is there any place in particular that you want to go?"

"No, we can just hit up a corner deli in the business district."

"Alright, well I'm off, I'll see you in a few hours. Have fun in your next training session with Rip."

Jason grabbed his Wild Card suit and left the lair, heading down to police headquarters.

In San Guatalaharo the last truck has left this morning with old, young, sick and wounded on it heading for the next village to the south. There was only one road in these rural parts of the jungle and Power and his men had to go through this town to get to them. This was a task that Vapor wanted to make very difficult. One of the scouts is just getting back from his nightly mission and reporting back to Vapor.

"They are breaking camp this morning, it looks like they'll be coming here tonight."

"Good, we'll be ready for them. You've done a great job with this information; go get some sleep now. If you're hungry, there's some stew left over from this morning's breakfast."

The tired scout nodded his head and walked over to the middle of the town center where a large pot was hung over a fire as he helped himself to a heaping bowl of stew. Vapor watched as the boy did this and then looked around at the rest of the people left in the town. They all looked scared, but they didn't complain. It was like pitting a snake against a lion, but a viper's bite can be very potent.

She felt a certain responsibility to these people as if they were from her own village or part of her family. Why did she feel the need to put such great weights on her shoulders? Maybe it was her hatred for Power or maybe it was the fact that she valued freedom above all else for herself and for her people.

"Put the sentinels out on post and send the marksmen into the woods to take up positions. The rest of you know your tasks to be done. Eat up and steel your hearts and your minds, for tonight we do battle."

Jason walked into police headquarters and up to see Chief Dixon.

"Hey Chief, I'm here to answer the call for Eon, she's on a special case right now."

"Oh, alright then Wild Card. Well, it's the same report as before over at the Hellfire Bar. I've been meaning to ask you, how did your little visit go last time you were down there?"

Chief Dixon sat back in his chair with a smile on his face and folded his arms.

"The guy is nuts! He came up to my armpit, but I saw him trash this guy that looked like a pro wrestler. There's also something about him that gives me the chills and the patrons aren't too friendly either."

Dixon leaned in on his desk with a serious expression on his face.

"Whatever it was that you saw him do the other night, I've seen him do much worse. You don't have to do this alone, I can send a few armed men down with you and..."

"No, that's alright Chief you don't have to do that. I think it might escalate into a bigger problem than it is already. One thing I don't want to happen is to have unnecessary people get hurt. I'll try and talk with him tonight, but I have the radio to call if I need backup."

Jason turned to walk away, but then turned back to face Dixon.

"I can't really explain it Chief, but when we met eye to eye I saw more there than just the red contacts. It was almost as if there was a glint of respect in there for me. I know it sounds crazy, but I just have to do this alone."

Chief Dixon nodded his head in realization.

"You just make sure you radio in if you need to, it can get pretty rough out there."

The day went slowly for Jason and Havanna with the anxious feeling of battle to come. Jason especially was having a hard time with it, even coming down with an upset stomach. Out to lunch with Toria, she could tell something was wrong with him.

"Jason, I just told you the entire morning of training and I don't think you heard a single word."

"I'm sorry Toria, I'm just a little side tracked. I have to go back to that Hellfire Bar tonight."

"You look really worried, why?"

"It's the owner, that guy they call the Demon. He's not that big, but he's so calm, cold and...and...precise that I feel way out of his league just standing next to him and I think he knows it."

"Jason, if you need me to, I'll go down there and trash the entire..."

"No, it's alright Toria. Believe me, I know you'd tear through it like a bull in a china shop. This is something that I have to do on my own. I can face down a 3,000lbs wolf and this 170lbs guy gives me the creeps."

"Jason, I'm not letting you go to get put back in the hospital again. I happen to like you like this."

"That sounds really great doesn't it Toria? Hey guys hold on, I'm gonna go get my younger girlfriend and she'll beat the crap out of you. That would look great, maybe I could tell one of the news reporters. 'Wild Card scared to do his job', what a headline."

"Jason you're a stubborn bastard and believe it or not, that's one of your attractive qualities. If you come back looking like Hell and you're too sore to kiss me for a month, I'm going to really be pissed at you."

"Thanks for being so caring Toria, that's one of your good qualities. I better kiss you now, just in case I can't later."

They both laughed as Jason planted a big kiss on Toria's cheek. They both finished up their sandwiches and then went their separate ways. Toria went back to the lair to continue her training and Jason decided to go for a walk to clear his thoughts and get ready for what was to come tonight.

Chapter 4

It was around dusk when the first scout reported back to Vapor that Power and his men were coming. It wasn't too long after that the sound of motors could be heard. Vapor ran to the edge of town where the jungle started and waited by the road. She heard gunshots ring out as they ricocheted off the metal of the trucks. Then the familiar sound of a popping tire could be heard, followed by a crash into the brush. The snipers that she had set up took out one of the vehicles. That was just the sound she was waiting for as she ran off into the jungle towards the crash. The rest of the trucks passed by as she saw them through the trees, they would hit the roadblock soon.

Vapor jumped back onto the road when the vehicles had went by and ran as fast as she could towards the crashed truck. When she arrived, the snipers were in a shooting match with Power's men in the truck. Some of his men were hiding around the back of the truck for cover. She could see that there were about 10 all together. Coming up from behind them, Vapor threw one of her disorienting capsules down in the middle of them. The men started firing wildly and staggering around not knowing their surroundings. This was easy work for Vapor and her curved daggers, all the men were dead in under a minute. The snipers came down out of the trees to join her, all of them grabbing the soldier's weapons and heading back towards the village.

    Power sat in the front of the lead truck and saw the roadblock up ahead consisting of rocks, brush and sharpened sticks.

    "Sir, up ahead is the roadblock and we need to clear it or the tires will go."

    "Yes, it does need to be cleared soldier, press your foot to the accelerator as hard as you can."

    The driver of the truck gave Power a questioning look, but didn't dare to say anything.

    "Don't worry soldier, we have spare tires to fix the flats. We're going to pave the way for the others in this little shit hole of a town."

    The truck plowed ahead, blasting through the roadblock as well as blowing out the front tires and bending the axle. However, the sacrifice worked as the 4 other trucks poured into the village.

Vapor and the snipers arrived to the sound of gunfire. She stopped just outside the village out of breath.

"Shit, they broke through the roadblock! We may be too late already."

In Harborside, Jason was just getting on his Wild Card suit. Toria was resting now after a full day of training with Rip. She looked on at Jason, as he got ready with a frown.

"I'll be back later tonight Toria, don't worry."

Wild Card left the lair and began to head south.

Back in the lair, Toria didn't say anything to him before he left. He already knew she was upset about this so-called meeting tonight. Toria lay back on the couch and shook her head.

"Stubborn bastard!"

Wild Card picked up the pace as he moved through the city to the south end. He was feeling good tonight; he had been preparing his mind all day. When the suit was on, he was Jason Card no longer. He was Wild Card and he wasn't going to let this guy intimidate him. A little over half an hour later, he arrived at the Hellfire Bar. He stormed into the bar, past the glaring of the bikers outside and ran into the doorman.

"Stay out of my way Pal, I'm looking for Demon."

"You might want to change your tone or you might be crawling out of here."

Wild Card just couldn't stand it anymore, the patronizing or the lack of respect from these clowns.

"I'm gonna ask you one more time, where's the Demon?"

The doorman just stood there and folded his arms. Wild Card nodded his head a couple of times at this gesture and smiled. He then grabbed the doorman under his armpits and threw him into the bar with a loud crash as chairs broke and a neon sign was shattered. The doorman who lay on the floor quickly grabbed a boot knife and threw it at Wild Card. The blade bounced harmlessly off the Kevlar on his stomach. The 2 steel bars came out and as Wild Card raised them over his head to come down on the doorman, a voice rang out over the music and the noise.

"Stop! Your business is with me, not him."

Wild Card stopped to see the Demon step out from a small room in the back. The Demon took off his sunglasses to reveal those piercing red eyes and showed a toothy smile. In a look of shock, Wild Card could have sworn that the guy's canine teeth were longer than they were supposed to be. That didn't matter; he was here on a job and wasn't going to be intimidated. Wild Card raised the sharpened steel bar and pointed it at the Demon.

"You and I have some business to discuss, outside now Demon!"

In San Guatalaharo, the battle rages on. Simple farmers riding on horseback using tools implemented as weapons against the advancing soldiers. One farmer embedded a rake into the chest of a soldier, while another stabbed one in the head with a pick. The soldiers came pouring over the town and became overwhelming, firing machine guns at the people. Vapor ran ahead of them to the side under the cover of the approaching darkness. Before the soldiers could get to the group of farmers that awaited them as sitting ducks, Vapor threw out a dozen of her fear capsules. Although it was a large chunk of her inventory, it created a smoke screen that the soldiers ran through. When they came out the other side, they were all frozen with fear and the farmers charged them with shovels and spades.

Screams of slaughter were heard in another area of the village north of Vapor's location as soldiers gunned down farmers. The 2 snipers that were with Vapor in the jungle gave chase behind the soldiers and unloaded on them with the guns they had picked up from the dead soldiers of the truck that crashed.

The village was dark and full of screams and sporadic gunfire in the night. The ground began to turn a brownish red in the moonlight. Through all the chaos, Vapor looked for Power; but he was nowhere to be seen. She ran to help a small contingent of farmers that had managed to get guns away from 4 soldiers, but were now fighting with knives. Vapor ran at them with both curved daggers out. She wasn't flashy, but she was quick and precise. The soldiers never had a chance against her as the blades glistened in the moonlight. Then over the crest of a small hill, there came at least 30 men armed with machine guns pointed at them. Out in the open, there was nowhere to go, they were all sitting ducks. There was no choice, but to put their hands up and surrender. Then she saw him coming behind the soldiers over the crest, Power casually walked with a smile.

"Miss Del Rio, always the wrench in the works? This time it will cost you as well as this pathetic little village."

Vapor had grabbed 2 capsules before she put her hands up; they were both disorienting ones.

"Why do you continue to do this to us Power? We have done nothing, all we want is our freedom and our homeland back."

"My dear Havanna, you are simply and unfortunately in the way."

Vapor started to wrinkle her nose a little and began inhaling deep breaths as if she was going to sneeze. As she brought her hands down to cover her face, she threw the capsules down and held her breath as they broke. The guards as well as Power immediately became disoriented. Vapor took advantage of the situation and immediately cut down 2 of them as she broke away, taking their guns in the process.

"Retreat! We must fall back to the next village!"

As Vapor ran back to the vehicles that were already in the back of the town in case of this, gunfire erupted behind her. More soldiers were coming over the crest and dominating the battle. A feeling of sickness washed over her as she watched the carnage while starting the jeep. The village had fought bravely, but in the end the soldiers had the victory. There was nothing she could do to help them now and those that could make it to the next village, had to push on. Vapor knew sooner or later, her and her people were going to run out of room to run and it infuriated her that Power knew that. She forced the thought out of her mind as she sped down the dirt road to fortify the next village. They would fight Power every step of the way, even if it meant losing. As long as there was resistance, that meant that there was at least hope. This gave Vapor a small comfort as she drove off into the night.

Outside the Hellfire Bar Wild Card waits and watches as the Demon with his sunglasses back on, steps outside to meet him in the street. Demon stops about 10 paces away from Wild Card and stares at him.

"There have been complaints about the activities that go on here during the night and it's my job to see that it doesn't continue. I need you to come down with me to the station, just make it easy on yourself and cooperate."

Demon remained standing and watching, but still didn't say a word. Wild Card approached him with both of his bars out and motioned for him to move along beside him. When the Demon didn't move, Wild Card grabbed his leather jacket by his left shoulder. The Demon reached back with his right hand in a fist and belted Wild Card in the chest, sending him tumbling in a backwards somersault. With surprising speed, Wild Card got to his feet and slugged Demon in the face, breaking his sunglasses. With the Demon recoiling from the blow, Wild Card sent a roundhouse kick to his chest. Recovering fast, the Demon grabbed Wild Card's foot and with a big smile kicked out Wild Card's standing leg and dropped him on his back.

The Demon walked in a circle around Wild Card with a smile on his face. Full of rage, Wild Card shot up with a steel bar in his hand and went to bring it down on the Demon's head. To his utter shock, Demon grabbed the bar with lightning reflexes and twisted it out of his hand before he could react. Demon reached up and grabbed Wild Card by the throat and brought him to the ground, pinning him to the concrete.

"Look Kid, I was just playing around with you and then you try to hit me in the head with this hunk of metal!"

Demon looked at Wild Card's bar in his hand and then threw it across the street in disgust. Still holding Wild Card by the neck and pinning him to the ground, Demon leans in really close to his face with those gleaming red eyes and elongated canines wrapped in a smile. Wild Card couldn't move, he didn't dare to; he was petrified with fear.

"Go play hero somewhere else Kid, down here you'll just end up getting hurt. You go and tell Dixon that if he wants to talk with me, he can come down here and see me himself. If not, I don't want to see anybody else coming down here and harassing me or I'll send the next guy out in a body bag. I hope I make myself crystal clear, now go get your toy and get out of here before I get angry."

Demon let up on Wild Card's neck and stepped back a few paces. Wild Card got up slowly holding his neck and glaring at the Demon. He walked across the street and picked up his bar. He wanted to attack him again and bring him to justice, but he had a gut feeling that would be a bad idea.

"This isn't over Demon!"

"Yes it is Kid, you don't want to push it."

Wild Card turned away and started walking back to the east side. Demon bent down and picked up his shattered sunglasses and began to laugh as he looked at them. Under his breath he exhaled a sigh.

"Well Kid, you got some guts coming down here like that and I respect you for it."

Toria awoke to the lair entrance being slammed open. She got out of bed and lit a few candles as Jason started to throw his Wild Card equipment into the corner of their room.

"Jason calm down, you're going to wake up Rip."

Jason ignored Toria, climbed into bed and turned away from her blowing out the candles.

"Jason what happened out there tonight, are you all right?"

"I don't feel like talking about it Toria, I just want to go to bed right now."

Toria knew that it took a lot for Jason to get upset, so she decided to leave him alone. After he calmed down, she'd speak with him about it in the morning. She lay back down, put her arm around him and closed her eyes.

Morning came for Vapor and her people, but it brought no comfort. She had stopped in the next small village called Tiharo and sent most of the others on their way. After a refueling stop in Tiharo, the trucks that they had stolen from Power should carry them to where the Jungle Road meets up with a main road and to civilization. She knew full well that Power could not be stopped by her small band of fighters that remained from San Guatalaharo. That's why she had sent a message with one of the villagers that were on the trucks back to civilization. At all costs, they must wire a message to Harborside in America and get a hold of Eon. Vapor knew of no one else that could help in this corrupted area of the Colombian jungle.

She also knew that if she left as well, Power would destroy all these rural villages in his wake just for his own pleasure and the chance to get to her. She would stay and fight him and his soldiers, to try to slow them down as best as she could. It was a long shot, but maybe through her efforts the message to Eon would get through. If they could combine forces, maybe they could stop Power from destroying all of these rural villages along the Jungle Road. Vapor knew that she was a harbinger of death wherever she went until Power was stopped. Just as San Guatalaharo had fallen, so too would be the case in Tiharo. It angered and sickened her as she looked around at the innocent farmers.

There were only 50 men left from the last village that were ready and able to fight. They had picked up some weapons from some dead soldiers in the last battle, so they could still do damage. Vapor checked her own supply of capsules and she was down about a third of her supply with no place to restock. She would do what she could until she could do no more. With a sigh, she led the fighters to meet with the locals of Tiharo and prepares to dig in and fight the enemy again with fresh bodies.

As morning came in the lair, the brewing of coffee that Rip had started awakened Jason and Toria.

"Hey you big lug, you in a better mood this morning?"

"Yeah, I think I just had to sleep it off that's all."

"You want to talk about what happened down on the south end of town last night?"

"It's twice now that I've run into this guy and neither time was a good moment in Wild Card's career. This guy they call the Demon, he moves with incredible speed and has the reflexes of a cat. He's got the strength to back it up too, I saw him knock a 300+lbs guy off his feet with one punch! Last night I tried to take him in on the complaint, but he pretty much made me look like a fool. I feel like I'm stuck between a rock and a hard place here. I don't want to fight him again, the guy's just flat out nuts. At the same time, I don't want to go to Dixon and tell him I can't do it. What's worse is I don't want to run to my little girlfriend for help. I just wish I could handle this problem on my own and be done with it."

"Look Jason, if you don't want me to go down there then I won't; but something has to be done about it. I didn't wipe out the gangs of this city just so another tyrant could do as he pleases. Just tell Dixon what happened and he'll have to send in a squad of officers to deal with this guy, that's all. Jason, nobody wins all the time; not even I do. When Power got the best of me, I didn't even want to admit it to myself; especially after what happened to Jax."

"I know Toria, my pride is hurt more than anything else. I'm telling you though, there's something not quite right about that guy. The boys at the gym hit like a truck and I can trade punches with the best of them, but I've never seen anybody throw a punch like this guy."

"I'll stay out of it Jason, it's your deal and I'll let you take care of it."

"Thanks Toria, lets go get some breakfast."

They both walked into the kitchen to greet Rip who was all smiles. She had the griddle out and was making waffles. Jason had temporarily forgotten about the Demon and how he was going to take care of all of this. This had brought a smile to his face; he loved waffles.

This morning a mysterious group had entered the city by way of train through the night. They had set themselves up in a hotel with all adjoining rooms.
"Tonight we will begin to look for Rip and begin the process of avenging what she has done."

Chapter 5

It was a long day that felt like deja vu to Vapor. Here she was again in a little rural farming village, with limited fighting resources and Power would be on his way. On a positive note, the fighters had captured at least twice as many guns as they started out with. With the extra weapons that they had stolen, Vapor sent out 6 snipers this time into the jungle along the road. She also utilized more scouts to get more updated accounts of Power's movements.

In another effort to slow down the soldiers, Vapor had the locals create a roadblock that Power's men couldn't just smash through this time. They were chopping down trees and laying them across the road, using the horses and chains to drag them into place. Vapor had 2 trucks left in her possession as well as a jeep after she sent off those that couldn't fight in Power's trucks. She parked them on the other side of the roadblock. If things went bad, there wasn't enough room to get everybody out. The thought of inevitable death for these innocents weighed heavily on her shoulders.

The order was given to cease work at 5pm so all could gather for food and a meeting. The women that stayed behind who would not leave their men, slaughtered livestock and a hearty meal was served. Nobody wanted to think it, but most knew this may very well be their last meal. Vapor stood up to address the fighters.

"I feel we are better prepared now than we were in San Guatalaharo. I also want to thank you for giving me shelter and food for myself and the other fighters. We were in desperate need of sleep and nourishment. We will be there tonight fighting, bleeding and dying with you. I will not tell you that this will be a glorious battle of victory. The reality is we are outnumbered and outgunned against trained soldiers with state of the art equipment and weapons. You are all good patriots and because of that you all are willing to fight until the end. Let those that live this night tell the tale for years to come of the brave few that fought the terrible horde. They will attack us at night because they have special glasses that allow them to see in the darkness. This gives them more of an advantage, but we will use the jungle to ours. We will not face them directly, but instead fight 100% guerrilla warfare tactics. It is likely that they will destroy your homes, but you will take as many as you can for revenge!"

In the ashes of San Guatalaharo, Power surveys the destruction that his soldiers have caused. As he walks, he comes across one of his fallen soldiers and he stops. Bending down he sees that a rake has been embedded in the soldier's head. He reaches down and removes the rake and throws it so far that it disappears into the jungle.

"A farming tool is no match for my soldiers! Call the men to arms lieutenant, it's time to destroy another one of those pathetic villages."

In the lair, Rip, Toria and Jason are sitting down to dinner.

"I'm very pleased with what you've achieved Toria, you are an incredibly fast learner. With your heightened senses, I've taught you how to hear the faster beat of a heart, see the twitch of a muscle under clothes, to feel the presence of another warrior. I feel you are well on your way to using the Foresight."

"Sorry to jump in here, but let's just say Toria and I get into a little argument. Is she going to be able to read my mind?"

Toria looked at Jason with a sly smile and quickly raised her eyebrows several times.

"No Jason she will not be able to read your mind; she'll instead be able to read you."

"Well that's a comfort. Anyway Toria, I wanted to tell you that I'm going back out there again tonight. I'm going under cover, I have to know what this guy's deal is. I just want to follow him and see where he goes. He never comes out during the day, the guy's a psycho."

"I know I told you this is all your case, but you have the radio and I'll be listening. I believe in you, you've saved my hide more than once; just be careful."

"I know; I'm just going to get a location to come back to so I don't have to keep going to that bar. I'd ask Dixon, but nobody knows where he lives. However, if I see him drive into a graveyard and climb into a coffin to sleep; I'm getting the hell out of there and giving you the case."

Toria put her hand on his with a little smirk.

"Thanks Hun."

Jason stood up and started to get ready. He wore the Wild Card top under a loose fitting shirt and tucked his bars in a holster he made that went across his back.

Later that night, the Hellfire Bar was as busy as ever. Jason rounded the familiar corner, which was his third trip down here and looked on from a distance. He had brought a small set of binoculars with him, part of his camping equipment that Toria hadn't managed to destroy. Scanning outside the bar he had found what he was looking for, Demon's bike. Jason knew the direction that Demon took off when he left, so he placed himself in a more strategic location across the way. Now it was just a waiting game to see when the Demon would leave.

Rip watched as Toria paced back and forth doing up her braid.
"I know you're worried Toria, but you need to relax."
"I can't do that knowing that this guy is as dangerous as Jason says he is."
"Why don't we go for a walk and get some fresh air, it will do both of us some good."
"Alright Rip, but the radio is coming with me."
Toria and Rip go topside and start to head down to the business district to hit up a late night cafe. Once they settle down into an outside table with 2 coffees, Toria gets lost in the sight of all the people out enjoying the warmer weather. After a

few minutes, a group of 5 men dressed in dark clothes approach their table.

"Eesveneetye Rip, kak dela? What a stroke of good fortune it is meeting you here."

A look of shock and terror come across Rip's face. She begins to look around nervously, as if scanning the immediate area.

"How did you get here and where is your new master?"

"Please, please, let us be civilized Rip. After all, this is a highly public place."

Toria stood up and got right in the man's face.

"Rip and I were having our own conversation and if you're so concerned about making a scene then you had better turn around and keep walking."

"Is this another one of your students Rip? You should teach her some manners."

"Toria, these men are not as they appear to be. They are highly dangerous, I suggest we remain calm."

The man flashes a smile and walks back to rejoin the others.

"We'll see you later Rip, please enjoy your coffee."

The 5 men turned and walked away, disappearing in the crowd of people.

"Who are they Rip and why are you so worried?"

"Toria, there's no time for a full explanation. Trust me, we are in grave danger and must get out of here now. There are more of them and we are being watched, we can't go back to the lair."

"All my weapons are back at the lair, how am I supposed to fight these guys without them?"

"Alright, I'm going to stay here and you're going back to the lair. Use your speed and knowledge of the city to lose them through alleyways. Once you get back to the lair and get your weapons, meet me back here. I'll be in the business district on the move trying to lead them away from you. You see the clock tower over there? I want you to go meet me there in one hour."

Rip reached over grabbing Toria's hand and mouthed the word "wait". Rip got up and walked into the coffee shop. Toria looked around nervously and after a few minutes Rip came out and secretly passed a note to Toria under her hand. She mouthed the words, "read it after you leave" to Toria and then sat back down. Toria got up and began to walk out of there. Once she was just out of the business district, she started to run. Once she went through a few alleys and side roads, she stopped to read the note from Rip.

"They would have been listening to us, do <u>not</u> meet me at the clock tower in one hour, instead meet me at the city park in 30 minutes."

When Toria thought she had lost them, she made a break for it back to the lair. As soon as she got into the open streets, gunfire erupted around her. Quickly she dove back into the alley she came out of. Four armed men with machine guns came into her view from across the way. Toria had wondered how they had gotten those through customs. She watched as one of the men bent down and picked up the note that had fallen out of Toria's shirt when she back flipped into the alley. There was nothing she could do; she was pinned down in the alley. Then she heard one of the men call out to finish her off. As the other 3 men moved into the alley, Toria jumped and caught the lower rail of a fire escape and quickly made it to the roof of the building as bullets rained in the alley below.

From the roof Toria could see the men walk into the alley after they stopped shooting. She could also see the other gunman make his way towards the city park. She was just across from one of the lair's manhole covers, but she was up 10 stories. It was too high to jump from, even for her. She couldn't go back down into the alley because the armed men were still milling about and worse yet, she was running out of time.

Just as Jason was getting comfortable, he heard an engine start up. He looked through the binoculars and confirmed that it was the Demon.

Demon never stayed too long and Jason was banking on that. As soon as Demon went by, Jason was on a sprint. He could see him on the straight-aways and hear him around the bends. One thing he had on his side was a good working knowledge of the south side of the city. After Jason lost him, he had followed him far enough before the Demon got out of his sight to know the general location of where he might be.

    Jason went on another 15 minutes before he entered a section of the south end that you didn't even want to send your enemies to. He could smell the exhaust from the bike, so he knew he was close. There was a random gunshot in the distance, a scream in the night and the sound of bums clanking wine bottles.

    "You're in the wrong place tonight, you look lost."

    Jason turned around to see 3 gang members holding out knives with guns tucked into their pants. He was thankful that he had on the Wild Card top underneath.

    "Look guys, I don't want any trouble here. I'm just passing through, so keep on walking."

    They all laughed and began to surround him.

    "Sure, we'll be on our way just as soon as we see what you got that's worth while."

    Jason didn't wait for another word before reacting. He grabbed the closest guy by the arm that held the knife and immediately broke his wrist. Another one ran at him with his knife and Jason threw the first guy into the oncoming blade. The first guy was impaled in the stomach. Jason looked up to see the third one reaching for his gun and ran to tackle him before he could pull it out. As they both went to the ground, Jason punched him in the face and instantly knocked him out cold as the back of the guy's head bounced off the concrete. Jason heard the second guy that stabbed the first running behind him. With a fast kick, Jason slammed his foot into the second guy's kneecap with a loud crack. Jason stood up and connected with a powerful uppercut to floor the second guy out. Just then Jason heard clapping down the street in the shadows. As he looked over, a familiar figure emerged into the light, the Demon.

"Don't worry about them, they won't be missed."

"Look Demon, I didn't come here to fight you. I'm not here as Wild Card, it's off duty."

"Relax Kid, I just came to ask if you wanted a drink?"

Sounds of engines could be heard coming down the Jungle Road. Vapor was waiting just off the road into the trees in front of the roadblock. Sounds of machine gun fire could be heard from the snipers hidden in the night-covered treetops.

However, this time the soldiers were firing back at them. One truck was taken out, but the others reached the roadblock. This time they stopped. Soldiers came pouring out of the trucks to make it around the roadblock. Vapor went to work and threw down a fear capsule to the side of the roadblock. Four soldiers ran through it and immediately stopped in their tracks. Vapor cut them all down before they could take their next breath. Unfortunately, she was spotted and the other soldiers started to fire at her. Vapor grabbed the guns off the fallen soldiers and ran through the village, disappearing into the jungle again. She met up with other members of the village and handed out the 4 guns to those that had none.

    Fires were lit all throughout the village in random spots so the villagers could see the soldiers moving through the town. It worked too, as the soldiers flooded the village; they were in plain sight of the farmers. The soldiers met no resistance, not a single person was around. The villagers watched them through the trees. The soldiers were moving cautiously, pointing their guns into the abandoned huts. Vapor had instructed the snipers to follow up behind them and between the snipers and the farmers, they would sandwich the soldiers. All the villagers knew not to attack until the soldiers arrived. Vapor knew they wouldn't arrive until they dealt with the truck that they had shot the tires out on. She began to wonder how they fared and then she wondered no more.

There was a loud shriek in the air to break the stealth of the night. This was the sign they all waited for, that meant the snipers had arrived. The soldiers looked up and behind them, but it was too late as gunfire erupted all around the soldiers. At least a dozen soldiers went down in the first few seconds; the rest took shelter behind huts and returned fire. However, their night vision was thrown off because of all the random fires in the village and was blinding them. For the time being the villagers had the upper hand. In a truck away from the battle, still on the Jungle Road waits the angry Power.

"Lieutenant, what's going on out there, I hear a lot of shooting. Over."

A lieutenant's voice came over the radio mixed with static and rapid gunfire.

"They have us pinned down sir. They're in the jungle and we can't get a fix on them. We also couldn't get around the roadblock this time either, so we're all on foot. Over."

"I want you to retreat out of there and switch to fire bombing. Over and out."

Power slammed down the receiver nearly breaking it.

"So Miss Del Rio, you are a resourceful one. You and the damn Kayden girl have a lot in common. Am I to be plagued with entities such as these wherever I go on this wretched planet? Let's see how you think your way out of this one."

The soldiers began to retreat back to the trucks behind the roadblock. The snipers began to unload on as many soldiers as they could before they made it to safety. The villagers saw this and became elated.

"We've got them on the run, come on let's finish them off."

In waves they came running out of the jungle into the village after the soldiers. Vapor watched in horror as every villager gave away his or her position.

"Wait, you don't know if this is a trap! They may not be retreating, hold your positions!"

Vapor ran as best she could through the jungle at night. Nobody could hear her over the gunfire and blazing fires. Her vision was limited to shadow movements here and there. Off in the distance she heard engines start up again and then a loud explosion, one after the next. There was a loud whistle and then tremendous explosions in the village. Houses were blown apart and the oil from the fires the villagers had lit was being spread in all directions catching fire to everything that it touched. The villagers couldn't get back to the jungle in time and Vapor watched as bodies flew through the air and were blown apart. The roadblock was blown apart as well and trucks were rolling in. Vapor dropped to her knees with her mouth open as she watched fire rain down from the sky. She was witnessing her worst fear; it was as if Hell itself was being unleashed on these innocents.

Chapter 6

    Jason followed the Demon back through a few alleyways to a small hole in the wall of an abandoned building. The Demon pointed to a ratty old couch and motioned to Jason.
    "Go ahead and have a seat."
    Demon grabbed a can off a 6-pack and handed it to Jason, it was warm.
    "Is this where you live?"
    "No, but this is part of my turf and that's close enough for you."
    "So, you knew that I was following you?"
    Demon smiled and took a long drag on his beer.
    "Tell me Kid, why do you keep pushing down here? I'm not going with you and Dixon and his boys couldn't care less about what happens down here."
    "I guess I was just curious really. I was there that night you fought that enormous guy. I saw you knock him off his feet in one punch, how did you do that?"

Again the Demon smiled and took a drag on his beer. Just then Jason's radio went off and he heard Toria's voice come over the speaker.

"Jason, are you there? I've got a problem back here..."

Jason listened as Toria filled him in on the situation.

"I'll be there as fast as I can Toria, just hold on."

Demon finished his beer, crushed the can and threw it back into the building.

"Well, it looks like our interview is over; no sharing secrets tonight. Come on, follow me and watch your step."

Demon took Jason through some more alleyways until they came to a motorcycle on its side covered in garbage.

"I've got bikes here and there in these alleys, I'll let you borrow this one. Its got a few problems, but it'll run and get you there faster than on foot."

"Thanks Demon, I'll take care on it and bring it back when this is over."

"Don't worry too much about it, it's not really a first class ride."

Jason started the bike and took off back to the east side.

Rip was waiting for Toria in the city park under one of the trees near a bench. At this time of the night it was sparse and it had been half an hour. She heard footsteps coming, but it was more than one pair. Rip knew there was no use in hiding and stepped out from behind the tree.

"At least I took you away from all those innocent people."

"Yes Rip, that's your misfortune."

"What did you do with Toria?"

"Oh, when she dropped this note, I grabbed a few of my men and came to meet you here. I'm not sure how she's doing right now, but at the time I left her in the capable hands of 3 of my associates. Now why don't you make this easy on yourself and just come with us. I'd rather not do this the hard way."

Rip looked on as the 2 men flanking her opponent pulled out guns and pointed them at her. Maybe in her early days she might have made a move against them, but she didn't want to risk it. There might be a better opportunity later to escape; she just hoped that Toria was all right.

"Have it your way, I'll go along peacefully to see your boss."

"Excellent, I knew you were a bright one."

On top of the building near the lair, Toria watches the armed men looking around in the alley.

"Where the hell did she go, she couldn't have just vanished."

"What about that fire escape, maybe she went up to the roof?"

"Well, she's not down here anymore. Give me a boost up to the ladder, I'll go up and check it out."

Toria heard every word and began to look around. There was an old antenna on top of the building. It wasn't her axe, but it would have to do. Toria ripped the antenna from its bolts and snapped it into a few smaller pieces. She grabbed one of the longer rods and waited by the edge of the roof near the fire escape. As the gunman neared the top, Toria reached over the edge and threw the rod at him. The man was caught by surprise as the thin steel rod embedded straight down through the middle of his head. There wasn't a single sound at all, he died instantly and slumped over on the landing he was on.

Toria peeked over the edge of the building to see if the other 2 had noticed, they hadn't. The landing was just below her, a single set of stairs away. She carefully and quietly climbed down to the landing without the others noticing. Toria was taking the gun sling off the dead body when she heard the men down below calling to their comrade.

"What are you doing just sitting there, go up to the roof. She's no threat, don't worry about it Varislav."

The men were answered with gunfire from up above. Even in the dark, Toria had enough light to see her targets. Just like with everything else, she had perfect aim. The men dropped down dead in the alley and Toria quickly climbed down the escape. She grabbed the guns and started to run to the lair when she heard a motorcycle coming. Staying hidden in the alley, she waited for it to pass. When she heard the engine quit and saw that Jason stepped off the bike, she ran out to greet him.

"Toria, thank God you're all right! Where did you get all those guns?"

"Never mind that, when did you buy a motorcycle? No time for questions now, Rip's in danger and we need to get our suits on."

The night continued to rage on in the southern jungles of Columbia. Vapor began to gather as many people as she could get into the waiting trucks on the south end of the village.

"They've broken through the roadblock! Go south as far as the trucks will take you, those that stay will not see the light of morning!"

Many men voluntarily stayed behind to fight to the end. As the trucks slowly filled up with wounded and those that couldn't fight, the firebombs continued to fall. There was no sign of any of the soldiers, but the entire village was leveled. Vapor even filled up the single jeep and sent them on their way. There was no more transportation for anyone else out of the village unless they hijacked another one of Power's trucks. After the last truck had left, the grenades stopped falling. The villagers that remained stayed hidden in the trees, not daring to go anywhere near the demolished village. Fear was the only driving force that kept them going and the only thing that kept Vapor awake from her lack of sleep.

"This may be an opportunity, they have stopped the bombing and probably think we're dead."

Vapor thought over the situation and agreed with the farmer.

"I had no idea Power had these kind of resources, I should have expected as much from the corrupt local officials. It's as if we are fighting our own military under the control of Power. Our only hope of escape is to capture one of those trucks, maybe 2 if we're lucky. Alright, we all go as a team and storm them, they won't be expecting that."

Just as the villagers began to move, they spotted soldiers coming around the destroyed roadblock with large tanks on their backs and long thin guns connected by tubes to the tanks. The ends of the guns were lit on fire in an ever-burning flame.

"Oh my God, they have flame throwers! They are trying to flush us out of the jungle."

Two dozen soldiers emerged with flame throwers and in seconds fire was forced into the jungle in long plumes 50ft across, setting ablaze anything that it touched.

"We need to make a frontal assault, the jungle is no longer safe. We have no choice, but to engage in direct combat!"

Vapor still had about 40 men left at her command and she was determined to use them.

"Half of you take out the soldiers with the flame throwers, the rest of you come with me to attack the trucks."

As Vapor took her 20 men forward, she feared what might be waiting on the other side of the destroyed roadblock.

Rip was seated in a chair with her hands bound when the blindfold came off. She was face to face with the leader of these men. He had his white robes on with the red headscarf around his face. Rip glanced at the medallion that hung around his neck and recognized it at once.

"You are here to pay for your crimes against the Cult when you killed Master Temovich. Do you remember that fateful night Rip?"

"We had many missions as mercenaries, sometimes our paths crossed with the Cult of 16. You must understand that fights would be inevitable, especially if we had opposing interests.

Besides that was a long time ago, the Soviet regime has since fallen. I can't be expected to answer against these terms when I was under orders so long ago."

"Yes Rip, the Soviets have fallen, but not the Cult of 16. Our history goes back a long way in time, long before Lenin and his Soviets. We remember all that transpires and you will be held accountable for your actions."

"I think you're just angry because a non-member defeated one of your own and you can't stand it. The great legendary fighters of the Cult of 16 and one of their leaders die at the hands of a mercenary."

"We are a new generation of fighters from those days and I assure you that the Cult of 16 is still alive and well throughout the world. When Temovich died, I took over control of the Russian division of the Cult. You are subject to my laws now. You will be taken back to Russia with us and executed on one of the Cult's sacred altars. It is the only befitting punishment for your crimes. We leave at sunrise and if you should try to escape, we will cripple you, keeping you alive in agony until your execution."

Rip remained silent; she was all too familiar with how the Cult of 16 worked.

The Demon returned to his home or what passed for his home. Lost in the maze of all the abandoned buildings on the south end through the alleys is where the Demon's own personal lair dwelt. The entrance was well hidden, but big enough for his bike to fit. Once inside he pulls the books out of the side bag on his bike and drops them on the table. The table also held multiple skulls of animals as well as people. Hanging in random arrays from hooks were animal bones and feathers. Large red candles were a major part of the décor as well as pentagrams on the floor. There were multiple small bookcases throughout the dwelling full of books all dealing with the occult and black magic. Demon lit some candles and sat down in the center of a large pentagram barefoot and shirtless.

"Jason the Wild Card, you are an ambitious one."

Demon laughed to himself in his recollection.

"You remind me of myself about 10 years ago."

Closing his eyes and touching his middle fingers to his thumbs, he starts to relax his breathing. Before long, he is unaware of the world around him and is lost in deep meditation.

Jason and Toria emerged from the lair, both in their alter ego suits.

"Alright Jason, we've got to get to the city park. That's where I was supposed to meet Rip, but if they've gotten to her already she might not be there. At least we can look for any clues that might be left behind."

"Hop on the bike Toria, we can get there faster than even you can run."

Eon climbed on the back of the bike and they took off, making it to the city park in a short amount of time. They both got off the bike and began to search for clues.

"There's nothing here Toria and I don't see any signs that they ever were."

Eon had her eyes closed not listening to Jason. She was inhaling deeply and turned to look over at a park bench under a tree.

"Over here Jason, I can smell her scent."

Both of them walked over to the tree, but Jason held up his hands and shook his head. Eon bent down to the ground and began looking through the grass.

"They went this way and I know she went against her will because I'm picking up other sets of tracks."

Eon got up and followed the near invisible tracks as far as Jason could tell, to the dirt road that entered the park.

"Right here Jason, the tracks stop and here in the dirt are tire tracks. It looks like a vehicle stopped and then took off again. Go grab the bike and we'll see where this leads."

Eon and Wild Card followed the tracks back through the east side of town all the way to the harbor. It was here that they found a lone van parked near one of the piers. There was nobody else around and that worried them both. As they started to approach the van with their weapons out, Eon stopped suddenly.

"Wait Jason, I hear ticking in the van. Jesus, it's a decoy; they set us up!"

Just as both of them started to run, the van exploded in a big fireball that turned into a small mushroom cloud. Debris fell all around them, but they were both all right. High above on a side road looking down on the harbor, was a man holding a detonator in his hand. With a sour expression, he walks back to the passenger side of a vehicle to his awaiting partner.

"Well, did you get them?"

"No, the girl stopped as if she could hear the bomb and they both started to run. I had no choice but to detonate it and hope to catch them in the blast radius, but I didn't."

"Master Sergey will not like this."

Both men stayed silent as they drove off down the road.

Eon and Wild Card got up and dusted themselves off. Each looked over the other to make sure both of them were uninjured.

"I can't believe they tricked me, I followed a decoy. We must have missed the switch on the road. Damnit! Now we don't have any more leads, it's one big dead end."

"Come on Toria, let's go back to the lair. Maybe Rip got away and is waiting for us there."

"I doubt it, but I don't know where else to look. Let's ride the same route back to the park; maybe I'll see where they made the switch."

Chapter 7

In a rural part of Columbia, the trees are burning high into the night sky. Sounds of gunfire filled the ears of Vapor and her men as they charge around the broken roadblock. She has to trust that the villagers behind her can take out the soldiers with the flame throwers; she needs all of her attention here. As Vapor and her men round the corner, they are confronted with a line of trucks coming down the Jungle Road in the distance. However, as good fortune would have it, the snipers are standing over the bodies of dead soldiers.

"What do we do, they're coming with more men? Power has called in reinforcements, his reach is long and he can pull men from anywhere it seems."

Vapor looked around and assessed the situation as fast as she could.

"You men with me go back and help the others kill off the soldiers with the flame throwers. Then I want you to get in these 2 trucks and head down to the next village and warn them that Power and his men are coming. They need to evacuate, we're not going to be able to stop him. He has camps set up here to the coast and all the way east to Suriname. It will be like fighting a never ending supply of mercenaries backed by our own military's weapons."

"We can handle that, but what will you do?"

"Don't worry about me, I'll try to buy you some time."

There are 3 trucks behind the roadblock and as the villagers ran to help their comrades, Vapor took off for the truck on the end. Getting in, she sees that the keys are still in the ignition. Putting the truck in reverse, there is just enough room on the Jungle Road to turn around in a 5-point turn. Facing the oncoming truck, Vapor shifts the truck into drive and puts the pedal to the floor. The truck starts to gain speed as best as it can on the bumpy terrain. The driver of the lead truck can't believe his eyes as he sees one of their own trucks barreling down on him.

"Commander Power, it seems one of our own trucks has been hijacked by the enemy and is on a crash course with the second wave. Over."

"You have my permission to blast it out of the way soldier. Over and out."

The driver quickly puts down the receiver and starts to bark orders at the soldiers.

"Get the grenade launcher up and ready fast, we need to take care of this oncoming vehicle."

The soldiers in the back scurry to get the gun loaded, mounted and through the canopy of the truck. They begin cranking the gun up when they can hear the other engine in the distance. Vapor shifts the truck again, gaining maximum speed directly at the lead truck. The driver stops the line of trucks to give the soldiers more time.

"Hurry up with that gun, it's almost here!"

The soldiers crest the gun over the canopy and crank the barrel down on the oncoming truck and look to aim.

"You fools shoot at it! Fire! Fire!"

The driver leaps out of the vehicle as Vapor's truck slams into the lead truck just before the soldiers can get off the shot. Before impact, Vapor leaps out of the speeding truck as well and tumbles through the brush and trees of the jungle. She turns to watch as her truck hits the other with such force, that the back end of her truck flips over the top of the front of it and lands directly on top of the other lead truck. The soldiers inside are crushed under the crunching and grinding metal. Vapor lays there hurt from her leap out of a speeding truck and impacting with the jungle trees. Combined with the little sleep that she's had and the constant fighting, the whole world fades to black and she slumps over.

Eon and Wild Card speed back to the city park on the motorcycle that Demon lent to Jason.

"Toria, are you picking up anything?"

"Nothing Jason, but I have an idea. I think these guys want Rip for something, so I don't think they would kill her outright or they would have done it in the park. They instead took her somewhere, which means that she's probably still alive. These guys also had an Eastern European accent, let's go to police headquarters and get a print out of all the flights coming and going from there. With any luck, we may be able to catch them at the airport."

"Alright Toria, you go to police headquarters and I'll go check back at the lair. If she's there, I'll radio back to you either way."

"You got it Babe, remember to be careful if you run into them. Rip said they weren't what they appeared. I don't know what that means, but I saw the look in her eyes and heard the worry in her voice."

Jason nodded and slowed down the bike. Eon jumped off and started to run towards headquarters, while Wild Card took off back to the lair.

As Wild Card neared the manhole entrance to the lair, he saw 3 men that fit the description of these goons. They were coming out of the alley carrying their dead comrades. Wild Card pulled up across the road under a streetlight.

"Hold it right there guys, you're coming with me to see the police."

The men looked at each other and laughed, they all turned towards Wild Card and stood there defiant. Wild Card got off the bike and shook his head with a sigh.

"Why is it people never want to listen, they always want to do things the hard way. Well, you're in luck because I'm in the mood to do things the hard way."

Wild Card pulled out his steel bars and stood across from them with only the distance of the street separating them. One guy stood in front of Wild Card, while the other 2 started to flank his sides.

"This isn't a chess game guys, don't think you're getting in position on me!"

Wild Card ran at the thug to his left with one bar raised over his head. The thug didn't let Wild Card get near him, with a jumping roundhouse kick; he connected with Wild Card's chest and knocked him back but not down. His armor absorbed most of the blow and again the steel bars were up, but this time for defense. The thug sent a flurry of kicks and punches at Wild Card, who blocked some of them with his bars. However, some of them got through and this time a spinning sweep kick knocked him off his feet. Wild Card quickly rolled to his feet as a stomping foot came down hard on the pavement next to his head, just missing him. As he got up, Wild Card swung a bar in a wide uppercut arc that caught the thug in the chest. To Wild Card's amazement, the thug just staggered back some.

"Well come on Pal. I've got more where that came from right here."

Before Wild Card could go on the offensive, he is kicked in the back from the thug behind him. The kick sent him into the thug that he was fighting who delivered a hard punch to his face, which sent him reeling. He was still on his feet, but he was dazed. The thug across the street took the opportunity to run at Wild Card in a flying jump kick that sent Wild Card crashing into the side of a building. Wild Card began to get up slowly, but his assailants ganged up on him and began to kick him while he was down. All Wild Card could do was protect his face from the lethal blows.

Then from behind them, the sound of a motorcycle could be heard. As the attackers turned to look, it was too late for one of them. The motorcycle flew through the air, hitting one of the thugs in the chest and crushing his body under its mass against the nearby building. After the crash of metal and concrete subsided, all that remained was a bloodstain against the wall with a dead body under the crumpled bike. The other 2 thugs turned towards the direction from which the motorcycle had come. There standing 30ft away in leather and sunglasses, unmoving and uncaring was the Demon. One thug stayed near the fallen Wild Card, while the other one ran at Demon.

    Demon waited, still not moving, as the attacker got closer. With a flying jump kick, the thug launched himself at Demon. At the last second, Demon threw a punch with such force that it snapped the thugs leg and spun him around 360 degrees in the air. Before the thug landed on the ground, Demon grabbed him out of the air and broke his back over his knee. The impact severed the thug's spinal cord and killed him instantly. Demon dropped the body and began walking towards the thug by Wild Card. The thug pulled out a long thin knife as he watched Demon approach. Wild Card shot up like a rocket and broke the thug's forearm with his steel bar. The knife went flying through the air and the thug went for a roundhouse kick on Wild Card. Wild Card met the kick with his other steel bar and drove his elbow into the thug's face. Before the thug had a chance to get his bearings, Wild Card brought the bar down on his head, which knocked him unconscious. As soon as he fell, Demon grabbed him by the back of the head and drove his skull into the side of the building, killing him.

"Whoa man, thanks for coming to my aid, but you didn't have to do that the fight was over."

"Yes I did, trust me."

"Ok, ok you had to kill him. You know Demon, I don't know if I should call you my hero or be scared to death of you. What are you doing down here anyway?"

"Your girl made it sound pretty serious down here, I just thought I'd check up on you. You seem to like getting in over your head."

"Oh Demon I didn't know you cared, I'm touched really."

Demon just looked at Wild Card with a stern expression and then cracked a smile.

"Let's just say you remind me of myself when I was about 10 years younger."

"Hey, I'll take that as a compliment, by the way I'm sorry about your bike. At least it went out in a blaze of glory and took out one of those bastards."

"Like I said, I've got more bikes around here and there. So, did you find what you were looking for?"

"No and it's a who not a what, she was one of Toria's mentors. I was going to see if she was in the l..."

Wild Card quickly bit his tongue and thought a moment before speaking again.

"Well, I thought she might be on this side of town, but I guess not."

"Alright Kid, it looks like you've got things under control."

Demon started to walk away when both of them heard fast footfalls like someone was running. They both looked over to see Eon running towards them.

"Hey Toria, did you get any flight numbers?"

"Yeah, but there are so many, we'd be there guessing all day with the flights leaving here and for other flights to bigger cities taking flights abroad. I guess it's as good as any right now and the first flight is at 6am. That's in 3 hours, so I say we get some sleep before spending the day at the airport with our fingers crossed. I take it Rip wasn't here, but it looks like you ran into some company."

"These guys were collecting their comrades out of the alley. By the way Toria, I'd like you to meet somebody; this is the one they call Demon."

Eon's eyebrows rose as she turned to the man in leather.

"So, you're the guy Jason's been talking about."

Wild Card flashed Eon a look and a smirk came over Demon's face.

"I'm Eon, good to finally put a face to the name. You know Jason, you don't look too banged up after this fight, nice job."

"Oh, I would have looked a whole lot worse if Demon hadn't shown up. He did his usual 'beat the crap out of everybody' thing and here they are."

"Let's see if there's any clues on them, um, you check the guy under the motorcycle."

Demon was already on it, as he pulled out keys from one of the thug's pockets. He looked at the name engraved on the key and smiled as he tossed it over to Eon. Eon grabbed the key and looked down at it, Demon stood up and approached both of them.

"If you guys want to take a chance and stay up, the Westmoore Hotel is a little dive on my end of town. You might find who or what you're looking for there. At the very least you could get some information."

Eon took the key and put it down her boot.

"What about you?"

"What about me?"

"Aren't you going to come with us and check it out?"

"Why, do you need me?"

"I just thought you might want..."

"Hey, just because I did a nice thing; doesn't mean I'm a nice guy. I'm sure you two can handle it from here. I'm heading back to my place; take Swift Street down about half a mile past my bar. You go ahead and take the bike Kid; you and your girlfriend will get there faster. I'm gonna take a slow walk home and enjoy the night air."

Eon and Wild Card climbed onto the bike and started it up.

"Thanks Demon, I owe you one."

"I have a feeling you'll be owing me more than that, try and stay on your feet in the next fight."

Wild Card smirked and took off towards Swift Street on the south end of town.

The bouncing of the truck on the Jungle Road woke Vapor up, she was groggy and her body ached. Looking up, she saw that there were villagers all around her looking down at her with concerned looks.

"I remember the crash, we were in the jungle..."

"The snipers went back for you and brought you to the truck. The stunt you pulled bought us enough time to get away with a good amount of distance between us and them."

"Thank you, where are we now?"

"We are on our way to the next village. We've just left one, telling them to evacuate like you said. We're taking shifts driving and going through the night into the morning until we come to the main road junction. We found 4 gas tanks, each one 10 gallons on the supply rack in the truck. This will take us into the city where Power would not dare attack for fear of international intervention. Nobody cares about the little rural towns along the Jungle Road, but attacking a city is a different story."

"I'm not so sure he won't attack, but I hope you're right."

Back at the crash site, one of the lieutenants gets on the receiver to the Commander.

"Commander Power, we are unable to get through the crash in time to catch the enemy. Over."

"Our enemy is very resourceful lieutenant, I will take care of things myself on that matter. In the mean time, I want you and the men to continue to get through the crash site and move south along the Jungle Road. Over and out."

In the truck that Power sits in, he puts down the receiver and contemplates the situation.

"Sir, would you like to go back to base, or should I continue to push on south?"

"No more advancing tonight, it's getting into the morning. We let a group of farmers get away from us tonight under Vapor's command. Miss Del Rio is starting to anger me almost as much as Miss Kayden. We'll head back to base and I have a few phone calls to make, I'm not to be disturbed during the ride back."

"Yes sir, we should be back at base within an hour."

Power picks up the receiver and punches in some numbers on a dial board.

"Sergeant, I have need of your men in the south. I want you to take a group of 100 men up the Jungle Road from the south end and head north. Some of my trucks have been hijacked and I want you to intercept them. You are to assemble the men at once and no matter the cost, do not let them reach the end of the Jungle Road."

Power sets down the receiver and smiles, keeping his hands folded over one and other.

"I underestimated you before Miss Del Rio, now you'll have no place to run. You'll be hunted by the north and now by the south. You'll have no supplies or food and your only course of action will be to take to the jungle and that will be certain death."

Back in the rebel trucks, Vapor is still too weak to even sit up.

"Rest Havanna, by the morning we'll be on our way to the city."

Vapor closed her eyes and smiled, with her mind at peace, she immediately fell into a deep sleep.

At the end of the Jungle Road, less than 100 miles away from Vapor's trucks are more of Power's soldiers heading north. However, in the major city of Mitu, the survivors of San Guatalaharo and Tiharo have arrived safely. The villager with Vapor's message finds his way to a police station in the city. After taking up a small collection from the other villagers for payment, the message is sent out to the Harborside police department in the northeastern US.

"Eon. Please come to Columbia. Serious trouble with Power and soldiers. See transmitted coordinates. Many are dead. More will die. Help us. Vapor."

The transmission was faxed through that morning at 3am. One of the guards on duty grabs the fax report without reading it and sets it on Chief Dixon's desk for him to read when he comes in.

Chapter 8

Wild Card and Eon pulled up at the Westmoore Hotel on Swift Street. It was about as sleazy as a dive could get. The neon sign only flickered half of the letters and there was trash all over the parking lot. The building itself had seen better days with a sagging roof and in bad need of a paint job. Most of the door numbers were ripped off the doors, gutters were hanging and there was spray paint all around the side of the building.

"Well, if you want to be discrete, I guess this is the place. You were right about these guys Toria; they remind me of master ninjas dressed in tuxedos. If Demon hadn't shown up, you probably wouldn't recognize me."

"I'm glad he showed up then. None of the lights are on in any of the rooms and the front office is closed for the night. I'm going to put my ear to the doors to see if there's any sign of life. Why don't you go around the back and check it out."

Wild Card walked around the back of the hotel and saw that there were several vehicles parked there, a couple cars and a van with tinted windows. He decides to look into one of the vehicles and starts with one of the cars. He doesn't find anything out of the ordinary and decides to check out the van. Just as Wild Card approaches, the van starts up and gunfire erupts all around him! He's hit in the chest with a bullet and knocked off his feet. The Kevlar and steel suit keep him alive, but he knows it will leave quite a bruise. Wild Card climbs behind one of the cars and stays down with his bars in hand. Eon quickly comes around the corner and tumbles behind the car with Wild Card.

"Jason, are you hurt?"

"No, I was lucky, they hit me in the middle of the chest."

"You're still making bad jokes, I guess you're fine."

The van begins to peel out and make its way around to the front of the hotel.

"Toria, the van!"

"I see it Jason, stay here in case it's a ploy."

Eon makes a run for it around the front of the hotel after the van. Armed men follow her that were shooting from the back of the hotel, outside in the surrounding bushes. Wild Card hears their feet coming around the side of the car and he gets ready. As the first one passes, he cracks him in the shins with the steel bar. With the crack of bone, the gunman goes down and Wild Card is confronted with another one immediately. Before the surprised gunman can get a shot off, Wild Card drives his other steel bar through the thug's stomach. Gunfire sprays out from a third thug and again Wild Card dives behind the car. All goes silent for a moment and Wild Card hears a gun hit the ground.

"Why don't you come out here, I'm unarmed. Or are you going to wait and ambush me as well?"

Wild Card slowly peeked over the car and saw the man holding his hands up and smiling.

"Come on, let's fight this out the old fashioned way. We've gotten what we came for, you'll just be a bonus."

"I was hoping you might say something like that."

Wild Card walked out from behind the car and faced the man 20ft away with his bars held firmly in front of him. The thug became serious and bent down in a fighting stance and waved Wild Card on in a taunt.

Eon took off in a sprint after the van as it peeled out of the hotel driveway and headed out of town towards the open highway. Being on the run, Eon had to take an extra second to steady her hand and take careful aim. Just as the van began to pull away from her, she released 2 throwing knives that blew out both the van's back tires. In a wild skid, the van swerved off the road and spun around 180 degrees in the dirt where it halted to a stop. Eon began to approach slowly and since she didn't have her axe with her, she pulled out her Bowie knives. Stepping out of the back of the van was a man holding Rip and a knife to her throat.

"I'm not sure who you are, but you're interfering with something much bigger than you know."

"Let her go and you can go your own way and I don't have to interfere anymore."

At that moment a car drove up, one of the cars that was parked in the front of the hotel.

"If you follow us or deflate any more tires, I'll kill her."

Without hesitation, Eon threw one of her throwing knives at the man's head. As if he had a perfect read on the blade, he brought up the knife from Rip's throat and deflected it away. Rip tried to free herself, but the blade was immediately replaced at her throat. In pure shock, Eon watched as the man smiled and got into the car with Rip.

Wild Card and the thug circled each other in anticipation. It was Wild Card who attacked first with a thrust to the man's stomach. The thug moved to the side and grabbed the steel bar, but before he could pull it from Wild Card's hand; the other bar wasn't far behind as it came down on the thug's forearm with a crack. The thug went into a spiral sweeping kick that Wild Card jumped, but the thug immediately jumped back up with a spinning roundhouse kick that caught Wild Card in the ribs sending him to the ground. The thug didn't stop there; he followed it up with an overhead axe kick to Wild Card's head. The force of the kick nearly knocked Wild Card's helmet off as it bounced off the pavement. The thug reached down and grabbed Wild Card and threw him into the side of the car, denting the door panel.

Wild Card was dazed, but otherwise he was all right. He stayed down on a knee and feigned weakness as a trap for his opponent. The thug took the bait and Wild Card could hear heavy footsteps running towards him. At the last second, Wild Card turned and faced the oncoming thug while standing up on his feet. At the same time, he swung up his steel bar in a wide arc like an uppercut. Putting everything he had into the blow, the steel bar connected with the side of the thug's head. The force of the hit sent the thug off his feet, landing on his back. The fight was over, permanently. As Wild Card walked over and looked down, he could see the thug's head split open as blood ran onto the black pavement.

Wild Card looked over his shoulder as he heard more footfalls behind him. At first he held his breath, and then relaxed as he saw it was Toria rounding the corner of the hotel. Eon saw the bodies and Wild Card standing over them.

"Nice job Jason, I wish I was as lucky as you were. They've got Rip and took off in one of the cars from the front of the hotel. I don't know where these guys came from, but I saw this guy deflect one of my knives right out of thin air. It seems every one of them are trained fighters in some type of martial arts. Let's get back on the bike and follow them, but we have to get Rip away from them before any confrontation. After what I saw, they're more dangerous than I thought and this isn't going to be easy."

"Alright, let's get going then. I'm feeling good right now with a big chip on my shoulder."

Demon made his way back to the south side of the city and began to head towards his bar, the Hellfire. It was a typical rowdy night with bikers swarming the place. Once inside, Demon was greeted by the doorman and sat at the bar with his patrons.

"What can I get for you boss?"

"Just a beer, whatever's handy."

Demon took a long pull on the drink, and then looked ahead seemingly at nothing. His thoughts wandered to the events of tonight and the foes that he faced. He was familiar with the fighting styles and guessed on the organization, but he hoped that he was wrong. If it was who he thought it was, Wild Card and his girlfriend Eon were going to have a hell of a time. Some of the boys approached Demon with darts in their hands.

"Hey Demon, how about a couple games?"

"Not tonight guys, I've got some thinking to do."

Demon tipped back his beer and slammed it down on the bar. It was a hot night and he wanted to lay low. Getting up from the barstool and getting nods from the bartender and the doorman, he left to walk back to his place.

    The car holding Rip and her captives raced down a dark and lonely road. The car held Rip, the mysterious leader named Sergey and 2 of his thugs. The car was heading north away from the city.
    "What do we do about this problem Master Sergey?"
    "We can't carry on the execution ceremony as I had planned in Russia, so we'll do it here. This student of yours Rip, she's good and won't let us continue our work and it won't wait till morning when we leave at the airport."
    Rip was bound and gagged, but she managed a little smile.
    "Continue to drive for an hour north, after which we'll consecrate a site in the woods for the execution. Get on the phone and contact the other groups and tell them to meet us out here and to look for the car along the road. Tell them we'll be 3 miles due north of the car in the woods. After we get dropped off, one of you will need to take the car 3 miles back. Take a route back to us through the woods, in case they're following. If they are, the distance should buy us enough time to get the job done before they find us."

"Master, the girl and her friend have already taken out 9 of our numbers, we are only at half strength."

In a fit of anger, Sergey slammed his fist into the car door and barked at his underling.

"Then get a hold of the men that are left and get them up here!"

Wild Card and Eon raced after the men who took Rip, when the motorcycle began to sputter.

"Toria, I think we have a problem with the bike."

"What do you mean, are we out of gas?"

"No, but Demon did say that this bike was a junker. Let me pull it over to the side of the road in that clearing and take a look at it."

Wild Card began to tinker around with it, but wasn't having any luck.

"Sorry Toria, but I don't have any tools and it's dark out here."

"Well that's just great, now how are we supposed..."

Eon stopped and listened in the distance down the road.

"Hey, there are a couple vehicles coming down the road."

"Really, I don't hear anything, are you sure?"

"I hear a lot better than you do Jason, remember? I'm going to take a look down the road from the top of that tree."

Eon jumped to a lower branch, flipped up to the next branch and within seconds had climbed to nearly the top of a 60ft tree. After about a minute, she returned back to the ground and ran over to Wild Card.

"Jason, it's the same models of cars we saw at the hotel and there's 2 of them. I'm going to try to ambush the lead car."

Wild Card watched as Eon ran across the road and up about 10ft in a tree. At this point, he could now hear the cars coming down the road and pulled out his bars to get ready just in case. As the lead car went by, Eon threw a throwing knife at the driver's side front wheel. The tire blew out and the car swerved into the ditch. The car behind managed to screech around it and continue on. Three thugs emerged out of the car looking around in wonderment as well as a little dazed. Eon still stayed in the tree and called out to them.

"Tell me where you're meeting your boss and I'll let you go. If you try to fight me, it'll be the last thing you do. I'm tired, my friend has been kidnapped and I'm not messing around here."

The thugs were unable to pinpoint her exact location, but at least they had her general whereabouts. Eon's question was answered with bullets as all 3 of the thugs fired away from side arms they pulled out. Eon jumped down to hide behind the tree she had climbed. When the shooting stopped, the thugs stood there in the road trying to listen. All the while Wild Card was watching from across the road, crouched down behind a bush. The moonlight was plenty enough for Eon to see her targets as she peered around the tree, they were in her sights. The next thing that Wild Card saw was all 3 of the thugs drop down dead with the only sound being the thunk of the throwing knife breaking through their skulls. The next thing that he heard was Eon's boots hitting the pavement of the road and walking up to the car.

"Jason, get in the car and crank the wheel around while I try to push it out of the ditch."

All Wild Card could do was shake his head; being scared to death of what his girlfriend could do was something new to him. Especially when she was in a bad mood and didn't get enough sleep. Wild Card walked up to the car and got in the driver's side seat through the passenger's side because the driver's side was so far in the ditch that he couldn't open the door.

"Toria, this thing's in the ditch pretty deep."

"I've got to at least try Jason, please just crank the wheel for me."

As Wild Card lined up the wheels for Eon, she jumped down into the ditch and crouched down to get a good purchase on the frame. Eon dug her feet hard into the side of the ditch to brace herself and began to push with all she had on the large Cadillac. Again Wild Card was stunned as the car was actually moving up and out of the ditch. Eon was straining hard and it was slow going, but it was moving and before long it was out of the ditch and back on the road. Eon climbed out of the ditch and rested her hand on the hood of the car, letting out a big sigh. Wild Card got out of the car and took a look at the front wheel that was flat as a pancake.

"Well, all I have to do is get the spare tire on there and we've got a ride again."

Eon smiled and nodded her head in agreement.

Vapor woke up an hour and a half later and saw that light was beginning to shine through the holes in the canvas cover on the back of the truck.

"We passed the last village on the Jungle Road about 15 minutes ago, so everyone has been warned of Power's coming. Only another couple of hours and we'll hit the city, the gas is holding up and we should make it."

However, 10 minutes later the rebel villagers rounded a corner only to be faced with a roadblock and armed soldiers. The roadblock was made of large spiked tripods that were scattered for at least a quarter of a mile; they looked like anti-tank devices. The lead driver hit the brakes as soon as he saw the block and soldiers.

"There are soldiers up ahead and the road blocked, we'll never get through!"

Vapor could see through the holes in the canvas that soldiers were running to the trucks and surrounding them. She could hear that there were a lot of them, much more than her rebels. They were shouting and waving guns in the air.

"Look, they want us to surrender ourselves in the name of Power. We didn't come this far, not to make it now. Radio to the other truck and tell them to get ready for a surprise attack. I want all guns out, hit the deck of the trucks and shoot through the canvas. Once we take out the men that have surrounded us, I want everyone to make a run for it into the jungle. Scatter on either side of the Jungle Road and keep firing as you move. They may take the vehicles, but we'll make it hell for them to take us alive!"

The other truck was radioed to and the fighters did exactly what Vapor had instructed them to do. On her signal, the rebels let the surrounding soldiers have it. Hot lead was fired from both sides of the truck. Soldiers went down in a red mist that painted the edge of the jungle. The commanding officer saw this and began barking orders to his troops that were positioned behind the roadblock to attack the trucks. As those soldiers were moving up, the rebels were pouring out of the trucks and firing at them. Both sides lost fighters in the barrage of bullets that lasted several minutes. After which, the rebels that survived the initial assault made it into the jungle.

Once the shooting stopped, the soldiers reclaimed the stolen trucks. Then the soldiers slowly began to creep into the jungle with their guns at the ready. The extra humidity in the air was choking and a telling sign that rain was coming. Even the insects could feel it and momentarily stopped pestering both sides. As if that had been enough warning, a typical jungle downpour began. The rain felt good on their sweaty unwashed skin, but it got in their eyes and dulled their senses. There was one more reason that the rain couldn't have come at a worse time and that fact was cursed possibly a little too loud by Vapor.

"Damnit! Why did it have to rain now?"

"You don't like the rain Havanna? After days of fighting in this heat, I say the rain feels good."

"It's my capsules, the chemicals can't rise in the air and spread in the rain as heavy as this one is. The rain will force everything into the ground; all my capsules will be useless in this. Hush now, I hear one of their radios in the distance."

Vapor and the few fighters that she was with listened intently, waiting for a firefight. As they watched, they saw that the soldiers turned back. Vapor knew what this meant and it terrified her.

"Remember Tiharo when the soldiers left, do you recall what followed?"

The rebels looked at her with wide eyes and murmured the words out.

"Fire bombing!"

"Radio the others, we need to charge them before they can start!"

An explosion went off not too far from them and screams could be heard.

"Now, now, let's move!"

The rebels started to charge in the heavy rain while more explosions went off around them. Little did they know that the commander of the soldiers had his men behind the trucks with machine guns pointed into the jungle waiting for them. The rebels charged while firing their own weapons and the rain was drowned out by both sides shooting their weapons and the continuous firebombs that left holes in the jungle canopy. When each side was close enough to see the other, the commander gave the order and every soldier there fired into the jungle. More of the rebels went down in bloody screams, while the rest dove on the jungle floor.

"Havanna, they mean to kill us all!"

Vapor saw the look on these poor farmers that overnight had become warriors. She saw the toll that the fighting had taken on them and the longing of how they wished to return to a normal way of life. Looking at the man that lay next to her, she nodded and the man gave her his gray shirt. Vapor tied the shirt to the gun and held it up as high as she could. If they stayed to fight, more would die and that was something that she just couldn't live with. She had seen the hell that is war, smelled the burning bodies and heard the agonizing screams. They would haunt her forever, but if she could help it, no more would die today. Vapor had no choice, but to accept the situation and trust her adversaries would acknowledge the rules of war. As she waved the gun with the shirt high in the air, she yelled out as loud as she could the words that she never thought that she would say.

"We surrender!"

Eventually the shooting died down and the soldiers moved in pinning the rebels down with their hands behind their heads face down in the mud. Vapor caught a glimpse of the commander's face as she was being forced down into the mud and he had a large sadistic grin on his face. The feeling she had of letting down the rebels was worse than a thousand bone crushing blows, the only feeling worse was the fact that she couldn't do anything about it.

Chapter 9

Once the spare tire was on the car, Wild Card and Eon were once again after the kidnappers.

"Jason slow down, there's one of the cars parked on the side of the road. Why is there only one car, where did the others go? Why don't you drive up a little ways and see if you can find the others, I'm going to get out and check around here. Radio in either way and let me know what you find."

"Alright, just be careful out there in case it's an ambush."

Eon got out of the car and saw that the first rays of sun were just starting to hit the landscape. With a Bowie knife in one hand and throwing knives in the other, she cautiously began to enter the woods near the parked car. Wild Card drove on ahead, keeping his eyes open for the others.

Once Eon entered the woods, she was immediately able to pick up the scent as well as see the driver's path. She began to jog through the woods as fast as she could without losing the trail. Then the trail got really hot, so hot that Eon stopped moving. She looked around the woods, he was in the immediate area she knew it. Rip's training had taught her to use her senses she didn't think were possible with the Foresight. Eon stopped and listened with the ears of a fox, looked with the eyes of a hawk and smelled the air with the nose of a bloodhound. She began to slowly walk into the woods deeper, changing her direction slightly. Then as she was about to pass by a tree, she stopped and she was amazed that she could hear it. The faint pounding grew more rapid the more she focused on it. She could hear the beating heart of her hidden opponent and knew he was about to strike.

With a single powerful, fluid movement, Eon spun around and thrust out the long Bowie knife in the time it takes a person to blink. Not a single noise was heard, only the contorted expression on her opponent's face. Eon had driven the Bowie knife through the thug's throat and did it with such force that he was pinned to the tree behind him. She withdrew the blade and the body slipped down. The epiphany in the realization of what Rip had taught her, made her one of the most deadly predators to rival any on the face of the planet. As Eon stood there in awe of the power called the Foresight, Wild Card's voice came over the radio.

"Toria, I found 2 other cars up ahead on the side of the road. Nobody appears to be in them, at least not at first glance. I'm about 3 miles up the road from where I dropped you off."

"I'll be right there Jason, this was just a distraction anyway. Wait for me to get there before you go into the woods."

About a quarter mile into the woods from where Wild Card was, stood Sergey dressed in his robes and head wrap with his triangle medallion out. He was standing in a clearing with 2 guards, chanting an ancient ritual. Rip was still tied up and gagged at the base of his feet.

"This area is now purified and may be used as substitute ground for the Cult's ritual."

The guards helped get Rip into position by laying her on her back, holding her shoulders and feet down.

Eon arrived in less than 5 minutes up the road to meet Wild Card.

"Come on Jason, I just hope we're not too late. They'll be in the woods and they couldn't have gotten too far."

Wild Card followed Eon as she picked up the trail easily. After several minutes Eon stopped and turned behind her to whisper to Wild Card.

"Be on your toes Jason, they're around here."

A spray of bullets filled the morning woods as both Eon and Wild Card dove to the ground.

"Hold on Jason, I see movement up in that tree over there."

With a perfect tumbling somersault to her feet in one fluid move, Eon released a throwing knife that flew like a rocket at its intended target 150ft away. The knife hit the thug hard enough to go right through his chest as he dropped out of the tree dead. Bullets again sprayed the forest floor and this time one of them connected. Wild Card was hit in the upper thigh and let out a yell. His armored suit protected him, but it still felt like he was hit with a baseball bat without any protection.

"Jesus Christ, that stings!"

Both of them crawled behind a tree and stayed down on the ground. Eon shook her head in frustration.

"We don't have time for this, I'm not even sure if Rip is still alive."

"Why didn't you just blast that second car with one of your nitro blades?"

"I couldn't Jason, remember it's too hot for them in the summer. The nitroglycerin is too unstable; I had to keep them in the freezer. It's a nice thought and I wish I had, but I'll have to make due with what I've got. Anyway, these guys aren't gonna move; they're already set up in a good defensive position. You stay here, I'm going to go around and try to get a better shot at them."

Before Wild Card could say anything, Eon was gone in a flash. Again the bullets hit the ground, but none of them could hit Eon as she ran ahead to a better position. As she dove head first behind a tree, she then peered around and saw a good angle to fire at another shooter in a tree. She reached for one of her throwing knives on her chest, but there weren't anymore. She still had some on her thighs, but she had to be careful not to run out. There was no telling how many more thugs there were in here. She knew that it couldn't be that many because there weren't that many vehicles, but still she had to pick her shots.

At the ritual site, the gunshots could be heard. Sergey remained calm as he pulled out a dagger from his cloak and held it above Rip.
"Now Rip, your killing of Master Temovich will be avenged. I promise you it will be a quick embrace proper of a warrior's death."
Sergey began to chant again in an old ancient tongue while he still held the dagger over Rip. She tried to squirm and free herself, but she was still tied and had a guard on either side of her.

Out on the Jungle Road in Columbia, 65 miles shy to the end of it; Vapor and her rebels are being collected into the trucks after being tied up. There were only 30 fighters left, half of their numbers had died in this terrible unforeseen encounter. Vapor had hidden her daggers in her cloak and was surprised that they didn't check her. The soldiers did confiscate the guns, but other than that nobody was checked. After all the rebels were secured, the commander walked into the back of the truck that held his prisoners flanked by 2 soldiers with machine guns. He stood there with his hands on his hips and a large grin on his face.

"Please sit back and enjoy the ride, we have a long journey back to San Guatalaharo. If any of you decides it's a good idea to try to escape or fight back, you will be killed without question."

With a smug laugh, the commander jumped off the back of the truck and the hatch closed. Two armed soldiers stayed behind in the back to keep an eye on the prisoners. As they moved on, the men began to get anxious waiting for the unknown; but didn't dare speak or call attention to themselves. Vapor was tired beyond words; she was absolutely exhausted. Her head hung, but how could she sleep now? There was no use in doing anything at this point, she decided to bide her time and wait for an opportunity.

After an undetermined amount of time, the trucks came to a stop. The commander appeared once again and the hatch of the truck came down. They were in the last village of the Jungle Road.

"I've just gotten a call from Commander Power and it seems he has deemed it a waste of resources to carry you all back to San Guatalaharo. It seems he is only interested in one of you. The rest are free to go in this village, a gracious gift by any standard."

"No, we will not let you take Havanna to that tyrant to face alone. She has been our savior and given us courage when we thought we had none."

All the rebels stayed on the truck and didn't move. They were loyal and stayed by their leader to the end. Vapor was touched by this display of devotion, but this was a gift and she had a better chance of getting away herself than worrying about the other fighters.

"You must do as he says and not worry about me. Take your freedom and go to the city with the others. You know Power is coming regardless and will destroy every village along the Jungle Road. You should all be proud; you fought better than any of these so-called soldiers. Remember, I'm not dead until I can no longer draw breath."

Vapor tried her best to stay strong and smile as she spoke. One of the rebels knelt down beside her and put a hand on her shoulder.

"It is because of you that my family was able to escape this place and it's because of you that I will see them again. You are the greatest warrior that we have ever seen and I believe that this is not the end. Should you ever need us again, we will all be there at your command."

All the fighters nodded in agreement. The commander was growing impatient and fired a warning shot into the air.

"Move now or I'll kill you all myself and just say I let you go!"

The rebels all filed out of the truck one at a time under gunpoint of several soldiers. After they were out and Vapor was the only one left in the truck, the soldiers climbed in and sat with guns pointed at her. As the hatch went back up, the rebels stood by the side of the road and watched. Vapor's eyes had caught the rebel that had spoken to her before the canvas flap went back down over the truck.

"Should you ever need us again..."

The other trucks were ordered to go back to their post and resume their stations at the southern end of the Jungle Road. Only a single truck that held Vapor, a handful of soldiers, the commander and a driver continued up the Jungle Road. Even though things looked bleak for Vapor, she could breathe a sigh of relief at the fact that at least the rest of the rebels were safe. Her hands were bound, guns were pointed at her and all the fight seemed to be out of her. The odds didn't look good, but she hoped at least the message to Eon had made it through. At least someone could continue the work that she had started.

Eon lined up her shot and before the gunman in the tree knew what hit him, the throwing knife had passed through his chest. Another dead body fell from a tree and hit the ground. Eon scanned the woods, but she couldn't tell if there were any more.

"Jason, can you see any from your angle?"

"No, I think we're clear, but I can't tell for sure."

There wasn't time to waste on waiting and wondering. Eon made a decision to go for it and ran through a clearing; it was then that she heard it. The shifting in the tree as the third gunman turned to fire at her was all she needed to hear. Eon began to tumble to the side as bullets bounced just inches from her feet. The gunman stopped shooting to take aim as Eon was still in the clearing and running for the cover of a tree. He smiled, there was no way she was escaping his shot this time. As he lined up his shot, suddenly the gun was knocked right out of his hand as a steel bar went flying through the air and landed on the ground next to the gun. The thug quickly climbed half way down the tree and tumbled the rest of the way to the ground in a mad dash for the gun. At the same time, Wild Card was running after him to make it there first. The thug reached down to pick up the gun and Wild Card collided with him like a freight train and they both tumbled to the ground.

The thug elbowed Wild Card in the face and did a back flip to regain his feet. Wild Card shot up to his feet as well and grabbed a hold of the gun trying to wrest it away from the thug. The thug let go of the gun, which sent Wild Card falling backwards to the ground; losing his balance. The thug pulled a side arm from his pants and pointed it at Wild Card as he was falling. Wild Card saw it coming and winced in anticipation, but before the shot was fired there was a wet ripping sound. Wild Card looked up to see Eon standing there behind him with a bloodied Bowie knife as the torso of the thug fell to the ground, followed by his legs.

"Jesus Toria, maybe you could have waited a little longer to make it more suspenseful."

"Come on you big lug, I picked up their trail down through these grouping of trees."

As Eon and Wild Card broke through the trees into a clearing, they saw Sergey standing over Rip with thugs on either side of her. Sergey stopped chanting and turned to face them both.

"You've interrupted the ritual and interfered with the Cult for the last time."

"Jason go get Rip, I'll handle this chump!"

Eon threw 2 of her last throwing knives at Sergey, who deflected one into the ground and the other into a tree with his knife. Laughter followed and a horrified look on Eon's face as she stared at the man in the robes.

"I thought we've been over this before, did you think it would succeed again?"

Eon drew out both of her Bowie knives, holding one upright and the other pointed down.

Sergey met her in the clearing and they circled each other.

Wild Card ran at the other 2 thugs, who stood up to meet him in a fighting stance. The words of wisdom from Demon echoed in Wild Card's head, '...try to stay on your feet...' Both of them came at Wild Card at the same time in a flurry of kicks and punches. Wild Card let the suit take a lot of the blows and countered with his bars. One thug grabbed his wrist and leaped up and put his legs around Wild Card's arm, which made Wild Card bend down. The thug tried to wrestled away one of the bars, while the other thug ran at him in a jump kick. Wild Card let go of the bar and met the jumping thug in the air catching him across the knees with his other bar. As the thug went down, Wild Card got behind him and put his bar across the thug's throat. The thug grabbed the bar to get it away from his throat, but he was no match for Wild Card's strength and began to choke. The other thug stood up and threw Wild Card's bar into the woods and came after him. Wild Card held the thug he had in front of him to use as a shicld from the other thug. While at the same time, Wild Card cranked up hard on his bar and heard the crushing sound of the thug's trachea. The thug fell to the ground as his life passed from him. Wild Card now faced the lone thug with a single steel bar, as they circled each other.

Meanwhile, Eon and Sergey were locked in a deadly combat with each other. Sergey made several swipes at Eon's head and midsection, Eon able to parry the slashes with her Bowie knives. She countered with a thrust, but Sergey side stepped faster than she could believe and grabbed her arm. Eon came overhead with the other Bowie knife pointed down at Sergey. He caught Eon's wrist and kicked her in the stomach, sending her tumbling. As she fell back, the arm that Sergey was holding was also his knife hand and he cut a long slash across her arm as she fell.

Eon got to her feet and held her arm, looking at Sergey who had a devious smile on his face. She came at him again swinging the knives in a figure 8 pattern. The tinging sound of metal on metal as Sergey blocked and attacked and Eon parried and countered. It was Eon who smiled now, as Sergey couldn't keep up with her barrage of knife attacks.

"Come on Sergey, faster, you need to be a lot faster than that."

Inevitably, Sergey couldn't keep up and one of Eon's blades cut him across the front of his knuckles. Sergey pulled back for a moment and Eon followed up with a thrust from the other Bowie knife, driving it right through his forearm. As she pulled the knife out, Sergey dropped his blade and stumbled back grasping his arm. Eon confidently walked towards him and kicked his knife away.

"Your speed, it's incredible! If you kill me, the Cult will hunt you down. You'll be a damned woman like Rip is."

Wild Card was thankful that the thug he was fighting was unarmed because he was dangerous enough. The thug did a spinning roundhouse kick, which Wild Card met with his steel bar on the thug's shin. An audible crack could be heard as the thug's tibia broke. Still the thug remained on his feet, but held up his bad leg and staggered. Wild Card was impressed by his pain tolerance and decided to test it further. Wild Card advanced, but to his surprise, the thug jumped at him. Being off balance, the thug tackled Wild Card to the ground; got around behind Wild Card and put his arms around his neck to choke him. The thug was unable to penetrate through the neck guard that Wild Card had attached to his helmet. So, wrapping his legs around Wild Card's waist from behind, he latched on and ripped the helmet off.

Wild Card was in no position to get to the thug that was behind him and the thug began to punch him on the top of the head. Wild Card reached down and grabbed the thug's broken leg that was wrapped around his waist and twisted it. The thug screamed in pain and latched onto Wild Card's neck, while at the same time letting his feet drop. Wild Card danced around trying to get the thug off his back and from around his neck. He slammed him into the trees, tried to flip him; but it wasn't working. The world started to spin and Wild Card went limp in the thug's stranglehold.

As he did so, he took his hands from under Wild Card's neck and grabbed the side of his head intending to break Wild Card's neck. Little did the thug know that Wild Card was feigning the fact that he was unconscious. Wild Card spun around and faced the surprised thug and wrestled him to the ground. The thug kneed Wild Card in the chin to get out from under him. Both men stood to face each other, but Wild Card wasn't waiting around to even let the thug breathe. He came at the thug with punch after punch combination, back to the most comfortable fighting style that he knew---boxing. Wild Card's punches were thunderous and powerful and as the thug staggered barely on his feet, Wild Card unloaded a massive uppercut on the side of his face. The thug's head snapped back with a crack and he fell to the ground motionless.

Eon kicked Sergey in the chest and knocked him 10ft across the clearing.

"I don't know what cult you're talking about or where exactly you came from, but it's over now. Go back to wherever you came from and never come back here, or it'll be much worse."

Eon turned towards Rip, Sergey made a dash for his knife. In faster than the time it takes to blink, Eon spun around and threw one of her Bowie knives at Sergey. The blade entered the back of his skull and the point exited out his forehead. Sergey dropped down to the ground dead.

Eon raced over to Rip and helped Wild Card get her bonds off. Rip looked up at both of them and flashed a weak smile.

Chapter 10

Eon, Wild Card and Rip all took one of the cars back to the lair.

"Toria, you do realize you have to report all these dead bodies to Dixon."

"Yeah I know; I'll catch up with him later today. I want to get some sleep first and something to eat."

As they pulled up a street away from the lair, they got out of the car and walked the rest of the way to the lair as not to draw attention. It was early morning, just before the heavy rush hour traffic started up. They were lucky only the early birds were out getting in a jog or some breakfast before they went to work. They all climbed down into the lair and Jason began to make some breakfast.

"God, what a night! I'm not making any coffee because I'm going straight to bed after this with a couple ice packs. Then after I get up, I want to try and track down where those guys came from."

"Yeah, Sergey said the Cult would hunt me down if I killed him. I don't know what the hell he's talking about."

Rip looked up from sipping her water. She was fine, just a little tired.

"I haven't been on an adventure like that since the old days. Over breakfast I'll fill you in on the details of the Cult that the late Sergey was talking about."

Eon and Wild Card looked very interested as they sat down with English muffins, toast and orange juice.

"They are called the Cult of 16. They are the most deadly cult in the world. Their membership is small and very strict to get into. They are international and each member has diplomatic immunity. The symbol of the Cult is an upside down triangle intersected by 3 equal dividing lines. If you look at the triangle, you can make out a combination of 16 triangles, hence their name.

The Cult has a hierarchy among themselves and is used as mercenaries on the highest level. Usually political powers may call on them for an assignment. Those that seek them out in whispers and shadows only know them. Our team ran into them a couple times, as we were mercenaries too. However, I was the only one that was capable of their levels of combat. One of the requirements to even try to enter their ranks is that you must hold at least a 4th degree black belt in your chosen art form. This is just the basic level and the level of those you fought.

I will try my best to break down their hierarchy for you. First there are 6 regions, each region covers one of the inhabited continents. Each region is comprised of 3 divisions and then further divided into 3 groups per division to better spread their ranks across the continents. Within each group there are 17 members, this is the base number of fighters to take on a given assignment. Each one of these groups has a leader, which would have been Sergey. Tournaments are held each year in secrecy for membership into a group as well as tournaments for existing members to move up in the Cult's ranks.

I will start from the ground up in my explanation. I told you about the basic members, this comprises 918 fighters of the 1,000 total members in the Cult's organization, you can think of them as foot soldiers headed by a group leader. Since there are 9 groups in each region and 6 regions, which means there are 54 group leaders in the Cult around the world such as Sergey. Now there are only 53, but Sergey will be replaced. The next level up from the group leaders are the division leaders. Since there are 3 divisions in each region and 6 regions, there are 18 division leaders throughout the world and these are among some of the best fighters in the world. Then beyond the division leaders are the region leaders and there are only 6 of them, they represent the greatest fighters on each continent and give command over the divisions, who in turn give orders to the groups.

    Each year a special tournament is held called the 'Master of All' and it brings together the 6 region leaders of the world as well as 2 of the greatest division leaders to fight in a bracket style tournament for the title of the greatest fighter in the world. The winner is given the title of 'Master of All' and is given a great secret; I'll come back to that. Four Elders, holding court in Asia, head the entire Cult and all disputes of the Cult go before them. They are also the judges of the Master of All tournament. Each of the 4 was once Masters of All, voted in by their peers. They hold that position until death, then another post Master of All is elected to take their place.

    Each of the 1,000 members holds a ranking that is decided in the tournaments, the lower the number, then the better fighter you are. The 4 Elders hold the ranks of 1-4, but the number 5 spot goes to the current Master of All and is the greatest fighter in the world. When I was in the loop ages ago, it was a fighter from South America, and then I heard it changed hands to a fighter from Asia. Today I don't know who holds the current title, but they are all deadly.

Now once a fighter becomes the Master of All, he is given the Cult's greatest secret. That is the chemical formula to forge the strongest weapons in the world. Years ago when the Cult was established, a rare mixture was created by accident during the forging of a sword. The sword took on a red tinge and was stronger than any substance that it came in contact with. The sword could cleave stone and was even tested on a diamond. As the sword came down, the diamond was shattered. The red tinge of the Master of All's weapons of choice are his signature to his status. When a Master of All passes away or becomes an Elder, his weapons are locked away in a vault that the location is unknown. Each weapon in the vault is a past Master's of All and regarded as an artifact in the eyes of the Cult. They are treated as such with shrines dedicated to each former Master of All inside the vault. Only the Elders know the location of the vault and have taken a vow of death before they ever reveal it to another.

Long before my time, I heard of a Master of All passing away and his weapon was stolen by a Cult group leader and tried to be reproduced. The attempt failed as any test on the metal could simply not be done; it was as if the metal itself didn't want to be reproduced. These are only legends, but to my knowledge the only way to create the substance is to forge it from scratch.

There is one other item to mention about the Master of All. The Elders give them, the location of the underground maze that holds what's called the 'Invincible Oil'. During the discovery of the reddish substance that they called the 'Secret of Krasnaya', also developed was this so-called Oil. Supposedly when the Oil is applied to the skin, the wearer is impervious to swords and blows. Something about the harder you hit, the denser it becomes. This part of the legend has never been recovered and I've heard that more than a few Masters of All have died in their quest for the Oil. The temptation to wield the greatest offense and to wear the greatest defense, were too much of a pull for the poor souls that met their fate."

Jason and Toria had changed out of their outfits after breakfast, while listening to Rip.

"So Rip, why do they want to hunt me down if I killed Sergey?"

"Sergey was a group leader and any Cult member that holds a leadership spot, group, division or especially region are of importance to the Cult. That means the other members will seek retribution for the death of one of their leaders. It also depends on the circumstance and if you can be identified, but you killed the entire group. Though not to worry, if you are tracked down, you are given the option to prove yourself in battle. If you are victorious, then you are free to go, as you are deemed worthy to have taken the life that you did. I on the other hand would have been killed in a ritualistic style because I'm too old to fight anymore. Well, I'm too old to fight that caliber of a warrior."

Toria got up and walked into her bedroom and came back out holding the medallion she had found in the cave where she fought the giant wolf.

"I found this in the cave system out in the western woods. It's just like the one Sergey wore; only this one came off a skeleton wearing similar robes. There was a stone table with what looked like dried blood on it with stone chairs and chains on the walls. There was even strange writing on the walls in a language I've never seen before."

Rip's eyes widened at the sight of the medallion. She took it from Toria and rolled it over in her hands to inspect it.

"You've found a secret sacrificial chamber of the Cult. It's places like these that they take their victims or targets to kill and dispose of their bodies. They are very well hidden in this manner; the public thinks that the person has just disappeared. It is a place like this that Sergey wanted to take me, but couldn't because of you. That writing you saw on the wall was the same that Sergey was chanting as he held the blade over me. He was purifying the area since it wasn't a sacrificial chamber of the Cult. They have their own secret language, just as any other nationality would have. It's taught to the new members if they are worthy enough to join their ranks after the annual tournament."

"How do you find out where one of these tournaments are and when they are taking place?"

"You need to ask the right people and do some research on your own. It was said that the sacrificial chambers were so well hidden that the Cult never feared being found in one of them. Because of this, they would place important items or bits of information hidden within the chambers. Doing this, spread the wealth of the Cult throughout the world. In case their main vault was ever breached, loss would be minimal."

"That sounds like a great idea! Hey Jason, how about after we rest up; I take you back over to the caves and we can explore the chamber inside?"

"Sure Toria, but let's push it off a couple of days, I'm whipped."

"Alright, that's fair enough. Oh Rip, when I was in the chamber, I took this medallion off one of the skeletons that had a dagger in his chest. Did the Cult ever go after one of their own?"

"It's quite possible, just as pirates often turned on each other. I doubt that it was a usual practice, but I'm sure that it happened from time to time. No organization, even the Cult of 16 is above corruption at some level."

"Well, that's all fascinating stuff, but right now it's time for a little shut eye. After my first run in with the Cult, I'm pretty tired."

Just as all 3 of them were getting ready for bed, Toria's radio went off.

"Eon, this is Chief Dixon, good morning. I just walked into work for the day and saw that there was a fax sent in from a city in Columbia and it's addressed to you. It looks very urgent, you might want to come down here and check it out. Does the name Vapor ring any bells with you?"

Toria and Jason looked up at each other in surprise. Toria walked over to her suit and picked up the radio.

"Yes Chief, I know that name. I'll be right down, just give me a few minutes."

Toria put down the radio and let out a big sigh.

"All I want is some damn sleep!"

"You want me to go check it out at headquarters for you?"

"No Jason, but thanks though. I'll just run down there and see what she has to say. Hopefully, it's telling me that the plan we had to fool Power worked and she was able to free her people. At least keep your fingers crossed that's what she says."

Toria decided to go out in regular clothes, after all she was just going to read a message.

Towards the other end of the Jungle Road in Columbia, the truck that has been carrying Vapor has just reached San Guatalaharo. Vapor was sleeping and jerks awake at the sudden stop of the vehicle. She's still groggy as she hears footsteps outside and then the canvas flap is pulled out with the hatch lowered. The commanding officer was standing there, still wide awake and wearing a big smile.

"Wake up Miss Vapor, it's time I delivered you to Power himself."

Vapor was led out of the truck by soldiers at gunpoint and thrown to the ground. Her strength was gone, so she just collapsed in a heap. Laughter could be heard around by soldiers and the commander. They picked her back up by her arms and walked her into the main tent that Power was using as his temporary headquarters in the area. The commanding officer walked in and saluted to Power's officers.

"I bring the rebel, the one they call Vapor to Commander Power."

Swiveling around in a large chair behind a large desk was the tyrant Power. A formidable sight, instilling fear on all who beheld him.

"Bring her in here and place her in that chair."

The officers did so at once, holding Vapor roughly and pushing her into the chair. A large grin appeared on Power's face.

"You may remove her bonds and leave us, I don't think she's going anywhere."

The soldiers looked at each other and hesitantly removed Vapor's bonds and all dismissed themselves from the tent. Power walked in slow circles around the chair that Vapor sat in. He held his hands behind his back and all the while wore that smile on his face. Vapor sat with her head hanging, looking down at her hands in her lap. Power approached her, cupping his hand under her chin and raised her head up to look at her face.

"You've been a very busy little rebel, dear Havanna. You are a troublesome little pest, what am I to do with you?"

Power walked away from her and stood near his desk, turning to face her.

"Please stand up Havanna, here is your chance. It's just you and me in here, why don't you see if you can finish the job. You have your little capsules and your knives, make use of them."

Power watched as Vapor raised her head in anger and slowly stood up. He continued to smile at her as she pulled out her dagger with a couple of capsules. Then her head wavered and she stumbled some. She tried to catch herself, but she lost her balance due to the spinning in her head and the weakness in her legs. She fell to her hands and knees, the knife and capsules bounced on the floor away from her. She stayed there with her head hanging low. She had endured more than any person could ask for and just simply needed rest, medical attention and a good meal. Power began to laugh uncontrollably at the fallen girl in front of him.

"That's quite enough Miss Del Rio, I'm sure the mind is willing. Unfortunately, I'm going to have to lock you away in this steel cell and take your toys. These little capsules of yours are very interesting, why even I fell for one of your illusions. Guards, come in here! Please escort Miss Del Rio to the steel cage in the corner. Clean her up, bandage any wounds that she may have and give her a meal. She will stay here in the tent with me, but I wish to speak with her when she's coherent."

The soldiers did what Power had said and Vapor was placed in the steel cage. There was a cot in there as well as a bottle of water and a bucket with a rag. As the soldiers placed her on the cot and began to take her weapons, the entire world went black. Vapor fell into a deep sleep; it was the only thing that mattered at this point.

Toria had made it to police headquarters in no time at all, she wanted to get back and get some sleep.

"Hi Chief, where's the message you wanted me to see?"

Chief Dixon handed Toria the fax and watched her face as she read it. Toria looked up and away after she finished it and there was a long pause. Dixon stood up and walked over to a map print out and handed it to Toria.

"These are the coordinates that they sent, it's in the middle of the jungle in the country of Columbia."

"How fast can you get me to the nearest city, and I need to bring the axe?"

"We can fly you in on official police business, but after that, you're on your own. New country, new rules, we can offer you no immunity or protection."

"I understand, just get me there and I'll handle the rest. If this is a shot to get Power and save lives, then I have to do it."

"We'll have a flight ready for you this afternoon. Stop by the Harborside airport at 3pm for take-off."

"Thanks Chief, while I'm gone call on Wild Card if you or the city need anything."

Chief Dixon nodded his head and watched as Toria walked out the door and began to head back to the lair. All she wanted to do was sleep, but before that happened she had some explaining to do.

Chapter 11

Once Toria made it back to the lair, Jason and Rip were already sleeping. She felt terrible, but she had to wake Jason up and tell him that in 7 hours she was going to be on a flight to South America. She nudged him gently so he wouldn't wake with a start.

"Jason, I'm sorry you can't sleep right now, but I've got to tell you some news."

"Jesus Toria, I just got to sleep. Why don't you just climb into bed and tell me after we've both had 8 hours of sawing wood."

"I'd love to Jason, but by that time I'll be 35,000ft in the air."

Jason turned and looked at Toria with a confused look on his face, he was awake now.

"Maybe I didn't hear you right, did you say you were going to be in the air?"

"That message from Vapor was a cry for help. I don't think Power bought the idea we came up with and I guess she's been in this little war with him ever since. From the sounds of it, she's also losing this little war and needs my help. Power's back on a rampage and people are dying, I can't turn her down."

"Oh my God, so you have to chase Power all over the world is that it?"

"We both know that Vapor is a pro and if she says it's bad, then it's bad. If this is a shot for me to get Power again and save lives, I've got to take it."

"Toria, when you fought him and his gangs here in Harborside; you had the lair to come back to. There was a place to recuperate, eat, sleep and prepare for battle in your forge and lab. If you go out there, you've got nothing and nowhere to go if things get bad. Not only are you fighting Power and his new little army, but the very environment of the jungle itself."

"I realize that and Vapor has been doing that ever since she left here, she needs some relief. I know it feels like I'm just springing this on you, but it was just sprung on me as well. I needed to tell you as soon as I found out because my flight leaves in 7 hours."

"I know you need to get supplies together, pack and prepare, but I don't think that will take 7 hours to do. Why don't you lay down here with me for at least a few of them, even the great Eon needs a little sleep."

Toria smiled and climbed into the bed next to Jason.

"You know, that's exactly what I was thinking."

On the south end of the city, Demon was just rolling out of bed. Breakfast consisted of whatever was available off hand. Demon got on his bike and decided to check out the sleazy hotel he knew that those thugs were held up in. He had been up throughout the night thinking about it and had to know. The roar of the motorcycle in the alley during the early morning awoke all the bums with a jump as it echoed through the entire block.

It didn't take him long to arrive on the scene of the hotel and to his surprise, it was swarming with cops.

"Well, it looks like they found what they were looking for. With all these cops around though, I'm not gonna find what I'm looking for."

Demon happened to notice a couple bodies being carried out to an ambulance, it was them he was sure of it. Those were the same guys he'd fought with Wild Card and it looked like this time the Kid stayed on his feet. Demon hung back and watched until the last of the cops left the scene. Then he searched the area for clues of any sort. He didn't find anything in the hotel itself or the parking lot, but then he took a walk out into the surrounding woods. There on the ground, next to a tree was a dark head wrap. Demon picked it up and felt the material through his fingers, staring at the fabric.

"The Cult of 16 is back, they were after Wild Card's friend. She must be someone really important politically that has a hit put on her, or she pissed off the Cult somehow."

Demon took the scarf and rode off back to his place.

Just waking up in a steel cage in Power's tent, is an exhausted Vapor. She sits up from the cot and looks around, confused as to where she is. Any wounds that she had sustained were cleaned out and dressed.

"Ah, it's good to see that you are up and about Miss Del Rio. Here, let me offer you something to eat."

Power grabs a bowl of fruit and places it at the base of the cage for Vapor to take. Vapor just stares at it in disgust and glares back at Power.

"What, you don't trust me? I can assure you that I haven't poisoned the food."

Power bent down and picked up an apple; he took a large bite out of it and threw it back in the bowl.

"There you have it, nothing to worry about here. Please, eat until your little heart is content."

Power watched with a smile as Vapor grabbed at a banana, peeled it and finished it in about 30 seconds. As she was still chewing, she reached out to grab an orange and began to peel that.

"Now let us talk as civilized people do, I have a proposition for you..."

"No deal Power, either you let me out or you kill me. Which ever you choose, there will be another that will rise up and take my place."

"You haven't even heard me out yet my little upstart. The offer is not just about you, but your people as well. I will leave this area in Columbia, from here to the southern portion of this Jungle Road here in the rural parts. The people you fight for and protect may resume their lives as they did before my arrival."

"This all seems too good to be true, what do I have to do for you?"

"All I ask is that you work for me in whatever tasks I assign you. You will be a wealthy girl and live like a queen, the riches of this land can be yours."

"I already know the riches of this land, I don't need to get anything from you."

"Then perhaps you'll do it for the people, you are a bleeding heart after all. If you do not accept my offer, more will die. I will destroy all that is left in this rural area of the jungle, right up to the cities. After that I'll use the entire area to grow my profits and become even more of a rich man. Think hard on my offer because if you refuse, all those deaths are on your head. There is none that can stop me and you know it. You however, will not be around long enough to see that. I will have you executed by a firing squad."

"Someone will stop you, someone will rise against you!"

Power smiled and walked over to the edge of the steel cage.

"I will let you have that hope if it lets you die easier. You will have 24 hours to think about it, after that I'll make the decision for you."

Power walked out of the tent and in came 4 guards that stood around the steel cage, holding their weapons at the ready.

Toria woke up after a few hours of sleep and looked over at Jason. He was still sleeping, but he'd wake up as soon as she started to move. However, even though she would have loved to stay right there in bed, she knew she had to get ready for this mission ahead of her. Toria eased out of the bed and crept into the forge and lab to start getting ready. Jason and Rip were both light sleepers and trained to be ready at any moment they heard noise. So, it didn't take long for both of them to meet in the kitchen due to the noise that Toria was making.

"Well Rip, she's getting ready to go to Columbia, it looks like Vapor is in trouble with Power and his soldiers down there."

"She is ready, my training with her is done. I would have liked to practice a little more, but she's the fastest learner I've ever seen."

"Will you be leaving as well, or will you be staying for a while?"

"No, I'll be going back to Russia as soon as I can. It won't be safe here in Harborside since one of the groups in the Cult has fallen. They will no doubt hear about it quickly and may know already. My presence here makes it unsafe for all of you because I believe more will follow. They will either look for me or for Toria. You also had a hand in this as well and they may come looking for you. You should stay low and out of sight for the coming months or at least until Toria gets back."

"I can't do that, I'm a defender of the city. I can't run and hide waiting for more of those Cult members to track me down. Besides, I might be able to get some help while Toria's gone if I need it."

Toria emerged from the lab with a couple bags packed. She stood there in her street clothes with her hair down. Rip approached her with a smile and placed her hands around Toria's shoulders.

"I'll be leaving shortly after you. Your training with me is complete; you are an exceptional warrior and will need to call upon your training in the following days. Jax was right about you; you are the brightest star. You should feel very content, he would have been very proud of you."

Toria and Rip embraced in a hug; there was a small tear in Toria's eye.

"Thanks Rip, you've given me an edge over Power and in the rest of my life. Take care of yourself, I won't forget you."

They both smiled at each other and Rip looked behind her over her shoulder at Jason who looked on. Rip excused herself back to the guest room she was staying in to give them some time to part ways. Toria dropped her bags and gave Jason a hug.

"Jason, I need you to do me a favor while I'm gone. I told Dixon to call on you if he or the city needed anything. Also, can you go to the bank and take out $1,000.00 and give it to the bums on the south end of town near the old billiards hall?"

"That was one of Sal's old hangouts, why do you want me to do that?"

"If not for them, you might be a dead man. They told me a secret way to get into the building when Vapor held you prisoner. I told them I wouldn't forget what they did to help."

"Sure, I can do that, is there anything else?"

"Yeah, stay healthy, strong and safe for me. I'll be thinking about you the whole time I'm there."

"Don't worry about me, just focus on the task at hand. You're going into a war zone; you need all your wits about you. I'll be thinking about you enough for the both of us anyway."

"I'm not sure how long I'll be gone, but I'll come back as soon as I can. I left the nitro and poison blades in the freezer because of the heat. If there's an emergency and you need to use them, just don't let them linger too long outside the freezer."

One last hug and Toria slung her bags over her shoulder and grabbed her axe.

"I love you Toria, take care of yourself."

"I love you too Jason, I'll see you soon."

Toria opened the hatch and with a last look and a smile, she was gone. Rip came out of her room and came up behind Jason, who was still looking at the closed hatch.

"The big fish now enters the ocean."

Toria arrived at police headquarters just before her flight left to go over the details with Dixon and be driven over to the airport.

"We can fly you into the closest city, which is Mitu. From there, you'll be on your own to track down the location of these coordinates. Take this handheld GPS; it'll help you through the jungle.

Now, we're keeping this undercover, which means that the consulate won't know of your arrival. For all they know or care, you're just another tourist. When you're ready to come back, just wire us here through a police station or post office down there. I'm giving you these credentials so they'll let you contact us directly. This'll show you're an officer of the United States when you present this. Once you get into Mitu, I suggest you set up a home base there. The axe will stick out like a sore thumb, but what can you do. Once you drop your bags there, you can go out and search for this Vapor. One more thing, try not to call too much attention to yourself. We don't need an international problem in the media over this."

"I got it Chief, I'm ready when you are to go."

"How do you feel about all this?"

"I'm anxious to get down there and find Vapor, as well as a second chance to get Power. I'm also excited, this is my first time out of the country."

Jason walked out of the lair and started to make his way down to the south side. He was on foot, since the police had taken the vehicle and his motorcycle crapped out on him. He knew the bar wouldn't be open in the afternoon and he didn't know exactly where Demon lived. Demon wasn't the kind of guy that you just picked up the phone and called. There was a reason he was so hard to get a hold of, he kept his secrets well. So, he decided to leave a note for him on the door of the Hellfire to meet him tonight. When he arrived, he was surprised to see Demon was already at the bar.

"Demon! I didn't expect to see you here at this hour, shouldn't you be sleeping?"

"I was making a run over to the hotel you fought those clowns at. On my way back, I had some work to do here. What brings you to this part of the city?"

"Actually I came to talk to you about that. A mutual friend of ours is in trouble and Toria is going away for a while out of the country and I came by to ask you a favor. I know you're a solo guy and anything around here I know I could handle, but there seems to be more to it. Those guys that we fought..."

"They were from the Cult of 16."

"How did you know that?"

"Like I said, I was just checking out over at the hotel. I picked up this head scarf and I recognized it as one of theirs."

"So, you're familiar with the Cult of 16?"

"Yeah, you could say that. If you're coming here to ask for help when they send more to come after you, I understand. It's not a question if you want my help, you're going to need it."

"How do you know they're coming back and how do you know so much about them?"

"That's a story for another time, maybe you'll get to hear it. The thing is, you killed a group leader of the Cult. You not only killed a leader, but you took out the whole group. I'm sure the Cult knows what happened by now and they'll be sending in the cavalry. It sounds like you know a little bit about the Cult, so know this; they won't stop until they're appeased. They have a region to represent each of the populated continents and 3 divisions per region with 3 groups per division."

"I know, our friend Rip filled us in on how the hierarchy works."

"Well, one of the North American divisions is close to around here. If you thought going up against a group was hard, try a whole division. Look, I'll help you out for a couple of reasons. First you need some practice against some real fighters. If you're gonna call yourself a 'hero', then you better learn to fight better than you do. One thing you got going for you is you're as strong as an ox and when you swing those bars, it causes a lot of damage. So, I see a lot of potential in what you can do. The second reason is, I've got a deep rooted history with these guys and it's not full of fond little memories."

"We should stick together then, do you have a phone?"

"No, I really never was much for talking to people."

"So, how do I get a hold of you then?"

"Get creative, I'm sure you'll get a hold of me when the time comes. Are you walking, where's the bike I gave you?"

"It quit on me up this road and probably is still where I left it. It was late and at the moment, I didn't really have the time or the tools to tinker with it."

Demon gathered some things from the bar and put them in his saddlebags on the bike.

"I'm just getting out of here now, why don't you hop on the back. I'll take you over to my buddy's garage. He takes all the junk bikes around here for parts and puts together some really nice ones. If you're gonna be hanging with me, you need something more reliable. Maybe we'll even customize it to more your style, come on let's go."

Jason got on the back of the bike and played it cool, but inside he was a kid in a candy shop.

Vapor sat and looked around her cell, searching for a way out. She had been there for at least an hour, she couldn't tell. The guards rotated on and off, so there were at least 4 of them with guns trained on her at all times. She couldn't even make a move without drawing attention to herself. The cage itself was solid steel with a lock and deadbolt on the outside. It would be useless to try to escape; she didn't even have her weapons. It looked like she was at the mercy of Power's option.

Vapor's mind was already made up; there was no way she would sell out to Power. Little did he know that all the villages left had been warned of his coming and were clearing out as she sat there. It gave her comfort in knowing that. She never thought she would go out like this, in front of a firing squad. By this time tomorrow, Power would order her execution. Knowing it was her last day; she began to think of strange things. Even petty things such as should she look defiant when they shoot her or close her eyes? Would it hurt, or would she die quickly?

She thought back on her rebel freedom fighters and smiled. Remembering their offer, she wished they were here now. Would they come, would they follow the truck all the way back to San Guatalaharo? Could they even get in here, let alone make it past the soldiers on their way back from dropping her off? It was all a pipe dream; nobody was going to come. Her story would live on in the tales of those that survived these attacks. She wished she knew if the message had reached Eon or not and that Eon could succeed where she could not. If she did get the message and she did come and defeat him, Vapor's only regret was that she wouldn't be able to look down and see Power's dead carcass. At least there was a window across her cage, she wanted to look out and see the world as long as she could. Vapor was left there in the cage to the sound of jungle birds and keeping her hopes alive.

    The car pulled up to the airport and out stepped Toria, Dixon and 2 other cops.
    "Alright Eon, you've got all the paperwork you need. Keep it in a safe place, if you lose it; you might be swimming back home. Of course I wouldn't put that one past you."
    "Thanks a lot for setting this up for me Chief. I talked to Jason and if you need him as Wild Card, he'll be ready for you. Well, take care and hopefully I'll see you soon."
    Toria made her way to the private jet that would take her to Columbia. She watched as the ground crew made last minute checks on everything.
    "Good afternoon Miss Kayden, I'm Captain Thompson and I'll be your pilot. We've got a tail wind, so we should arrive a little early. Is there anything I can get for you before takeoff?"
    "No I'm fine, just anxious to get to Mitu."
    "Have you ever flown before?"
    "No this is my first time, is it that easy to tell?"

"Not to worry, you're in good hands. It's a smaller plane, so you'll feel the turbulence a little bit more; but it won't be too bad. If you're ready, I just have to do a quick check up here in the cabin and we'll be ready for takeoff."

The pilot disappeared into the front of the plane. Toria looked out the window and waved to Dixon, who waved back with a smile on his face. Captain Thompson's voice came over an intercom above her head.

"Just remember to buckle up back there, I wouldn't want you to get jostled around any."

Toria laughed to herself, it was obvious that the Captain didn't recognize her as Eon. He could slug her in the face as hard as he could and she still might not even get a bruise, but she put the seatbelt on anyway. About a minute later, the engines started up and Toria could feel the roar of the plane. Captain Thompson's voice came back over the speaker.

"We're looking at a 5 hour flight Miss Kayden, the good news is there's no time difference. We'll arrive a little after dinner, but not to worry, there's some food here on the plane."

Toria became lost in thought; there was so much going through her mind. For one thing, she'd never been out of the country before and really didn't have time to study up on Columbia at all. She wondered if she would be able to find Vapor or even if Vapor was still alive. Or maybe the coordinates she had were old news by this point and Vapor had moved on, how would she find her then? Then her mind drifted to Jason and how he would cope. She remembered when she was away for less than a week, what he looked like after his fight with the Steel Link. Toria shook her head, she knew she should just focus on one thing at a time and that first thing was to get a place to stay in Mitu. From there she could venture out, after all anything could happen. That's why they call it adventure; even the best-laid plans can't predict everything.

    The plane began to take off down the runway. Toria took a deep breath and got ready for some international adventure.

End of Book III

Next: The Eon Chronicles Volume 2:
A Crucible for Justice